THE TEST OF GOLD

HEARTS OF GOLD SERIES BOOK 1

RENEE YANCY

PRAISE FOR THE TEST OF GOLD

This sweet Gilded Age romance shines with Renee Yancy's attention to historical detail bringing depth to the story. The settings in 1897 New York, Newport, and Chautauqua drew me into a complex time of contrasts in wealth, poverty, power and helplessness

~ Susan Page Davis, author of the Prairie Dreams Series and Maine Justice Series

OTHER TITLES BY RENEE YANCY

Have Cash, Will Marry: A Gilded Age Novella

The Battlefield Bride: A Civil War Novella

The Irish Bride: A Potato Famine Novella

A Secret Hope: A Novel of Ancient Ireland (Sword & Spirit Series Book 1)

The Fury of Dragons: A Tale of Roman Britain (Sword & Spirit Series Book 2)

More Precious Than Gold (Hearts of Gold, Gilded Age Series Book 2)

On the Trail of Love, a contemporary road trip romance

For my longtime pal and high school buddy,

Mike Emminger,

I couldn't have a better superfan than you!

Fire is the test of gold; adversity, of men...

Seneca (c.3 BC-65 AD)

1

April 1897, New York City

Evangeline Lindenmayer slipped through the marble halls toward her favorite room at 660 Fifth Avenue. Somehow the library had escaped the lavish attention to detail Mama and her architect had opulently bestowed on the other 149 rooms in the Petit Chateau.

The massive oak doors opened on well-oiled hinges, and the papery scent of books and leather enveloped Lindy. Sunlight streamed through the leaded glass windows and sparked off the gold lettering on the book spines. Her shoulders relaxed, and she gave a contented sigh. Such riches! In a lifetime, she could never read all the books here.

Her copy of Robinson Crusoe lay in the overstuffed chair where she'd left it the previous afternoon. Her mother had summoned her just as Robinson had been enslaved by a Moorish pirate.

And one didn't disobey Vera Lindenmayer.

Lindy had waited all day to discover his fate. Curling in the chair, she lost herself in seventeenth-century Africa. Sometime later, she closed the book and sighed.

"Is all well?" A tousled blond head peeked over the back of a leather Chesterfield sofa, and then a young man sat up and rubbed his eyes.

"Oh!" Lindy dropped the book and sprang to her feet, her hand at her throat. "Who might you be? What are you doing here?"

The man stood hastily and clutched a book against his black frockcoat. "I'm so sorry. I didn't mean to startle you. I must have fallen asleep."

"You did startle me, sir. And an unwelcome shock it was too!"

He reddened and took a step back. "Please forgive me. My name is Jack Winthrop." He glanced at the bookshelves. "Mr. Lindenmayer has kindly offered me the use of his excellent library while I'm studying for the ministry at Union Theological Seminary." He gulped and ran a finger around his collar.

"Oh." That sounded like Papa, with his tender heart.

"I'm also taking classes at Columbia, where the new anthropology department has recently opened."

Lindy's mouth fell open. Not one but two colleges. Does the fellow even know how fortunate he was? Oh, to have been born a man. It isn't fair.

"Please accept my heartfelt apologies for startling you, Miss..."

"Lindenmayer. Evangeline Lindenmayer."

"I'm pleased to make your acquaintance, Miss Lindenmayer.

"Winthrop, you said? Are you related to Reverend Joseph Winthrop at St. Thomas?"

The young man nodded. "He is my uncle."

Lindy examined him a moment. The edges of his sleeves were shabby and his blond hair a trifle too long, falling over his collar, but something undeniably attractive about him telegraphed itself to her.

"I recognize you now. You usually sit at the back of the church."

Mr. Winthrop nodded. "That's right." He retrieved his hat off the sofa. "I'll be going now. Sorry to intrude."

Lindy laughed. *He looks like a dog caught with the Sunday roast in his paws.* "Don't leave, Mr. Winthrop, you won't be disturbing anyone. The only books Papa reads concern the care and breeding of horses, and my mother never comes in here. I'm the only one who frequents it with regularity. But aren't you going to be frightfully busy with classes at two different colleges?"

His face brightened. "I thrive on it, actually. It's a great privilege to attend both the university and the seminary. My uncle has generously made it possible."

"Do you have other family besides your uncle?"

"My mother."

"I don't believe I've seen her with you."

A shadow darkened his face. "She isn't well. Not strong enough to attend the service on Sunday morning."

"I'm sorry to hear that. And your father?"

Mr. Winthrop smiled faintly. "My father died when I was seven, and Uncle Winthrop took us in. My father was his younger brother."

He crossed the distance between them and plucked her book off the floor. "Allow me." He glanced at the title before he handed it to her. "What did you think of Mr. Crusoe's adventures?"

My, he's tall. Lindy sank onto her chair as a qualm went through her middle. *Mama would have a conniption if she knew a man like Jack Winthrop was given permission to use the library.* Having a conversation with a man Lindy hadn't been officially introduced to wasn't done in society circles. But he's not exactly in my social class, and he did introduce himself. Quite nicely at that. And I'm seldom able to discuss books with anyone.

She pushed the thought of her mother firmly out of her head. "Won't you sit down, Mr. Winthrop?"

He nodded. "Call me Jack," he said, as he took the chair across from her.

"I couldn't possibly, sir."

"Of course not. Forgive me. But what about Robinson's adventures?"

She considered his question. "I found it interesting Mr. Crusoe often felt guided by something or someone else. And that gave him hope amid hopelessness."

Mr. Winthrop arched an eyebrow. "Indeed, Miss Lindenmayer."

Lindy frowned. "You are surprised to find I have an opinion, Mr. Winthrop?"

He smiled. "No, delighted. I thought young ladies such as yourself, were restricted to the latest treatise on manners and ballroom dancing."

Lindy wrinkled her nose. "If my mother had her way, books on etiquette would be my only reading material."

Dimples appeared when he smiled, transforming his serious face. "I'm surprised to see you inside on such a beautiful day. Do you not ride the Promenade on sunny afternoons?"

"Only when I must." She shrugged. "I'd much rather be here with my books than outside for the entire world to see and criticize." Mama never lets me forget for a minute that I have the Lindenmayer family reputation to uphold.

"You speak of your books as if they are old friends."

"They are indeed my friends, to be read and enjoyed again and again."

Mr. Winthrop leaned forward. "Do you mind if I ask what your favorites are?"

She laughed. "I read almost anything. Right now, it's Heinrich Schliemann's account of his excavations in Greece, searching for the lost city of Troy."

Mr. Winthrop smiled again. "So, you're interested in archaeology too? Unusual. What else do you read?"

Those dimples were devastating, and the intent look in his brown eyes produced a curious fluttering under her breastbone. "I love books about adventure, whether it's Gulliver's Travels or The Count of Monte Cristo."

"Those are some of my favorites too. Have you read Ben Hur?"

"I haven't."

"Miss Lindenmayer, you must read it. Let me find it for you." He jumped up and pulled the rolling ladder to the east corner. "I glimpsed it the other day searching for something else. Now, let's see."

He ran his fingers over the leather spines, murmuring to himself. He had a long straight nose, a square jaw, and eyelashes entirely too long for a man.

"Ah! Here it is." He descended the ladder and held out the book. "Perhaps when you've finished, we could discuss it?"

She swallowed hard at the eager look on his face. "That would be lovely."

Mr. Winthrop pulled a watch out of his waistcoat and glanced at it. "Five o'clock. This last hour has flown. I must take my leave."

Lindy jumped to her feet. "Five o'clock? Oh no!"

She ran out the library, down the marble staircase, and across the vast two-storied hall toward her mother's Régence salon on the other side of the mansion. Stopping outside the glass and bronze doors, she undid her hair ribbon, gathered the escaped curls, and retied the knot at the nape of her neck. Then she shook out her wrinkled skirts and sighed. *I'm in for it now.*

Vera Lindenmayer sat near the French windows at a tea table cluttered with silver spoons and delicate porcelain cups. Her French chignon hadn't a hair out of place, and her coral earbobs perfectly matched her tea gown. She didn't look up at her daughter's hasty approach but continued to leisurely feed a bit of pastry to the Pomeranian on her lap.

"Mama, I—"

"Be silent." Mama pressed her lips together and glowered at Lindy. "Your punctuality leaves much to be desired, Evangeline." Her sharp eyes took in Lindy's disheveled figure. "From the look of you, a person would think you care nothing for your appearance."

"I'm sorry, Mama—"

"You know we haven't much time left before our trip to London this autumn. I've worked hard to make your debut perfect, but it's obvious you care nothing for my feelings."

"That's not true, I—"

"Enough of your excuses, Miss." Mama took a sip of tea. "What engaged you so completely that you forgot your poor mother? I'll speak to Miss Kendall. If she can't keep track of you, I will have to engage another governess."

"It's not her fault, Mama." Poor Miss Kendall. Her lumbago had flared up, and when she'd fallen asleep in her chair, Lindy had tiptoed out to give her elderly tutor some much-deserved rest. "I finished my lessons and went to my room for a moment. I fell asleep." *It wouldn't do for Mama to know just how much time I actually spend in the library.*

Mama narrowed her eyes. "Is that so?"

"Yes, Mama." When she took a step closer, the Pomeranian growled and bared its teeth. "Please don't blame Miss Kendall."

"Your actions affect others, Evangeline. Never forget that."

How could she forget? Her mother never missed an opportunity to remind her.

Remember who your father is, Evangeline. Don't do anything to bring shame on this family.

People are watching. You must always be gracious and elegant, a lady in all respects.

One of these days, you will marry into the aristocracy, Evangeline. You must be ready.

"I haven't forgotten, Mama."

Her mother sniffed. "Do you remember we're off to Paris next month to choose your gowns at the Worth salon? When we return, you'll accompany me on my social calls. All of them."

Lindy groaned inwardly.

"Smile, Evangeline. No one wants to see a dour debutante."

Lindy tried to smile. "Yes, Mama." What else can I say? I've always tried to do what you expect.

"I trust you will come down to dinner punctually tonight. And have your maid do something with your hair. It looks a fright. And your corset isn't laced tight enough."

"Yes, Mama."

Lindy waited a moment, but her mother had returned to the plate of pastries, murmuring to the dog. Lindy sighed and left the salon.

Just another day in the Lindenmayer chateau.

2

A faint scent of lavender lingered after Miss Lindenmayer fled the room. Jack Winthrop hadn't expected to meet anyone in the library, and especially not someone like Evangeline Lindenmayer. She'd been quite animated when speaking of her favorite books. He could barely stop himself from staring at her lovely face and eyes—what color were they? A sort of fascinating blue-green. Had Otto Lindenmayer known his daughter used the library when he had offered the use of it? Jack shook his head. He certainly wouldn't tell him.

He slipped out the delivery entrance at the rear of the mansion and made his way to the street. Other high society folks like the Lindenmayers attended St. Thomas Episcopal Church, where his Uncle Winthrop held the office of senior pastor. Such a fuss of fur and feathers surrounded the daughters of these families, the girls whispering to each other behind their gloved fingers and peeking over the rim of their fans at the young men in the assembly. After the service, a group of these young women would invariably burst into titters at some comment, while their mothers looked on with an indulgent air.

They were like hot-house roses, raised in luxury and given the best of everything. He couldn't imagine any of them had read Robinson Crusoe, let alone have an intelligent thought about it. A few of these girls had even made cow's eyes at him, but he always handled it the same way—a stiff little bow and then turn politely away, which usually provoked more smothered giggles. How silly they all seemed.

But not Miss Lindenmayer. She didn't fit with these other girls in the least.

She had beauty and brains. Intelligence shone through her beautiful eyes, and she was thoughtful, taking the time to think about his questions before answering. And she loved to read—how amazing was that? She was like a rare jewel, shining among the rocks, or a star that blazed brighter than any other in the night sky—

"Uscire di strada, signore!"

Jack scrambled onto the curb as a two-wheeled cart clattered past, flinging dirt onto his trousers and narrowly missing his toes. This wouldn't do. Jack gave himself a shake and pushed his hat firmly onto his head.

"Hey!" Someone poked his arm. "You wanna pretzel?" An elderly woman in a tattered headscarf fixed him with shiny black eyes. She pointed to the pretzels stacked over dowels on the tiny pushcart. "Nice and fresh. You buy?"

Jack stared at the street cluttered with fruit stands, olive-skinned moppets, and swarthy men with drooping mustaches selling peppers, strings of garlic, and onions from wooden carts. The gaily-painted wooden shop signs snapped into focus.

Peruzzi Olive Oil. Banco P. Caponinigri. Giovanozzi

Formaggio. Jack blinked. He'd gotten turned around in the opposite direction on Park Avenue, veered off Fourth, and walked all the way to Grand Street in Little Italy.

He'd been shanghaied by the stunning creature in the Lindenmayer library.

"Ciao," said the Italian lady.

3

L indy tossed her hair ribbon onto the dressing table where her maid Claudine waited, hairbrush in hand. "Where have you been all afternoon, chérie?"

"In the library." Lindy sank onto the bench and quickly straightened as her corset pinched her midriff.

"No lessons?"

"Miss Kendall's napping, the poor dear."

In the mirror, Claudine arched a perfectly plucked eyebrow. "Does your maman know?"

Lindy shook her head.

"Be careful." Claudine shook a finger at her.

"What she doesn't know can't hurt her." If her mother discovered Mr. Winthrop's presence in the library, she would definitely forbid Lindy to go there. No one could know, including Claudine, normally privy to everything going on in Lindy's life since becoming her personal maid ten years ago.

Lindy closed her eyes and submitted to the soothing ministrations of Claudine's hairbrush, thinking about Mr.

Winthrop. Such a charming young man. Imagine taking classes at two colleges at the same time. Will he be in the library every day?

Claudine finished brushing and tied Lindy's hair with a fresh ribbon. "Voilà!" She stood back to admire her handiwork. "Now, what shall you wear for dinner?"

"Oh, anything. The blue, I suppose."

Lindy stood, and Claudine unbuttoned the day dress and slipped it off, leaving Lindy in her unmentionables. She wrinkled her nose. "Mama said my corset strings aren't tight enough."

"I tried to tell you this morning, chérie."

"I know. But I can't bear it so tight."

"You must if you're going to be a fashionable young lady." Claudine ran her fingers down the smooth basque of her own dress and spanned her waist with her hands. "You don't want to look like une vache, do you? A—how do you say... a cow?"

Lindy laughed. "Of course not. But I can't breathe!"

"It's the price of beauty, chérie. Come now."

Lindy rose and took hold of the chair back. Claudine loosened the ties and pulled the chemise underneath smooth against the skin. "Ready?"

Lindy braced herself as Claudine tightened the laces from top to bottom.

"There." Claudine gave a final tug and tied the laces. "Tout fini."

The simple, blue silk dinner dress went on next. "You're charming, ma petite," said Claudine. "Soon, we'll be putting your hair up every day."

Lindy nodded. After the September debut marking her entrance into adulthood, society would consider her fully a woman and ready for marriage. Though, she'd begun to have doubts about her mother's plan to marry her to a British aristocrat. Lindy checked the clock. Nearly seven. During the week, Papa insisted the staff serve dinner at seven o'clock, instead of the more fashionable eight.

Lindy ran down the marble staircase and halted at the bottom. It wouldn't do for Mama to see her running through the house. She entered the dining room as her father seated her mother. He smiled and held her chair out, then gave her a quick kiss on the cheek. "How's my girl?"

"Fine, Papa."

Mama ran her sharp gaze over Lindy and gave an approving smile. "Very good, Evangeline." She nodded at the butler. "You may begin now, Percy."

"Yes, madam." He signaled the footman to bring in the soup.

Percy served her mother first. Mama took a sip of the beef consommé and rolled it around her tongue as if tasting a fine wine. "Hmm. Too much salt. Tell Cook to use a lighter hand next time."

Percy nodded, his smooth-shaven face bland and imperturbable. "Yes, madam."

He ladled out the soup to Lindy and her father and then took his place against the wall.

The consommé tasted delicious, rich, and redolent of fennel. Mama could find fault in anything.

"Now, Otto." Mama waved her silver soup spoon at him. "Have you remembered Evangeline and I are going to Paris next month for the ball gowns?"

"Of course, dear."

"Have you checked on the flowers for the debut ball?" Otto nodded and spooned consommé at the same time.

"Good. I've decided on roses, lilies, orchids, jasmine, and orange blossoms. White roses and orchids, of course."

Five different kinds of flowers. Mama liked to do things to the extreme.

"Certainly, my dear. But..."

Her mother's head snapped around. "But?" She raised an eyebrow.

Papa laid his spoon down. "Jasmine and orange blossoms will be nearly impossible to obtain in October."

Mama sniffed. "That's why I'm telling you now, Otto. Surely some country has spring while we have autumn. South America? Don't they grow that sort of thing down there?"

Papa spread his fingers on the white tablecloth and paused, the ends of his mustache quivering. "But my dear, the cost will be prohibitive. Aren't there other white flowers that will do? Chrysanthemums, perhaps? They grow in autumn, don't they?"

"Chrysanthemums?" said Mama in a withering tone.

Papa blinked several times. "Well, maybe not chrysanthemums but perhaps—"

"As if I would use chrysanthemums for my only daughter's debut. The idea!" Mama glared at her husband.

The butler silently withdrew. Poor Papa. Only her mother could reduce him to stuttering when she turned that flat-eyed glare on him.

Lindy sat straighter. "I think mums would be perfect, Mama. Why not? They're lovely."

Her mother's lip curled. "The very word 'mum' is despicable. And what would you know about planning a debut, Evangeline?"

Lindy shrugged. "Nothing."

"Well then. I suggest you leave it to me." She exhaled hard through her nose. "This is the most important event in the life of this family, Otto, your daughter's debut into society. It must be perfect."

Papa sighed. "Yes, dear."

"I expect the jasmine and orange blossoms to be here the day before the debut."

Her father nodded and returned to his consommé, his face downcast.

Mama tossed her head. "Sometimes, I think I'm the only person who truly cares about this family's name and Evangeline's marriage."

Lindy bit her lip. *It always comes to this.*

Percy slunk into the dining room, carrying the salad course.

"Stop that!

Lindy dropped her spoon. "What?"

"Biting your lip. So unattractive."

"I was thinking about something."

Mama frowned. "What?"

Lindy shook her head and picked up her spoon. It usually didn't do to confide anything to her mother. She had a habit of turning it around on a person when least expected.

"Evangeline, answer me. What could you possibly be concerned about?"

Why can't Mama realize I have feelings, too?

"Answer me."

Lindy hesitated. *Mama had been young once. Could she understand my apprehension?* "What if I don't meet the right man? What if... I don't like any of them?"

Her mother burst out laughing. "Oh, Evangeline. We'll meet the right man."

Lindy's cheeks flamed. "Mama, I'm the one who must marry him. What if I don't love him?"

Papa choked on a bite of his salad.

Her mother pressed her lips together. "That's only in fairy tales, darling. If you're fortunate, you'll come to care for each other in time. Like your father and I did. Isn't that right, Otto?"

Papa swallowed hard and cleared his throat. "Yes, dear," he croaked.

THE AFTERNOON SHADOWS had lengthened by the time Jack arrived home at his uncle's brownstone on the Upper East Side. After leaving Miss Lindenmayer and getting completely turned around in the opposite direction, he had headed north, striding as quickly as he could manage, having no spare pocket money for an omnibus.

He usually joined his mother for afternoon tea, but teatime had passed long ago. He gave a wide berth to two young boys throwing jackknives on the grass in a game of mumblety-peg and sprinted up the steps into the house.

Their red-haired Scottish maid, Jenny, appeared to take his hat and coat. She folded it over her arm and lifted a ruddy eyebrow. "Himself wants ye in his study."

"Thank you, Jenny."

"Ye canna go in lookin' like that, sir."

He followed her scandalized glance to his trousers, where mud clumps clung untidily to the black wool.

"Wait here, sir, while I fetch ye a cloth." She hurried away toward the kitchen. What did his uncle want with him now? He usually only saw his uncle at supper, and even then, the conversation dragged. Jack sighed. Nothing's going to change any time soon.

Jenny returned with a damp cloth, and over Jack's protestations, swiftly wiped away the offending mud.

"There," she said, with a final flick of the cloth. "Aye, ye'll do now."

"Thank you, Jenny," he said, with all the dignity he could muster, and headed for the rear of the brownstone, where his uncle's study overlooked a leafy courtyard. He knocked quietly.

His uncle's deep voice rumbled through the door. "Come."

Jack entered the study. A bailiwick of order and decorum, hundreds of books sorted by size and subject lined the walls. Not a spare pen nib or scrap of paper littered his uncle's desk. The leather blotter lay squarely in the center, and the red lacquered desk objects – an ink blotter, a pen cup, a stamp box, and a letter opener—were lined up with military precision at the front of the desk, each item exactly four inches from the next. His uncle sat at his desk, crouched over a book, a pen in his other hand, and the inkpot lid open. "Ah, there you are, boy."

"My name is Jack, Uncle."

"Yes, yes, so it is." He pushed away the book he'd been studying and picked up an envelope. "Sit down." He peered over the top of his spectacles at Jack. "Your midterm marks have come in."

"Yes, Uncle."

"Sit, please." Reverend Winthrop shrugged. "Not bad. Could be better." He cast a steely glance at Jack. "Latin got the best of you, boy, hey?"

Jack shrugged. "Not at all." He grasped the handle of the ink blotter and absently rolled it back and forth on the desk. "I enjoy it."

His uncle frowned and pursed his lips, then stared pointedly at Jack's hand.

Jack dropped the blotter hastily.

His uncle retrieved it and nudged the handle until it lined up perfectly with the other objects, restoring the careful symmetry of the desk.

Then he scowled and shifted in his chair to scrutinize Jack. "I think you can do better. You've got to hold up the Winthrop name." He sniffed. "Even if your father couldn't." Jack stiffened. His father had been dead for fifteen years, yet to this day, his uncle could never resist an opportunity to belittle him. He clenched his jaw and stood. "There is no need to castigate my dead father. I intend to do my best to honor the Winthrop name," he said through gritted teeth. "Is there anything else?"

"Tut-tut." His uncle clicked his tongue with disapproval. "Always so proud and sensitive. You'll have to get over that if you expect to follow me into the ministry."

The last thing I want to do is follow in your footsteps, Uncle. But this wasn't the time or place to make such a statement. And his uncle wasn't exactly a model of humility. Or sensitivity. "You'll have to have some faith in me, Uncle. That is your area of expertise, is it not? Faith?"

His uncle pursed his lips, and his eyes narrowed. "Don't forget, I'm paying for your education." He rapped gnarled knuckles on the desk. "And I always expect a return on my investments."

"Yes sir." His hand touched the doorknob behind him. "Is that all, sir?"

"How is the library at Lindenmayer's? Meeting your needs?"

"It's excellent, sir. Everything I could hope for."

"Yes. Capital of Lindenmayer to offer the use of it."

"I met his daughter today."

Reverend Winthrop's head swiveled around. "His daughter?" His eyes bored into Jack.

"Yes, briefly. Apparently, she loves to read."

"Now, you listen here." His uncle fixed him with a chilling stare. "You've no reason to speak to her. Avoid her at all costs."

"Uncle, we only exchanged a few words. I hardly think-"

"Stay away from her."

"Whatever you say, sir."

His uncle waved a hand at him. "That's all."

Why did every encounter with his uncle have to be so difficult? As if he was still a little boy and not a grown man. Jack exhaled hard. One year to go, and he would graduate. The sooner he finished school and could strike out on his own, the better. Until then, he would have to endure his uncle's condescension.

He took the stairs two at a time and headed to the spacious bedroom at the front of the brownstone. Softly, he knocked on the door. When no answer came, he pushed it open. His mother lay asleep, her slender form barely making a bump under the blue coverlet. He tiptoed to the bed.

She lay on her side, her hand under her cheek and her hair in a long silver braid down her back. If it weren't for the pallor of her skin and the color of her hair, she might have been a young woman. A faint smile curved her lips, and a pang went through his chest. Until a few months ago, she had been hale and hearty and fully committed to being Uncle Winthrop's hostess and housekeeper.

She woke then, and held her hand out to him, her smile deepening. "Hello, dear. How long have you been standing there?"

He pulled a chair close and sat down. "Not long. I'm sorry I missed our teatime."

"That's fine, son." She sat up and pulled another pillow

behind her. "I know you're busy with your studies. Have you had a good day?"

"My college grades arrived."

"And?"

"My mark could have been a bit higher in Latin. Otherwise, I've done well."

"Then I'm sure Joseph remarked on that."

"He remarked on the Latin grade. And reminded me of my responsibility to bring honor to the Winthrop name."

"That sounds like your uncle."

Jack snorted. "Pompous and didactic?"

His mother shook her finger at him. "I know he can be rather heavy-handed at times."

"I'll say," muttered Jack.

"But he has been good to us, son."

"I know, Mother. I don't mean to criticize, but in every discussion we have, he always somehow manages to denigrate father."

His mother sighed. "It's true there was no love lost between them. I remember well the arguments they would have." Her gaze flicked to him. "And I don't suppose it helps that the older you get, the more like him you look." She reached out and gently brushed the troublesome lock of hair off his forehead, then glanced at the sepia photograph on her dressing table. "He had that same forelock."

His father's serious face stared at him out of the silver frame. "I wish I could have known him." The few memories he had of his father grew dimmer with each passing year.

"He would have been so proud of you."

Jack patted her hand. "Enough about me, Mother. How's the cough today?"

"Better, I think. The new medicine is helping."

If only it were true. She'd lost so much weight her

cheekbones looked like sculpted marble. And the hand she lifted to push away a tendril of hair appeared almost translucent. He could swear the sunlight passed right through it. But she hadn't coughed once since he'd entered her bedroom.

He took her hand, determined to be light and gay for her sake. "I met a girl today."

"Indeed!" The sparkle returned to her clear gray eyes, and she sat forward. "Tell me about her."

"She's the daughter of the Lindenmayers. Her name is Evangeline."

"Hmm. One of the society people from the church."

"Yes. But she's different."

"She must be, if she attracted your attention." She smiled at him. "I know you don't care for most of the young ladies at church."

"That's true. But Miss Lindenmayer loves to read, and we had an interesting discussion about books. I think you'd like her."

"I'm sure I—" she broke off, snatched a handkerchief from her sleeve, and pressed it to her mouth. But not quickly enough for him to miss the bright red blood on her lips.

He stood, helpless, as the coughing episode erupted. Her slender shoulders shook with the force of the spasm, over and over, until it finally waned, and she sank exhausted onto the pillow, gasping, her forehead beaded with sweat.

The door burst open, and his uncle rushed in. "Anna!" He halted when he caught sight of Jack at the dresser, wetting a cloth with the water in the pitcher. "Are you—"

She flapped her hand at him, not yet able to speak. His uncle plucked the wet cloth from Jack's fingers and approached her. He took a seat on the edge of the bed and gently sponged her face.

The sound of her ragged breathing tore through Jack's chest, and he clenched his fists, wishing for the thousandth time he could do something to help her.

"She's fallen asleep," his uncle said. "We must let her rest."

Jack leaned over and kissed her pale cheek. "I love you, Mother," he whispered. "Sleep well."

4

The library door opened, and the whistled strains of "A Mighty Fortress is Our God" floated over to Lindy. Mr. Winthrop turned the corner a moment later, carrying a book under his arm. "Good morning, Miss Lindenmayer." He nodded at the book in her lap. "Are you enjoying Ben Hur?"

"Yes, very much."

A frown creased his brow. "Are you well?" His brows knit together. "You look a trifle pale."

Lindy fingered the cover of her book. *A proper gentleman never remarked on a lady's health or lack of it. But no one else in the house ever seems to notice anything amiss with me.*

Mr. Winthrop bit his lip. "Forgive me. That was presumptuous. I do hope you haven't been ill." He rolled his eyes. "There I go again. Please excuse me. I'll leave you to your book."

He turned to go.

"No, wait. Would you like to sit down?"

"If I'm not interrupting you."

"Please." She indicated the wing chair across from her. "May I ask how your mother is feeling?"

He sighed. "About the same. She is consumptive, Miss Lindenmayer. Although my uncle has had the best physicians attend her, there seems to be little they can do for her horrid condition."

"Oh." She twisted her hands in her lap. "I am so sorry to hear that. I will pray for her."

"Thank you. I'm not ashamed to say I covet every prayer for her healing I can get."

She glanced at the book in his hand, thinking to change the conversation to a happier tonic. His shoulders had slumped when he spoke of his mother. "Pascal's Pensées."

"Yes. Do you know it?"

"I do."

He nodded approvingly. "And what were your thoughts when you finished it?"

When has anyone besides Miss Kendall asked my thoughts on anything? "It's wonderful. He writes so beautifully."

"The book was published posthumously.

"I didn't know that."

"Yes. Pascal was passionate about his Christianity and de- fending the faith. He died before he could finish the book. A close friend put his notes together. Apparently, Pascal suffered from ill-health all his life, and died at the age of thirty-nine."

"His thoughts on the vacuum inside of us—what was it exactly?"

"I love that too. Here, let me find it." He paged through the slim volume. "Page seventy-five." He cleared his throat. "'What else does this craving, and this helplessness, proclaim but that there was once in man a true happiness, of which all that now remains is the empty print and trace? This he tries in vain to fill with everything around him, seeking in things that are not there the help he cannot find in those that are, though none can help, since this infinite abyss can be filled only with an infinite and immutable object; in other words by God himself.'"

He let the book slip to his lap. "Compelling words."

She nodded. "I think I know what he means by man trying to fill that void with things. Riches, houses, jewels. I see it everywhere around me here in New York. In the society my family is a part of. Each ball, each mansion, must be more magnificent than the one before. And my mother —" She broke off. It wouldn't be polite to burden Mr. Winthrop with her doubts and questions, and in any case, the last subject she could discuss with him would be her mother.

"You were saying?"

Her cheeks turned hot. "I'm sorry... you must excuse me... I don't know why I'm dithering on like this."

"My dear Miss Lindenmayer, you're not dithering. You're sharing your heart with a friend. At least, I hope you count me your friend."

She did, she realized. Perhaps the only one who might understand. She nodded slowly. "It's only—I ponder these things and have no one to discuss them with. My father is always busy with his horses. My best friend, Madeleine, doesn't have thoughts like mine. All she's concerned about is beaus and ball gowns."

"What about your mother?"

She snorted and then clapped her hand over her mouth. "Excuse me! But that's too funny, really. She'd laugh at me."

His brown eyes grew serious. "I give you my word. I will never laugh at you."

All his attention centered on her as if she were the most important person in the world. As if her thoughts truly interested him. "My mother spent most of her adult life craving something she didn't have. Entrance into high society. After she married my father, she set about procuring that entrance, by beating the grande dame of society at her own game."

Mr. Winthrop crossed one long leg over the other. "Hmm. And how did she accomplish that?"

"She arranged a ball. The most magnificent masquerade ball anyone had ever seen. Mrs. Astor hadn't received my mother, but Mrs. Astor's daughter, Carrie, had a part in one of the quadrilles. But when no invitation came for Carrie from my mother, Caroline Astor had to send her calling card and meet my mother, so her daughter could attend the ball. Mrs. Astor came too. The city talked of it for months, according to my mother. She's been in her element ever since."

"Do I detect an undercurrent of disapproval?"

She twisted her hands in her lap. "There's only one thing left Mama craves. Ever since I was a little girl, my mother's dream has been for me to marry into the aristocracy, preferably of England. A duke or an earl, at the least."

"A duke?" Mr. Winthrop frowned and leaned forward. "I don't understand."

"It's the final thing she covets. Don't you see? A title! She wants a title in the family. And I'm the one who must consummate her desire."

Mr. Winthrop's eyebrows rose.

She'd said too much. Confided too much. He would think her insolent and ill-bred to speak so of her family. She jumped up out of her chair. "Have you explored the rest of the library, Mr. Winthrop?"

He blinked at her sudden change of conversation but rose gamely to his feet. "Why, no, I haven't."

"Let me show you how we organized it. In the event you ever need to look up anything outside your current studies." Without waiting for his answer, she walked to the closest wall of books. "Let's see. This entire section is Greek and Roman histories. American history. British military campaigns."

She moved on to the next wall of books, talking too fast. "Works of fiction and poetry. I know we have some early first editions. Swift and Byron, to name two."

What on earth was the matter with her? Blathering like an idiot. But she couldn't seem to stop. The tour ended at the west wall, filled with science tomes from astronomy to zoology. She had run out of words. Now what should she do?

"It's quite spacious, isn't it?"

She stole a glance at him. He waved a hand. "It takes years to acquire a library like this. Or did he inherit them?"

Lindy's shoulders relaxed. "Surely, you've heard the term nouveau riche, Mr. Winthrop? My father has only acquired his wealth in the last thirty years, the opposite of patrician bluebloods like the Astors and the Stuyvesants. When my mother built this house, she had the architect fill the library with all the books a proper gentleman should have."

"Oh..." Mr. Winthrop stammered. "I beg your pardon."

"Don't allow that to disconcert you. Both you and I benefit from this library, inherited or not."

"That's true." He walked to a gilded display case set in a corner and pointed to the objects nestled inside on black velvet cloth. "And whose are these?"

She joined him at the case. "This is my curiosity collection." She turned the tiny key in the lock and opened the glass door. "My Uncle Henry's home, Mahicantuck, is in Hyde Park, and I used to hunt for fossils in the river bed and the bluffs above." She plucked a pale gray rock out of the case. "This is a trilobite." A small, segmented body lay embedded in the stone.

"I spent summers with my uncle when I was a little girl. My interest grew from there. Most girls want trinkets for their birthdays, but I always wanted these old historical things. My father would surprise me every year with something new for my collection, like these Roman bronzes from Pompeii for my ninth birthday. He gave me this piece of amber when I turned twelve." She picked up a golden lump. "There's a fossilized insect inside."

Mr. Winthrop peered into its clear depths. "Ah! I see it. A dragonfly. Remarkable. And what in tarnation is this creature?"

He pointed to a peculiar stuffed animal on the bottom shelf, with overlapping scales, a triangular head, and tiny clawed feet.

Lindy laughed. "That is queer, isn't it? It's an armadillo, an animal found only in Texas and the southern United States. That's not a birthday present."

"I'm relieved to hear it." Mr. Winthrop smiled at her, and that curious flutter went through her breastbone again. "I've heard of a 'cabinet of curiosities,' but I'd never seen one. I don't suppose you hunt for fossils anymore?"

She sighed. "I certainly won't find any in New York City.

But I'd love to go on a dig sometime." "A dig?" His eyes widened.

"An archaeological excavation. Like the one Mr. Schliemann worked on in Greece. I'd love to go to Egypt. Or Rome."

He grinned. "Miss Lindenmayer, I know what a dig is.

We're kindred spirits, for I plan to go on a dig myself. It's part of the curriculum at Columbia. But it's difficult for me to picture you spending all day in the hot sun, getting your hands dirty, and living in a tent!"

She laughed. "I know it sounds odd, but that's my idea of heaven."

"You've become quite animated speaking about archaeology, Miss Lindenmayer. Feeling better now?" This time he didn't apologize for remarking on her health.

She observed his open, honest face and smiled back. "I do now."

5

M ay 1897

JACK GLANCED at the empty dining chair across the table. For the last fortnight, his mother hadn't been strong enough to come downstairs for supper and grew steadily weaker.

The windows of the dining room were open to the spring air, and the fresh scent of newly-turned flower beds drifted through. Children played on the street outside as the days grew longer. But in this room with his uncle, silence lay heavy like a tomb. Only the clink of silverware against the china gave any evidence of life.

Jack's thoughts went to the library in the Lindenmayer mansion, where earlier this afternoon, Miss Lindenmayer had shared some details of her life with him. Funny, he'd never thought about what life might be like for the high society young women in the church. That they would marry a man of their parent's choosing. But what about love? His parents had married for love. And then his father had died young, leaving his mother in a precarious position with no means of support. If it weren't for his uncle...

"Have you no conversation this evening?" His uncle glowered at him, his lower lip thrust out in a most unpleasant way. His surliness had increased in direct proportion to his mother's worsening condition.

Startled, Jack tore his thoughts back to the present. "I'm sorry, Uncle."

"What are you thinking about?"

Do I dare answer honestly? He laid his fork down. "My parents actually. Their marriage."

His uncle's face screwed up into a frown. "A mistake from the start."

Jack blinked, not expecting such a blatant statement of disapproval. "Pardon me, sir? A mistake?"

"They were never suited." His uncle chomped viciously on a piece of beef, swallowed it, and speared another piece. "Never should have been allowed."

"Never should have been allowed?" Jack choked out.

"Stop repeating everything I say. You heard me."

"My mother would never say that. She loved him. And he her."

His uncle glared at him. "She was too young to see how shallow he was. My brother swept her away with his smooth charm and pretty words. And then what does he do? Goes out and gets himself killed."

"He could hardly have planned that," cried Jack, fury rising in him.

"Stop shouting." His uncle helped himself to another serving of beef. "It's fortunate for you and your mother I took you in."

Jack swallowed hard. Calm down. Don't rise to the bait.

His uncle would never have voiced these thoughts if Mother had been at the table. Until now, he'd never realized how much of a buffer she'd always been between them. And as her illness worsened, the crotchetier his uncle became.

"Yes, Uncle, it was." He swallowed the bitterness and forced himself to say the next words. "Thank you."

"Humph."

For the next few moments, they ate in silence.

"Why the deuce don't you get a haircut?" Across the table, once again, his uncle glared at him.

Jack took a deep breath. His uncle required a monthly accounting of the stipend he gave Jack, a paltry amount out of which Jack paid for his clothes and shoes, and all the other assorted items a young man needed. His uncle knew right well what Jack did with the money. Rarely did he have even a penny left over.

An old Bible verse popped into Jack's head. "A gentle answer turns away wrath." He smiled wryly. "I'll get one this week, sir."

His uncle pushed his plate away so sharply the fork slid onto the tablecloth. His fingers trembled when he plucked it from the cloth and threw it onto the dish.

"Uncle Joseph," said Jack gently. He laid his hand over his uncle's. "I'm worried about her too."

The anguish in his uncle's eyes made Jack wince.

His uncle groaned. "I don't know what I'll do without her," he whispered.

"I know." Jack swallowed. "I can barely stand to think about it. But Uncle, we'll go through it together."

"Yes. We must support each other." He started to say something and then hesitated. "I haven't been kind to you, Jack. I took you into my home, but it was all for Anna. But in these last few weeks, I've realized you and Anna are the only family I have."

Jenny entered the dining room to clear away the plates. His uncle rose. "Come into the parlor. There's a matter I want to discuss with you."

Jack followed his uncle to the little-used room with horsehair sofas and heavy portiere curtains. A baby grand piano stood in the corner. His mother used to play after dinner when she had been well, everything from the lyrical notes of Debussy to the rousing chorus of Daisy Bell and her bicycle built for two.

His uncle went over to the piano and trailed a finger across the cover's shining wood. "Your mother is not improving." He turned, his jaw clenched. "There's a sanitarium in the Adirondack mountains at Saranac Lake. I'd like to take her there this week." He sat abruptly, as if his legs couldn't hold him. "If you agree with my plan, that is. Your mother sets a great store by you, Jack," he said gruffly.

"Of course, Uncle. If there's anything to be done, we must try."

His uncle's shoulders sagged. "Thank you. There's a theory that fresh mountain air can be curative for consumption. After her last coughing spell, I've been beside myself with worry."

Jack nodded, studying his uncle's face. There were deep lines around his mouth he hadn't noticed before, and more gray in his hair. A sudden thought dawned on Jack. "You love her, don't you?"

His uncle smiled faintly. "Since the day I first laid eyes on her." He stared into the distance over Jack's shoulder. "But she never saw me. Your father was the charming one." He sighed. "I suppose that's why I've been so hard on you. You're so like him." He looked directly at Jack. "And then in other ways, you're nothing like him. You're a hard worker, Jack, and a good student."

Jack blinked, unaccustomed to hearing praise from him. "Thank you."

His uncle stood and squared his shoulders. "The arrangements will be made tomorrow. I'll take good care of her."

6

P aris, France

LINDY TOOK a wistful breath of the lilac-scented air and wondered what Mr. Winthrop might be doing at the moment in New York City. Would he like Paris? It was heavenly to be here in spring, the breeze soft and sweet enough to use an open carriage. The chestnut trees had burst into full bloom along the Avenue de l'Opéra, and sunlight filtered through their newly-minted leaves, dappling the street with muted light.

"Do stop fidgeting, Evangeline. A lady must always be calm and collected."

"But it's so lovely, Mama, isn't it? The trees are breathtaking."

Her mother glanced up from the leather-covered notebook in her lap and waved a gold pencil at her. "I haven't time to notice the trees, Missy. I'm busy thinking about all the dresses and ball gowns you require for the season."

Lindy bit her lip. How unfortunate to miss such a glorious morning.

The landau turned off the Avenue de l'Opéra and onto the Rue de la Paix, stopping before number seven. The coachman handed them down. Two dapper young men in frock coats greeted them and opened the double glass doors. A grand marble staircase swept up to the second floor, carpeted in a rich crimson red, and lined with exotic palms.

A vendeuse clad in black satin met them at the top of the stairs. "Bonjour, madame et mademoiselle." She ushered them through several drawing rooms. Black and white silks in glass cabinets filled the first room, with silks in a rainbow of colors in the second. The third contained velvets and plush of all types and opened into the airy and spacious salon, where the natural light reflected off the mirrored walls.

Live mannequins strolled about the room in the latest designs. The vendeuse sat next to Mama, pointing out the particular charms of a piece of lace or a striped brocade bustle on the models gliding by.

Lindy squirmed on the upholstered bench next to her mother, trying to find a position that would allow her to take a deep breath. The corset encased her from ribcage to hips, tightly boned and laced up the back.

"Bring that girl closer." Her mother nodded at a slim blonde mannequin in a vision of white tulle and embroidered white rosebuds. Mama stood up to examine the gown more closely, fingering the rosebuds.

"The skirt is watered silk, madame. You see how elegantly it drapes." With a deft hand, the vendeuse turned the girl to indicate the small train. "Simple, but bewitching."

"That might do." Mama turned to Lindy. "Stand up, Evangeline." When Lindy did so, her mother tipped her head to one side, considering. "Yes. That's the one." The vendeuse glanced at Lindy, who shrugged.

A maid brought a silver tray of tea and sweetmeats for the ladies' refreshment while the mannequins disappeared to change into the ball gowns. A debutante's gown must be white, but ball gowns were different. Here there was a myriad of colors to choose from. This would be Lindy's first ball gown.

One by one, the slender mannequins glided into the salon. Lindy eyed a gown of ice-blue damask trimmed in embroidered lace and pearls, with rows of crystal pendants on the sleeves. Next, a model twirled through the salon in a gown of deep cherry-pink satin hemmed in black fur, with beaded iris designs on the skirt. Short, puffy sleeves of mousseline de soie were tucked under ruffles of beaded satin.

Mama nodded her head at the pink gown. "That might do for the Christmas Ball. But I don't like the sleeves. Could they be lengthened?"

The vendeuse nodded. "Of course, madame." She snapped her fingers at another girl who brought a thick book of illustrated pattern pieces. Together they leafed through its pages. "This one." Mama pointed to her choice.

"Excellent, madame."

More models entered the salon. A gown of yellow silk brocade with embroidered tassels design caught her mother's eye. Lindy shuddered. The gown had gigot sleeves—huge puffed sleeves of velvet—in an apricot color, with a large silk taffeta bow at the breast.

"That's perfect."

Lindy swallowed hard. "Mama, I don't care for it."

Her mother turned, eyebrows raised. "And since when do you know anything about selecting a gown, Evangeline?"

"I hoped I might be able to choose something for myself since I'll be the one wearing them."

Mama pressed her lips together. "You need a gown like this, Evangeline. It helps disguise the inadequacy of your figure." Her gaze dropped to Lindy's bosom. "If you know what I mean."

The vendeuse shot a glance at Lindy and then looked away.

Lindy's face flamed, and she took a deep breath.

"I do the thinking, Evangeline. Your duty is to obey."

She glared at Lindy until she murmured, "Yes, Mama." Why did I think today would be any different?

A burly figure in a paisley silk smoking jacket swept into the room. "Ah, forgive me, madame." Charles Frederick Worth removed his black velvet beret and swept her a low bow. "Business unavoidably detained me, but I am here now and at your service." He took the seat next to her mother and smiled at Lindy. "Now, where are we?"

"I've chosen the debut gown already, monsieur. We're looking at the ball gowns now."

"Exceptional." He nodded to the live mannequins, who once again began their slow amble around the room.

Her mother selected several more gowns. All to Lindy's distaste. But it was no use to say anything. Lindy shifted on her bench. It would be over soon.

Then a model went by, and Lindy sat up straighter. This gown was different. Simpler. Celadon silk ruching rippled in waves over the bodice, a pale blue-green, with delicate undertones of soft gray, like the sea outside their Newport mansion, Seaside. The skirt draped over a smaller bustle than was popular at the moment and flowed to the ground in a silken sweep. Silvery chrysanthemum petals embroidered at the hem reflected the light. The décolleté left the arms bare while diamanté beading on the soft shoulder straps sparkled softly.

"May I see that one?" Lindy couldn't believe she'd spoken up again. Next to her, her mother exhaled hard.

Mr. Worth stood up. "Mademoiselle has a wonderful eye. Come here, Sophie."

The gown was even lovelier up close. The silk had a translucent, ethereal quality. Mr. Worth lifted a fold of the skirt and held it against Lindy's cheek.

"It matches your eyes perfectly, mademoiselle."

Lindy fingered the silk. "The color is amazing."

"It's called 'Eau de Mer.'"

She didn't dare look at her mother. "I will take this one, monsieur."

"I congratulate you on your choice."

Mama's upper lip quivered, but she held her tongue until they left the salon. Then she clamped her hand on Lindy's arm. "Whatever possessed you in there, Evangeline? I have never been so insulted. And by my own daughter!" She squeezed Lindy's arm hard. "You will not do that again, Miss, I assure you."

Lindy wrenched away from her mother's grasp and glared at her. "I don't understand why you won't allow me to make some choices for myself. It's only a gown, Mama."

Her mother flushed dark red. "Are you contradicting me, Evangeline?"

Lindy exhaled forcefully. "No. I'm not. But Mama, I won't always have you at my side to—" *To tell me what to do.* She took a step back. "I have to learn sometime. Why not now?"

Mama shrugged and pulled her sable stole around her shoulders. "There's too much at stake here to indulge your childish whims. Once we make a suitable match and you're married, you may choose to wear whatever you like." Her mother reached out and tucked a curl behind Lindy's ear. "Even then, dear, I'm sure you'll still need me. I imagine I will be making quite a few trips abroad to oversee things."

She held her hand out to the footman, who assisted her into the landau.

Lindy clenched her jaw. Her mother had to control everything. If the day ever came that Lindy refused to do her mother's bidding, the resulting explosion would be bigger than the fireworks over the Brooklyn Bridge on Independence Day.

7

N ew York City

JACK HAD IMMERSED himself so completely in his study of Ephesians he didn't hear the knock at the door.

"Are ye in there, sir?" A more rigorous knock sounded. "Sir?"

"Come in, Jenny."

"A letter's come for ye."

"From who?"

Jenny drew herself up to her full height of five feet and glowered at him. "I dinna ken, sir." She sniffed. "I'm not in the habit of readin' other people's mail—I can tell ye that."

"Don't get your knickers in a twist now, Jenny. You know I didn't mean that."

"I'll thank ye, sir, to leave me knickers out of it." She waved the letter at him. "But since ye're askin', I believe your mam wrote it. I smell roses." She dropped the envelope on the desk in front of him and left the room.

Jack breathed in the summery scent of his mother's eau de toilette and opened the letter.

MAY 12, 1897, Saranac Lake

DEAREST JACK,

WE ARRIVED SAFELY LAST EVENING. I am staying in a little house called a "cure cottage" on the grounds of the sanitarium. A nurse stays with me. Her name is Betty, and she is most pleasant. The cottage has two porches, one open and one glassed-in, so I might 'take the air.' Your uncle is staying at an inn in the village, although he is here most of the day with me, and quite attentive. All the staff is cheerful, with not a sour face among them.

I am writing this after lunch, and I must stop soon and take a rest. Even if it were not a scheduled rest time, I fear the noonday dinner would compel me to somnolence, for never such a heavy dinner have I seen! We had roast beef, and mutton, and some type of wild game, which I declined, much to the consternation of the server, who seemed to take it as a personal affront. Then there was creamed spinach, peas, lettuce with lemon juice, and mashed potatoes. And then, for a sweet, a huge baked rice pudding. I am bursting at the seams, my dear. I shudder to think what breakfast items await me tomorrow.

.   .   .

ALWAYS YOUR LOVING,

MOTHER

JACK DROPPED the letter onto his desk. Did she know his uncle loved her as more than a sister-in-law? She sounded cheerful. But his mother always put a gracious air on everything.

He closed his eyes. Dear Lord, bless her. Heal her. Fill her with joy in Your presence. Remove this sentence of death from her.

Then he laid his head on the desk and wept.

HIS CHURCH HISTORY textbook held Jack's attention, but even so, when the library door opened, he looked up at once.

"Good morning, Mr. Winthrop."

Is it my imagination, or does she look even lovelier than ever?

Instead of her usual long tail of hair tied back with a ribbon, her curls and waves were swept up into a thick chignon. It emphasized her exquisite cheekbones and the long slender line of her neck.

He stumbled to his feet. "Good morning, Miss Lindenmayer." The calmness of his own voice surprised him. As if he hadn't been eagerly waiting for the last fortnight to see her again. "How was your trip to Paris?"

"Productive." She wrinkled her nose. "As far as my mother is concerned, anyway."

"Did you enjoy yourself?"

She sat down. "I did. It's a wonderful city, especially in the spring. And what about you? Are you well?"

"Yes. Quite well."

She eyed him and then tipped her head to one side, scrutinizing him. "Are you sure?"

"Why do you ask?"

She blushed then, a delicate pink suffusing her face and neck. "It's just—" She shrugged. "You look sad."

And he'd thought he'd done a good job of hiding his feelings. "You're perceptive." He sighed. "It's my mother. My uncle has taken her to a clinic in Saranac Lake. She isn't doing well."

"I'm so sorry. Has she written?"

"Yes, I've had a note this morning." He patted the pocket of his coat.

MAY 12, 1897, Saranac Lake

MY DEAREST SON,

THE DAYS ARE PASSING AGREEABLY ENOUGH. I rest quite a bit, and sometimes if the evening is fair, your uncle pushes me about in a wheelchair. My days are full with rest periods, doctor appointments, and something they call therapy, which is simply another name for spending your time making things no one could possibly use or want. I made an embroidered coat hanger today, and I think I will give it to you when I come home. I do so long to see your handsome face. I think my coughing spells are not as bad as they were.

Always your loving,

. . .

MOTHER

"SHE SAYS her cough is better. But I know she wouldn't tell me if it wasn't."

"Not wanting to worry you."

"Yes."

Miss Lindenmayer sat and smoothed her skirt. "You and your mother are close."

"We are. I wish you could meet her," he blurted out. "I know she'd like you."

Miss Lindenmayer's eyes widened. "That would be an honor. But..."

"I know. We don't inhabit the same society circles."

"That's not it, Mr. Winthrop." She leaned forward. "As an unmarried woman, I am chaperoned and watched every moment I leave my home. It wouldn't be possible." She smiled. "But if it were up to me, I'd love to meet her."

Jack smiled at her. "Then, I suppose I'm fortunate you are not chaperoned here in the library."

A glint sparkled in her eye. "That you are, sir!"

"What are you reading now?" He glanced at the exotic cover of the book in her lap.

"A Thousand Miles Up the Nile. Have you heard of it?"

"Can't say I have." He sat down across from her. "Interesting?"

"Oh my, yes. It's Amelia Edwards' account of her trip up the Nile in a houseboat."

He rubbed his chin. "Wait a moment. I do know that name. As a boy, I read one of her ghost stories. The Phantom Coach. Scared the heck out of me."

"Oh? I will have to look into that. I love a good ghost story." She plucked a pencil from the side table and jotted the title down in a notebook. "Her writing is amazing. I've just started it, but already I'm entranced. Listen to this from the first chapter."

BUT WHAT HAD memory to do with rains on land, or storms at sea, or the impatient hour of quarantine, or anything dismal or disagreeable, when one awoke at sunrise to see those gray-green palms outside the window solemnly bowing their plumed heads towards each other, against a rose-coloured dawn? It was dark last night, and I had no idea that my room overlooked an enchanted garden, far-reaching and solitary, peopled with stately giants beneath whose tufted crowns hung rich clusters of maroon and amber dates. Yonder, between the pillared stems, rose the minaret of a distant mosque; and here where the garden was bounded by a high wall and windowless house, I saw a veiled lady walking on the terraced roof in the midst of a cloud of pigeons.

"CAN'T you just see it? I feel that I'm there."

"It sounds fascinating." Mr. Winthrop smiled and held out his hand. "May I?"

She handed him the book, which he perused for the next several minutes, examining the many drawings and reading some of the prose.

Then he closed the book and handed it back to her. "May I borrow it when you've finished it?"

"Of course."

A glint came into his eyes, and he smiled mischievously.

"You certainly have a great interest in Egypt. Perhaps you'd like to see a mummy unwrapped?"

She wrinkled her nose. "Goodness, no, I don't think so. They were mummified as part of their death ritual. It seems wrong to disturb that." She smoothed a fold in her skirt. "But it is a dream of mine to see Egypt someday. The Sphinx. The Great Pyramid. The Valley of the Kings."

"Then, I hope you are able to."

"It isn't likely." Mama's plans for me don't include a trip to Egypt.

"But I can just see you riding a camel in the Egyptian desert, in a khaki skirt and a pith helmet on your head, notebook in hand."

She smiled. "I've never admitted that secret hope to anyone, Mr. Winthrop."

"Then I'm honored you shared it with me." His brown eyes deepened as he gazed at her. "Hold on to your dreams, Miss Lindenmayer."

Her heart turned over in her chest.

Mr. Winthrop, you almost make me believe it's possible.

8

J ack drove his uncle's carriage down Madison Avenue toward the Grand Central train depot on Forty-Second Street. Thousands of glass panes composed the iron and glass roof of the train yard and cast a soft, coppery glow of lamplight into the night.

He checked the time on the clock in the center of the largest tower. Seven twenty-seven, his uncle had telegraphed. Although his mother had been away only three weeks, it seemed much longer. Her last letter had been positive, but still, some nameless feeling of dread had surrounded him since he read it.

MAY 19, 1897, Saranac Lake

DEAREST JACK,

.   .   .

I DON'T WANT you to worry needlessly, but I think the fresh air of the mountains has done its best for me. Actually, I don't think I should be able to endure many more days of sanitarium food. Mutton chops were served for breakfast today. Did you ever? If consumption doesn't kill me, the food here certainly will.

I don't mean to seem frivolous, my dear son. I miss you.

I've been away from home long enough. It's time to come home.

EVER YOUR LOVING,

MOTHER

LORD, what's happening? He tried to tamp down the dread and focus on positive things. He repeated to himself 2 Timothy 2:7. "For the Lord has not given us a spirit of fear, but of power, and love, and of a sound mind."

Then his uncle emerged from the depot, wheeling the chair his mother had spoken of. She sat motionless within its wicker embrace, only the pale oval of her face showing from her cocoon of blankets.

His uncle approached and laid a gentle hand on his shoulder, and somehow Jack pushed away the despair that washed over him. "Hello, Mother," he said.

She stirred then and gazed at him with such a sweet look of love that tears welled in his eyes. She seemed even more ethereal than she had been before. Her slender hand emerged from the blankets toward his face. "My darling son, how happy I am to see you."

He leaned over and took her cold hands in his. His throat smarted, and he didn't trust himself to speak.

"Take me home, son."

Wordlessly, he gathered her in his arms and lifted her from the chair, her weight negligible. A sob caught in his throat then, and he stopped, unable to go on. His uncle came behind and pressed his shoulder hard. "Let's get her home, Jack."

Jack nodded. His uncle got into the carriage, and Jack handed her in to him. He swung himself up into the seat next to her. She laid her head on his shoulder and sighed.

JACK CARRIED her upstairs to the blue bedroom. Together, they removed her coat and shoes. She had traveled in her nightclothes.

"She was too exhausted to dress this morning," his uncle whispered.

They laid her in the bed, where she curled up on her side.

"Please open the windows, Joseph. I want to hear the crickets."

His uncle protested. "You'll take a chill."

She only looked at him. His shoulders slumped, and then he raised the window sashes, letting the tender night breeze into the room.

"I must leave you for a bit, Anna." He turned and left the room, leaving the door ajar.

Jack pulled a chair close to the bed, and she held out her hand. He sat and took it into his own. She closed her eyes and drifted off to sleep.

One glance at her in the depot had confirmed the truth.

The dark smudges under her eyes. The skin stretched tight over her cheekbones. Perhaps it had been there all along, but he had chosen not to see it. Now the evidence struck him in the face like a blow.

One solitary lamp burned on her dressing table. The crickets chirped in the grass below, and birds sang their evening song in the big chestnut tree outside the window. The lace curtains blew gently in the breeze while he held her hand. Hot tears ran down his cheeks until exhaustion overcame him, and he laid his head on the blue silk coverlet and fell asleep.

Her fingers caressing his hair woke him. The lamp had burned out, but a silver moon had arisen in its place and shone its sweet, silver light onto her pillow. She smiled tenderly at him. "My sweet boy, it grieves me to see you taking on so."

Fresh tears welled in his eyes. "Mother..." He swallowed hard, unable to go on.

"Death comes to all of us, dearest. Part of living is dying."

He shook his head. "You're too young! There's so much life left for you to live."

She nodded, and her fingers tightened in his hair. "It's not for us to choose, my darling. Look at me."

He obeyed.

"I know where I came from. And I know to whom I am going. I'm not afraid. I'm expectant. Can you understand that?"

He nodded.

"Be happy for me?"

He smiled through his tears. "You'll be well at last."

"Yes, my darling," she said, stroking his head. "I will be healed. And I will be with Jesus. My healer and my beloved." A smile curved her lips. "And I will see my dearest John again."

A FEW HOURS LATER, she lapsed into a coma. As her breathing grew more labored, Jack didn't leave the bedside. He prayed and softly sang her favorite old hymns. His uncle had come in silently and sat in a chair on the other side of the bed. Together they kept watch through the long hours of the night.

The first notes of birdsong in the chestnut tree had begun when she suddenly sat up in bed. "Do you hear them?' She looked at Jack, her eyes bright, and her pale cheeks flushed a lovely pink. "Oh, it's so beautiful..." She lay on her pillow, and a smile curved her lips. "They're singing, Jack. Welcoming me... home..."

She gave a little sigh, and her hand went limp in his grasp.

Jack pressed her hand to his lips. "Goodbye, my dearest mother," he said. "Good-bye."

9

After they returned from Paris, Mama decided the time had come to dismiss Lindy's tutor. Now Miss Kendall's bags sat in the great marble hall, brought by a footman, and Lindy waited to say goodbye to her tutor. A warm spring rain drummed outside the massive glass and bronze front doors of the mansion, sending showers of pink crab apple blossoms fluttering to the pavement.

Huffing, puffing, and a smothered exclamation announced Miss Kendall. She rounded the corner at the staircase landing, lugging a bulky carpetbag with a violent pattern of pink cabbage roses.

Lindy ran lightly up the stairs. "Miss Kendall, you should have called for assistance." She took the bag from her teacher. "Oof—!" She shook a finger at Miss Kendall. "This is much too heavy for you." She dragged the bag down the stairs and dropped it near the others, then went to take her tutor's arm.

"Well," wheezed Miss Kendall, "I've not had difficulty with these stairs before. Perhaps it's the notion I'm going into retirement." She pulled the lapels of her traveling jacket down. "I think I've collected everything." She took a deep breath. "My, Evangeline, how you've grown." Her eyes misted over. "I'm going to miss you."

Lindy kissed her old teacher on the cheek. "And I, you." She smiled. "What shall I do without you?" When Miss Kendall had first come to the Lindenmayer chateau, Lindy had been seven years old. Miss Kendall had seemed tall and severe then. And now Lindy towered over her teacher.

"You'll do fine if your mother has anything to say about it." Her brown eyes twinkled at Lindy.

Lindy grinned. "And we know she has a lot to say about it, don't we?"

Percy entered the hall. "Excuse me, Miss Lindy. I've called for the carriage. It's being brought around now."

Lindy nodded. "Very good. Thank you, Percy."

The butler bowed and walked away. Miss Kendall glanced about the hall. "Oh, I have so enjoyed living here, Evangeline. But I won't miss all the stairs, that's certain."

"Are your arrangements made satisfactorily?"

"Yes, dear. I'm going to my sister in Hackensack. Her husband died a few years ago, and she's been lonely. Her children have all moved away. We'll be two old ladies, sitting in our rocking chairs on the porch, watching the world go by." She rummaged through her carpetbag and pulled out a brown paper parcel. "I have a small gift for you." She placed it in Lindy's hands. "I hope you enjoy it."

Lindy pulled the paper aside to reveal two books covered in blue Morocco leather and gilt bindings. A pictorial design of elephants stamped in gold adorned the first cover and a gold python the other.

"It's The Jungle Book, by Rudyard Kipling. I know how

much you love your adventure books." Miss Kendall winked. "I hope you'll think of me when you read it."

"I'm sure I will. Thank you." Lindy threw her arms around the plump figure of her teacher and hugged her. "And I have something for you, too." She plucked the envelope off the hall table.

"Now, I know my mother settled your account and gave you a small pension for your retirement." She smiled at her teacher. "However, in my opinion, it was a paltry sum. So, this is from my father at my behest." She handed the envelope to Miss Kendall. "Please, open it."

Miss Kendall opened the envelope, removed the check inside, and stared at it. Tears sprang to her eyes, and she clutched her chest. "Oh, my goodness. Oh, my goodness!" Her free hand groped for Lindy. "Evangeline, I don't know what to say. How can I ever thank you?"

Lindy patted her hand. "I wanted to be sure you had what you needed. My father said you should contact his lawyer, Roger Stone, who will help you decide where to invest it."

Miss Kendall retrieved her handkerchief and dabbed at her eyes. "You blessed girl."

"No, no, Miss Kendall, please. Enjoy your retirement. You've certainly earned it!"

Miss Kendall nodded. "Thank you, dear." She tucked the check into her purse. "Au revoir!"

Miss Kendall opened her umbrella and descended the stairs with a decidedly lighter step. Lindy closed the door and sighed.

Her schoolgirl days had come to an end.

～

WITH HER FATHER in Colorado on business and her mother away for the day on the planning committee for a Patriarch ball, Lindy had the house to herself. A perfect rainy day to spend in the library with a cozy fire and a good book. She headed up the vast marble staircase to the second floor, where she curled up in her favorite chair and opened The Jungle Book.

Sometime later, her stomach growled. The light slanting through the windows told her it was late afternoon. She had read from breakfast to teatime. The adventures of Mowgli had been so exhilarating she'd scarcely noticed the passage of time. Instead of ringing, she took the shortcut on the service stairs to the basement kitchen.

The cook and the maids were having their tea and jumped up when she appeared in the kitchen. "Land a' mercy," said the cook, straightening her floury apron. "It's Miss Evangeline! We didn't hear you ring, miss, beggin' your pardon."

"I felt like a walk, so I didn't ring. Could you send some tea to the library?"

"Right away, miss."

"Please don't hurry. Finish your tea. I'm sorry to have interrupted you." She went toward the back stairs, rounded the corner, and there stood a wet Mr. Winthrop, water dripping from the brim of his hat, pulled low over his eyes.

"Oh!" She had never expected to see him here, but of course, he would use the service stair at the rear of the house, instead of calling at the front. She hadn't given any thought about how he arrived at the house. Had her mother ever seen him? The library was tucked away off a hallway, away from the more heavily traveled corridors, almost as an afterthought.

"Why, good afternoon, Miss Lindenmayer."

"Good afternoon, sir."

"I'm surprised to see you here."

"I ran down to order tea."

Molly turned around the corner and stopped short. "Excuse me, miss." She went toward the kitchen after casting one backward glance over her shoulder.

Lindy hesitated a moment. Surely offering him a bit of refreshment couldn't hurt. "Would you like to join me?"

Mr. Winthrop's normally ruddy face was pale, and his eyes bloodshot. He sighed. "I wouldn't be good company for you today. I—" He broke off and bit his lip, turning as if to go.

"I insist," said Lindy. "Please go up, and I will pop back and have a word with the cook."

She didn't wait for an answer but went to the kitchen and stuck her head in the door. "Nan? Would you add some sandwiches and a sweet to the tea tray? And another cup, please."

Nan raised an eyebrow but only nodded.

Lindy climbed the stairs. Something was wrong. Of all things, it looked as if Mr. Winthrop had been crying.

NAN SET A KETTLE TO BOIL. "Did you hear that?"

Molly nodded. "That handsome Mr. Winthrop was in the hall just now. Looked upset. I guess she's asked him for tea."

Nan rolled her eyes. "It's a good thing her mother ain't here. She'd never have allowed it. If I didn't know better, I'd think he was sweet on her."

"And her on him," said Molly.

Nan returned to the wooden table where a mound of

proofed dough waited and gave it a punch. "The missus would sure enough have a fit if she knew." She flipped the dough and sifted flour over it.

"Well, I ain't goin' to tell her." Molly shook her head. "I stay as far away from her as I can get. She's scary, is what she is."

∾

MR. WINTHROP HAD POKED up the fire when Lindy returned to the library.

"Tea will be here shortly." She seated herself.

He nodded but didn't speak, and stood staring into the fire. A few minutes later, Molly entered wheeling a tea cart laden with covered dishes,

"Thank you, Molly."

The maid bobbed her head and left. Lindy pulled the tea cozy off the silver pot. Steam curled from the spout. "How do you take your tea, Mr. Winthrop?"

He didn't answer. "Mr. Winthrop?"

He turned then. "I'm sorry. Just a bit of cream and a lump of sugar. Thank you." He dropped into the chair and reached for the cup. His hands shook so badly the cup clattered against the plate.

"Dear Mr. Winthrop, what is wrong?"

He swallowed hard and turned slightly away. "I don't think I can speak of it." He set the teacup onto the cart. "Perhaps I should go before—" He drew a handkerchief from his pocket and mopped at his eyes.

"Perhaps it would do you some good," she said gently. "What is it one of the poets said? 'Shared joy is double joy; sorrow shared is half sorrow?'"

He looked her then, with such a world of pain in his

brown eyes that she had a sudden urge to take his hand. "My mother died this week." He caught his breath and swallowed hard.

Lindy set her cup down. "I am so sorry, Mr. Winthrop." She touched his sleeve softly. "So very sorry."

"It wasn't unexpected. She had been ill for months now. But I didn't realize, even knowing death approached, how hard it would be when it actually happened." He twisted the handkerchief between his fingers. "I wasn't prepared."

How did one prepare for something like that? She had never experienced the death of a loved one. She cast about in her mind for something comforting to say and couldn't find anything.

But he didn't notice she hadn't spoken again. "The funeral is tomorrow. I wouldn't be here except I have an exam on Friday and I must study."

"Surely they would allow you to take it at another time?"

"I didn't ask. Mother wouldn't have wanted me to. She was thrilled when my uncle made it possible for me to undertake my studies." He paused. "Thank you, Miss Lindenmayer." He smiled faintly. "I do think the pain has ease a bit, speaking with you. It just... feels so odd."

"What does?"

"Knowing I have no parents now. They're both gone." He sighed. "I hadn't realized what an empty place that would leave in my heart."

Her own heart twisted in her chest. "I hope the happy memories you have will see you through this time."

"Thank you, Miss Lindenmayer, for your understanding."

"Have you eaten today?"

He blinked. "I haven't, actually."

"Well then," she said, refreshing his tea. "You cannot let

these go to waste." She piled cold chicken sandwiches and a biscuit with plum jam on his plate. For a few minutes, they ate in companionable silence while the fire crackled. Then Lindy cut the gooseberry tart and gave him a generous slice. After he finished the tart, he put his napkin down and sighed. "That was delicious. I didn't realize how hungry I was." He stood up. "I'll find the book and be on my way. My uncle and I are finalizing the arrangements tonight."

"When will the service be?"

"Friday morning at ten o'clock."

"At St. Thomas?"

"Yes." He searched her face. "You've been so kind, Miss Lindenmayer."

"I've tried to do what any friend would do."

"Yes." He smiled then, faintly. "I'm glad we're friends." He turned and headed off toward the east bookcase where the religious texts were kept. "Good day then."

She smiled and nodded. "Oh wait—"

He poked his head around the bookcase. "Yes?"

"Did your mother have a favorite flower?"

He smiled then, a genuine smile that reached his eyes. "Daisies," he said. "She always loved daisies."

10

J une 1897

THE DREADED SOCIAL calls had begun. Lindy and her mother were at home today, ensconced in her mother's gold and white salon. They had already received four ladies. And now the butler entered with yet another card on the silver tray and presented it to Mama. She glanced at the name. "Show them in, Percy."

The butler nodded, and a few moments later, Mrs. Charles Goulet, her mother's best friend, swept into the room on a wave of perfume, followed by her daughter, Madeleine. Mama and Mrs. Goulet exchanged air kisses on the cheek and sank onto the same overstuffed sofa.

Her mother waved a hand at Lindy. "Darling, why don't you take Madeleine to your room? The trunks from Paris came this morning. I've sent Claudine up to unpack them."

"Ooh!" Madeleine jumped up, clapping her hands. "I can't wait to see your gowns."

Lindy allowed her friend to take her hand and tow her out of the salon. Laughing, hand in hand, they climbed the marble staircase and went along the hall leading to Lindy's bedroom on the west side of the house, their feet noiseless on the thick Persian carpet.

Trunks reinforced with wood slates, brass hardware, and leather edging lay scattered about the bedroom. All stamped with the gold Louis Vuitton monogram, LV.

Claudine greeted them. "Bonjour, mademoiselles."

"Bonjour!" replied Madeleine. "So exciting, is it not? All the way from Paris." She turned away and surveyed the bedroom. "I'm always amazed at how spartan your bedroom is, compared to the rest of the mansion, Lindy."

Actually, none of her family's bedrooms were highly decorated. Except for her mother's, of course. A riot of lacy pink silk and carved cherubs lavished every corner of Vera's immense bedroom.

Lindy nodded. "I know. But I like my room. It's a haven from the rest of this monstrosity my mother has built." She clapped a hand to her mouth. "Oh, pretend I didn't say that."

Madeleine giggled. "But I like flourishes and furbelows."

"I know you do." Silken flounces covered Maddie's dress, and she wore a huge taffeta bow on her blond ringlets. "You look like a bonbon from the bakery. All spun sugar and ribbons."

To some eyes, Lindy's room might be plain and ordinary, but the cream silk wallpaper and the simple lines of the furniture suited her fine. No painted boiserie here, no marble columns, no tapestries, and definitely no cherubs. Just one simple, restful painting—Capriccio Padovano by

Bernardo Belloto. Watered silk draperies covering the floor-to-ceiling windows, and a banquette seat upholstered in bottle green velvet built into the window gable. "It suits me perfectly."

Claudine gestured to the trunks. "Where would you like to start, chérie?"

Lindy shrugged. "It doesn't matter. Anywhere."

"Oh, the ball gowns first, Claudine!" Madeleine hugged herself. "Mine should arrive any day now.

Claudine opened the nearest trunk, carefully lifting the domed lid to disclose a heap of tissue paper. Claudine untied the silk ribbons holding everything in place and lifted out the cherry-pink gown with black sable trim.

Madeleine gasped. "Oh, it's beautiful." She fingered the fur. "So soft."

"I hate it." Lindy wrinkled her nose. "But I suppose it will keep my ankles warm."

"Oh, you. It's the latest style, darling."

"I don't care. I think it's awful."

The hem had a swatch of the silk basted to it, to match the color for dancing slippers. Claudine carried the gown away, and Madeline opened another trunk to reveal a mass of silver-spangled white tulle. A white satin sash set off the bodice, trimmed with roses and pink hearts.

"Oh," breathed Madeline. "You'll be a vision in this, Lindy."

"Perhaps, but a vision of what? A valentine?"

Madeleine giggled. "Very droll. A vision of loveliness, of course!" She lifted the lid of the next trunk, untied the ribbons, and rooted around under the tissue for the next gown. Yellow satin appeared.

Lindy groaned. "See what you think, Maddie." Out came the gown with the huge, apricot gigot sleeves.

"It's quite chic, Lindy."

Lindy shrugged. "There's enough material in those sleeves to make another dress. Honestly. I'll be lucky to fit through the door sideways."

"Oh, Lindy, you are too much."

Claudine opened another trunk. "Oh, là là! C'est charmant." She lifted out folds of celadon silk.

"That's the only ball gown I chose for myself." Lindy took the dress from Claudine and turned to the mirror, holding it against her. The silver embroidery at the hem sparkled in the sunlight.

Maddie sighed. "It's perfectly dreamy." Then she spied a smaller trunk off under the window seat emblazoned Madame Suzy. "Oh, I adore Madame Suzy!" The first hatbox revealed a cerise silk velvet bonnet with trailing ribbons and black lace butterflies on the crown. "Oh my, it's gorgeous. A perfect color for you, with all that glossy dark hair. May I try it on?"

Without waiting for an answer, Madeleine placed the hat on her curls and went to the cheval mirror in the corner, turning her head this way and that.

"Maddie."

"Yes?"

"Do you ever have questions about this life we lead?"

Madeleine raised an eyebrow. "What do you mean?" She turned to the mirror, admiring her reflection.

"I mean this." Lindy waved her hand over the trunks spilling their multi-hued riches. "One of these dresses cost more than a score of men earn their whole lives."

Maddie frowned. "My goodness, whom have you been speaking to?"

"No one."

"Then how do you know that particular fact so surely?"

"I read the newspapers."

Madeleine laughed. "Darling, how boring. You definitely must stop that."

"But Maddie, haven't you ever had the urge to do something different with your life? Something useful?"

"Useful?" Maddie frowned. "I don't know what you mean."

"To help others. Something that will have meaning at the end of your life?"

Maddie came over and laid a cool hand on Lindy's forehead. "You must be taking a chill. I can't think why else you'd be speaking this nonsense."

"Truly? You never think on these things?"

Madeleine shook her pretty curls. "Never. I think about marrying an English lord, having a beautiful wedding, and a spectacular honeymoon." She laughed. "Oh, and a spectacular trousseau, all French, from my unmentionables out!" She dropped a kiss on Lindy's cheek. "Come, darling, I want to see these on you."

Madeleine tugged her toward the dressing table, pushed her onto the bench, and blithely tried the hats on her.

Lindy stared at her reflection. For as long as she could remember, her mother had planned Lindy's future marriage. The masquerade ball was her earliest memory.

She had crept out of bed to the musician's gallery on the second floor and pressed her face between the marble balusters of the balcony to watch the glittering figures below.

Thousands of American Beauty roses and white orchids swagged the walls of her mother's golden ballroom. Massive chandeliers of ormolu and crystal blazed overhead while the flames from a thousand tapers glimmered from candelabras and multiplied their tiny points of light in the tall leaded windows.

One figure in the sparkling gold ballroom drew Lindy's attention again and again—her mother, dressed as a princess in a cloth-of-gold gown embroidered with pearls and silver beads. The diamonds adorning her neck and décolleté sparked rainbows in the candlelight.

Mama looked up and spied her, then smiled and waved. A moment later, Lindy smelled her mother's jasmine perfume.

"Now, my darling, what are you doing out of bed?" Her mother's arms went around Lindy's shoulders.

"I want to see the queen, Mama!"

Her mother laughed, a tinkly silver sound. "That's right, darling. The queen is coming. So, I mustn't stay here long."

"Who are all these people?"

"Why, that's Joan of Arc. See there?" Mama pointed to a tall woman clad in shimmering silver mail. "And there goes Elizabeth the I of England." A woman in a brilliant red wig crowned with a diamond tiara had entered the ballroom, with a ruff of lace a foot deep around her neck.

Lindy stood on tiptoes to get a better look. "Is that the queen you're waiting for?"

"No, darling. I'm waiting for Queen Caroline Astor."

"Is she a real queen?"

Mama nodded. "In her own way, she is indeed a queen."

"How will I know her?"

Her mother rose to her feet and smoothed the gold cloth of her skirt. "When you see all the guests part to let her through. Then you'll know. Then we'll know."

"Know what, Mama?"

"If she has accepted us."

"How will we know?"

Mama smoothed a curl out of Lindy's eyes and kissed her cheek. "If she smiles, darling. If she smiles, then everything will be all right."

The queen had to smile then. So Mama would be happy. "Go to bed after that, my sweet lamb."

"Yes, Mama."

Her mother swept out of the gallery and reappeared in the ballroom below a few moments later. Papa, looking so handsome in his white tie and tails, waited for her near the massive marble fireplace at the end of the ballroom where the receiving line had formed.

More and more guests entered the ballroom, and still, the queen hadn't come. Lindy's eyes grew heavy, and she'd almost fallen asleep when the buzz of conversation in the ballroom dimmed and then rose to a new high. Lindy sat up. The crowd of gorgeously costumed guests parted to allow a statuesque woman in midnight blue silk approach Mama. Diamonds covered Queen Caroline from her tiara to her slippers and dripped from her earlobes and wrists. A hush fell over the crowd as the queen held her hand out to Vera, who shook it heartily and bent forward to whisper in the Queen's ear. Lindy held her breath.

And then it happened.

Lindy gasped and clapped her hands. Now Mama would be happy. All she had spoken of since Christmas was the masquerade ball. Even on Lindy's birthday a few weeks ago, her mother had worried and fussed through the party that the ball might not go right.

But all was well. The Queen had smiled.

Maddie snapped her fingers in front of Lindy's face. "What are you daydreaming about?"

Lindy blinked.

"I called your name three times." Maddie frowned and

scrutinized her. "You must be coming down with something. Shall I get your mother?"

"That's not necessary. I'm fine." Lindy rose from the dressing table. "It must be nearly time for tea. Let's go down."

She followed her chattering friend through the marble halls and down the staircase to the régence salon. She had never questioned her mother's love for her or the plans for the future marriage. But suddenly, the future had arrived, and the doubt inside her grew like a canker—a little bigger every day.

How do I tell my mother I no longer want any part of the plan?

11

A blur of luncheons and tea parties had filled the last four weeks. But finally, her mother had a private engagement that didn't require Lindy's presence.

Her shoulders relaxed when the oak library door closed behind her. Even the air here seemed different from the rest of the mansion. Quiet, peaceful, and orderly. And she had the rest of the afternoon to herself since she couldn't make social calls alone. Thank goodness.

A blond head popped up from the leather sofa near the fire. "Good afternoon, Miss Lindenmayer."

"Good afternoon, Mr. Winthrop." Her pulse skipped a beat. "I haven't seen you—since your mother's passing." She could have kicked herself. Perhaps he would have preferred she not mention that sad day. "How are you faring?"

Mr. Winthrop left the sofa and took a chair across from her. "I am well."

Her heart missed another beat. She could barely remain polite and ladylike when his nearness kindled heart palpitations. He did look chipper—rosy-cheeked and bright-eyed. "I'm so glad to hear it. I was concerned about you, after—"

"My mother's death."

"Yes." Oh, why did I say anything?

"Thank you for your kindness." He smiled then, revealing his dimples. "I want to tell you something."

Her mother's face rose before her. I should discourage him. Instead, she waited for him to continue.

The faint scent of sandalwood from his toilet water drifted to her nose when he leaned toward her. "I had an epiphany one night after the funeral. I'd been sitting up late, studying." He smiled faintly. "I felt so weary and alone. I had the garret window open, so perhaps it was only a stray breeze that ruffled my hair." He glanced at her. "I hope you will not think me irrational, Miss Lindenmayer, but it seemed to me my mother touched me gently, as she used to stroke my head when I was a little boy." He swallowed as if a lump had risen in his throat. "And then the terrible emptiness disappeared. And as sure as I had ever known anything, I understood in my heart she was alive, with God in heaven, and I rejoiced."

Her own heart responded with another thump. "How marvelous."

"And that is why I can truly say I am well." He studied her. "I've been meaning to ask you something, Miss Lindenmayer. The most enormous bouquet of daisies arrived at the church on the day of the funeral, tied with a blue silk ribbon. But no card arrived with them."

Lindy smiled. "You've found me out. I sent them, I confess." How could I send a card when no one can know of my clandestine association with you?

"How thoughtful. Of all the flowers there, the daisies meant the most. To me, I mean."

"I'm glad I could give you a moment of joy on such a sad day."

"Thank you."

Mr. Winthrop regarded her with such an intent expression, she turned away. It seemed he grew more handsome with each visit to the library. *I'm going to drown in those brown eyes if I'm not careful.*

"What are you studying today?" She kept her voice light. "A history of Martin Luther. I've an exam on ecclesiastical history this week and must spend every waking moment with my nose in a book."

"Don't allow me to distract you then." She retrieved her copy of The Jungle Book and curled up in the red leather chair. But even Mowgli and his escape from the Bandar-Log couldn't distract her racing thoughts. The entire week had been an endless round of luncheons, teas, and long afternoons spent in mindless conversation about subjects that had no import.

Mr. Winthrop hummed under his breath as he flipped pages and took notes. *How wonderful it must be to follow your heart and study the things that pleased you. His research of Luther had engaged him completely. What a noble profile he possessed.* He turned to her as she admired it.

Lindy's cheeks flamed, and she hastily returned to Mowgli. *How awful to be caught staring at the fellow.* Her throat thickened. *What's wrong with me?* She was about to cry. Fumbling in her pocket for a handkerchief, she failed to notice Mr. Winthrop until he stood next to her.

"Dear Miss Lindenmayer, is anything amiss?"

She shook her head and burst into tears. *Oh, horrors! And of course, she didn't have a handkerchief.* But she couldn't restrain them, and she didn't try. Instead of fleeing, he reached into his coat pocket and handed her a large cotton handkerchief, then pulled up a chair and waited while she sobbed into it. She seldom cried. At that thought, she sobbed harder.

Finally, the deluge ended. Mr. Winthrop hadn't moved, and she had wet the handkerchief clear through with her tears. She wiped her eyes with a damp corner and then blew her nose with a loud honk. He raised an eyebrow daintily when she stole a glance at him, and she giggled.

Mr. Winthrop laughed then too. She started to return the handkerchief, but Mr. Winthrop stopped her.

"No, you keep it," he said hastily, and that sent her off into another gale of laughter.

"Oh, oh—don't make me laugh anymore, please." She waved him away, holding her sides. "No more faces." She hiccupped. "You must excuse me. I've been out of sorts this week." She tucked the crumpled hankie into her pocket. "I'll return this to you, Mr. Winthrop. Many thanks. I had better let you resume your studies. The history exam?"

He nodded but made no move to get up. "You've listened and encouraged me during my bereavement as a true friend. If you have need of me, if it would relieve you to speak about it..."

"Oh, no, I could never presume to do that." It just wasn't done. Open her heart to this young man who regarded her with such deep kind eyes? According to her mother, this type of conversation should never take place between a young man and woman.

"We are friends, are we not?"

"Yes." But a young woman in my society circle doesn't dare confess her deepest thoughts to anyone.

"Surely it would unburden you to speak about it. What

did you tell me when my mother died? 'Shared joy is double joy; sorrow shared is half sorrow?'"

"But that was different, Mr. Winthrop. I would never compare the sorrow you felt at your mother's death to my foolish thoughts."

"Perhaps they are not foolish. Let us examine them."

She sighed. "You are quite persistent."

"Tenacity is one of my strengths. And sometimes, my weakness."

Her pulse picked up a pace. Did another meaning underlie his words? Why did it seem an invisible line tightened between them, drawing them closer?

She stood abruptly and put the chair between them. "If you must know, I was sitting in envy of you at your studies."

"Envy?"

"Yes. The paths open to me as a woman are few. But you may study anything that pleases you."

"Within means and reason."

"Yes."

"If it weren't for the benevolence of my uncle, I wouldn't be in school."

"True. But you always have that possibility, don't you see? I am denied that." Her fingers tightened on the chair. "You may seek to do anything you wish, go here or go there with impunity and choose your own calling!" Mr. Winthrop's eyes widened at her strident tone. I'm making a mess of things. What did it matter? In a few days, she'd head to Newport for the short summer season, and wouldn't see Mr. Winthrop for two months. Perhaps it was for the best. "I've said quite enough. Good day, sir."

She fled the library as quickly as she decently could, her spine straight, and her head held high. Only when she reached the safety outside the doors did she pick up her skirts and run.

JACK TAPPED his pencil on his knee. He had detected her sadness as soon as she walked into the library. The way she held herself, as if she might shatter if she relaxed her shoulders. The rosy blush in her cheeks had disappeared, and her complexion had grown pale. Each day he had eagerly looked for her, but until today he hadn't seen her in nearly a month.

How difficult it had been to keep from touching her as she wept. More than anything, he wanted to take her in his arms and do all in his power to take her pain away. His fingers had twitched with the effort to restrain himself.

I've done it now.

Fallen in love with a girl I can never have.

ugust 1897, Newport, Rhode Island

GRAY LIGHT FILLED the usually sunny breakfast room at Seaside, the Lindenmayer's Victorian "cottage," as Lindy's mother called the three-story marble mansion. Lindy and her father drank their tea and read the newspapers while the white- capped sea roared outside the French doors. The wind had risen steadily since yesterday, and a possible hurricane forecast had made Mama decide to leave early for New York instead of staying the last two weeks of August. The maids had stayed up all night to pack the trunks.

For nearly two months, Lindy had resolutely pushed all thoughts of Mr. Winthrop out of her mind. Her mother had kept her occupied with endless rounds of luncheons, teas, and picnics on the beach. Perhaps he had forgotten about her. She had been rather abrupt the last time she had seen him. She had even stayed away from the library at Seaside, choosing instead to read on the beach or in her bedroom to avoid reminders of him. But for all that, a butterfly still hatched in her stomach at the thought of returning to New York City.

Percy brought in a silver tray laden with letters for Papa.

He flipped through the stack, opened one, and gasped.

"What is it, Papa?"

He rubbed his forehead and scanned the telegram again. "It's from my brother, Henry. Our brother Kurt is dead."

"Oh, Papa, I'm so sorry." She jumped up and wrapped her arms around his shoulders. "Uncle Kurt was your youngest brother, wasn't he? I thought you didn't know where he was."

"We didn't. My brother Henry received notice of his death a week ago. He's been living in Brockport, New York. On the Erie Canal, of all places. He died in a measles epidemic."

"How sad." She kissed her father's cheek and sat next to him.

Otto smiled wistfully and patted her hand. "Kurt never wanted anything to do with our family after he had a falling out with Henry about selling their oil refinery to Rockefeller. But there's more."

Mama entered the room in a Japanese morning kimono. "More what?"

Otto handed her the letter.

She read it quickly. "Oh my. And there's a daughter!" Her father nodded. "And Henry's her guardian. Imagine."

Mama laughed. "I can't image Henry being responsible for a young girl."

"So, I have a cousin," said Lindy. "What's her name?"

"Emma. She's twenty. Apparently, Kurt contacted Henry

years ago out of nowhere and asked him to be her guardian. Then we never heard from him again. Until now."

"Will we get to meet her?"

Vera frowned. "Is there to be a funeral? I don't relish a trip to the far end of western New York State right now."

Lindy touched her father's arm. "We could visit Aunt Gertrude in Buffalo afterward. I haven't seen her since I was twelve." Her German grandmother had lived with her aunt in Buffalo, and up until her grandmother's death, visits between New York City and Buffalo had been regular family outings.

Mama pursed her lips. "You'll see her soon enough. She'll be here for a fortnight in October, before your debut." She rolled her eyes. "As if I won't have enough to do with the preparations, I'll have to entertain your sister during the busiest two weeks of my life."

"Now, dear, Gertrude can entertain herself," said Papa mildly. "She's always been a self-sufficient woman."

Mama smirked. "I'll say. Playing the stock market like a man."

Papa rubbed his chin. "Well, she was good to you when we were first married. Stayed in New York after the wedding and introduced you to all the highest society friends she had."

Her mother nodded begrudgingly. "That's true. Although she hot-footed it out of here as soon as she decently could."

"She never cared much for New York City."

"But why Buffalo of all places? It's full of Poles and Italians."

"And Irish. And Germans too, like us, liebchen." He raised his silver eyebrows at his wife.

Lindy smiled at her father's term of endearment. Her

parents rarely displayed affection, and sometimes she wondered what had drawn them together in the first place.

Mama smiled. "You're right, Otto." She sighed. "I'll do my best to get along with Gertrude. But for heaven's sake, I hope she'll leave her social reform causes in Buffalo."

"Will there be a funeral for Uncle Kurt?"

Papa shook his head. "Already taken place. Last Thursday. Emma will be arriving at Mahicantuck this week. Poor child." He sighed heavily. "I'll talk to Henry. Perhaps they'd like to come to New York for Christmas. Meet the rest of the family?" He raised an eyebrow at Mama.

"Of course, Otto. I'll send an invitation right away. It's a good thing we're returning early. So much to do before the debut. I'll need every extra minute to be ready." She glanced at Lindy. "Six weeks until your debut. Are you getting excited?"

Lindy carefully placed her teacup onto the saucer and didn't answer immediately. "Mama, I'm not sure how I feel about the debut."

Her mother frowned. "How you feel? What on earth do you mean, Evangeline?"

"I mean, I'm not as excited about it as you are."

Mama's mouth dropped open. Her father lowered his newspaper and peered at her over his spectacles.

Lindy swallowed hard. "I'm not at all sure I want to be presented to society."

"Wh—WHAT?" Mama sputtered. "Are you being impertinent, Miss?" She glared at Lindy.

Lindy shook her head. "No. But there never seems to be an ideal time to discuss it. I should have spoken sooner."

Her father laid the paper on the table. "Then, let's discuss it now."

Mama slammed her hand on the table, and the silver

rattled. "What is there to discuss, Otto?" She turned to Lindy, the loose knot on top of her head quivering. "You're making your debut next month, and that's all there is to it."

Lindy struggled to remain calm. As a child, she had done whatever possible to stay in her mother's good graces and avoid her formidable temper. But she couldn't avoid it now. "I'd like to go to college." There. She'd said it.

Mama's eyes bugged open. "College? What put that idea into your head?"

Mr. Winthrop did, but I can't say that. "More women are enrolling now."

"Not the women in this family."

Lindy sighed. How could she make her mother understand?

Mama turned to her father. "Well, Otto? Do you have anything to say about this?"

Papa stroked his chin and considered both of them. "It's possible you could do both."

Vera heaved an exasperated sigh and rolled her eyes. "Hear me out, Vera." He turned to Lindy. "Your mother has dreamed of your debut for so long. It would be cruel to change the plan now."

Mama nodded.

"Make your debut as planned, and then we can discuss the possibility of college afterward."

Her mother's head swiveled around. "Afterward? Not possible. The London season! I have it all planned."

"Well then..." Papa rubbed his chin. "The following year. Would that be acceptable, Vera?"

Her mother smiled faintly. "Perhaps." Her eyes narrowed as she turned to Lindy. "Perhaps you'll meet your prince and fall in love. Then you'll forget all about college."

I've already met him.

Lindy blinked. She had tried so hard to forget Mr. Winthrop this summer, and he popped into her head as if he was next door.

"What's wrong, sweetheart?" Papa laid a gentle hand on her arm. "You look like you've seen a ghost."

13

N ew York City

LINDY WOKE EARLY the morning after the return trip to New York, even though they had arrived home quite late the night before. A herd of escaped cows loitering on the train tracks in Connecticut had resulted in a wait of several hours before the farmers rounded up the stray bovines.

She pushed the coverlet aside, rang for Claudine, and went into the closet where the day dresses Mama had chosen in Paris hung neatly in their muslin bags, the sleeves and skirts stuffed with tissue paper and sandalwood sachets to keep the moths away.

Not blue. Perhaps the pink? The pink silk faille had narrow sleeves and a deep yoke of lace on the bodice. She pulled the muslin aside on the next dress. Pale lavender and cream stripes peeped out. That might do. She pulled the dress out and went to the cheval mirror to hold it against her when Claudine arrived, her eyes puffy from lack of sleep.

"Bonjour, chérie. Up early, no?"

"I'm sorry to wake you so early. Could you help me dress and then go back to bed?"

"Back to bed?" said Claudine. "Your Maman would have my head."

"She won't be up for hours. I'd dress alone if it weren't for that infernal corset."

Claudine's gaze focused on the day gown in Lindy's hands. "You've chosen your own outfit?" She cocked her head to one side and scrutinized Lindy. "What are you up to so early, chérie? And why the sudden interest in what you wear?"

"No particular reason." Lindy turned away. "Let's begin so you can go back to sleep."

Claudine clicked her tongue and shook her head. "Very well."

Lindy washed her face and hands, donned a clean chemise and unmentionables, and turned so Claudine could lace the corset.

When she finished, Lindy measured her waist with her hands. "I think it could be a bit tighter."

Claudine's eyes widened. "Qu'est-ce que ç'est? Tighter? The girl who can't breathe in her corset suddenly wishes it tighter? What has happened to you overnight?"

Mr. Winthrop happened. "Perhaps I'm beginning to take more of an interest in my appearance, as Mama wishes. After all, I will soon make my debut." If only Claudine would stop asking questions.

"Very true. Well then." She loosened the laces and pulled.

"Oof." Lindy gasped. "Too much."

"Non. This is perfect." She lifted the mass of lavender silk and dropped it over Lindy's head before she could protest again, then buttoned her into the bodice. "Lovely, chérie. You have quite a neat figure now."

Lindy stuck her tongue out, and Claudine laughed. "Come, let me do your hair." She unplaited the long braid and ran the brush through the mass of waves and ringlets.

All night Lindy had fought with herself over whether she would go to the library this morning. And then as soon as her eyes opened, she had jumped out of bed and gone to look at the day dresses. I have to see him. The good intentions of the last eight weeks faded away, and the butterfly in her stomach multiplied into a whole brood.

WHEN SHE REACHED THE LIBRARY, she stopped, took a deep breath, and straightened her shoulders before opening the door. No Mr. Winthrop in the leather chair near the fire. She hummed a little tune, thinking he would pop up from the sofa where he sometimes reclined.

But the only person in the library was a maid dusting the books in the historical section, who murmured a "Good morning, miss" and scurried out.

Lindy sank into a chair and then hurriedly straightened when the corset edge bit into her hipbone. The walnut bookcases gleamed in the bars of pale sunlight streaming through the leaded windows. Perhaps it was too early? She checked the clock. Seven a.m. Poor Claudine. Lindy hoped she had gone back to bed.

She jumped up and went to the casement window facing

Fifth Avenue. Though early, horse-drawn carriages filled the street, and pedestrians hurried on the sidewalks toward their destinations. Pressing her face against the glass, she examined the pavement for a solitary figure in a frockcoat. But Mr. Winthrop was nowhere to be seen.

Perhaps classes weren't held during the summer. She bit her lip. She hadn't considered that. September was two weeks away. Maybe she should keep her resolution and give up seeing him.

She gritted her teeth and steeled herself against peering out the window again.

Honestly, Lindy, have some self-respect.

She tossed her head and marched to the door, pushing it open with considerably more violence than necessary just as someone pulled it open from the other side. Lindy stumbled and crashed through the doorway, knocking her head on the solid oak, barely aware of a tall figure that grasped her arms to keep her from falling in a heap.

"Miss Lindenmayer! Are you hurt?"

Her vision went white at the corners and then cleared to reveal Mr. Winthrop gazing at her, his brow furrowed. The heat of his hands burned through the thin silk of her sleeves, and her knees buckled. Mr. Winthrop dragged her to the nearest chair and snatched up a magazine lying on the library table to fan her.

Her head hurt like the dickens. Surely there would be a bruise. How would she explain that to her mother? She groaned, and Mr. Winthrop threw the magazine down.

"I'll call for your parents."

"No!" She tried to keep the note of panic out of her voice. "No, don't. I'm fine."

He hesitated, his hand on the doorknob. "Are you quite sure?"

With an effort, she sat up and tried to appear normal. "Quite sure." Of all days to ask Claudine to tighten her laces. She could barely breathe for the smothering constriction around her ribs.

Mr. Winthrop plucked his hat off the floor and sat down, smiling ruefully. "I am so sorry, Miss Lindenmayer."

Lindy rose and stood on tiptoe to check her reflection in the mirror over the fireplace. A purple lump the size of a walnut had risen on her forehead close to her hairline. She had definitely gotten the worst of it.

"How will you explain that to your mother?"

Lindy laughed. "She already believes me to be clumsy. I shall tell her I absentmindedly walked into a wall or something. She says I'm as 'graceful as a gazelle,' but of course she means exactly the opposite."

Mr. Winthrop fiddled with the band on his hat. "You're in the library quite early this morning. I didn't think you were leaving Newport until next month."

So, he remembered when she would return from Newport. She sank into her chair. "The hurricane. My mother wanted to come home early."

"Oh." He nodded.

Now what? Mr. Winthrop sat across from her, but all the scintillating conversation she'd thought to have with him had flown out of her head, along with any semblance of gracefulness.

Her head hurt. She sighed. Before she saw her mother, she had better get some ice on it. "I must go."

He stood when she did. "Please take care of yourself." He paused. "I look forward to resuming our book discussions." He smiled. "I have a few new suggestions for you."

His eager face raised a lump in her throat. "Mr. Winthrop, I..."

"Yes?" He took a step closer, and she caught the faint scent of sandalwood.

"I won't be able to spend my spare time in the library much longer. My debut is looming in a few weeks, and my social calendar is full."

"Oh, I see." He nodded. "Of course. And afterward?"

"I'll be going abroad for the London season. I'm not sure when we'll return." She gritted her teeth. Might as well say it now. "And then, if I meet a man my mother approves of..." She broke off. She should never have come to the library this morning. What had she been thinking? There was no chance that she and Mr. Winthrop could ever be together. She should have stayed away and let their affair of the heart die a natural death.

The smile dropped off Mr. Winthrop's dear face. He swallowed hard and twisted his hat in his hands.

Tears stung her eyes, and she shook her head fiercely. I can't cry now. She clenched her hands so tightly, her nails pierced her palms. "I have so enjoyed your company. But this must be..." She couldn't say the words.

He searched her face. "Goodbye?"

She ducked her head, not trusting herself to look into his eyes.

"Miss Lindenmayer, it has been my great pleasure to make your acquaintance. I hope you will continue to think of me as your friend."

She nodded mutely.

"At a difficult time in my life, you gave me something to hold on to. So, I will leave you with this verse, from Shakespeare."

His fingers gently raised her chin then, and the tears overflowed as she looked into his eyes. "'I count myself in nothing else so happy as in a soul remembering my good friends.'"

He released her chin and put his hat on. "Goodbye, Miss Lindenmayer." A moment later, he slipped silently out the door.

"Goodbye, Jack," she whispered.

14

J ack strode along the sidewalk, heedless of the foot traffic. She had said goodbye. And she had wept. Was it possible she had feelings for him? He could barely consider it.

And then, of all the confounded things to do, he left her with the verse from Shakespeare. She must think him a ninny. A fop.

He should have declared his love for her right then. He halted, turned on his heel, and ran straight into a brawny workman carrying a tin lunch pail, which made crunching contact with Jack's kneecap.

"Watch where you're goin', fella!"

The workman straightened his cap and hurried around Jack, who stood irresolute.

Should he go back now? But she wouldn't be in the library, would she? She'd have had to attend to the bump on her forehead.

He'd missed his chance. He probably would never see her again.

Unless it was in the society pages of The New York Times.

15

September 1897

"COME ALONG, Evangeline. They're here. I saw the carriage pull around the back."

Her mother rose and smoothed her skirt. Lindy hid a smile as she realized her mother was tightly laced and rather short of breath as a result. Mama hadn't inherited the tall athleticism of her German ancestors but possessed a figure more like Kartoffelknoedel, the German potato dumplings she was so fond of. Hortense, her mother's French maid, must have had a frightful time pulling the corset strings tight enough to suit her mistress.

"We'll receive your aunt in my salon."

Lindy followed her mother across the marble hall. Yes, her mother had definitely taken pains with her figure this morning. Her waist looked at least two inches smaller. It could only be due to the arrival of Aunt Gertrude.

Her mother's Pomeranian greeted them when they entered the salon. Mama perched on the edge of a straight-backed chair instead of reclining on her usual place on the chaise lounge, and the confused lap dog ran in circles, yapping at her feet. Her mother pushed a tendril of hair off her face. "Is it hot in here, Evangeline?"

"Not really, Mama. Here." Lindy retrieved a magazine from the chaise lounge and fanned her flushed mother. "Better?"

"Yes. I think so." The Pomeranian jumped at her skirts, whining. "Not now, Lily." Mama pushed the dog away with the tip of her shoe. "Go lie down." Whimpering, the Pomeranian slunk away to its satin pillow by the window.

Doors slammed outside the salon. Mama slowly got to her feet and straightened her figure, elongating her neck and thrusting her shoulders back.

Papa opened the door for Aunt Gertrude, who strode in, cloaked in black Persian lamb with a matching toque. "Vera, how lovely to see you again."

The two exchanged kisses before Gertrude turned to Lindy. "My goodness, Lindy dear, you're all grown up." She held Lindy's hands out to the side and examined her with a merry smile. "She's enchanting, Vera. She'll be the belle of the ball. What a lovely family, Otto. You've done well for yourself."

"Please, Trudy, sit down." Papa urged her into a comfortable chair.

"I've sent for tea," said Mama. "How was your journey?"

"Lovely. Beautiful weather, coming from Buffalo, and all the trees in their glorious colors."

A gentle knock sounded at the door, and Mary Ann rolled the teacart in.

"Thank you, Mary Ann." Mama dismissed the maid with a nod and began to serve.

Lindy sipped her tea and studied her aunt. Ruddy cheeked, with the same deep-set brown eyes and silver hair as her brother. Rather a long nose for a woman, but it seemed to suit her. A pair of silver pince-nez perched at the end of it, and she had strong eyebrows and a decided chin. All in all, not beautiful, but striking. You would certainly notice her in a crowded room.

She shed the Persian lamb coat and hat, revealing a sleek traveling suit of silver-gray tweed. Lindy nearly choked on her tea. Aunt Gertrude wasn't wearing a corset. The tiniest bulge of middle-aged fat rolled at her middle in the loose traveling suit, and she had no waist to speak of. At least, not the tiny hourglass waists seen in New York society, on young women and old alike. Mama's lips pressed together primly. Obviously, she'd noticed the same thing.

"Have a cookie, Aunt Gertrude." Lindy picked up the plate and passed them to Aunt Gertrude, trying not to meet her mother's gaze.

"Oh no, thank you, dear." Aunt Gertrude set her cup down. "I think I'd like to get settled in my room, and then I'm going to take a long walk. Would you like to join me?"

"You can't be serious, Gertrude," Mama protested. "No fashionable woman walks in New York. You can take my carriage. I've a lovely new pair of matched fillies."

"No, no, no. I've been sitting all morning on the train." Gertrude stood up. "I need some fresh air. Lindy?"

Lindy didn't dare look at her mother. "Certainly, Aunt Gertrude."

"Very well, then." She looked at her watch. "Three-quarters of an hour ought to be enough to get settled."

"I'll come to your room then."

"Perfect!" She glanced at Lindy's feet. "Mind you wear something sensible to walk in, dear."

Mama rose, her head held high. "Allow me to show you to your room. I've put you in the Michelangelo suite."

They left the salon. Papa looked at Lindy, and his silver mustache quivered. "It's going to be an interesting visit."

LINDY RANG FOR CLAUDINE. Of all the numerous ball gowns, tea gowns, and afternoon dresses her mother had ordered in Paris, several walking suits had been among them, meant for the season in London. And suitable shoes. She went into the dressing room and searched the rows of silver dancing slippers, velvet bedroom mules, leather boots, and ankle boots. There they were, on the bottom rack. A two-tone, flat-heeled pair of leather shoes.

Claudine entered the dressing room. "Chérie? You rang for me?"

"Yes. I'm going to walk with Aunt Gertrude, so I need to change."

"Certainly." Claudine moved into the second part of the dressing room. "Which one do you prefer?" She held up two choices.

Lindy considered them. Which one would be more comfortable? "The green, I think."

A few moments later, she stood before the cheval mirror and examined the walking suit. Soft green wool, with a long tunic-like jacket, belted smartly around her waist and buttoned with two large jet buttons. Long sleeves turned at the cuff to reveal black-and-white striped lining. A smaller bustle, with a shorter and wider skirt allowed for stepping off curbs and getting into carriages.

"It's quite comfortable, actually."

A hat of black straw matched the outfit, wired in a flowerpot shape, with a hat band of iridescent green silk adorned with a peacock feather.

Claudine unpinned Lindy's hair and twisted it into a higher coil to fit under the hat and secured it with several hatpins. "Voilà! Très charmant."

The east wing of the mansion held the Michelangelo suite and the other guest bedrooms. As she turned down the corridor, Percy and another manservant hustled a painting at least eight feet long and as tall as they were along the hallway. The butler's normally smooth features were flushed, and he had removed his jacket, revealing large wet spots in the armpits of his immaculate white shirt.

She'd never seen him without his formal frockcoat.

"Percy, what on earth?"

"Madame Gertrude's wishes," Percy gasped, without slowing down. "Careful, Edward! Don't push."

Grunting, the men continued down the hallway, followed by two grooms lugging a rolled tapestry on their shoulders. A parade of kitchen maids came after, all loaded with various impedimenta from the Michelangelo room.

"What's happening, Molly?"

Molly shrugged and grappled for a tighter hold on the marble statuette of Venus in her arms. "I don't rightly know, Miss Evangeline. Madame said something about too much... ornamentation in the room?"

Oh my. Mama will be furious.

"We're taking all this to the storeroom," said Mary Ann, her arms filled with folds of burgundy damask.

Lindy squeezed against the wall, avoiding two menservants hoisting an overstuffed chair between them. Her mother had taken special care with the Michelangelo room, personally choosing all the tapestries, painting, and statuary on a trip to Italy.

Aunt Gertrude appeared at the door of her room as the final servant departed carrying a hefty pair of putti, plump Italian angels designed to sit on a shelf and stare benevolently onto the room's inhabitant. Lindy stifled a giggle.

Aunt Gertrude waved at her. "There you are, my girl. Ready for our walk?

Lindy stepped into the Michelangelo room, now nearly as plain as her own bedroom. Without the heavy damask drapes and the valances normally swagged across the window, sunlight streamed into the room from the tall casement windows, now wide open.

"I do hope your mother won't mind that I've reordered the room." Gertrude surveyed the nearly bare chamber. "I simply can't think with that much fuss and feathers around me."

Lindy smiled. "Don't tell her. It's much more spacious and brighter now. I see you've kept one painting."

"A Bellini landscape," said Aunt Gertrude, noting her interest. "One of the few Renaissance painters I actually admire."

"I'd mention that particular painting if Mama asks how you like your room."

Gertrude nodded. "Indeed, I will." She glanced at her wristwatch. "Dear me, let us be going. Teatime will be here before you know it, and I must have my walk before your dear mother presses cake and pastries upon me!"

THE SOUTHERN END of Central Park lay three blocks from the Lindenmayer mansion. Aunt Gertrude walked rapidly, swinging her arms, and before long, she had marched ten and then twenty steps ahead of Lindy.

Lindy increased her stride, but her lungs wouldn't cooperate. "Aunt Gertrude," she called breathless, "wait, please." She stopped, a stitch in her side. Aunt Gertrude whirled about and marched toward her. "What is it, dear?"

"I can't walk that fast." Lindy tried to massage the stitch in her side through the corset. "I'm sorry."

"Oh. Of course." She took Lindy's arm and steered her toward a park bench near the pond. Lindy sank onto it and groaned.

Aunt Gertrude sighed. "Drat those corsets. We have to get women out of them, that's all there is to it."

Lindy burst out laughing and then grabbed her side. "Oh, don't make me laugh."

"I'm perfectly serious, dear girl." She leaned closer. "I never wear one myself."

"I'm sure I wish I didn't have to." Lindy sighed. "But you know Mama."

Aunt Gertrude's lips twitched. "I do indeed know your mother." She pressed her lips together as if to stop herself from saying more, and pointed to several small boats coasting slowly around the pond. "Now there's something I'd dearly love to try."

A pontoon boat in the shape of a magnificent white swan sailed across the pond, powered by a man turning the paddle wheel with his feet.

"Oh, the swan boats? Would you like to go on one?" That would certainly be easier than trying to walk in this corset.

"I'd like to drive one."

Lindy gasped. "Oh, I don't think that would be wise. Someone might see." If her mother heard she or Aunt

Gertrude had been paddling a swan boat, she would have a conniption.

Aunt Gertrude turned toward her, an amused smile on her face. "Really, dear? Who might that be? And why should I care?"

"Well..." sputtered Lindy. "I don't know who, specifically."

Gertrude smiled. "You'll have to pardon me, Lindy. I haven't cared much about what other people think for a very long time."

Imagine not caring what people thought of you! Lindy could hardly fathom it. The public's perception of the Lindenmayer family mattered greatly to her mother. "How did you learn not to care about others' opinions, Aunt Gertrude?"

Her aunt gazed out over the pond. "It was an evolution, I suppose." She adjusted a fold of her skirt and shifted on the bench. "I certainly didn't plan it."

Lindy sighed. "How lovely it must be not to care what other people think of you. To do what you like."

"I can't always do what I like, my dear." Gertrude smiled. "And it wasn't lovely, in the beginning."

"Would you tell me about it?"

Gertrude patted Lindy's sleeve. "Your mother would never forgive me for putting ideas in your head. She's already worried I've induced you to take a walk with me."

"She'd be surprised to know I have a few ideas of my own, Aunt Gertrude. But she doesn't listen to me."

Gertrude scrutinized Lindy. "There's more going on inside that pretty head than you've let on." She folded her arms, a glint of amusement in her eye. "Well then, what do you want to know?"

"The part about not caring about what people think of you."

Gertrude crossed her arms across her chest and stared across the pond. "I suppose it started in 1863 when my fiancé died on Cemetery Ridge. He had survived the first two days at Gettysburg, only to perish on the third day of the battle." She sighed. "My dream of marriage and children died with him. I was twenty years old."

Only two years older than Lindy. Over the years, she'd heard her parents speak of Aunt Gertrude losing her fiancé during the Civil War, but as a child, it hadn't touched her as it did now. She squeezed her aunt's gloved hand gently. "I'm so sorry, Aunt Gertrude. How terrible for you."

Gertrude smiled. "He was such a handsome man. Full of life! And so sweet to me. He was my first and last love. I could never look at another man after that." She smiled wryly. "Not that there were many marriageable men left after the war." She reached under her collar and pulled out a gold locket on a fine golden chain. Inside a painted miniature of a young man with a sunny smile and a dashing mustache gazed out. A lock of blond hair lay under glass on the opposite side. "This is all I have of Stephen now."

She closed the locket. "My father died shortly after the war ended. He didn't see well, and I used to read the financial papers to him. That's how I learned about banks and bonds and stocks. He left me a small inheritance, and against the advice of my brothers—" She winked at Lindy. "I began to invest my money. Cautiously, of course." She laughed. "It amazed Otto to learn I'd actually made a profit on a smart investment. My real independence began then."

"When you didn't care any anymore about what people thought?"

"That took longer." Gertrude smiled ruefully. "People

whispered behind my back at dinners and parties. I was the odd one, you see, being interested in 'manly' things. It bothered me at first. Then I grew used to it. I had no use for parties anyway. Or fancy clothes, or most of the things society women are interested in these days." She kissed the locket and slipped it under her collar. "But enough about me. Are you excited about your debut?"

Lindy shrugged. "Mama is more excited about it than I am, unfortunately."

"Oh? Why?"

Lindy hesitated. "I know I should be, but actually, I'm rather dreading it."

Aunt Gertrude nodded. "Go on."

"Mama has so many plans for me. And I don't seem to have a say in any of it."

"Your mother does have a rather forceful personality." Aunt Gertrude laughed. "I've been the target of it at times. So, I can only imagine what it's like for you."

"Yes, well,"—Lindy broke off— "she means well." Doesn't she? Does Mama truly have my best interests at heart? "She wants me to marry a duke."

She regretted the words as soon as they slipped out.

But Aunt Gertrude simply nodded. "And what do you want?"

Jack.

"Someone I can't have."

"You have a beau? Does your mother know?"

"Oh, my goodness, no. I didn't mean that." She wiggled her toes on the path. "Someone I met this past year. But Mama would never approve." The image of Jack's merry brown eyes made her wince, and a harsh wave of longing for him washed over her.

"Is it truly impossible?"

"I've recently said goodbye to him." Lindy stood abruptly. She couldn't start thinking about Jack now. Each day she somehow managed to push him to the farthest reaches of her mind, but thoughts of him still popped up unexpectedly. When she saw dimples on a face or a man with a blond forelock falling over his forehead.

"I can't speak about it, Aunt Gertrude."

Beyond the pond, children ran through the fallen leaves on the park path, shouting to one another. The tang of wood smoke filled the air. The end of the year fast approached, and there was no help for it. Life marched on.

"Mama will be wondering where we are. She's probably about to dispatch one of the grooms to look for us."

Aunt Gertrude stood and linked her arm through Lindy's. "Don't lose heart, darling. Sometimes life has a way of working things out."

CLAUDINE HELPED Lindy dress for dinner. Mama would be going all out with a guest in the house. Had she discovered yet that Aunt Gertrude had stripped the Michelangelo room? Lindy hoped not.

She chose a dinner dress of bronze brocade silk with gigot sleeves and rust velvet trim. Not really her color, although it did make her eyes seem green rather than gray. But Mama would be pleased to see her in it.

Percy had seated her mother when Lindy walked into the dining room. The chandelier and the candelabras on the sideboard infused the room with a golden glow. Her mother's best china, Royal Copenhagen's Flora Danica, adorned the table, with Tiffany sterling in the Audubon pattern to compliment it. A massive silver cache-pot filled with blue hydrangea and purple phlox graced the center of the table, with green Amaranthus trailing over its sides.

"The flowers are lovely, Mama. You've outdone yourself."

Her mother beamed at the compliment. "Thank you, darling."

"I agree. Most charming," said Aunt Gertrude. "But wherever do you find hydrangeas in October?"

"Otto procures them." Her mother bestowed a queenly smile on her husband. "Every week he ships them in for me." She nodded at Percy to begin serving. "I know you'd prefer something simple for supper, Gertrude. I hope roast chicken is agreeable."

"Perfect. One of my favorites."

"And your room? I trust it's comfortable?"

"Oh, quite." Aunt Gertrude looked sideways at Lindy. "I love the Bellini landscape."

Mama nodded. "I chose the Bellini myself."

"Yes, Lindy told me."

"And how was your walk this afternoon?"

"Very illuminating. I quite enjoyed Lindy's company."

The conversation continued in this vein, and Lindy stopped listening. Until Aunt Gertrude mentioned women's voting rights while waving away the rich sauce that accompanied the roast chicken.

"Come, come, Gertrude." Papa frowned. "You don't mean to say you advocate the vote be given to women? It's an inane idea."

"Inane to you, perhaps, Otto." Aunt Gertrude set her fork down. "Don't you think I'm capable of forming my own judgments?" She stared down her long nose at her brother.

Papa raised an eyebrow and applied himself studiously to his dinner. "You, yes. You've always had your own opinions. But my own dear wife and daughter have been more gently raised."

"By gently raised, I assume you mean heads filled with flowery nonsense?"

Papa exhaled hard through his nose. "Now, Gertrude..."

Gertrude removed her pince-nez and looked at Vera. "Certainly, there have been occasions when you would have liked to vote, Vera."

Mama pressed her lips together, then smiled wryly. "Much as I hate to admit it to you, yes, I've thought about it."

Papa bristled and thumped his wineglass on the table, leaving a large purple spot on the damask cloth. "What?" He turned to his wife. "You want women to have the vote?"

"Yes, Otto." Her mother smiled smugly. "Haven't I always said a woman's intellect is equal to that of men?"

"You can't be serious." Papa waved Percy away as he approached with a napkin to mop up the wine.

"Calm yourself, Otto." Aunt Gertrude smiled. "It isn't likely to happen in New York State anytime soon, even though we collected 600,000 signatures in '94, which the state legislature ignored. But I think it will happen by the turn of the century. An appropriate time, don't you think, Vera?"

Her mother nodded. "A new century. And a new age for women."

"Tosh," muttered her father under his breath.

"What was that, Otto?" Mama smiled sweetly.

"Nothing." Papa signaled Percy for more chicken. "What other outlandish thoughts do you have, Gertrude? Or perhaps I shouldn't ask."

Aunt Gertrude shook her fork at her brother. "Well, since you did ask, I do have something else on my mind this evening." She glanced at Lindy and then addressed Mama.

"Since you believe a woman's intellect is equal to a man's, what do you think about young women being able to choose their own husbands?"

Mama choked, her face turning red. She took a sip of water and regarded Aunt Gertrude with the same basilisk glare she often favored Lindy with. "Are you thinking of anyone in particular, Gertrude?"

Oh no. A terrible premonition crept over Lindy. Oh no, no, no, please don't say anything.

"Lindy told me of the plan to marry her to a duke." Aunt Gertrude smiled pleasantly. "Don't you think it possible she could choose her own husband?"

Mama turned to Lindy, her gaze pure, hard steel, and her eyes flattened at the corners. "What have you done?"

Lindy clenched her hands together under the table. "I wasn't aware it was a secret, Mama."

"It's private family business. Not to be discussed with outsiders." Mama tossed her head and transferred her malignant gaze to Aunt Gertrude, who continued calmly eating.

"Vera," her father said. "Come now, Gertrude isn't an outsider."

Mama reddened and flicked a finger at Percy, who immediately left the dining room, followed by the footmen.

Aunt Gertrude placed her fork on her plate. "I apologize for asking the question. I hoped we could discuss it, that's all. No doubt, you have the best of intentions toward your daughter."

"But I would like to discuss it." Lindy couldn't believe she'd spoken the words aloud.

Her father's eyes widened. "I don't think this is the time or place, sweetheart." His eyes pleaded with her.

Her mother had gone dangerously silent across the

table. Lindy pressed her shaking hands on the table to stop the trembling. "I have reservations, Mama. About my debut. I do want to please you, but I'm growing up. I'm no longer a child. I have thoughts and opinions of my own."

Mama sniffed. "And where did you get them, I wonder?"

"I read the newspapers. I read books. I have some knowledge of what is going on in the world."

"And a little learning has gone to your head?"

"No. But it's made me think. And as you said, it will be a new century soon. A new age for women. I'm going to be part of that new century." She swallowed. "I must make some decisions for myself."

"I suppose you're speaking of college?"

"That's part of it."

Mama smiled. "Well, darling, that's not so hard. Let us make a deal, as your father would say. You make your debut and go abroad with me. And then, when we come home, you can make your plans to go to college."

Lindy blinked. "Truly?"

Her mother nodded. "Certainly. Now that wasn't so hard, was it?" Mama rang the little bell to summon Percy. "You may serve dessert now."

A silver tray with a molded baba au rhum made its entrance, but Lindy barely tasted it. Her mother had suddenly agreed to allow her to go to college. It was a miracle. And all due to Aunt Gertrude.

Across the table, her mother oohed and aahed over the baba, smiling widely. But instead of smiling, Aunt Gertrude wouldn't meet Lindy's gaze. Why was that?

16

Jack leaned against the lamp post across the street from 660 Fifth Avenue, as carriage after carriage drove up and discharged gorgeously gowned and top-hatted inhabitants at the glittering entrance to the Lindenmayer mansion. Hoping for a glimpse of Miss Lindenmayer, he searched every window again and again, without success.

"Here, boyo, what are you about, loitering here?"

Jack turned. A policeman regarded him with a rather jaundiced eye. Jack nodded toward the mansion. "I stopped to listen." Laughter and music drifted out the open windows, and he recognized the beginning of a waltz. "It's such a lovely evening for a stroll." No need to mention he'd been standing here for the last two hours.

The policeman gave him the once over, his narrowed eyes not missing a detail of Jack's plain frockcoat. "You live in this neighborhood?"

"On the Upper East Side. With my uncle, Joseph Winthrop."

"Do you now?" The policeman tucked beefy fingers into

the belt girding his ample waist. "And would that be the pastor of St. Thomas Episcopal?"

Jack glanced at the brass name badge on the officer's wool coat. "Yes, Officer McConnell."

"And you might be?"

"Jack Winthrop." He repressed an impatient sigh and glanced sideways toward the house. Wait! There—was it her? A young woman in a sparkling white gown, her dark hair swept up on her head, in conversation with a man in white tie and tails. He clenched his fists and peered closer, not caring what the policeman might think.

"Ah." McConnell's gaze followed Jack's. "Quite the party, isn't it? But not for the likes of us, hey?"

Jack didn't answer, straining to determine if the girl was Miss Lindenmayer.

"There's fifty of us coppers here tonight, hired special for the ball. To keep the riffraff away, mind."

Jack continued to scan the windows. Maybe if he ignored the officer, he'd go away. Then he gasped. There she was!

"Hmm." McConnell followed Jack's startled gaze. "Oh, boyo, I understand now. In love with the colleen, are you, laddie?"

Jack exhaled hard. "Is it that obvious, Officer?"

"It is, lad. That it is." McConnell gazed toward the Lindenmayer mansion. "Love's grand, isn't it?" He tapped Jack gently on the chest with his baton. "Right, then. I'll be off now on my rounds. I trust you'll not be here when I come through again."

"Yes, Officer. Thank you."

Officer McConnell crossed the street and headed off down the sidewalk.

Jack looked at his coat and plain boots. How he'd love to

march into the mansion, announce himself as a friend of the debutante, and steal her away for a dance. What a commotion that would cause. He supposed he'd be unceremoniously thrown out. Perhaps arrested. How would he explain that to his uncle?

He kicked a stone and sent it skittering into the street, and slowly walked away. At the corner, he turned and gazed at the Lindenmayer mansion. Every window blazed with light. Miss Lindenmayer lived and breathed only a few hundred feet from him, but she might as well be on the moon for all the good it did him.

17

T he night of the debut had arrived, after years of Mama's dreaming and planning.

Lindy stood in the second-floor musician's gallery while the orchestra tuned their instruments behind her. Since the disastrous first evening of Aunt Gertrude's visit, her mother had kept Lindy busy with social calls and luncheons every day. And at dinner each evening, her mother determinedly kept the conversation light. No serious topics allowed.

Now her mother flitted about the ballroom below like a moving jewel shop, the pale green satin of her evening gown barely discernable under the diamonds adorning the front of her capacious bosom. She wore a diamond tiara tipped with pearls the size of hummingbird eggs, the former possession of Catherine the Great, Empress of Russia. Mama gleamed with scintillating light every time she moved.

It occurred to Lindy that this might be the only ball she attended where her own preferred mode of dressing meshed with her mother's wishes. As a rule, a debutante wore a dress all of white, with simple jewels, so the virginal beauty of the girl herself received all the attention.

Her mother glanced up. "Evangeline, your father wants to see you in his study."

Lindy nodded and took the marble staircase to the cozy oak-paneled room. She knocked on the door and entered.

Papa stood next to his desk, resplendent in white tie and tails, his mop of unruly silver hair combed into submission and even his mustache waxed. "Sweetheart, you look absolutely beautiful!" He grinned. "It doesn't seem all that long ago I dandled you on my knee. And now here you are, ready for high society."

"You look quite handsome yourself, Papa." She straightened his silk tie and gave his striped waistcoat a pat. "I suppose you'll be dressing like this quite a bit in the future if Mama has her way."

Her father groaned and rolled his eyes.

"Papa." Did she dare voice her doubts to her father? "I wanted to talk to you about some—"

Mama swept into the room on a cloud of jasmine scent and beamed at Lindy. "It's finally here—the night we've waited so long for! The first step in our plan, Evangeline. Soon we'll be off to London for the season and then,"—her smile grew wider— "we'll find you the earl or duke we've been dreaming of!"

Lindy smiled automatically. Her mother had worked tirelessly to ensure Lindy's debut was a success. The invitations for the ball had gone out last week on heavy cream vellum with elegant copperplate printing.

Mr. & Mrs. Otto Lindenmayer

    Request the pleasure of your company

On Friday evening, September 25, at 9 o'clock.

THE CHATEAU HAD ENDURED a frenzy of cleaning under the gimlet eye of her mother. Nearly every room on the first floor of the mansion had been pressed into service. Adjacent to the ballroom, the drawing room had been set up as a refuge for the gentlemen—since no gentleman could smoke in the presence of a lady. Her mother's régence salon would contain refreshments throughout the evening—small canapés and tiny sandwiches, cream puffs and the like, plus coffee and iced lemonade.

Mama turned. "Do you have the gift, Otto?"

Papa smiled and retrieved a silver box from his desk. "I hope you like it, sweetheart. We chose it especially for you." A diamond and aquamarine necklace lay inside on white velvet. Three strands of perfect pearls hung from the jeweled clasp, joined to a cabochon aquamarine in a platinum setting of diamonds.

"It's breathtaking." Lindy turned to her mother. "Mama, help me?"

Instead, her mother glared at Papa and scowled. "That isn't what I chose, Otto. The color's wrong."

"No, it isn't." He took the necklace and turned Lindy around to fasten the jeweled clasp. "You're wrong. It's perfect. Look."

Instead of the usual bright blue color, the aquamarines in the necklace remained in their natural state—a gorgeous, translucent sea green with just a hint of blue.

"They match her eyes exactly."

"Humph." Mama sniffed. "No one will even know what they are." She swept out of the room. "I can't leave you to do anything right!"

Papa shrugged. "I guess I know what color my daughter's eyes are."

"You're so thoughtful, Papa. Thank you."

She kissed her father's cheek, and a shy smile lit his face. "You like it?"

"I love it. It will always be my favorite jewel."

He grinned at her compliment and tucked her hand into his arm. "I suppose it's time to face the lions. Er... I mean, the ladies."

"Oh, Papa." She squeezed his arm, and off they went.

The crystal chandeliers sparkled over a fairyland of potted orange trees, ferns, and palm trees, interspersed with tiny electric lights that transformed the ballroom. The flowers were white and cream, in honor of the debutante. Roses, lilies, orchids, chrysanthemums, jasmine, and orange blossoms, all were giving off their exotic fragrances in a heady mélange, sure to make some of the ladies swoon.

Lindy stood between her mother and father to greet the guests. Dressed in the latest fashions from Paris, the ladies of New York society sparkled in satin and silks in every hue of the rainbow, and like Mama, seemed to be wearing the entire contents of their jewelry box all at once.

Mama's pinch on her arm brought Lindy out of her reverie. Mamie Oelrichs approached in the receiving line. Next to Caroline Astor, Mrs. Oelrichs was one of the most important hostesses and leaders of society. Mama straightened her already impeccable posture as Mamie swept up to them in a gown of peach silk crepe overlaid with gold tulle. A diamond dog collar encircled her wrinkled neck, ropes of pearls and diamonds decorated her deep décolletage, and a tiara, of course, accentuated with peacock feathers, graced the coils of her graying coiffure.

Mamie nodded to Papa and exchanged kisses with Mama in the European fashion, one on each cheek.

Then she turned to Lindy. Lynx-eyed, she scrutinized Lindy's appearance for several long moments, from the crown of her head to her white silk dancing slippers. Mamie tipped her head to one side and pursed her lips. Then she smiled and waved her jeweled fan. "Exquisite! You've outdone yourself, Vera."

Mama smiled and favored Lindy with an approving glance. Lindy bit her lip. She was a commodity to be traded to the highest bidder. At least that's what it felt like. *What's wrong with me? Most girls would be over the moon to have a debut ball like this.*

Aunt Gertrude stood at the back of the ballroom in a simple gown of silver lamé, a head taller than the rest of the ladies. Instead of a tiara, white orchids adorned her coiffure, looking suspiciously like the same orchids decorating the ballroom walls. In a sea of fussy gowns and opulent jewels, Gertrude stood sleek and unadorned, a cool star amidst a galaxy of overheated suns. Between the sheer number of bodies and the burning candles, the heat in the ballroom had risen uncomfortably. A long line of guests stretched to the French doors from the hall. Though she longed for the peaceful silence of her bedroom, Lindy greeted the guests, outwardly calm, while a question thrummed through her brain like the endless bubbles in a glass of champagne.

How can I tell Mama I don't want any part of high society?

After what seemed like hours, the interminable line of guests had been received and formally introduced. The official ceremony of the debut ended, and the dancing could begin. The orchestra struck up a lively waltz, and a posse of young men in tie and tails besieged her, clamoring for a dance. Her mother-of-pearl and silver filigree dance card filled within moments.

Maddie's brother, Charles Goulet, claimed her for the waltz already in progress. With excellent skill, he swept her into the flowing rise and fall of the dance.

"You're looking especially beautiful tonight, Miss Lindenmayer." He gazed at her with admiring eyes.

"Thank you, Mr. Goulet."

"Are you enjoying your evening?

"Very much so."

"I hope I shall be able to have another dance with you this evening. Your beauty is ravishing."

Lindy resisted the urge to roll her eyes. *Is this what I have to look forward to? Fatuous comments from slick young men?*

"So is yours."

He blinked, considering her comment. Lindy had been instructed by her mother to reply to these sorts of statements with a modest thank-you and downcast eyes. *What tosh.* She smiled to herself. Her father's word quite accurately described the situation.

"Mr. Goulet, would you mind if we didn't speak? I'd like to enjoy the dance."

He shrugged and fixed his gaze somewhere over her right shoulder. At the conclusion of the waltz, he bowed to her and hurried off.

Walter Rockefeller claimed her next, and the same insipid line of conversation ensued. "How lovely you are tonight, Miss Lindenmayer. I've been waiting a long time to have this dance with you."

"A blue moon, I'm sure." Immediately the identical look of ruffled incomprehension slid over Mr. Rockefeller's smooth features. She wasn't playing the game correctly. "Let's dance, shall we, Mr. Rockefeller?"

He gulped and nodded. Lindy did the same thing with the rest of the young society gentlemen who asked for a dance. And as a result, she enjoyed the dancing. Having escaped the need to make banal conversation, she could lose herself in the dips of the waltz and the fast steps of the mazurkas. And her mother was none the wiser.

Her father claimed her for the last dance before the orchestra stopped playing at midnight, when the elegant supper would be served. He beamed at her. "You seem to be enjoying yourself, sweetheart. I wasn't at all sure you would."

A pang went through Lindy at the hopeful expression on her father's face. Of course, she couldn't tell him what she had done to ensure an enjoyable evening. "It's been lovely, Papa. Thank you."

When the waltz ended, they were near the tall windows overlooking Fifth Avenue. The servants had been quietly opening the casements to relieve the stifling heat in the ballroom, and a delicious stream of fresh air washed over her. "Let's stay here a moment, Papa." She pressed closer to the open window and sighed as the breeze cooled her hot cheeks.

"Only until the gong sounds, sweetheart." He checked his pocket watch. "It's nearly midnight. Only three infernal hours to go."

"Oh, Papa." She laughed and kissed his cheek. "You're not cut out for this any more than I am."

The dinner gong sounded then, three times, its wavelike notes swelling over the ballroom.

Papa bowed to Lindy and held out his arm. "Shall we then?"

Lindy curtsied. "Yes, Papa."

Arm in arm, they went together to find Mama and lead the way into supper, where Mamie Oelrichs commandeered her mother, and Papa ended up in conversation with Caroline Astor.

Aunt Gertrude popped up at Lindy's elbow. "Sit with me for a bit. How is your evening progressing?" They retreated to a settee in a cozy corner of the salon with their plates.

Lindy smiled at her aunt. "Do you truly want to know?"

Gertrude smiled conspiratorially. "I do."

"I've had much instruction from my mother as to how a lady converses with gentlemen at a ball like this." She took a bite of roast pheasant. "But I never imagined how boring it would be." All those discussions with Jack have spoiled me.

Aunt Gertrude laughed. "Oh my, yes, I do remember how it could be. Even now, for a woman my age, the same rules apply. I choose to ignore them."

"Yes. And so did I." She recounted for her aunt how she had stopped the dialogues cold with her request for no conversation.

"Be careful. You'll make a name for yourself as a difficult girl." Gertrude's knowing smile betrayed her approval.

Across the crowded salon, her mother spotted them and began to thread her way through the throng. Aunt Gertrude had seen her too. "Lindy," her aunt said quickly, "I want you to know if you ever decide to go a different way, my home will always be open to you."

Then her mother stood in front of them, imperious in her jewels and green satin. "Come along, Lindy, you mustn't allow yourself to be monopolized now."

"Soldier on, darling," said Aunt Gertrude under her breath as Lindy's mother led her away.

18

October 1897

"Good morning, chérie."

Lindy rolled over and opened her eyes at Claudine's voice. A faint gray light showed at her bedroom window. She hadn't awakened this early since her sleepless night waiting for Santa Claus when she was five years old. But sailing for London meant rising early. Thank goodness there had been no ball last night.

Heavy fog pressed in at the windows, and Lindy couldn't see anything beyond a few feet outside. After a hurried breakfast, she went upstairs to change into her traveling suit. When she came downstairs again, she found Mama supervising the loading of the hand luggage. The trunks had gone on ahead yesterday. As soon as Lindy and her mother had dressed, Claudine and Hortense had left to properly attend their mistress' clothing and belongings on the ocean liner.

Mama stamped her foot. "Do hurry. We're going to be late." She glared at the footman, who fumbled the hatbox and nearly dropped it. "Yes, madame. I apologize for the delay."

Sputtering, Mama allowed the footman to hand her into the carriage. Lindy stepped in after her. "Really, Mama, must you terrorize the staff?"

Mama sniffed. "In time you'll discover, Evangeline, if you want something done right, you must do it yourself."

Lindy bit back a retort. "Calm down, Mama. We have plenty of time."

"Oh, wouldn't you know the chauffeur would fall ill with influenza at the most inconvenient time."

Lindy rolled her eyes. "Really, Mama, is there a correct time to contract an illness?"

"Oh dear, dear, dear. We simply cannot be late."

Lindy patted her mother's arm. "Please don't worry. I'm sure James can get us there in time."

Fog lay heavy over the city, occasionally lifting to reveal a glimpse of the streets of Manhattan before again dropping its ghostly fingers over the carriage. Mama had her notebook and gold pencil out, muttering to herself.

While her mother fretted, Lindy remembered the hasty way she had told Mr. Winthrop goodbye. Could she have said it any differently? Would she ever see him again? She closed her eyes and let her head lean against the cushions. She didn't want to think of it right now.

She must have fallen asleep and woke when Mama rapped sharply on the front wall of the carriage. "Where are you taking us, James? Stop at once."

The carriage jerked to a stop. Lindy lifted the lace curtain over the glass. The fog had dissipated, but the sky remained gray and cloudy. Instead of Pier 54 and its bustling three-story terminal, this wharf seemed abandoned. Weeds grew between the cracks of the rough planking, and the smell of neglected fish nets penetrated the glass.

The carriage door opened. James stood, clutching his hat in his hands, his eyes wide. "I'm sorry, madame," he sputtered. "I'm afraid I've taken a wrong turn in the fog." He swallowed. "I'll step over and speak to one of those sailors to set me right." He pointed to a few men loitering about the wharf.

"Step smartly," snapped Mama, and James slunk off. Mama leaned against her seat. "Just wait until I speak to your father about this. Close that door."

Lindy reached for the door handle and then stopped. The broken windows of the decaying terminal leered at her like eyes in a scarred face. She shivered in the cold air and peered harder at something moving on the ground. Lindy gathered her skirts and stepped out of the carriage.

"Where are you going, Evangeline? Come here!"

"Just a moment, Mama." She shut the carriage door, cutting off her mother's remonstrations, and crept toward the ramshackle building in the lightening gloom. A rusty iron fence ran along one side of the building out toward the dock. Old newspapers and dead leaves blown by the wind had collected on the lee side, and there lay three sleeping boys, barefoot and threadbare, sleeping on a pile of rags. Lindy gasped. They couldn't be more than six or seven. Their dirty faces were pinched, even in sleep, and their poor little feet were grimy and calloused.

"Oh dear," she whispered.

"Miss Lindenmayer." James appeared at her elbow, accompanied by a man in striped socks, a wool seaman's cap, and several days' growth of beard. "Come along now. We'll be late."

"Wait." Lindy turned to the sailor. "What are these boys doing here?"

The sailor glanced at the children. "Well, miss, looks to me like they's sleeping."

"But... but what are they doing here?"

The sailor raised his eyebrows. "I don't take your meaning, miss."

"Where are their parents? How could they have left them alone in such a..." She pulled her collar closer about her neck. "In such a terrible place?"

The sailor blinked. "They don't have no parents, miss."

"What? Then where do they live?"

He shrugged. "They lives right here. They're wharf rats." Lindy exhaled. "Wharf rats?"

"Yes, miss. Why, there's gangs of 'em, roaming the docks. Orphans or abandoned, all of 'em."

Lindy shook her head helplessly. "But how do they live?"

The sailor's eyes narrowed. "What's an orphan or two?"

His contemptuous gaze flicked over her body and returned to her face.

James pushed in front of the sailor. "That's enough, you scallywag. Go on about your business."

The sailor retreated a few steps. Lindy stared at the abandoned boys. How could she help them? Then she remembered the small change purse in her reticule and fumbled for it in her coat pocket.

Her fingers closed over the coins. She pulled them out and faced the sailor. He stared at her, a cocky grin on his face.

She swallowed hard. "Sir... would it be possible... could you—"

Her mother opened the carriage door and glared

through it like a gorgon. "Evangeline!" she screeched. "Come here at once."

James cast a nervous look back. "Please, miss," said James. "She'll sack me for sure."

Lindy held out her hand to the sailor. "Could you buy them a hot meal? And perhaps... some shoes if there's enough left over?" She dropped the coins into his palm.

The grin left the sailor's face, and he stared at the silver dollars in his hand. "Are you sure, miss? This is a lot o' money."

"I'm sure."

The man's lips twisted. "Alms for the poor, is it?" He turned and spat on the wood planks at his feet. "Trying to clear your conscience? It'll take more than this."

"It's all I can do for the moment. I'm sorry to have to ask you to do it for me."

The sailor scrutinized her, and then his face softened. "Blimey, if I don't believe you." He laughed shortly, then pulled a silver medal on a chain from under his shirt and kissed. it "On my life, and the Blessed Virgin, I'll do it."

Next to her, James' foot tapped with suppressed impatience. "Please, Miss Lindenmayer, we must go. Now."

"Thank you."

She steeled herself not to turn and look at the boys again and allowed James to lead her to the carriage.

"What's gotten into you?" Her mother glared at her. "What were you doing?"

Her mother would never understand. Lindy didn't answer, but shook her head and closed her eyes instead.

She understood the concept of poverty. She'd read about it in books and the newspapers. But never before had she been starkly brought face to face with it as she had just now.

She groaned inwardly. The image of the poor starving boys had been indelibly branded on her soul.

19

L ondon, England

THEY HAD BEEN at the Savoy Hotel in London for two weeks, in a pleasant suite of rooms that overlooked the River Thames, all blue and gold silk damask, and gold taps in the bathrooms.

Mama bustled into Lindy's boudoir with a triumphant smile on her face. "I'm so pleased about the invitation to the ball tonight." She sank onto the bed, waving the card in her hand. "Thanks to Minnie Paget. Lady Paget, I should say. She has proven to be most true to her American friends."

Mama heaved her considerable bulk off the bed and went into the dressing room. "The Prince of Wales will be there. I must find a way for you to be introduced to him. Claudine, come right away, I need you."

Claudine looked up from the linen she had been folding and winked at Lindy. "Mais certainement, madame."

Mama paused at the doorway. "Evangeline."

"Yes, Mama?"

"I do hope you'll perk up for the ball. You've been positively gloomy since we arrived. Remember—"

"I know, Mama. No one likes a dour debutante."

"Well then. I hope to see an improvement in your attitude."

"Yes, Mama." Lindy turned to the mirror at the dressing table. Even amid all the fuss of docking in Liverpool and the traveling to London, checking in at the Savoy, and getting ready for a full docket of balls and luncheons, she hadn't been able to expunge the memory of the ragged boys asleep on the cold ground. Their pinched faces and chilblained feet had even appeared in her dreams. Mr. Winthrop had said there was much work to be done in the poorer sections of New York. And now I've seen it for myself.

Lindy grimaced at her reflection. Another ball tonight. Another endless evening of introductions to English men looking for a rich wife. She'd already received three proposals. Of the three, her mother favored Lord Higginbottom, but his liver-colored lips and reddened eyelids repulsed Lindy, and she had refused to consider it.

Mama had received the rejection with good grace. "This is only the beginning, Evangeline. And he's only an earl, after all. You'll have other offers."

Lindy rolled her eyes. An earl wasn't good enough for her mother. It had to be a duke.

Her mother's stringent voice followed her through the connecting door to her own suite. "I've chosen the white and silver tulle for you."

Lindy shut the door and sighed as Claudine emerged from the dressing room. "What is it, chérie?"

"Nothing. Only Mama and her usual fuss over things that have no import."

Claudine glanced out the window. The sunlight had disappeared. "It's getting late. We must begin if you are to be punctual."

After a long soak in a scented bath and Claudine's administrations to her coiffure, Lindy stood before the mirror while Claudine dressed her in the ball gown.

"Magnifique!" Claudine clapped her hands. "C'est fabuleux! You will be the belle of the ball tonight, chérie."

"Only one of many belles." Lindy examined her reflection. The elegant silver-spangled tulle gown showed her waist to perfection. She had chosen the aquamarine and diamond pendant as her only jewel, although she had allowed Claudine to weave a single strand of diamonds into her dark hair.

"You will be the most beautiful of all." Lindy laughed and kissed Claudine's cheek.

"I want to hear all about the prince when you return."

"It will be quite late. Why don't you go out this evening and explore? I'm sure Pierre would be happy to escort you, hmm?"

Claudine blushed. "Merci. I will then."

Mama opened the connecting door and entered the room, resplendent in a burgundy velvet gown trimmed with gold lace and a collar studded with diamonds and rubies at her throat. More diamonds adorned her wrists and coiffure. "Mama, you needn't wear all your jewels at once. You won't be able to move with all that on."

"Don't be cheeky." Mama's gaze fixed on her. "Apparently, I need to wear the jewels to represent the Lindenmayer family as you have decided not to. I want you to make a good impression on the duke."

"He's already married, Mama, to a princess."

"Don't you think I know that? Honestly, Evangeline, do you have any interest in your future at all? The prince may introduce you to an eligible suitor."

She did have an interest. It's just wasn't the same as her mother's.

Mama snapped her fingers at Claudine. "Bring the cases. She needs something else."

"No, Mama. This is enough. Perhaps I will dazzle the prince with my simplicity."

Her mother sighed. "You're quite wearying, Evangeline. My mind cannot keep up with your strange ideas."

"It's not my idea, Mama. It's Leonardo da Vinci's. He said 'Simplicity is the ultimate sophistication.'"

"I don't care a fig who said it. Let us be off."

She swept through the doorway and disappeared. Claudine slipped the evening cape over Lindy's shoulders. "Do try and have fun, chérie," she whispered.

THE GRAND BALLROOM of the fashionable Langham's hotel on Regent Street gleamed in colors of cream and gold. Towering Renaissance pillars circled the room, and shimmering crystal chandeliers lit the gay scene. Several American families were there, including the Goulets. Maddie waved to her across the ballroom, and Lindy noted with amusement that a troop of admirers already surrounded her pretty friend, including the rejected Lord Higginbottom. Lindy's own dance card soon filled up.

Her current dance partner, a young baron with prematurely gray hair and a lisp, had stopped near the French doors bordering a garden. Out of breath after a waltz and a mazurka, Lindy excused herself and walked onto the terrace. The scent of night-blooming jasmine intoxicated her, and although she knew she shouldn't go anywhere unaccompanied, the garden lured her like a hummingbird drawn to the throat of a lily.

Bay trees lined the twisting paths, adding their subtle scent to the fragrance of roses and jasmine. She passed one alcove and started as two intertwined figures shifted and moved. She hurried to the terrace to sit on one of the marble benches, drinking in the scented air.

"All alone, my dear?"

A short and stout figure with a luxuriant white beard beamed at her. Medals and ribbons covered his chest, and his bald head gleamed in the moonlight.

She rose to her feet and swept a curtsy. "Your Grace!"

The Prince of Wales waved a hand at her. "Prettily done. May I join you?"

"Of course." She moved over to make room, and he sat his considerable weight onto the bench with a little sigh. "I'm not as young as I used to be. These dances are murder on my feet." He smiled and pulled a silver case out of his pocket. "Do you mind?"

"No, not at all."

The prince lit a slim cigar, puffing a few moments until it drew. "You're an American girl, then. Are you enjoying your stay in our 'Merrie Olde Englande'?"

"Yes, Your Grace, very much."

"Here to find a husband?"

Lindy grimaced. "If my mother has her way."

The prince guffawed. "Oh, you American girls. I quite enjoy my conversations with you. Always have something to say, don't you? Not like our homegrown English roses." He crossed his legs. "So, who have you set your cap for, then?"

"No one, Your Grace. If I could choose, I wouldn't marry right away."

"Indeed." He scrutinized her. "Which family are you from?"

"The Lindemayers, sir. I am Evangeline Lindenmayer."

The prince puffed on his cigar. "Ah, yes, the Lindemayers. Your father made a fortune out west, wasn't it? Mines or something?"

"Yes, Your Grace. Silver and copper."

"Hmm. Still at it, is he?"

"Yes, he stays quite busy."

"Is he here with you tonight?"

"No, sir. I am here with my mother."

"She sounds formidable, Miss Lindenmayer. I should like to meet her."

Lindy repressed a grin. That would send her mother to exalted heights. "She would be honored, Your Grace."

The Prince of Wales stood and threw his cigar into a rosebush. "Then do let us go in." He held out his arm.

Oh, my. Won't Mama be surprised?

All eyes focused on them when they walked in from the terrace. The Prince of Wales turned and contemplated her face in the glow of the chandeliers. "Why, you're beautiful, my dear. Perfectly charming."

"Thank you, Your Grace."

Mama stood in an alcove near the French doors, ecstasy blooming on her face.

"I see my mother, Your Grace."

He turned his head as Mama approached, her plump body encased like a sausage in her burgundy silk gown. She dipped a deep curtsy to the prince.

"Your Grace, may I present my mother to you. Mrs. Vera Lindenmayer."

The Prince of Wales took her mother's gloved hand and dropped a kiss on the back of it "I'm charmed to make your acquaintance, Mrs. Lindenmayer. I am enjoying the company of your dazzling daughter and her frank speech."

The beaming smile on Mama's face turned into a frown. "I do hope she didn't offend you, Your Grace."

The prince shook his head. "Au contraire, Mrs. Lindenmayer, she is a delightful young lady, to be sure." He looked up. "Ah, Hampshire is here. I'll introduce you."

A man in impeccable white tails approached. High of forehead, with wavy blond hair and a cleft in his firm chin, the man smiled, revealing beautiful white teeth.

"Ladies, this is the ninth Duke of Hampshire, James Alexander Bentley." They dipped a small curtsy. The duke took each of their gloved hands in turn and kissed them.

Her mother's breathing quickened, and the diamonds on her bosom flashed. But she didn't reply immediately. No doubt, the shock of meeting not one but two persons of English royalty had rendered her temporarily speechless.

"Hampshire, this is Mrs. Vera Lindenmayer and her daughter, Miss Evangeline Lindenmayer. They are here to enjoy our brief London season."

"How lovely to meet you both."

Mama recovered her powers of speech. "Such an honor."

The Duke of Hampshire bowed to them. Fresh-faced, with a straight nose and hazel eyes, he had a disarming smile. "How pleasant to meet you." His gaze settled on Lindy as the notes of a waltz sounded in the ballroom. "Do you like to dance, Miss Lindenmayer?"

"It depends on the partner." She caught a glimpse of her mother watching her and flashed the young duke a brilliant smile.

"I think I'm up to the challenge." He held out his hand,

led her to the dance floor, and proceeded to whirl her through a waltz with so many dizzying turns that she fell breathless into a chair when it ended.

She plucked the ivory fan hanging from her sash and waved it with vigor at her hot cheeks. "I don't think I've ever danced a waltz like that."

Hampshire laughed and took the chair next to her. "Then, you approve of my partnering skills?"

"You passed with flying colors."

"Shall I bring you some refreshment?"

"No, thank you, I'll just sit here a bit to recover."

"Where is that famous American vigor I've heard so much about, Miss Lindenmayer?"

"I'm afraid I left it on the dance floor."

"I hope you're able to retrieve it, for I fully intend to dance with you again." He smiled at her. "How long will you be in London?"

"Another week, perhaps two." *Until we meet the desired aristocrat.*

"Excellent. Perhaps I will have the pleasure of seeing you again."

"That would be lovely."

Her mother lurked behind a potted palm not far away, peering through the fronds. The diamonds in her coiffure glinted as she nodded and whispered to Mrs. Goulet next to her, fabulous in a gown of emerald brocade.

Lindy turned away from her mother's smiling face and cast about for some suitable topic of conversation.

But the duke spoke first. "You live in the city of New York, I understand?"

"Yes."

"And what do you do there for pleasure, Miss Lindenmayer?"

"I read a great deal. And bicycles are becoming quite popular."

The duke's jaw dropped. "You don't mean to say you ride a bicycle?"

She laughed. "No, but I'd love to try."

The duke smiled. "I can't picture a lady on one of those contraptions." The notes of a quadrille struck up. He stood up. "Would you do me the honor?"

There was no help for it. She stood and took his arm. The duke commandeered the rest of her evening, insisting on rewriting her dance card until the gong sounded at midnight, announcing dinner.

The Prince of Wales led the way, and not far behind, Lindy entered the dining room on the arm of the Duke of Hampshire. Mama joined them.

Scarlet silk swagged the windows and covered the dining tables set with crystal and gold plate. Silver epergnes of white roses adorned each buffet table, laden with chafing dishes of sirloin tips and creamed oysters, lobster salad, tiny roast potatoes, salmon mousse, and roast quail. Desserts had their own special table with chocolate soufflés, fresh strawberries and cream, bonbons, and glacéed fruits. A magnificent ice sculpture of a swan graced the table, with a space carved out for fruit. Coffee, tea, and sparkling water were offered, as well as champagne and wine.

The duke smiled at Vera. "I am greatly enjoying your daughter's company, madame. I would like to invite you to be my guests at the Royal Opera House tomorrow night. La Traviata is playing."

Vera beamed at the duke and bestowed an approving glance on Lindy. "Why that would be lovely, Your Grace. Wouldn't it, Evangeline?"

A secret message lurked under Mama's smile. Accept or else.

Lindy bowed her head. "We would be honored, Your Grace."

"It is my pleasure." He tipped his hat and flashed a jaunty smile. "I will call for you at seven o'clock."

20

New York City

JACK GLANCED into the mirror above the washbasin and straightened his shirt collar as his uncle called up the stairs. "Ready, Jack?"

"Coming, Uncle Joseph."

He gave his hair one last pat, and took his frockcoat off the hanger, shrugging into it on the way downstairs. His uncle had pressed him into dinner at the home of an old friend, and had even rented a landau complete with a driver for the occasion, insisting Jack needed an evening away from his textbooks.

They left the house and entered the carriage waiting at the curb. His uncle pulled his gold watch from his waistcoat pocket. "Reverend Fogarty was always a stickler for being on time." He smiled. "Even worse than me."

"We daren't be late then." Jack closed the half-door of

the landau and relaxed against the seat cushions. "When did you last see him?"

"At a conference last summer. He married late in life and has a brood of children. All of whom we'll likely meet tonight."

"Such extravagance, Uncle, this carriage."

His uncle shrugged. "I thought it would do us both good to get out. You've been looking rather glum lately, my boy." He hesitated. "I know it's been hard, after... after your mother's death. Heaven knows I miss her terribly too." He stared out at the passing street. "But I also know she wouldn't want us to grieve, as the Bible says, as 'one without hope.'"

Jack smiled. "I agree. And it will do me good to get out of my messy study."

He couldn't tell his uncle that the lingering sadness of his mother's death compounded when Miss Lindenmayer had said goodbye and left for London. What was she doing right now? London was several hours ahead of New York. Probably dancing into the wee hours of the morning, dressed in a shimmering ball gown and sparkling jewels.

His uncle shook his head. "I don't know how you can think in there, Jack. It's the untidiest office I've ever seen. How on earth can you find anything when you want it?"

"I manage somehow, Uncle."

They lapsed into silence. The sidewalks brimmed with people walking with their children in the crisp autumn air. Dogs yapped at young men on bicycles, and he watched a mother comfort a crying toddler who'd lost her balloon.

The Brooklyn Bridge rose ahead of them, its elegant steel suspension cables glimmering in the sunlight. Birds wheeled about the soaring Gothic arches of the towers. The East River teemed with traffic, tugboats, sloops, brigs, and merchant ships from all over the globe. Once off the bridge, they drove through Brooklyn Heights to Cobble Hill, a leafy neighborhood of brick row houses, and stopped before 239 Fairborn Way.

A bluetick hound raced to greet them with hysterical barks, and then Reverend Fogarty stepped onto the front stoop to greet them. "Joseph! Welcome!"

A flock of children swarmed out of the row house, presumably the reverend's offspring, and a petite middle-aged woman, soberly attired in black silk, whom Reverend Fogarty introduced as his wife, Amelia. Reverend Fogarty himself, almost as round as he was tall, ambled toward them and grasped Uncle Winthrop's hand. "So good to see you, Joseph."

The reverend's genial demeanor abruptly shifted when he squeezed Jack's hand and gave him the once-over. It seemed his sharp appraisal missed nothing in that one instant, and then Reverend Fogarty pumped his hand enthusiastically, his beaming smile returned. "Indeed, you are welcome, young Jack. Come in! Come in!"

Jack allowed the reverend to sweep him into the row house amid a wave of childish laughter and the dog's frantic barking. A flurry of bustle and bedlam ensued in the narrow dark-paneled entrance hall until Mrs. Fogarty sorted things out—the youngest children sent upstairs to the nursery, the hound banished outside, and the three oldest children dispatched to the parlor.

"Now." Amelia Fogarty straightened the circle of lace on top of her head. "Do let us have some conversation before dinner. We are so longing to make your nephew's acquaintance, Reverend Winthrop."

Jack repressed a shudder as they entered the parlor, a bulwark of Victorian fashion. With windows fortified with lace curtains, draped with heavy brocade, and so overhung with pelmets dripping tasseled fringe, it was doubtful any stray beam of light had found its way into the interior in the last decade.

The three eldest children awaited them there, the two boys fidgeting on straight-backed chairs. Jack seated himself on a stiffly upholstered sofa and tried to find a comfortable position on its tufted surface.

"Reverend Winthrop, Mr. Winthrop, this is Stewart and Warren, our two middle boys."

The boys nodded, dressed in identical short pants, suspenders, and white collared shirts.

"And this is our eldest, Grace Marie."

The young woman inclined her head at her mother's introduction. "I'm pleased to make your acquaintance, Reverend Winthrop, Mr. Winthrop." She raised her head and smiled at Jack. She had an oval face under a coronet of braided chestnut hair, a tip-tilted nose, and a pleasing manner.

At his sister's polite words, the youngest boy glanced at Jack and burst into giggles. Stewart elbowed his brother in the ribs. "Stop that."

A rosy wave of color washed over Miss Fogarty's face, and she sent a murderous glance sideways at her sibling, who gulped and looked away.

Reverend Fogarty cleared his throat. "So, Joseph, what are you up to at St. Thomas Episcopal?"

Before long, the two ministers were deep into a conversation about the need for new pews and communion tables.

Mrs. Fogarty smiled at Jack. "Did you have a pleasant drive from Manhattan?"

"Yes, thank you. Brooklyn is beautiful in the summer with all the old trees growing together overhead."

"Oh, I agree," said Miss Fogarty. "As if you're in a leafy green tunnel."

Jack nodded. "Exactly."

Warren kicked Stewart, who yelped and grabbed his shin, and then both boys dissolved into giggles.

Jack chuckled. "Did I say something funny?"

Mrs. Fogarty bestowed a sharp glance at her sons. "You must excuse them, Mr. Winthrop. I'm afraid they spent far too much time in the blackberry patch this afternoon. I'm of a mind to give them a good dose of castor oil and send them to bed early."

The boys subsided at this proclamation and fixed their eyes on their boots. A servant peeked in the doorway of the parlor and nodded at Mrs. Fogarty, who rose from her seat. All the gentlemen stood. "Dinner is ready, gentlemen. Shall we go in?"

She led the way into the dining room, where an oval pedestal table draped in white linen took the place of honor. A gas chandelier hung above the table, its multiple lights reflected in the gold mirror over the sideboard, picking up glints of gold in the china and the red velvet wallpaper of hummingbirds enthroned among curlicues and scrolls.

"Tell us about yourself, Mr. Winthrop," said Reverend Fogarty, busy slicing the crown roast of pork. "How do you like your classes at Union?"

"They keep me quite busy," said Jack, as Miss Fogarty handed him his plate. "Thank you, Miss Fogarty."

"Your uncle tells me you're actually pulling double duty. Classes at Columbia as well."

"Yes sir."

"And what do you intend to do with your degrees?"

Jack hesitated. He hadn't spoken about the future with his uncle, who expected Jack to follow him into ministry. "I haven't planned that far ahead." He took a bit of the wild rice with roasted chestnuts that accompanied the pork. "Mrs. Fogarty, this is simply delicious. How do you find the time to cook like this with such a busy family?"

Mrs. Fogarty colored pink. "Why, thank you, Mr. Winthrop. Cooking has always been one of my favorite things ever since I was a little girl."

"As I can well attest to, my boy," said Reverend Fogarty, patting his ample tummy. "To look at me now, you'd never know I was once thin as a whip."

"And wait till you see what's for dessert!" burst out Stewart. Then he looked at his mother and shrank into his chair. "Go ahead, son." Mrs. Fogarty smiled at her youngest child. "Just this once."

Stewart turned to Jack and puffed his chest out before announcing importantly, "Minnehaha Cake!"

Grace Marie spoke up for the first time since Jack and his uncle had arrived. "Have you ever had it, Mr. Winthrop, Reverend Winthrop?"

A puzzled frown crossed his uncle's face. "Can't say I have."

"It's the boys' favorite. Surely you know Henry Wadsworth Longfellow, do you not?"

Uncle Joseph looked helplessly at Jack. "Help an old man out, will you, nephew?"

Jack chuckled. "I suppose it must have something to do with Mr. Longfellow's famous poem? The Song of Hiawatha?"

Grace Marie clapped her hands. "I knew you'd get it!" Then she turned red.

"Yes, it's named for his fictional heroine, Minnehaha," said Mrs. Fogarty smoothly. "And Grace Marie baked it specially for our dinner tonight."

"How fascinating," said Jack. "What is it made of? Acorns and bear grease?"

Stewart burst into giggles.

"It's a three-layer cake," said Grace Marie rather stiffly, "filled with raisins and almonds, and topped with a burnt sugar frosting."

"I was close then," said Jack, smiling at Grace Marie.

"Our Grace Marie is quite an accomplished cook, Mr. Winthrop. You should see the pies and cakes she turns out regularly. We must have you for dinner again soon."

"That would be lovely." Suddenly his shirt collar seemed abnormally tight. Stewart nudged Warren, and the two boys smirked at each other. His uncle and Reverend Fogarty exchanged a look as the maid came in to clear away the dinner dishes.

"Our Grace is an excellent seamstress too. Makes all her own clothes." Mrs. Fogarty delicately wiped her lips with her napkin and folded it carefully. "She'll make a wonderful wife for the right young man." She smiled at Jack.

Jack gulped. Surely some reply to this statement was expected. "Um... yes... that's splendid. I'm sure she'll... she'll make some young man very happy." It was definitely getting warmer in here. Would it be too obvious to check his pocket watch for the time? In any event, he still had to get through dessert before he could make his escape.

"Aah, there it is!" said Reverend Fogarty. The maid carried in the Minnehaha cake on a footed glass platter and set it in front of Grace Marie.

"Why don't you serve it, dear," said Mrs. Fogarty.

Grace Marie picked up the pearl-handled cake server. She cut a large slice and handed it to Jack. "Mr. Winthrop."

Jack reached to take the plate from her, and their fingers

touched. Grace immediately turned a violent shade of red, prompting more snickers from the boys.

Mrs. Fogarty rounded sharply on the two brothers. "Up to the nursery with you. I'll send your cake up there. Off with you now!"

The boys slunk from the room, and there was an uncomfortable silence for a moment.

"I hope I'm next, Miss Fogarty," said Reverend Winthrop. "I love raisins and almonds."

Miss Fogarty nodded and quickly cut him a large slice, then served the rest of her family.

"Now, where were we?" said Mrs. Fogarty.

THE EVENING FINISHED two hours later, after a piano recital by Miss Grace Marie, who also just happened to be an excellent pianist and singer.

"Goodbye! Goodbye!" The Fogartys waved from the front stoop.

Jack saw his uncle into the landau and then hauled himself in and signaled the driver to go. He turned to his uncle. "Uncle Joseph, if you ever do that to me again, I may disown you."

His uncle's shoulders shook, and he burst out laughing.

"I'm so sorry," he choked out, between gasps.

"You mean to tell me you had no idea?" Jack demanded indignantly.

His uncle scratched his head. "Well... I said you were a fine young man, that's all." A shudder of repressed laughter went through him again. "But then, now that I think of it, Amelia Fogarty has always been a woman to go after what she wants." He chuckled. "And I think it's you she wants, Jack, for her daughter."

"Don't accept any more dinner invitations, Uncle. I mean it. Or go without me. I don't like being ambushed."

His uncle calmed down. "Now, Jack, think about it. Grace Marie is a fine young woman, and you will need a wife one of these days. Doesn't do any harm to think about who you'd like to have for your future wife."

Jack leaned against the seat cushion and closed his eyes. "I'm not ready to do that, Uncle Joseph."

I already know who I want.

If only she were available.

21

L ondon, England

"No, no, no," wailed Vera. "I don't like it at all! Take it down and start again."

Lindy sent Hortense a sympathetic look. After being invited to the opera as the Duke of Hampshire's guests, Mama had been in a tear all afternoon, agonizing over gowns and fretting about jewels.

"Mama, please calm down. He's only a man, after all."

Her mother sniffed. "Only you would say that, Evangeline. This could be the most important night of my life. And yours." She caught Lindy's gaze in the mirror. "You'd better get to your own toilette. Your hair's a fright since you insisted on walking in the park this morning."

Lindy rose. "Yes, Mama."

When Lindy returned to her room, Claudine had the

purple velvet gown with the beaded irises laid out on the bed. "Does this please you, chéric?"

Lindy shrugged. Her mother had chosen it. But it did no good to say so.

Claudine brought out the jewel cases and unlocked them. "What will you wear with it?"

The contents of the cases gleamed in the light of the rose-shaded lamps. Diamonds, pearls, rubies. Parures and demi-parures of topaz and aquamarine. Gold chains with diamond accents and jeweled combs for the hair. Exquisite mother of pearl opera glasses. Bracelets of gold and platinum set with emeralds and amethysts. Even a tiara. A modest one compared to Vera's, which had diamonds big as filberts. A simple circlet of platinum composed Lindy's tiara, set with pavé diamonds and one single luminous aquamarine.

She chose the amethyst and diamond necklace, with the matching earrings, and bracelets to wear over the long silk evening gloves that were de rigueur. She had heard La Traviata last year at the Metropolitan Opera House in New York City. This social engagement she intended to enjoy, although most of her mother's social set went to the opera to see and be seen.

Lindy and her mother donned black velvet evening capes with hoods large enough to preserve their coiffures. A knock sounded at the door. The duke's carriage waited for them downstairs.

A splendid enclosed coach with the duke's coat-of-arms waited at the curb. The groom handed them in. The duke sat on the backward-facing seat, freshly barbered and resplendent in top hat and tails. The spicy note of lavender emanated from his linen.

"Good evening, madame and mademoiselle." He smiled,

and even in the dim light of the carriage, his teeth gleamed whitely. He waited until they had gathered their skirts and then knocked on the carriage wall. With a word from the groom, the horses trotted along the street.

"I trust you have had a pleasant day in my fair city, ladies?"

Lindy nodded. Mama gave her a tiny nudge. "Yes, Your Grace."

"And what have you found to occupy your attention?"

"The gardens are lovely, Your Grace. I took a long walk this morning to admire them."

The duke smiled. "I walked this morning also, Miss Lindenmayer. I find it clears the head after a long evening of dancing."

The carriage turned onto Bow Street and joined a line of carriages waiting to let their passengers alight. The magnificent facade of the opera house loomed outside the carriage window, dominated by six Corinthian columns supporting a pedimented entablature. Large round windows spilled golden light onto the stone staircase.

"Have you ever heard La Traviata, Miss Lindenmayer?"

"Yes, Your Grace, last year."

"And did you enjoy it?"

"Very much so."

The coach door opened. They stepped from the carriage, and the duke offered his arms. They made their way across the pavement toward the opera house. Tall niches set in a plain rectangular frame occupied each end of the building. She recognized Melpomene in the south niche, and Thalia in the north, the seventh and eighth of the Nine Muses of Greek mythology. Tragedy and comedy. They would hear both tonight.

They entered the great glass and iron foyer to the opera

house. Conversation buzzed in the room, mixed with the scent of perfumes and flashes of fire from the diamonds adorning the women. The men, elegant in their evening dress, formed the perfect foil for the kaleidoscopic colors of silk and satin on the ladies.

They ascended the grand staircase as the oboe sounded a penetrating note, and the orchestra tuned their instruments. The main opera house had the usual horseshoe-shaped audience area, with tiers of boxes around its outer perimeter. The grand proscenium arch delineating the stage shimmered in the glow of crystal chandeliers hung from the center of the domed ceiling, itself a marvel of gilt plaster.

An usher in crimson and gold livery escorted them to the duke's box, which wasn't a box at all but contained a small sitting room for gentlemen who wished to partake of a whiskey or a cigar. The loge from which they would observe the opera lay beyond the sitting room, with crimson velvet drapes pinned at the sides and three gilded chairs placed at the front.

A maid took their cloaks, and they entered the loge. The auditorium lay below them, nearly filled with patrons. The women shone like jeweled butterflies as they greeted friends and exchanged air kisses. Mama immediately drew her opera glasses and scanned the audience. "Oh, there's Minnie, directly across from us! My, what an ugly gown."

The duke smiled. Lindy grimaced and studied the program while Mama continued to survey the audience. "There's Elizabeth Rockefeller, in a perfectly hideous shade of green. It makes her complexion look positively jaundiced."

"Mama, please!" She made a sideways motion with her eyes at the duke.

Vera rolled her eyes and subsided. "Very well."

The duke laughed. "Please don't stop on my account. Your American candor is refreshing."

Vera smiled complacently, and Lindy swallowed the temptation to roll her eyes. Fortunately, the curtain went up and spared her from further speech. The lights dimmed, and the audience took their seats. The plaintive notes of the prelude drifted over the audience like the touch of a gentle breeze.

The "Libiamo" of act 1 began, an exuberant song extolling the pleasures of life. Lindy tapped her foot in time to the music. When the heroine, Violetta, pondered her experience with Alfredo and sang about falling in love, Lindy's heart soared with the coloratura soprano's notes. She wanted to be in love like that too. From out of nowhere, the winsome brown eyes and dimpled smile of Mr. Winthrop came to her.

Then the crescendo of Violetta's aria "Sempre Libera" cascaded through the room. "I must always be free!"

Thrilled, Lindy glanced sideways to gauge the effect of the aria on her mother and snorted. Mama had fallen asleep in her chair. Shouts of "Brava!" and a spontaneous burst of thundering applause crashed over them, and Mama jerked awake in time to see the curtain fall. Lindy stole a sideways glance at the duke. He fixed his attention on the stage, but a tiny smile played about the corners of his mouth.

Act 2 brought the songs of two people deeply in love, and Lindy hung on every note. And when Alfredo's father, Giorgio, appeared to convince Violetta to give up the love of her life, Lindy wished she could rewrite the opera.

"One day, his passion will die." Giorgio's voice hammered at Violetta to forsake Alfredo.

Finally, Violetta is persuaded to give Alfredo up. But Alfredo must never know. She writes a letter to Alfredo telling him she's returning to Paris. When Alfredo comes in unexpectedly, she gets flustered. She sings, "Love me, Alfredo, love me as much as I love you!" The desperation in Violetta's voice pierced Lindy to the marrow.

In act 3, Violetta won't return to Alfredo because of her promise to his father, although Alfredo pleads with her. He doesn't understand, thinking she is in love with the Baron, and he becomes despondent. Then Violetta sings, "Alfredo, you don't know how much I love you. But someday you will know, and I will be dead."

Act 4 began with Violetta on her deathbed, reading an old letter from Giorgio. Alfredo knows all and is on his way to her. Violetta sings, "Addio del passato." "It's too late. Goodbye to all my sweet dreams, I only want Alfredo." Tears fell from Lindy's eyes, and an aching pain welled up inside her as the mournful notes of the oboe lingered.

Then the door bursts open—Alfredo enters, and the lovers are reunited.

Lindy recoiled at a sharp poke in her side. Mama leaned in close. "Let's leave now."

Lindy shook her head. "This is the most important part. It's almost over."

Her mother frowned and settled in her chair, her face looking like curdled milk. On the pretext of rearranging her skirts, Lindy managed to turn her chair away from her mother.

Alfredo tells Violetta they will leave Paris, and she will get well. But it's too much for Violetta. Knowing she will die soon, she takes her portrait from her locket and gives it to Alfredo. Alfredo is overcome. Giorgio confesses his mistake and asks Violetta to forgive him. All three sing—soprano, tenor, baritone in tragic harmony. Violetta sits up, feeling stronger. "I'm going to live!" she sings. Then she falls dead on her couch. The music in the auditorium built to a fortissimo. Lindy's heart thudded along with the dramatic drum rolls. The curtain fell.

Deafening applause ensued. Lindy leaped to her feet, her hand at her throat. Tears streamed down her face. She and the duke clapped as shouts of "Bravo!" and "Brava!" filled the auditorium. The curtain opened, and the singers took repeated bows. The stage floor disappeared under bouquets of lilies and roses thrown upon the stage, and the stage manager presented the coloratura soprano with a huge bouquet of red roses.

Finally, the curtain fell and remained closed. Lindy's hands tingled, and she took a deep breath to calm herself, her heart filled with the conflicting emotions the opera had engendered.

The duke turned to her, smiling. "That was superb. Quite possibly the best I've ever heard it performed."

Lindy nodded. "Oh, I agree! My heart is still pounding after that final aria."

"Yes, it was wonderful. And now I hope you will be my guests at a late supper I've arranged at the Savoy?"

"We'd be pleased, Your Grace."

"Thank heavens," whispered Vera into Lindy's ear. "Why do these things have to be so long? And all that caterwauling! Like bedlam in a barnyard."

~

THE SAVOY DINING room was as full at midnight as it had been earlier in the day. A table laid with crystal and silver awaited them in a quiet corner. Hand-written menus lay at each place setting, silver ink on rose-colored paper.

· · ·

Canapés de Caviar
  Oeufs Mirabeau
  Poulet de Grains Grillée Diable
  Pêches Rose Chéri

When they were seated, the duke leaned toward Lindy and smiled charmingly. "I took the liberty of ordering earlier today."

He seemed quite sure of himself. The duke and her mother exchanged a glance, and Lindy frowned. Something didn't feel right.

Vera nodded at the duke, the feathers in her hair bobbing like a rooster's wattle. "I'm sure whatever you've chosen will be delicious, Your Grace."

"Thank you for your confidence in me. One of the finest chefs in all of Europe is here on London soil. The Savoy has lured Monsieur Escoffier from his beloved Paris, and we are all the richer for it. Perhaps we shall meet him tonight. He often comes out to greet his diners."

Champagne arrived at the table, a Moët & Chandon, in its own block of ice set in a silver urn. The waiter deftly covered the top of the bottle with a white cloth and uncorked the wine with a soft pop! He poured the sparkling wine into crystal flutes and replaced the bottle in its ice bucket.

The duke looked at Lindy and Vera and smiled. "To two beautiful American ladies!"

Her mother took a sip of champagne. "I hope we shall meet again. This has been a lovely evening, Your Grace."

The duke turned to her. "And what about you, Miss Lindenmayer? Is it your wish to meet again?"

Not for nothing had her mother tutored her all these

years to engage in mindless conversation. "I would be most pleased, Your Grace, should you choose to honor us with your company."

Her mother frowned. Perhaps Lindy had been two obsequious? The appetizer arrived then, and Lindy ignored her mother's glare. Mama had obviously set her cap for a duke. This duke.

The waiter set three tiny silver plates on the table, holding round pieces of toast covered with a piping of butter and a plump mound of black Beluga caviar in the center.

"The Canapés de Caviar, sir."

"Very good."

The canapés were delicious, as was the next dish, eggs gently cooked in anchovy butter and stuffed with tarragon cream.

"I trust my selections are light enough for a midnight supper, ladies?"

Lindy nodded, but this wasn't her idea of eating lightly. Two dishes so far with three kinds of butter. She would definitely be taking a long walk in the morning.

But she couldn't restrain herself when their waiter served the Poulet de Grains Grillée Diable. Tender slices of chicken with a mustard and cayenne pepper crust, surrounded by thin slices of lemon and served with a sauce of shallots and white wine.

"Mmmm." Then she blushed. "Excuse me, Your Grace.

"You like it?"

"My goodness, it's absolutely delicious."

The duke patted his mouth with his napkin. "I'm so glad."

The waiter whisked away the dishes and refilled their champagne glasses. A distinguished older man with a drooping white mustache approached their table, clad in striped trousers and an immaculate black frock coat. He carried a silver timbale, which he set in the middle of the table with a flourish.

"Monsieur Escoffier!" The duke rose to his feet and shook the gentleman's hand. "I congratulate you on another feat of gastronomic genius."

Monsieur Escoffier bowed. "Merci."

"May I introduce my supper guests? Mrs. Lindenmayer, from America, and her charming daughter, Miss Evangeline Lindenmayer."

Monsieur Escoffier kissed the hand of each lady. "Charmed, madame et mademoiselle." He gestured to the timbale on the table. "Maintenant, s'il vous plaît, le Pêches Rose Chéri."

He bowed again and left them to the dessert—peaches poached in vanilla syrup, covered with a puree of pineapple and champagne, and served icy cold.

When they had finished, Lindy lifted her champagne flute. "A delicious end to a memorable meal. Thank you, Your Grace."

"It has been my pleasure."

They left the dining room, walked into the lobby of the Savoy, and paused at the sparkling fountain that threw dazzling drops of water three stories high.

The duke bowed. "I will bid you good night then, ladies." He smiled at both of them, but his glance lingered on Lindy. "Adieu!"

He turned and left them, a sprightly erect figure with a noticeable bounce in his step.

"That went well." Vera snapped her fan shut and smiled at her. "You were perfect."

Lindy raised an eyebrow at her mother as they walked toward the lift. "Indeed."

"I'm sure he's interested in you, Evangeline."

The feeling wasn't mutual.

The lift door opened, and they entered the wrought-iron cage that would take them to their suite. Lindy yawned. She wanted to unpin her hair and shed her corset, get into bed, and not think about anything.

"Well, Evangeline?" Her mother gazed expectantly at her.

"Hmm?" Had she missed something?

"I said," her mother jutted her chin, "I think he fancies you."

"Well, bully for him." Oops. That was a mistake.

Her mother's face inflated like a balloon, seeming to expand as she thrust it into Lindy's face. "I haven't come all this way and made my plans for nothing, Evangeline."

Don't I know it. "Mama, I understand." The lift door opened, and she hastily stepped into the carpeted corridor. "All I want to do now is go to bed. You don't want me to look pasty tomorrow, do you? Who knows whom we shall meet?"

"True," her mother said. Mama drew the room key from her bag and unlocked the door. "You had better go straight to bed."

Lindy sent up a silent prayer. Thank you, Lord. Without another word, Mama opened her own bedroom door and retreated.

"Oh my." Lindy opened the bedroom door and leaned against it, suddenly exhausted.

Claudine poked her head up from the sofa in front of the fire. "How was your evening, chérie?" She sat up and stretched, then came over to Lindy. "Let's get you out of this."

Lindy laid her evening bag down and turned so Claudine could unbutton her. "I suppose it was a success—if you asked my mother."

"And if I asked you, chérie?"

Lindy hesitated. "I... don't know anymore." Claudine lifted the bodice away, and Lindy stepped out of the skirt. Claudine rapidly finished undressing her, and Lindy gasped when the unlaced corset fell away from her, and she could finally take a deep breath. At the dressing table, Claudine unpinned her hair and removed the jewels, and then brought a long silk nightgown. Lindy fell into bed.

"Good night, chérie." Claudine tiptoed out after opening the window near Lindy's bed.

A crescent moon hung in the sky outside her window. Her throat thickened, and astonished, she realized tears smarted in her eyes. Why?

Suddenly, she longed to be home, curled up in her chair in the library, not having to bother with all this formal stuff. It signified nothing. Talking endlessly about boring matters like the weather and who was going where and with whom. The season had just started, and all she wanted was for it to end.

Mr. Winthrop's cheerful face popped into her mind, and her heart gave an eager thump. To be able to speak to him right now and have a discussion that meant something. The realization rose like an iceberg to the surface of her mind, and she sighed.

I miss Mr. Winthrop.

22

A squeal from her mother's bedroom woke Lindy the next morning. It was still early, according to the sun slanting through her window.

Vera burst through the connecting door, her thinning hair in a careless knot. "You'll never guess! Oh, it's wonderful!" She dropped an envelope on the bed.

Lindy yawned. "It must be something special to have you this excited this early." Normally her mother never appeared before noon after a late evening out.

A lion and a unicorn on the envelope caught her attention. She pulled out an invitation with the same coat of arms stamped at the top.

His Royal Highness, the Prince of Wales
    Requests the pleasure of your company
    For a weekend at Sandringham House, Norfolk
    October 24 to 26, 1897

. . .

VERA SNATCHED the invitation out of Lindy's hands. "Isn't it marvelous?" She clasped a hand to her throat. "We've only been here a fortnight, and already we're invited to the Prince of Wales's estate!"

"How astonishing, Mama. Perhaps you should cable Papa and tell him the stupendous news."

"A capital idea. I'll do it at once." She turned and hustled into her bedroom, calling for Hortense.

Claudine shook a finger at Lindy, who shrugged.

THREE DAYS LATER, Lindy and her mother, accompanied by Claudine and Hortense, took the train north from London on their journey to Sandringham. There were several other American girls on the train, accompanied by their mothers and maids.

Mama sniffed. "That's Edith Pendleton." She nodded toward the front of the car. "It's only last year they were finally admitted to a Patriarch's Ball." She lowered her voice. "And now they're here in England. Do you suppose they're headed for Sandringham?"

"It's quite possible, Mama."

"Oh? Why is that?"

"Because the Prince of Wales is interested in Americans. American girls, in particular."

"Hmm." Her mother stared at Mrs. Pendleton and her daughter sitting several seats in front of them.

"Mama, did you think we would be the only Americans invited to the weekend?"

Her mother turned her gaze away from the Pendleton's. "I hadn't thought about it at all, Evangeline. It doesn't matter. You'll outshine them all." She patted Lindy's arm.

Lindy concentrated on the emerald fields and hedgerows passing outside the train window. What would her mother do if her carefully made plans came to naught? If the right earl or duke didn't materialize? If I refuse to do her bidding? Chilly fingers grazed Lindy's neck. They would have to go through all this again. The balls and open houses, the trips to Paris for the most fashionable gowns. The endless rounds of dinners and parties. She groaned mentally.

Help me, Lord. All I want to do is go home.

THE TRAIN PULLED into the Wolferton station with a hiss of steam. Mama gathered her things, humming, and brandished her umbrella. "I'm so glad I won't be needing this." She stepped out of the train car and took a deep breath. "It's a perfectly glorious day!"

Lindy followed her. The trees on the hillsides blazed in shades of scarlet, orange, and gold against a deep cerulean blue sky. A flock of wooly white sheep grazed in the distance, and the air held the crisp tang of wood smoke and apples. Lindy took a deep breath. If nothing else, the English countryside proved spectacular.

That evening the Prince of Wales greeted guests at the head of the receiving line before the ball, with his wife, Princess Alexandra, at his side.

He winked at Lindy when she approached with her mother. "My American friends! I'm so pleased you accepted my invitation." He turned to his wife. "My dear, the American ladies I told you about."

Mama and Lindy dipped a curtsy. "Mrs. Otto Lindenmayer, and my daughter, Evangeline."

The Princess nodded. Her blond hair had been woven into a regal coronet to fit inside her diamond tiara. "So nice to meet you. I hope you enjoy your stay at Sandringham House."

Vera and Lindy stepped away, and a woman in coral silk velvet came up to them. "Vera, you're here! I have some very eligible men lined up to meet Evangeline."

I don't want to be here. I'm suffocating.

The woman turned to Lindy, appraising her dress and outfit. "My word, child! What a beauty you've turned out to be." She smiled at Vera. "You should have no trouble finding her a husband, dear. Put your fears to rest."

"Minnie, I am in your debt. Both of us are, aren't we darling?"

Lindy nodded mechanically.

Lady Paget gathered the train of her gown with an elegant, gloved hand and linked her arm through Mama's. "Come then. Let's begin."

Lindy followed them into the ballroom. Smaller than Vera's golden ballroom on Fifth Avenue, it had a barrel ceiling and wainscoted walls with painted white paneling. The same paneling covered the curved ceiling. A large gallery ran the length of the back wall where the musicians sat.

"Now, let me see…" Lady Paget searched the room. "Ah, there's the earl." She lifted a hand.

A man with patches of pink scalp peeking through his pale hair approached. "Lady Paget." He bowed, and the ladies inclined their heads. "How delightful to see you this evening."

Lady Paget smiled. "It is my pleasure to introduce my dear friend, Mrs. Otto Lindenmayer, and her daughter, Miss

Evangeline Lindenmayer. My dears, Lord Richard Pierson, Earl of Derwentwater."

Solemnly they bowed to each other. The earl's brows and eyelashes were so pale as to be almost invisible, which, along with watery blue eyes, gave him an unfortunate appearance. Worse than that were the yellow particles of sticky stuff embedded at the roots of his lashes.

Lindy pressed her lips together. The ladies and the earl stared at her, and she realized he had asked her a question. The orchestra struck the beginning bars of a waltz then. "I'm sorry, I didn't hear you."

"Would you like to dance, Miss Lindenmayer?" The earl held out a gloved hand as if he already knew the answer. Vera raised her eyebrows delicately and gave an infinitesimal nod.

"I would love to," said Lindy.

The earl led her to the dance floor and expertly through the dips and turns of the Viennese waltz.

He smiled into her face. "Are you enjoying the English countryside, Miss Lindenmayer?"

"Oh yes. The trees are lovely."

Another turn and dip through the ballroom. "How long will you be here?"

Too long. "Another week."

"Very good."

"And then you return to America?"

"Yes." Thank goodness.

Lindy squirmed inwardly at the insipid repartee. But the subjects an unmarried woman and a young man could speak about were limited, and she didn't dare to sabotage the conversation as she had at her debut. *If I truly spoke my thoughts, Mama would have apoplexy.*

The waltz ended, and the earl gracefully deposited her

near the sofa where her mother and Lady Paget were in deep conversation.

Lady Paget clapped her hands. "You both looked so elegant during the waltz. I hope I have the pleasure of seeing you dance together again." She smiled at the earl daintily.

"I sincerely hope Miss Lindenmayer will allow me the honor." The earl turned an eager gaze on Lindy.

All her life, her mother had groomed her for exactly this moment. From the time she'd been a small girl, her mother had dreamed of a title in the family. And she had gone along with it, believing her mother's desires to also be hers.

But now, with the earl gazing at her like a besotted rabbit, Mama waiting expectantly for her daughter's perfect response, and Lady Paget looking as smug as the cat who had swallowed the canary, Lindy wanted to get up and run out of the room as fast as she could.

But instead, she said, "That would be lovely."

AFTER THAT, the earl monopolized her dance card. Vera beamed whenever a dance turn took them close to the upholstered bench where she sat. Lindy had danced with the Duke of Hampshire exactly once, a mazurka that left no breath to converse, and then the Earl of Derwentwater had immediately claimed her for the next dance, whirling close to the wall where the duke stood alone, watching the dancers. But not just any dancers. His narrowed gaze had locked on her like the stuffed head of the tiger that ruled the library.

She stumbled then, and the earl caught her. "Are you quite well, Miss Lindenmayer. Shall we sit?"

"Yes, please," she stuttered and stole another glance at the duke. He had risen from his seat and now stalked toward her, frowning.

"I'll get an ice, shall I?" said the Earl.

She pulled out her fan, the better to hide her face. "Yes, please... it is rather warm in here."

What had she seen? What had the duke been thinking as he gazed on her with such... ferocity?"

The duke stood in front of her. "My dear Miss Lindenmayer, are you quite well?"

She avoided the duke's gaze and fluttered the fan. "Very well, thank you." A stab of unease cut through her middle, and she winced when he took the chair next to her.

What was wrong with her? The duke had been most polite, and his actions had been that of a gentleman at all times. Perhaps her tight corset had affected her brain. Mr. Winthrop entered her mind again, and she gave herself a mental shake. Oh, why can't I stop thinking about him?

The earl returned with two cups of lemonade ice. "Why, good evening, Hampshire."

The duke stood. "How are you, Derwentwater?"

The earl took the vacated seat and handed Lindy the ice. "Excellent. I'm enjoying the company of one of our American friends. Have you met Miss Lindenmayer?"

"I have had the pleasure."

Still, she didn't look at the duke, concentrating instead on the coolness of the ice sliding along her parched throat.

"Well then," the earl said. "You know what a scintillating conversationalist she is."

"Indeed, I do. And I hope to have the opportunity to engage her in conversation again soon."

"I'm afraid you'll have to wait for another evening,

Hampshire. I intend to keep Miss Lindenmayer all to myself."

They're speaking as if I'm invisible. She stood abruptly. "Please excuse me, gentlemen." As quickly as she could, she made her way around the ballroom to where her mother sat.

"Mama, I need some air. Please, let us go out for a bit."

"Now, Evangeline?" Vera looked across the room, and Lindy stole a glance, too. The earl had moved on, but the duke stood in the same place, staring at her.

"Yes, Mama. Now."

Without waiting for an answer, she quit the ballroom and entered the main saloon.

Vera huffed after her. "Wait a moment, Evangeline. I don't think this is wise. It appeared something quite interesting was happening with you and the duke."

"I don't care, Mama. Your corset isn't as tight as mine." A footman opened the door to the garden, and she burst through it, taking as deep a breath as the hated corset would allow. The cool air hit her overheated cheeks, and she sighed and sank onto a stone bench.

Vera puffed her way up to the bench a moment later. "For pity's sake, Evangeline, what's come over you?" She plumped herself down next to Lindy, her breath rapid. "I'm too old to chase after you like this."

Slowly the heat in Lindy's cheeks dissipated. A gentle breeze wafted through the garden, bringing the spicy scent of pinks and delphinium.

"Are you ill?" Vera touched Lindy's forehead. "I do believe you're feverish. I don't care for the dampness of this English air. Claudine can make a tisane for you. Rosehip tea might help. Heaven knows, there's an abundance of roses around here." She sniffed. "The English certainly love their gardens, I must say. Each one blowsier than the last."

"Oh, Mama, the gardens are bewitchingly beautiful."

"So why are we out here, Evangeline? When there are two aristocrats ready to fight for you inside?"

Lindy bit her lip. Because I want to go home. But it was no use saying so.

"Well? Answer me."

"I needed a moment of... peace."

"Peace!" Vera snorted. "We're here to get you a husband, my girl."

"The highest of aspirations indeed."

"Now you're being deliberately saucy. I won't have it."

"I'm not being saucy, Mama. I'm tired of all this, the bowing and manners and balls and... I just want to go home!"

There. She'd said it. Mama's eyebrows shot up to her hairline. "Home! What on earth is wrong with you, Evangeline? What we're doing here is the culmination of our life's dream." Her mother stared at her. "After all I've done for you, the clothes, the lessons. Sacrificing my life so you may make an excellent marriage and bring a title into our family. I've lived almost my whole life for this."

Vera stood up, her bosom heaving. "And now you want to go home." Her lip curled. "No, my ungrateful girl, you're going into that ballroom, and you will be the charming young woman I've raised you to be." She tapped her foot on the pavement when Lindy didn't answer. "Now, Evangeline."

Lindy rose to her feet and silently followed the path toward the house. But when they entered the door, she turned left instead of right, across the Grand Hall, and ran up the stairs to her room. She opened the door, rushed in, and turned the great iron key in the lock. Gasping, she leaned her forehead against the door.

Several moments later, the doorknob jiggled.

"Evangeline." Mama was out of breath. "Come out immediately."

Claudine rose from the sofa, and Lindy held her finger to her lips.

"Evangeline? Are you in there?"

Lindy tore off her jewels and pulled the pins out of her hair, scattering them on the carpet. "Unlace me," she said, turning her back.

Silently, Claudine complied.

"I hear you, Evangeline. Open this door immediately!" Lindy nodded at Claudine, who unlocked the door.

Mama burst into the room. "What on earth is wrong with you?" Her eyes bulged in her flushed face as she took in Lindy's appearance. "Just what do you think you're doing, Miss?"

"Going to bed. I'm not feeling well."

Mama stood staring at her, her lips working soundlessly. Lindy could almost see the thoughts chasing each other through her mother's brain. How will she react?

Finally, her mother drew a deep breath. "Very well. I certainly can't have you missing the rest of this weekend. Go to bed. And you'd better be bright-eyed in the morning, Evangeline, do you hear me?"

"Yes, Mama."

Her mother stared at her a moment longer, and her eyes narrowed suspiciously. Then she opened the connecting door to her own bedroom, calling for Hortense.

Claudine quirked an eyebrow. "What's going on, chérie?: I don't want to be here.

But she couldn't say it, even to Claudine. "I'm tired, that's all."

Tired, and missing Mr. Winthrop.

23

Norfolk, England

LINDY WOKE SHORTLY after dawn and decided to dress and go for a walk in the gardens, accompanied by Claudine.

Mama's snoring reverberated in the corridor outside her room and quite a way down the hall. Only a few guests were about in the quiet house besides the servants. Lindy nodded to several people she'd met last night. Soon they were outside Sandringham's walls. There were two lakes on the estate, and she chose a path that would take her to one of them. Autumn in all its lush beauty and ripeness had settled upon the English countryside, the trees and shrubs creating vast swathes of gold, burnt orange, and scarlet among the evergreens.

"Are we in a race, chérie?"

Lindy turned. Claudine lagged a few steps behind, out of breath and cheeks flushed pink.

"I'm sorry, I didn't mean to walk so quickly." She pointed to a carved wooden bench in a shaded dell off the path. "Come sit for a bit and catch your breath."

The velvet grass sloped to the lake before them, bordered by weeping shrubs and Japanese maples. A faint mist hovered over the water, and here and there, a ring broke the glassy surface where a fish nibbled at an insect.

"It's peaceful." Lindy sighed. "So quiet."

"Have you something on your mind?"

"No. Yes. Oh... I don't know."

"Did something happen last night to upset you? You came upstairs rather early."

Lindy bit her lip. Supposedly a young woman of good breeding didn't confide in her maid. "I was fatigued, that's all."

Church bells rang in the distance, tolling the hour of eight.

"Are you rested enough to continue, Claudine?"

"Certainement, mademoiselle."

The neatly graveled path ambled through a copse of beech trees turned to molten gold by the sunbeams piercing the tree canopy overhead.

Claudine stopped to stare at the scene. "Oh, how beautiful."

"Isn't it? Like a fairyland. I almost expect to see a gnome pop up under that mushroom." Lindy pointed to a large brown specimen with a cap as big as her head. "Just there."

A black swan floated out from the spreading branches of a cypress and glided toward the middle of the lake.

"I've never seen one," said Claudine. Another swan swam out and joined its mate, stretching its long neck. "Two of them!"

"So elegant," murmured Lindy.

"They mate for life, chérie, did you know that?"

Lindy shook her head. "No." *Mated for life. If Mama has her way, I'll soon be mated for life too.*

Entranced, they stood and watched until the pair of swans swam of sight. The church bell tolled the half hour.

Lindy sighed. "I suppose we'd better get back. Mama will have a conniption if I don't eat breakfast before we go to chur—" She broke off, rooted to the spot. "Oh no. Quick, Claudine, over here."

Hastily, Lindy moved quickly up the bank toward the sheltered dell where they had been sitting. Too late.

"Good morning, ladies."

The Duke of Hampshire doffed his hat and bowed, freshly barbered and not a hair out of place. "I'm immensely pleased to see you this morning, Miss Lindenmayer."

"Yes, well, we're returning now. I'm attending church in the village with my mother. Please excuse us."

"Then perhaps I could escort you to the house?"

Lindy hesitated.

"Have I done something to offend you, Miss Lindenmayer? I shall be crushed if I have somehow managed to taint your good opinion of me."

Lindy shook her head. "No, Your Grace. I must be going." She took a step toward the path, and the duke fell into step beside her, with Claudine following behind.

"Surely you won't object if I walk along with you? Where did you disappear to last night?"

Lindy gritted her teeth. She didn't want to speak about this. "Disappear, Your Grace? What can you mean?"

She quickened her pace, but the duke kept up with her. "Miss Lindenmayer, why do I have the distinct impression you are trying to avoid speaking with me?"

She'd nearly reached the house, but she turned to face him.

"Miss Lindenmayer, please." He stopped and lightly touched her arm and then withdrew his hand. Lindy relented at the beseeching look on his face. If her mother heard of her rudeness, there would be the devil to pay. Perhaps she had imagined the frightening look on his face last night after all.

"You've done nothing to offend me, Your Grace. I'm pleased to have you escort me to the house."

His face lit up boyishly. "Thank you." The duke offered his arm, and she took it as birdsong filled the crisp air.

"Have you much snow in the winter season, Your Grace?"

"Occasionally, but our winters are usually mild, especially in southwest England, where my home lies. There the grass often stays green all year long. I hope to be able to show it to you one day." He turned and looked into her face as they reached the main door into the house. "Miss Lindenmayer, I hope you know how greatly I treasure our conversations." He placed his gloved hand over hers where it rested on his sleeve. "I—"

The front door opened, and a footman greeted them with a grave look. "Your Grace,"—he bowed— "a telegram arrived from the village for you." He offered a silver tray on which lay a single piece of paper.

The duke snatched it up, read it quickly, and turned pale. "I must leave immediately." He removed his hat and ran his hand through his hair. "My mother has had an apoplexy. She lies near death." He exhaled hard and read the telegram again.

"Your Grace, I am so sorry. Is there anything I can do?"

"I cannot think at the moment." He dropped the telegram and took her hand. "Miss Lindenmayer, I hadn't thought to be called away like this." He stared into her eyes, and his lips moved as if he would say more.

"Your Grace, you're in shock. Let us go inside. You may wish to send a message to your family."

"Yes, that's right. A message."

Lindy took his arm and led him inside.

The footman hovered behind them. "Shall I have your bags packed then, Your Grace?"

"Yes, thank you." The duke straightened his coat. "I must think."

"I'll leave you now, Your Grace. Unless there is something else I may do to assist you?"

"No, no."

Lindy curtsied and turned to go.

"Wait!" The duke caught her hand again, then dropped it. "Miss Lindenmayer." He searched her face. His brow furrowed, and he shook his head. "What to do, what to do..." He straightened his shoulders as if he had made a decision and drew himself up. "Miss Lindenmayer."

"Yes?"

"Wait for me." His eyes pleaded with her.

Butterflies swam in Lindy's stomach, and her breath caught in her throat. "Your Grace..."

He took her hand, and this time he didn't let it go. "I know I am being forward. But please, Miss Lindenmayer, whatever you do, don't accept the Earl of Derwentwater's suit."

Abruptly he turned and hurried up the staircase. On the landing, he turned and sent her one more beseeching look before he disappeared around the corner.

"Ça alors, chérie!" Claudine's eyes were as round as marbles. "What was all that about?"

Lindy shook her head slowly. "He was asking me not to marry the earl."

Claudine regarded Lindy. "Is there any danger of that?" Lindy thought of the earl's pink scalp and scabby eyelashes. "Absolutely not."

24

December 1897, New York City

TWO WEEKS HAD PASSED since their return to New York from London, and the Christmas season was already in full swing in the city. Mama kept her so busy with balls, dinner parties, and musicales there hadn't been any free time to steal away to the library. Lindy hadn't seen Mr. Winthrop in two months.

But she had thought about him every day.

Claudine hung the yellow silk gown with the tassel design on the skirt and hung it on the tall brass stand in the corner the bedroom. "Your mother chose this one, chérie."

Lindy wrinkled her nose. "I absolutely detest that gown. Put it away, please. I'm not wearing it tonight."

Claudine raised her eyebrows. "Then what is ma petite belle going to wear to the ball?"

Lindy walked into the closet. One entire wall held shelves of shoes and slippers, another displayed hats, toques, and picture hats with lace frills and osprey feathers. A wall of built-in drawers contained dozens of pairs of gloves in doeskin, chamois, and suede. At the end of this closet, another door opened onto a room with fragrant cedar walls, kept solely for the ball gowns. Enshrouded in muslin bags with sweet-smelling sachets tucked into their folds, and padded with tissue to retain the shapes of sleeves and bodices, they were lined up according to color on wide shelves.

"This one." Lindy pointed to a muslin bag at the far end of the shelf. Claudine picked it up and carried it into the bedroom, where she laid it on the bed. Carefully she removed the muslin bag, and the folds of celadon silk rustled out. "Oh c'est belle!"

"Mother had palpitations when I chose this gown in Paris."

"But what will Madame say if you go to the ball in this, chérie? She will not be pleased."

Lindy smiled. "She won't arrive until later in the evening. And by then it will be too late."

Claudine proceeded with the rest of Lindy's toilette, arranging her hair in an elaborate updo, and lacing her into her corset. When she finished, she spanned Lindy's waist with her hands. "Oh là là! Eighteen inches."

She slipped the gown over Lindy's shoulders and fastened the diamante clasps that held the slim shoulder straps. Lindy stood in front of the cheval mirror while Claudine clapped her hands. "You look like a goddess, chérie, like one of the women in Madame's paintings."

The sweep of celadon silk emphasized her slender figure and brought out the sheen in her dark hair. The neckline had deep décolleté, only proper in an evening gown.

Claudine tipped her head to one side. "Which jewels will you wear tonight?" She brought the leather cases and set them on the dressing table, unlocking them with a silver key she kept on a chain around her neck.

The aquamarine and diamond necklace set her father had given her on her debut would be perfect. Claudine fastened the necklace around her throat and slipped diamond pendant earrings into her ears. Long white gloves and beaded silver slippers with low heels completed the ensemble. Claudine brought out the black velvet evening cape, and Lindy was ready for the ball.

"Have a wonderful evening, chérie." She kissed Lindy on the cheek and winked. "Without Madame!"

THE DANCING ACADEMY was hosting the Patriarch Ball tonight. Papa would escort her, as Mama had another function to attend.

Scores of potted palms transformed the ballroom into an enchanted forest. Exotic plants bloomed from every corner, and banks of imported jasmine plants along the walls perfumed the air. Tiny electric lights strung through the garlands of smilax and ivy twinkled overhead.

Her father appeared at her side and handed her an iced lemonade. "I'm off to the smoking room, Lindy. I'm leaving you in Mrs. Pettigrew's capable hands."

"Enjoy yourself, Papa." She kissed her father's cheek, and he waggled his eyebrows at her. He despised these functions almost as much as she did.

Papa nodded to their hostess, who approached with a beaming smile, her bosom and wrists sparkling with diamonds and rubies. "I'll look after her, Mr. Lindenmayer. The smoking room is behind the musician dais."

Men weren't allowed to smoke in the presence of ladies, and a generous hostess always provided a special room for this purpose. Papa bowed and took his leave.

"What an unusual gown, Miss Lindenmayer," said Mrs. Pettigrew.

Lindy glanced at the celadon silk. "Thank you."

"It's a bit different than the ball dresses you usually wear, I think."

"Yes, it is." Because I chose it.

"There you are, Miss Lindenmayer, looking entrancing as usual." Charles Goulet took her gloved hand and pressed an air kiss on it. "Will you dance with me tonight? I hope your card isn't filled already."

Here we go. Let the vacuous conversation begin. Lindy touched the vellum card attached to her wrist with a white ribbon. "I have a few spaces left, Mr. Goulet. Shall I pencil you in?" She took the tiny gold pencil attached to the card.

"Yes, please."

"The mazurka? Or would you prefer the quadrille?"

"The mazurka, by all means. I shall conserve my strength in order to keep up with you."

"Monopolizing Miss Lindenmayer, are you, Charlie? Left any room for me?" Walter Rockefeller bowed to her.

Lindy consulted her card. "The waltz?"

"Perfect."

The two men walked away, and Mrs. Pettigrew nodded approvingly. "Don't fill all your spots, Miss Lindenmayer. You never know who might arrive later."

Lindy smiled. The quadrille was forming. Her father appeared, smelling of aromatic pipe tobacco. "Shall we, my dear?" He held out his arm to her. They joined the long line of couples that formed a stately procession down the center of the ballroom to officially open the ball.

The orchestra swept into the "Waltz of the Flowers" from Tchaikovsky's Nutcracker Suite. Charles Goulet tapped Papa's shoulder, and he graciously handed her over to him. With other glittering couples, they swirled about the dance floor in three-quarter time. Normally the weight of beading and embroidery and the heavy bustle on the skirt all combined to make dancing difficult. But the fluidity and lightness of the simple silk gown gave wings to her feet. The waltz finished too soon.

Charles Goulet smiled and cocked an eyebrow at her. "You're different tonight. Miss Lindenmayer. What are you up to?"

Lindy smiled demurely. "Nothing, Mr. Goulet. Enjoying the ball."

Someone tapped her shoulder. "Good evening, Miss Lindenmayer."

The familiar deep voice sent a shiver through her as she turned to find Jack Winthrop bowing to her, in evening dress of black tails and white tie.

"Why, Mr. Winthrop!" The phrase from the opera H.M.S. Pinafore popped into her head. Be still, my beating heart!

"You are surprised to see me?"

Oh, surprised and happy. "Indeed, I am." In the space of a moment, her heartbeat doubled.

"I don't normally come to these affairs, as I'm sure you know."

He smiled down at her, and suddenly the room seemed

quite warm. Lindy opened her fan to cool her cheeks. "What are you doing here?" *Can he see my heart beating out of my chest?*

"I wangled an invitation." He smiled at her, and the dimples in his cheek appeared. "I hoped you were going to be here tonight."

Her fan waved harder, keeping tempo with her rising pulse.

"And I hope this won't be unwelcome, but—I must tell you that you are so beautiful tonight it quite takes my breath away."

Darts of silvery happiness streamed through her. She bowed her head, her cheeks flushing. This wasn't the first time she had heard such a compliment.

But it's the first time I've cared about who was saying it.

"Forgive me, have I offended you?" He swallowed and took a step back. "I'm sorry, I shouldn't have been so forward." He ran a finger around his collar. "I'm no good at this sort of thing."

You're doing just fine. She smiled at him. "You haven't offended me. Actually, I—" *Dare I say it?* "I'm happy to see you, Mr. Winthrop." *I've missed you.*

"It seems ages since we've had our discussions in the library."

"Perhaps we could steal away somewhere here?"

His face brightened. "Could you?"

"Let's get an ice and find somewhere to sit where we won't be noticed."

He offered her his arm. "Allow me?"

After a quick inspection of the ballroom, she took his arm. No sign of Mama yet. Did he notice how Mrs. Rockefeller's head whipped around as they walked past her?

Standing with some other society matriarchs, Mrs. Pettigrew smiled at Lindy and then frowned as her gaze slid over to Mr. Winthrop.

Lindy sighed. "We seem to be attracting some attention."

Mr. Winthrop nodded. "I don't mind if you don't."

He secured two silver cups of pink ice and handed one to her, then glanced at the potted orange trees which decorated the salon and raised an eyebrow. "Where on earth do they get strawberries and orange trees in the middle of winter?"

She laughed. "Brought in by railroad or ship. From Florida or California. Would you like to sit down?" Lindy nodded at two chairs recently vacated in a nearby alcove, shaded by palm trees.

"Is that allowed?"

Not if my mother was here. "Just for a bit."

Lindy pushed her chair further into the screen of palms. "How are your studies coming?"

"Grueling. But I enjoy it."

"Do you hope to take the pastorate at St. Thomas's eventually?"

"It's a possibility. But what I'd like to do is take a poorer parish, somewhere in the city. There is so much to be done and not enough people to do it. But what about you? I haven't seen you in the library for the longest time. I've missed our book discussions." He cleared his throat. "What are you reading now?"

That troublesome lock of blond hair had fallen across his forehead, and the unexplainable desire to brush it off his forehead came over her. How handsome he was, and oh my, the intent way he gazed at her as if she were the most fascinating creature alive. He raised an eyebrow. "Miss Lindenmayer?"

She stared at him like a lovestruck cow. "Um... what am I reading?" Her mind went blank while she frantically tried to recall the last book she had started. "Oh yes, Around the World in Eighty Days," she said hurriedly. "Jules Verne."

"And are you enjoying it?"

"It's fabulous. What adventures Mr. Phileas Fogg and his valet are having." She bit her lip. "I envy them."

Mr. Winthrop fixed his serious, brown gaze on her. Of all the people in her life, why did she have the impression that only he truly listened to her?

He leaned forward. "You'd like to have some adventures of your own, wouldn't you?"

She sighed. "Living vicariously through others' adventures is the only way I'm likely to have them."

"And yet," Mr. Winthrop said slowly, "there are many who would give everything they have to be in your position."

"Because my family is wealthy, you mean?"

He nodded. "Yes." He smiled. "Now, I'm going to play devil's advocate."

Lindy raised an eyebrow. "Indeed?"

"I'm going to ask you a question I dare say no one else has ever asked you before."

"Very intriguing. But I may not answer."

"I hope you do." His brown eyes sparkled. "Just imagine, if you can, Miss Lindenmayer, that money, time, education, and the expectations of society have no bearing on you."

She narrowed her eyes. "That's difficult." Where was he going with this?

"Just try. Now. The question. If you could do anything in the world, if you had the freedom to choose what you could do with your life, what would it be?"

He was correct. No one had ever asked her what she would like to do with her life. The Lindenmayer household always assumed she would do exactly what her mother wanted.

"Miss Lindenmayer?"

With a start, she realized she had been staring into the distance, turning the question around in her mind like an intriguing new specimen while he waited for her answer. Waiting as if there truly could be an answer to such a question. "I believe you are trifling with me."

"Never." He laid his hand on her gloved arm. "I could never treat you that way. I hope you know by now that I regard you with the utmost respect."

A tiny gasp escaped her lips, and he quickly removed his hand. But the warmth of it lingered through her glove, and her cheeks grew hot.

"Forgive me. I don't mean to disconcert you. But I truly want to know."

"I'd be an archaeologist." The words shot out before she could think.

He grinned. "I knew it would be something fascinating." He looked into her eyes, and his grin faded to a wistful smile.

Her breathing quickened, and her heart resumed its double-time cadence. She turned her face aside. Can he see the effect he has on me?

"There I go again. Forgive me. What if we only discuss safe subjects?"

"What do you mean?"

"Only that I won't say anything to make you uncomfortable. Let's see... I could ask you where you've been these last two months?"

I should go. Mama might arrive at any moment. But her body didn't seem inclined to obey. "I made my debut two months ago. It's been a whirlwind of balls, luncheons, and social calls since then. My mother and I spent a month in London for the season there." She wrinkled her nose. "Truth be told, I'd much rather be in the library."

"You seem to be enjoying yourself tonight." He gave her a little smile.

"Perhaps it's the company."

He swallowed then and didn't speak, only gave her an intense glance. The notes of a slow waltz drifted into the room.

"Is your dance card filled, Miss Lindenmayer?"

She didn't need to look, but she drew the card on the ribbon and pretended to peruse it. "I do have an opening."

"When?"

She took a deep breath. "Now."

He stood up and held out his gloved hand. "Shall we?"

They reached the edge of the parquet dance floor, and he took her into his arms. "Ready?"

Another rapid survey of the ballroom. Her mother was nowhere in sight. "Yes."

They moved smoothly into the whirl of dancers as he swept her through the rise and fall of the steps. The other couples dancing around them blurred and receded into the background until she was only aware of him, the warmth of his hand at her waist, her fingers captured in his, his eyes gazing down at her as if she were the only woman in the universe.

"You're an incredible dancer, Mr. Winthrop." Did she imagine it, or did he pull her ever so slightly closer?

"Thank you. But I've never enjoyed it as much as I am this evening."

I never want this dance to end.

She opened her mouth to answer when Mama entered and scanned the ballroom. Oh no. "Mr. Winthrop, do forgive me, my mother has arrived. I must go and greet her."

At once, he brought her to a graceful stop. "Thank you for the dance, Miss Lindenmayer."

"No, thank you, Mr. Winthrop."

Hopefully, her mother hadn't spotted Lindy's dance partner.

"Mama. You're here."

Vera frowned and made a tsk sound with her tongue. "In the nick of time, it seems. Mrs. Rockefeller said you were dancing with a completely unacceptable man."

Lindy put on a demure face. "Unacceptable? What did she mean?"

"Don't play innocent with me, Evangeline. She didn't know the man. Probably someone who shouldn't be here at all. What was his name?"

"Umm... I don't remember."

"Fiddlesticks. What was his name?" Mama glared at her, her heaving bosom shooting sparks from the diamonds on her breast.

Lindy didn't want to say, and her mother definitely didn't need to know. "I don't remember, Mama. He said he was visiting from Philadelphia. That's why Mrs. Rockefeller didn't know him, I'm sure."

"Philadelphia?" Vera sniffed. "No wonder. Those Philly people have no class."

"Really, Mama. He was perfectly polite. Charming, actually. And doesn't your sister live in Philadelphia?"

"I won't have you wasting your time with someone like that."

Lindy sighed, trying to repress her irritation. "For pity's sake, Mama, there aren't any dukes here tonight. Or hadn't you noticed?"

Mama frowned. "Watch your tongue, Miss." Her mother's gaze dropped to Lindy's gown. "That's not what I chose for you, Evangeline. I told Claudine to lay out the yellow silk."

"I'm ready to go home now, so it doesn't matter. I've a slight headache. I'm going to go and cool my face."

She hurried away before her mother could say she needed a chaperone to accompany her. The French doors to the terrace were open, and the air cooled as she walked through them and found a seat.

"Lindy!" Madeleine appeared in a shimmering gown of ice blue satin with silver beadwork embroidery on the bodice. She flipped her lace fan at Lindy and sat next to her. "Who was that delicious young man you were dancing with, hmm? I've never seen him before."

"Maddie! You make him sound like he's something to eat."

"Well, he did look rather mouth-watering. So, who is he?" She leaned closer and whispered in Lindy's ear. "He never took his eyes off you."

"I didn't catch his name." *The second lie I've told tonight.*

"What?" Madeleine's eyes went wide. "Weren't you introduced?"

Here we go again. "Umm. In one sense, we were."

Madeleine giggled. "What are you up to, darling girl? And what are you doing way over here?"

"I felt stifled. Too hot. That's all."

Maddie cocked her head and scrutinized her. "Your eyes are shining. And you've the most beautiful pink blush in your cheeks. If I didn't know you better, I'd think you'd been dipping into the rouge pot." She stopped then and gasped. "Why, Lindy, you look—you

look   like   you've   fallen   in   love!   Evangeline
Lindenmayer!"

"What?" Lindy jumped to her feet. "That's ridiculous,
Maddie."

"Is it?"

Lindy tried to catch her breath. It was true.

I've fallen in love with Jack Winthrop.

25

L indy woke early the next morning and rang for Claudine.

Her maid bustled in and raised a slim eyebrow. "Up already, chérie?"

"I couldn't sleep." After coming home from the ball, undressing, and falling into bed, she had lain awake the rest of the night, thinking about her waltz with Mr. Winthrop.

Would he be in the library this morning as usual? Or was he still abed? Only one way to find out. She chose a simple pintucked white blouse and black wool skirt and then sat at her dressing table so Claudine could do her hair. "Just put it up in a simple chignon, Claudine. No fussing this morning."

"Oui, oui, mademoiselle!"

Two maids busy dusting the marble staircase and its carved stone wainscot greeted her. "Good morning, miss."

Lindy turned toward the library. No sign of her father.

He was probably already out at the stables.

She opened the library door. A fire crackled in the red

granite fireplace. In the colder weather, he liked to sit and toast his toes. Sure enough, a pair of feet emerged behind the side of a leather wingchair, stretched toward the fire. The feet straightened, and Mr. Winthrop stood up.

"Good morning, Miss Lindenmayer." He smiled at her, and her belly did the flip-flop thing again. "I didn't think I would see you this morning."

Now what should she say? It must be painfully obvious that she had arisen early and come to the library specifically to see him.

"I—I couldn't sleep."

"Too many waltzes and mazurkas?"

She laughed. "The last polka did me in."

"Would you like to sit down?" He gestured to the chair across from him. Then he slapped the side of his head. "Look at me, asking you to sit down in your own home."

She sank into the chair, not looking at him, and arranged her skirts. Now what? She stole a glance at him, and hastily looked away when their eyes met.

He cleared his throat. "Will you tell me something about your recent travels?"

That's a safe subject. "We spent the month of October in England. For the London season. Mama had it all arranged. I met oodles of aristocrats, earls, and counts. And the Prince of Wales."

"My word. Did you enjoy yourself?"

"Not really." I'd much rather be here in the library with you. She gasped as the thought flashed through her head.

"What is it?"

"Oh, nothing." She choked on the words. "Really. I'm fine."

"You looked as if you had a pain."

She blushed. Why ever had she come to the library this morning?

Because you wanted to see him.

"Oh!" She jumped up.

Mr. Winthrop rose to his feet too. "Miss Lindenmayer! Are you alright? What is it?"

What indeed? Her throat closed, and tears stung her eyes. "I had three proposals of marriage," she blurted out.

"Three?" Mr. Winthrop's eyes boggled. "Did—did you accept any of them?"

"It's not up to me, don't you see? Mother will choose my husband." She took a step and turned back, pacing. "Oh, I hate it so."

He swallowed. "I'm sure your mother has your best interests at heart."

"Tosh. She only wants what she wants. But I can never say that to her, though I think it all the time."

A long silence ensued. She pressed her lips together to stop their trembling. He must think her a terribly spoiled and ungrateful child. "There. I've shocked you, haven't I? By my impudent outburst and unfilial thoughts."

A pang went through her when he didn't answer. She collapsed into the chair, and a lump rose in her throat. "And that isn't even the worst of it." She clenched her fists.

He looked up then, his brown eyes serious. "You haven't shocked me. Far from it. But continue. What is the worst of it?"

Tears brimmed, and she shook her head, dashing them away. "Why, it's never knowing. Never knowing if it's just the money they want."

"The money?" Mr. Winthrop seemed dazed, a blank look on his face.

"Yes, the money. I'm an heiress, Mr. Winthrop. A considerable heiress. Five million to be exact."

His eyebrows went up. "I never realized... I never thought... about that."

"I can assure you that it is all these men think about. Oh, of course, they are impeccably polite. Their manners are perfect. But even when we're dancing, I can see the question in their eyes, 'how much is she worth?'"

A line appeared between his brows.

"So, how am I to know?"

He shook his head. "I'm sorry—how are you to know what?"

Her throat thickened. Was she a fool to think he could understand?

"Miss Lindenmayer?"

She slumped into her chair, all the stuffing gone out of her. "How am I ever to know if—if he truly loves me? For me? For me, and not the money?"

"There is one way you can know." His brown eyes were on her now. Intent. He reached out, touched her hand, and then quickly withdrew his fingers.

"Miss Lindenmayer, I never thought to speak of this." He stopped and cleared his throat. "I've so enjoyed conversing with you in the library this past year. I realized I was looking forward to seeing you. And slowly, that feeling of appreciation I have for your sweet personality and quest for learning has quietly transformed itself into something else."

He reached out and took her hand. This time he didn't let go, and her pulse jumped. "Quite simply, Miss Lindenmayer, I've fallen in love with you."

Warmth stole over her. Was it the fire, or—

Mr. Winthrop dropped to one knee and took both her hands, and she gasped at the contact of skin on skin. "Marry me, Miss Lindenmayer. Marry me, and you will never have to fear it's your money I want. I don't care about the money. I want only you." He bent his head over her hands and kissed them.

She should retreat. Scream or something, and run from the library. Instead, the tears she'd been holding inside streamed down her face. "Yes," she said. "Oh yes!"

Lindy found herself humming the next morning as Claudine did her hair. She looked at her reflection in the mirror, noting her pink cheeks and the shine in her eyes. It was true. She was in love! Her heart gave a little thump of joy only to collide with another thought. How am I going to tell Mama? She groaned.

"What is it, chérie? Aren't you feeling well?"

Claudine paused, hairpin in hand, and scrutinized Lindy's face in the mirror.

"I'm fine." Oh, dear Lord, give me strength. How can I tell her? Perhaps she should speak to her father first. Perhaps together they might be able to persuade Mama?

A soft knock sounded at the door, and Molly peeked in. "Your mother wants to see you in her salon, miss."

"Thank you, Molly."

After Claudine finished her hair, Lindy left the bedroom and slowly walked along the hallway, letting the smile fade, and arranging her features into a dutiful mask. As soon as she could, she must try to find her father and speak with him.

Her mother was arranging flowers, and didn't look up when Lindy entered the salon. "Evangeline, I've been meaning to speak with you since we returned from London. What did you think of the Duke of Hampshire?" She leaned over to pet Lily, enthroned on a cushion at her feet. Then she placed another spray of purple heliotrope in the crystal vase and stood to survey the arrangement.

Lindy chose her words carefully. "He is a charming man. I was interested to hear his views on the Labor Party."

Her mother raised her eyebrow. "You didn't actually discuss that, did you?"

"We did. Why?"

"It's not a seemly subject for a young lady."

"Why ever not, Mama?"

"He might think you're arrogant, showing off your knowledge."

"He mentioned it first, for heaven's sake."

"Oh." Mama finished her flower arrangement. "I have good news this morning. He's coming to America for a visit. I'm going to give a ball in his honor."

A tiny smile played about her mother's mouth. Lindy's heart slowed. Oh no. Something was up. "What are you so secretive about, Mama?"

Her mother smiled. "What do you think?"

Lindy swallowed hard. She should have seen this coming. All the hints her mother had dropped on the ship. "Please speak plainly."

Her mother's eyes sparkled. "I've spoken to the duke about a match with you. He's coming at Christmas to speak with your father and ask for your hand in marriage."

Lindy gasped. Her heart thundered in her chest. She couldn't take a deep breath, as if she had been punched in the stomach.

Mama rushed to her and took her hands. "It's what we've always dreamed of, Evangeline. Finally, it's coming true!"

The room swirled around Lindy, and nausea shot through her middle. She wrenched her hands out of her mother's grasp and turned away, the hot bile surging into her throat.

"What is it, Evangeline?"

"I... I..." She swallowed hard and took a deep breath.

Mama stopped and stared at her, eyes narrowed. "What's wrong?"

"I can't marry him."

"What?" Mama's mouth fell open, and her eyes bulged. "What are you saying?"

"I can't marry him, Mama!"

"Are you mad? This is what we've planned for. Why do you think we went to London for the season? It's a title, Evangeline. A title for our family! You'll be a Duchess!"

Lindy's fell into a chair and buried her face in her hands, shaking. How could she make her mother understand?

"Evangeline! Look at me this minute and tell me what's come over you."

Lindy swallowed hard. This was it. "I'm sorry, Mama." Mama frowned. "What do you have to be sorry for?"

Lindy wiped the tears off her cheeks. "I should have told you sooner."

Mama grew still and pulled a chair close to Lindy. "You will tell me what this nonsense is you're blathering. Now."

Lindy took a deep breath. "I'm already engaged, Mama."

"What?" shrieked her mother. "Engaged! How could you be engaged without my permission, Miss?" The Pomeranian sprang off the cushion, yipping hysterically. Mama jumped up and jerked the bell pull for the butler. "Percy!" she shouted. "Come here this instant."

The butler scurried into the salon, his eyes widening at the sight of Mama's red face and bulging eyes. Her mother's hand went to her throat. "For God's sake, fetch Mr. Lindenmayer immediately! Tell him it's an emergency!"

Percy hurried out of the salon, giving the deranged dog a wide berth.

Vera plumped herself onto a sofa across the room. "I don't know what mischief you've gotten yourself into, Evangeline. But when your father gets here, we'll get to the bottom of this coil. Shut up, Lily!" She glared at the dog, who retreated whimpering to its cushion and laid its paws over its nose. Mama crossed her arms over her heaving bosom and glared at Lindy.

Papa hustled in a moment later, carrying a curry brush and smelling of horse liniment. He went straight to his wife. "What is it, my dear? What's wrong?"

Mama stood up and pointed at Lindy. "I'll tell you what's wrong. Your daughter has told me she's already engaged."

Papa blinked. "Uh... engaged?" He turned and regarded Lindy. "How could that be? Has the duke already proposed?"

Mama shook her head. "No." She advanced on Lindy, who shrank into the chair. "Who are you engaged to, you foolish girl? Speak up. Now."

Lindy straightened in the chair and lifted her chin. "Jack."

Her mother frowned. "Jack? Jack Rockefeller? But you hardly know him."

"No, not Jack Rockefeller. Jack Winthrop."

Her parents stared at her. She could almost see the name tumbling through her mother's mind. Her father nodded. "Oh. Jack Winthrop." He looked at his wife. "Pastor Winthrop's nephew."

Mama stamped her foot. "What?" she screamed.

Papa retreated a step and rubbed his chin nervously. "The boy who uses the library."

Vera fixed the full force of her furious gaze on her husband. "What library?"

"Why, our... library. Oh dear." Her father sank onto an overstuffed chair and wrung his hands.

Mama turned red as a radish. "Otto..." she said through clenched teeth. "You go right this minute and write that boy he is not to set foot in this house ever again."

Otto remained in his chair. His face sagged. "How can I do that? He's studying for the ministry and needs the books in the library."

"Now." Mama slapped the table. Then her face lit up. "Send a maid to see if he's here now."

He shrugged and got out of the chair, avoiding Lindy, and left the room, his shoulders slumped.

Mama looked at Lindy. "Go to your room. You will write immediately to that boy and tell him you cannot marry him." Lindy got to her feet. Her knees shook. "I won't, Mama. I love him."

Her mother snorted. "Love? Please."

"It's true. I love him."

"How can you love him? How many times have you seen him?"

"I've known him for the better part of a year, Mama. He's become my dearest friend." Maybe she could explain what Jack meant to her. Make her mother understand. "He's different. He listens to me. We discuss things. Books. Ideas."

Her mother stared at her. "A year?"

Lindy nodded. "We were friends at first. And then, it became something deeper."

Mama's eyes narrowed. "How far has this gone?" Her mother took a step closer. "What have you done with him?"

Lindy shook her head. "Nothing, Mama—oh!" Her mother gripped her forearm hard and jerked Lindy toward her. "I repeat—how far has this gone? Has he had you? Answer me!"

Lindy winced at the pain in her wrist. "What? No! It's nothing like that. Mama, you're hurting me."

Her mother released her. "It's all right then. You gave me a turn, girl." She sank into her chair. "Write to him and tell him it's over. We will proceed with our plan for the duke."

Lindy clenched her hands to stop their trembling. "No, Mama. It's your plan. It's always been your plan, not mine." She drew a deep breath and faced her mother. "I won't marry the duke."

Lindy moved to put a chair between her and her mother. "I love Jack. We're going to be married. I'm sorry about your plans for the duke. I know you've always wanted a title for the family."

"We'll see about that." Mama's lip curled. "Go to your room. Get out of my sight!"

Lindy fled the salon and ran up the curving marble staircase to her bedroom. When the door closed behind her, she sank in a heap to the floor.

A moment later, she heard a footstep in the hall. A key turned in the lock outside.

27

J ack closed the commentary on the apostle Paul and opened his Greek grammar. Although the professor had promised a difficult exam next week, Jack had barely been able to focus on the text for the joy that bubbled through him every time he thought of Miss Lindenmayer accepting his suit yester- day. His head whirled every time he relived the moment when she had cried, "Yes! Oh yes!" It seemed like a dream, but this precious young woman would be his to love for the rest of his life. And she loved him.

He must speak with Mr. Lindenmayer soon. Perhaps he should write and ask for an appointment. That might be best. He stood and packed his books, intending to go directly home and write the note immediately.

A soft knock sounded at the door, and a maid entered. She bobbed her head. "The missus would like to see you in her salon, sir."

Jack blinked. Mrs. Lindenmayer wanted to see him? Mystified, he closed his book and followed the maid out of the library, down the carved stone steps, and across a vast marble hall filled with ornate mirrors and statuary on pedestals. "In here, sir." The maid pulled one of the bronze an glass doors open and ushered him in.

A ball of snarling orange fur lunged at him, and he jerked as a small dog sank its teeth into his pant leg.

"Get down, Lily."

The dog sat on its haunches and pulled harder, tearing the tweed cloth.

"Lily!"

The dog reluctantly turned him loose and retreated to the sofa where a plump woman in blue silk and dark hair piled high on her head stared at him like a banshee.

Otto Lindenmayer advanced toward him. "Mr. Winthrop." He held out his hand. "Good morning. This is my wife, Vera Lindenmayer."

"Very nice to meet you, ma'am." He bowed politely, trying not to stare. This was Miss Lindenmayer's mother with the iron will. He could see nothing of Miss Lindenmayer in the woman's curling lip and the imperious tilt of her head.

Vera didn't acknowledge the introduction. "Get to it, Otto."

Otto flushed red and took a step back. "Yes. Right." He cleared his throat. "I'm afraid my offer of the use of our library must come to an end. It... er... has come to our attention that you've made the acquaintance of our daughter, Evangeline, and—"

A ripple went through Jack. Had Miss Lindenmayer told her parents of their engagement?

"Oh, for pity's sake, Otto." Vera shook her finger at Jack. "Whatever designs you have on my daughter, Winthrop, you may forget about them right now. Leave this house and never return. Do not attempt to contact Evangeline in any way, or I will have you arrested."

"Vera, please—" Otto wrung his hands. "There's no need to be so rude, surely." He threw an apologetic glance at Jack. "I'm sorry, Winthrop."

"Leave. Now." Vera bared her teeth in a feral snarl. "Or shall I call the butler to escort you out?"

Jack planted his feet and stood his ground. He hadn't pictured himself asking for Miss Lindenmayer's hand in marriage like this. He turned toward Otto. "I love your daughter, sir. I want to marry her. I intended—"

"Be silent!" Vera heaved herself off the sofa and took a step toward him, the heavy jowls of her neck quivering. The lapdog growled at him menacingly. "I don't doubt you'd dearly love to marry Evangeline, but it will never happen." She sneered at him. "She's meant for someone far above your common station."

"Is she?" Jack turned on Vera. "How well do you know your own daughter, madam? She loves me and I her. We intend to be married, and you won't stop us."

Vera laughed. "You've already been stopped, sir. I intend to speak to your uncle about your less than honorable intentions here." She picked up a weighty vase from the side table. "Now get out."

When he didn't move, her eyes flattened, and her knuckles tightened on the vase.

"You'd best leave, Winthrop," muttered Otto.

Without a word, Jack turned and left. The door had barely closed behind him when the vase smashed to smithereens against the door.

～

THE BUTLER STEPPED FORWARD from behind a potted fern where he'd obviously been listening.

"Allow me to show you the way out," the man said, with no expression on his smooth face.

Jack nodded curtly and followed him through the massive hall, his footsteps echoing off the marble floor. When the bronze doors shut behind him with a final clang, he stood for a moment, trying to control his breathing. On the sidewalk, he turned and gazed up at the mansion, wishing he knew which room was Miss Lindenmayer's. Only yesterday, she had consented to marry him, and joy unspeakable had filled his heart. And now he stood outcast on the sidewalk. How had things changed from day to night so quickly?

He barreled along the sidewalk, hardly noticing his surroundings as his thoughts whirled. What should he do? What could he do?

Mr. Lindenmayer hadn't seemed angry. Should he start with him? Write a letter and request a private interview? His boots ate up the blocks as he continued to ponder the problem. Perhaps he should have gone immediately to Mr. Lindenmayer and pleaded his case before Mrs. Lindenmayer had had time to interfere. But from what Miss Lindenmayer had intimated about her mother, it didn't seem likely she would have consented anyway.

He stopped in the middle of the sidewalk. Should he seek advice from his uncle? Jack clenched his fists. What a coil.

People streamed around him bundled up against the cold in woolen mufflers and mittens. He had ended up on Sixth Avenue at Fourteenth, in front of Macy's department store. Red silk bunting and swags of holly decorated the huge display windows. Children stood with noses pressed against the cold glass. Porcelain dolls hung from string danced in the air overhead, while underneath a toy train merrily sped along its track past a tiny village, pulling its cars with the red caboose at the end, complete with a waving signalman.

Across the street, the scent of cinnamon kuchen and sweet almond paste wafted from the German bakery. The elevated streetcar zoomed past, adding the clacking of its wheels to the bells that jingled on the horse-drawn carts. Even though many ministers preached against it from the pulpit, the pro- motion of Christmas was in full swing. Everywhere about him were smiles and laughter, while inside his heart had turned as black as the lump of coal some parents threatened their children with on Christmas morning.

28

Her bedroom had become her prison. The kitchen sent up meals, and when the maid delivered them, a manservant accompanied her to ensure Lindy didn't escape. It had been murder to get out of her corset by herself the first night. Even Claudine wasn't allowed to attend her. Periodically she tried the door, but it remained locked.

Her window overlooked Fifth Avenue. But when she raised the sash, the snow-covered ground lay so far away she grew dizzy. She couldn't jump that far. An unfamiliar man in servant's garb walked into view and looked up at her window. She gasped and pulled her head inside. Her mother had stationed a guard below her window!

How could her mother do this? Did she actually think she could force her into this marriage?

Lindy paced from bed to chair to writing desk and back again the second day, trying to formulate a plan. She had to get a message to Jack. Why hadn't she thought of it yesterday? He must be wild with confusion right now, wondering what had happened.

She tried to gather her thoughts.

DEAREST JACK:

MY MOTHER LOCKED me in my room when I told her of our engagement. She is furious. Without informing me, she arranged a union with the Duke of Hampshire. He is on his way to New York right now.

My mother is stubborn, but I can be stubborn too. I love you, Jack. I will not marry the duke. Wait for me. Do nothing hasty. I will find a way to get out.

ALL MY LOVE,

LINDY

THE NEXT MORNING Lindy waited until Molly brought the breakfast tray. As the maid placed it on the bedside table, Lindy darted past the girl to block the bedroom door. Molly gasped and shrank back, her eyes wide.

"It's all right, Molly. I want you to do something for me."

Molly's eyes widened. "Oh no, miss. I'm not to speak to you. The missus gave me my instructions, she did."

"She won't find out. I want you to take a letter for me." Lindy tried to press the envelope into Molly's hand.

Molly put her hands behind her and backed away. Tears welled in her eyes. "No, miss, I'll lose my position. I can't do it."

"Could you pass it to someone else who could?"

"No, no, Miss Evangeline. She'd know. She's got them eyes in the back of her head, she does."

"Please, Molly, just this once. I'd be eternally grateful."

Molly shook her head. "I'd be in terrible trouble. Please let me pass."

Lindy sighed and moved away from the door. Molly fled the room. Lindy threw herself on the bed and wept.

The third day the guard brought all her meals into the room and returned to take the untouched trays out.

On the morning of the fourth day, the key turned in the lock as usual. Lindy didn't turn from the window.

"Evangeline."

Lindy clenched her jaw and didn't turn at the sound of her mother's imperious voice.

"Evangeline." Again that commanding tone. "Look at me."

Slowly, Lindy turned around.

Her mother studied her. "You look pale." She glanced at the untouched breakfast tray. "I hope you don't intend to starve yourself."

Lindy turned to the window. "I'm not hungry."

"Evangeline." Now her mother spoke in a coaxing voice. "Please be sensible about this. Jack Winthrop isn't a good match for you."

Lindy whirled to face her mother. "His pedigree is superlative, Mama, descended from the Puritans! You always said it was important to have a good name."

Her mother nodded. "I did say that. But he has no money, Evangeline. And no prospects."

"He's going into the ministry, Mama!"

Mama sat on the silken counterpane of the bed and smoothed her skirts. "An admirable vocation, to be sure."

"As long as it's not your son-in-law's, is that it?"

"You weren't raised to be the wife of a minister. Or educated for that purpose. And you know it."

Lindy swung around and clenched her fists. "Needle-work and painting lessons don't educate a girl for much, Mama. Classes in deportment and social etiquette don't prepare one to be useful. And I so much want to be useful." She choked back tears and kept her voice steady. "Please, try and under- stand. I want to be Jack's wife and minister at his side."

Mama sighed. "That's enough. It will not happen. I forbid it."

"What does Papa say?"

Her mother snorted. "What does he ever have to say? He'll do what I tell him."

A hard lump rose in Lindy's throat. She lurched away from her mother and sank into a chair. How could she change her mother's mind?

Vera stood up and smoothed the kimono over her hips. "You will marry the duke."

"I don't want the duke! I won't marry him." Lindy clenched her jaw and raised her chin. "You can't make me."

"You want to be a minister's wife, and yet you don't even know the Ten Commandments."

"What?" Lindy gaped at her mother.

"The Fifth Commandment, to be specific."

Lindy groaned. Honor your father and your mother.

Her mother smiled and walked to the door. Before Lindy could move, she had exited the room. The key turned in the lock. Lindy rushed to the door and jiggled the handle. "You can't keep me locked up for the rest of my life!" She pounded the door with her fists. "Do you hear me? You can't!"

There was no answer.

She collapsed to the floor. God in heaven, what am I going to do?

29

I'll go mad soon.

Her mother was stubborn. But she could be more stubborn. With a lot of pulling and pushing, she turned the bed around to face the window. Then she pulled the silk draperies open as far as they would go. Robin's-egg blue tinted the sky outside her window. She tried to pray.

Give me wisdom, dear Lord. What is your desire for me?

But all she could hear in her mind was her mother's droning voice. Honor your mother and father. Honor your father and mother. Honor your father and mother.

AFTER A RESTLESS NIGHT, she went to the window and threw the sash up. Pedestrians passed on the street below. Goose-bumps prickled her skin as cold air rushed in. She leaned out as far as she could and held onto the ledge with one hand.

"Help!" She waved her hand back and forth. "Help me!

Please!" She screamed as loud as she could. A couple walking by stopped and peered upward. "Please! Call the police—I'm being held a prisoner in this house! Help! Call the police! Please!"

The woman's mouth formed a perfect "O." Another man stopped, and the couple pointed to her.

"Help me!" She screamed with all her might. "Help me! Please!"

A small crowd gathered, and the blue uniform of a policeman appeared.

"Up here!" she yelled again and again. "Help me, please! I'm being held hostage!" Her voice gave out.

The policeman shooed the crowd away, walked toward the mansion's front door, and disappeared from her sight.

Oh please, God.

She went to the door and pressed her ear against it, but her bedroom lay too far away from the main hall to hear anything. She put a wrapper on over her nightgown and tried to brush some order into her hair. Then she waited.

It wasn't long until footsteps sounded outside her door. The key turned in the lock. Three menservants entered. One stood guarding the door, and none would meet her gaze. The other two went to the window, lowered the sash, and nailed it shut. Swiftly they did the same to the other two windows in the room. Without looking at her, they left the room. The key turned in the lock.

She flung herself at the door and beat it with her fists. "You can't keep me in here! Mama! Mama!" She hammered the door until her hands became bruised. She sank to the floor, leaving bloody trails on the pristine white paint.

"Jack," she whispered. "Oh, Jack…"

She saw no one. Only the guard who brought her meals and left the room as quickly as possible. Christmas decorations were going up on the gaslights in the street. Evergreen wreaths and red bows. Snow fell, melted away, and fell again. Perhaps she would grow old and die in this room.

How would her mother explain that to the duke?

She lost track of the days. It must be nearly three weeks now. Her body grew thin. She knew she should eat, but she had no appetite.

One morning she awoke lying in her window seat. Doors slammed in the hall outside. Excited voices penetrated the wall of her bedroom. Lindy pressed her ear against the door, trying to hear. Footsteps pounded up and down the stairs. The noise decreased after a while. She banged on the door, wincing at the pain in her bruised hands. "What's happening?" she yelled. "Papa! Papa! Please come."

No one answered.

Lindy curled up on the bed and fell asleep.

She woke the next morning when the key turned in the lock of her bedroom door. Instead of her mother, her Aunt Julia entered the room in a fashionable mauve day dress. The scent of fresh air lingered about her person.

"Aunt Julia. What are you doing here?"

Julia pulled her gloves off. "I came up on the train from Philly this morning."

"Why? Has something happened? I heard a lot of noise yesterday."

Her aunt gave her a sober glance. "Yes." She sank on the bed beside Lindy and sighed. "My goodness, you're a sight."

She gave her a gentle pat on the cheek. "I have bad news. Brace yourself."

"What is it? Tell me quickly."

Julia took her hand and held it tight. "It's your mother, Lindy. She's had a heart seizure."

Lindy gasped. "Oh no! Has the doctor been here?"

Julia nodded. "That's the commotion you heard yesterday. She fainted at the breakfast table and had to be carried to her room. The doctor examined her and said it's her heart. She's resting now."

"Is she going to die?" Lindy steeled herself to hear the answer.

"I don't know." Julia hesitated. "Lindy, your mother told me what's happened. It's likely that the shock of your refusal has brought this on."

Lindy clenched her jaw. "Did she tell you she's kept me captive in this room for weeks?"

Julia's face paled. "No..."

"I've seen no one. She's even set a guard at my door."

Her aunt shook her head. "I had no idea. Where is your father in all of this?"

Lindy groaned. Where was her father? Out in the stables with his prize horses, afraid to set foot in the house, most likely.

Julia sighed. "Never mind. I know my brother-in-law. When trouble comes, he's always been like a turtle. Retreats into his shell. Why he married your moth—" She stopped abruptly and shot a glance at Lindy. "Well..."

Lindy wrung her hands. "What should I do?" Possibly her mother lay dying. But it wasn't Lindy's fault. Was it? "Can I see her?"

Julia frowned. "I don't know. The doctor doesn't want her upset."

"I won't upset her."

Julia stood up. "Let me ask your father."

She left the room. Lindy ran her hands through her hair and shook her head. Had she caused her mother's heart seizure? She jumped to her feet and paced the room. Oh dear, God, help me to think!

A gentle knock sounded at the door, and Aunt Julia returned. "He says yes. Come. Let's fix you up a bit before we go in."

She sat Lindy at the dressing table, brushed out her hair, and loosely plaited it.

Lindy stared at her reflection. She had avoided the mirror for at least the last week. Her cheeks had hollowed, and there were dark smudges under her eyes.

"Here, darling." Julia held out a fresh dressing gown. "Put this on." She pulled the sash tight about Lindy's waist. "So thin you've become. We'll have to do something about that."

They headed toward the carpeted hall leading to her mother's bedroom. Her mother's bed, a huge canopied affair, rested in a corner of the chamber. The room, usually illuminated by a magnificent crystal chandelier and wall sconces, today had only a small lamp burning on the side table, and all the draperies closed up tight.

Papa sat by the bedside and looked up at Lindy's entrance. His normally spotless white shirt was wrinkled, and he wore no tie. Deep lines were graven around his mouth. He gave her a weak smile and then dropped his head into his hands. Mama lay underneath the silk counterpane, unmoving.

Lindy approached the bed. "Mama?" Her mother didn't react. Lindy touched her arm. "Mama. Please. Open your eyes."

Her mother's eyes fluttered open. She moaned and fastened her eyes on Lindy, then held out her hand. Lindy grasped it and sank to her knees next to the bed. "Mama, how do you feel?"

Her mother shook her head. "Tired." Her weak, shaky voice sent a dagger through Lindy's heart.

"What has the doctor said?" When her mother didn't answer, Lindy turned to her father. "Papa?"

Otto shrugged. "He thinks it's her heart. An attack of some kind."

"Will she get better?"

Otto sighed. "Time will tell, sweetheart."

Lindy drew a chair close to the bed and took her mother's limp hand in hers. The fingers were cold against her own warm ones. Could she have caused her mother's attack? Had the stress of the last three weeks affected her somehow? She had never seen her mother ill. Now the still silent figure in the bed made her throat swell. But hadn't Vera been partly responsible for her own illness?

Honor your father and your mother, that your days may be long upon the land which the Lord your God is giving you.

Had she forsaken her duty to her parents? To obey them and trust they knew what was best for her?

"Mama... do you need anything? Is there anything I can do for you?"

Her mother shook her head. Dark shadows ringed her eyes and stood out against her pale complexion.

Lindy bit her lip. "Mama, you must try to get well."

Her mother turned away, emitting a soft sigh. A tear rolled down her cheek.

Lindy squeezed her mother's hand. Dear God, was she dying? What can I do?

A thought gathered in her mind, and she swallowed hard. There might be only one thing that could raise her mother off her deathbed. "Mama... if I were to agree to marry the duke, would that help?"

Otto's head jerked up. "Lindy," he whispered. "No..."

Her mother's eyes opened, and another tear slipped from her eye. Weakly, she nodded her head.

Lindy drew a deep breath. She couldn't live the rest of her life, knowing she had been responsible for her mother's death. "Mama, if you get well, I will marry the duke."

LINDY WENT to breakfast the next morning for the first time in over three weeks. Mama had decorated the mansion for Christmas while keeping Lindy imprisoned. Garlands of pine and evergreens warmed the marble staircase and swagged the great entrance hall. A wax angel with silver wings graced the top of a tall fir tree decorated with glass ornaments and strings of silver beads. So many newfangled glass ornaments covered the trees that the branches drooped.

Pale bars of early sunshine slanted through the mullioned windows and illuminated the Flemish tapestries Mama had ordered from Europe and hung on every wall of the Gothic breakfast room. At least there were no painted cherubs in this room.

One of the maids bustled in and stopped short, her eyes wide. "Oh, Miss Evangeline, I didn't know you were here." The maid stared at Lindy a little longer than necessary, then hastily averted her eyes. "What would you like for breakfast?"

Her appetite hadn't returned yet. "Just coffee, Molly. And some toast."

"Coffee, miss? Not tea?"

Lindy frowned. Mama didn't like her to drink coffee, believing tea more ladylike. "Yes, Molly," she said firmly. "Coffee." Molly nodded and scurried off.

The butler entered and bowed to her. "Good morning, miss."

Lindy smiled. "Good morning, Percy." Always impeccably turned out, the sight of him in his crisp linen with not a hair out of place cheered her.

"May I say how lovely it is to see you downstairs, miss." His ears reddened. "Pardon me, miss. I've no wish to offend."

"No offense taken, Percy. Thank you."

Molly returned with a carafe of coffee and a plate of toast and butter, and placed it at Lindy's elbow, with a small pitcher of cream. "Thank you, Molly."

"Will that be all, miss?" "Yes. Thank you."

The maid didn't leave but stood with her hands behind her, staring at the floor.

"Molly? Are you well?"

The maid's cheeks turned as red as her hair as she twisted a corner of her apron between her fingers. "Well, miss," she stammered, "it's just that..." She glanced behind her and lowered her voice. "I'm sorry I couldn't help you, miss. You know... about the letter?" She gulped. "I was afeared for my position, miss..."

Lindy sighed. The poor child. Not only did Vera Lindenmayer have her daughter firmly under her thumb, but Otto and all the Lindenmayer servants lived in terror of her as well. "Molly, it's perfectly all right. I understand."

The maid heaved a sigh. "Oh, thank you, miss! Sure, and I'd do anythin' for you if I could."

"Thank you."

The maid fairly skipped out of the breakfast room. If

only all burdens could be relieved so easily. Lindy added cream to her coffee. She had consented to marry the duke. There was no turning back now. But if her mother got well, that would be reward enough. Wouldn't it? Her knuckles tightened on the handle of the creamer. Am I doing the right thing? She couldn't think straight.

Her mother entered the breakfast room in an elegant Japanese morning gown, her hair dressed in a French twist, humming under her breath.

Lindy's mouth fell open. "Mama?"

Her mother stopped short on the threshold, then swept the rest of the way into the room and seated herself across from Lindy. Her eyes were bright, her complexion glowing. This couldn't be the same woman dying in her bed last night.

"Good morning, Evangeline."

A terrible premonition flitted through Lindy. "Mama, how can you be up so soon?"

Her mother's cheeks were blooming. And she never wore rouge. That would be too déclassé.

Molly entered and bobbed before Vera. "Will you be havin' breakfast, then, ma'am?"

"Tea and toast, Molly, with a poached egg." Vera looked at Lindy's coffee cup and frowned.

Lindy stood up so abruptly the chair fell over. "I don't understand. Yesterday you were on your deathbed. What happened?" A thread of nausea curled in her throat. It couldn't be.

Molly froze and then tiptoed out of the dining room. Mama sat and smiled pleasantly. "You, Evangeline. You happened. You made me so happy that health returned to me almost instantly."

Lindy narrowed her eyes. She swallowed hard, trying to control the quiver in her voice. "Were you really ill?"

Mama lifted her chin. "I had lost the will to live. Until you gave it back to me."

Lindy's throat closed up, and her pulse thudded a slow drumbeat in her ears. She clenched her fists and faced her mother. "Tell me the truth. Was it all an act? A trick? To force me to marry the duke?"

Her mother drew a deep breath. "It's for your own good, Evangeline."

Lindy's chest heaved. "How could you? Mama, even you, how could you do that to me?"

Vera waved her hand. "Do sit down, Evangeline. Finish your breakfast."

"No, Mama. I won't."

"Calm yourself. It isn't good to get worked up like that."

"Like you, Mama? Like last night?"

Vera sighed. "Now who's putting on an act?"

Lindy breathed out hard and moaned. It had been all pretense. And she had fallen for it. Her mother had never been ill. She ran out of the breakfast room.

Her mother's voice followed her up the marble staircase. "It's done, Evangeline. I've telegraphed the duke this morning. He arrives next week."

LINDY RAN to her bedroom and locked the door. Two could play that game.

She pulled paper and pen out.

. . .

Dearest Jack,

My mother is forcing me to marry the duke against my will. But I love you and no other. We must make plans to run away together. I have a small inheritance from my grandmother. It should be more than enough for the two of us to live a quiet life together.

Write to me through my maid, Claudine Roget. Don't use a return address.

I wait to hear from you, my love.

Always,

Lindy

She rang for Claudine, who burst through the door a few moments later. "Oh, ma pauvre bébé." She wrapped her arms around Lindy in a fierce hug, then stood back to examine her. "So, she has starved you?" Her lips curved in a scowl.

"I had a tray sent up for each meal. But I couldn't eat."

"And no wonder." Claudine muttered something in French under her breath.

"Help me dress. And then I have a favor to ask."

After Claudine finished her hair, Lindy peeked out the long hallway. No one in sight.

She drew Claudine into the deepest dressing room closet, and pulled the letter out of its hiding place under her unmentionables. "I need you to mail this for me."

Her maid took the letter and gazed at the address. "Are you sure, ma petite?"

Lindy smiled grimly. "I've never been more sure of anything in my life."

30

T he next morning her mother announced they would travel to Newport earlier than usual. Something about needing to get the decorations "just right" for the duke. But Lindy knew her mother really wanted to get Lindy out of New York and away from any possible contact with Jack.

And so, they arrived in Newport that very evening, as most of the servants and maids had already been sent ahead to open the summer mansion for the Christmas season. Seaside was just that, a "cottage" on the sea with a hundred rooms built of Italian marble, and famous for its ballroom with three types of gold applied to the ceilings and walls alone.

Three days had passed since she'd sent the letter to Jack. Three days spent watching the clock, hoping, and daring to dream. It had taken every bit of skill she possessed not to let her secret joy shine through her eyes and her voice, lest her mother suspect anything.

The duke would arrive this afternoon.

A brief knock sounded at the door, and her mother

breezed in with Lily in her arms. "Excellent. You're up." She glanced at the Bible on Lindy's bed. "I've chosen the silver-gray silk for you."

Lindy nodded.

"Tell Claudine I want your hair arranged more loosely this morning. The pompadour is all the rage now. I wouldn't want the duke to think we aren't informed on the latest fashions here."

Lindy pressed her lips together. Right now, she couldn't care less about fashion. She glanced at the little ormolu clock on her dressing table. Nine o'clock. The mail usually arrived about noon. She closed her eyes for a moment and sent up a fervent prayer that Jack's reply would arrive today.

"Are you quite well, Evangeline?"

Lindy opened her eyes. Her mother stared at her, a frown twisting her lips. "You're not ill, are you?" She laid a cool hand on Lindy's forehead.

"I'm perfectly fine, Mama." Lindy shrugged her mother's hand away and stood up. "Ready to get on with the day."

Her mother beamed at her. "Excellent." She walked to the door and stopped to pull the bell rope for Claudine. "The duke arrives at eleven."

TWO HOURS LATER, Lindy waited in the hall with her parents. A groom had rushed ahead of the duke to announce his imminent arrival through the great iron gates on Bellevue Avenue. All the servants stood in two lines behind them, starched and laced to the nines. Papa had his morning coat on. Mama stood stiffly, her spine ramrod straight, not a hair out of place, and nearly vibrating with excitement.

There was a clattering outside, and the ducal carriage, emblazoned with the duke's coat of arms, pulled up outside. Of course, he would have brought his carriage with him on the ocean liner. That would certainly impress her mother's friends. Percy opened the entry doors and bowed. The duke strode in, wearing a fur coat with a Turkey red muffler around his throat, and bringing a blast of cold, salt-scented air with him.

"Ah, my dearest Mrs. Lindenmayer." Simpering, Mama dropped a small curtsy as the duke took her hand and kissed the back of it. "Enchanting as always."

"Welcome to our cottage, Your Grace." Her mother drew Papa forward. "May I present my husband, Otto Lindenmayer."

Papa bowed his head. "So pleased to meet you, Your Grace."

"It's my great pleasure, sir." The duke smiled, and his gaze fell on Lindy, waiting slightly behind her parents. "There she is."

Lindy curtsied. "Welcome to Seaside, Your Grace."

The duke took her hand and brought it to his lips. He dropped a kiss on it and then looked at her, searching her face. The cold air had flushed his cheeks, and an agreeable scent of balsam wafted from his person. "And am I truly welcome, my dear Miss Lindenmayer?"

There was an admiring gasp behind her from one of the maids, quickly squashed by a sideways glance from her mother. "Of course, Your Grace. I hope you enjoy your stay here."

"I do hope you won't always be so formal, my dear," murmured the duke under his breath for only Lindy to hear. "I'm simply salivating to know you better."

Ugh. Lindy curtsied again, giving her mother the opportunity to usher the duke forward. "Let me show you to your room, Your Grace. I'm sure you need some time to freshen up and rest a bit." She led the way up the marble stairway, followed by the duke and his male valet.

The servants dispersed to their respective duties, some to receive the duke's suitcases and valises.

Papa glanced at her. "So, this is the duke your mother hasn't been able to stop gushing about. Seems like a decent sort."

Lindy shrugged.

Her father muttered something under his breath and quit the room, leaving Lindy alone. Servants were still carrying in the duke's trunks, valises, and even a case of French champagne. It looked as if he had brought all his worldly goods with him.

She returned to her room and at half past twelve rang for Claudine, who bustled in a moment later.

"Anything?" Lindy asked as soon as her maid entered the bedroom.

Claudine shook her head. "Non. Not today."

Lindy turned away and bit her lip. Jack would answer. She knew he would. Now she would have to wait another long twenty-four hours for tomorrow's mail. The strain twisted her stomach and sent nausea spiraling through her.

She hadn't slept well last night, indeed the last three nights she had lain awake for hours, pondering the future and thinking about Jack. Now sleepiness washed over her like a warm blanket. "I think I'll rest for a while, Claudine." With her maid's help, Lindy changed out of the gray silk and let her hair down. A formal dinner party tonight. She would be seated next to the duke, naturally, under the inquisitive gaze of her mother's guests, all of whom would swoon over the fact of meeting genuine royalty. What a feat her mother had accomplished, having the Duke of Hampshire as a house guest for the Christmas season. The newspapers would be full of it tomorrow.

Lindy pulled the silk coverlet over her, rested her cheek on her arm, and dozed as the afternoon shadows fell across her bedroom window. When she awakened, a true headache had ensconced itself in the space between her eyes. She rang for Claudine. "Tell my mother I am ill, and beg leave to be excused from dinner." Claudine nodded and left the room after getting a cold cloth for Lindy's head.

A few minutes later, her mother entered the room and turned on the lamp. "I knew you were coming down with something this afternoon." She sat on the edge of the bed and examined Lindy. "Is it your monthly then?"

Lindy shook her head. "A raging headache."

"Ah. Likely to pass, then, by tomorrow." Her gaze narrowed as she stared at Lindy. "It isn't any more nonsense about that Winthrop boy, is it?"

Lindy shook her head. "No."

"Good." Mama stood up. "I'll have Claudine fetch some lavender oil. It's perfect for headaches." She paused at the door. "I expect you to make a complete recovery, Evangeline, for tomorrow night. Understood?"

Most of New York society would be here for the Lindenmayer costume ball. There was no way her mother would excuse her from that.

No letter came the next day.

But she couldn't plead illness to escape the masquerade ball tonight. Mama planned to introduce the duke to all the important New York society people. Sunlight fell across the bed, illuminating the masquerade costume her mother had purchased for her without her knowledge in Paris. More gold. I'm sick to death of gold.

Claudine entered the room. "It's time, chérie. The guests will be arriving soon. I need to do your hair."

"It won't take long. I'm not wearing that." She nodded at the costume on the bed.

Claudine's eyebrows rose. "Your mother will kill me. She gave me express orders."

"I'm sure she did." Lindy picked up the costume and snorted. "Cleopatra, indeed!"

Charles Worth had made the dress, of course. Embroidered gold scarabs adorned the train of black crêpe de chine. Gold and diamonds encrusted the bodice, with straps of emeralds and diamonds. Cloth of gold composed the square Egyptian headdress, with striped black and gold side panels studded with diamonds, crowned by an ibis with outstretched wings of diamonds and sapphires. The jeweled girdle over the hips gave way to more cloth of gold panels to the hem, and as if that wasn't extravagant enough, there was a jeweled ostrich fan to carry, and more diamonds and pearls to wear around her neck.

The only thing her mother had gotten right was the small diamond asp to wear around her upper arm. A prophecy of doom. Too bad it wasn't real. Perhaps she could have used the snake on the duke. Or her mother.

"Put it away, Claudine. It's impossible. Even if I agreed to wear it, I'd barely be able to move, let alone breathe."

Her mother always had a plan. If she had chosen Cleopatra for her daughter, what had she proposed to the duke for his costume? Marc Antony, of course. It should have been Octavian, who forced Cleopatra's suicide.

Dear God, help me to get through this.

Claudine lifted the costume and bore it away, groaning under its weight. "What will you wear then?"

"The Queen of the Night gown." At least she liked this gown. Midnight blue velvet, spangled with silver stars and the constellation of Orion on one shoulder in diamonds. A pale blue silk gauze scarf representing the Milky Way in diamanté, attached to one strap by a silver nightingale.

Claudine retrieved it and laid it on the bed. "C'est belle! Now come and let me do your hair."

Lindy sat at the dressing table while Claudine brushed out her hair and piled it on top of her head, then brought out the jewel cases. "There's a headband for this costume somewhere." She sifted through the contents and pulled out a silver circlet with a jeweled diamond star in the center. Claudine carefully placed it over her hair, so the star rested against her forehead. "Magnifique, mademoiselle."

Lindy smiled at Claudine. "No, you're magnifique, Claudine. Always there to support me."

Claudine dropped a light kiss on her cheek. "But of course, chérie. Are you ready to make your grand entrance?"

Lindy sighed. "As ready as I can be."

She rose from the dressing table, plucked the train in one hand, and made her way to the Grand Staircase, wrought iron and bronze, and finished with gilt bronze trophies modeled on a Versailles fountain. Her mother adored everything French, and especially anything from the time of Louis XIV. The duke was sure to be suitably impressed as he viewed the Lindenmayer wealth on display in her mother's "cottage."

Servants with blue and gold French livery and ridiculous powdered wigs scurried to and fro, their arms filled with American Beauty roses. Mama had even costumed the servants.

Opposite the foot of the staircase stood a bronze basin flanked by cherubs in front of a mirror backed with silver metallic leaf to represent flowing water. Two sets of double doors with French beveled glass opened to the Grand Salon, which served both as her mother's reception room and ballroom. The upholstery was green silk cut velvet, and the draperies bore the motif of Louis XIV—Apollo in a sunburst. The ceiling painting depicted Minerva, the Goddess of wisdom and war, snatching a youth from his love. How appropriate.

Two chandeliers wired for electricity lit the salon, suspended from decorative gold masks of Apollo. Huge carved wood and twenty-two-carat gold gilt panels dominated the walls, with scenes from classical mythology. An ornate clock based on Michelangelo's figures from the Medici Chapel in Florence stood on the mantel.

"Do you require anything, miss?"

She turned to find Percy in the same blue and gold livery as the other servants. His hair had been powdered too. She pressed her lips together to stop the giggle, and his chin rose a notch higher.

"Oh, Percy." She couldn't help it. The laughter rose in her throat and spilled out. "Oh, oh, oh! I'm so sorry, Percy. Oh!" She went off into another gale of giggles until she gasped for breath and had to hold on to the banister. Finally, she gained control and straightened up. Percy had stood quietly during her fit, but a tiny sparkle glimmered in his eyes.

"Percy, you're first-rate, you are."

"Thank you, miss."

She shrugged. "Thank you for that laugh, Percy. But now, I suppose I must face the music."

She didn't want to. But she had to. Guests were arriving,

and she must endure the reception line with her mother and the duke.

She straightened the folds of midnight blue velvet and entered the salon. Her mother stood near the fireplace, supervising last-minute placements of roses. She turned as Lindy approached, and her eyes widened. The duke turned then too. They stood together, wearing identical frowns, their gaze on her ball gown.

"What are you wearing?"

Her mother's vicious voice made the back of Lindy's neck cringe.

"Go to your room and change immediately. Do you know how much money I spent on that costume?"

But Mama had gotten everything she wanted, hadn't she? So what if Lindy didn't wear the costume her mother had chosen. Right now, Lindy couldn't care less. "A fortune, I'm sure, Mother."

Mama's eyes bulged at the bored tone in Lindy's voice. "Six thousand dollars. I've hired an armed detective to shadow you tonight. That's how valuable it is."

The duke's jaw dropped at her mother's last words. He wore a purple silk Roman toga that reached to mid-calf, with the imperial eagle of Rome embroidered in gold thread. Leather sandals shod his feet, with straps wound around his calves, and a wide leather belt girded his waist, with a golden sword thrust through it. A gold wreath of laurel leaves circled his forehead. Hail the conquering hero.

"Evangeline! Did you hear me?"

"Yes, Mother." Voices reached them. Mamie Fish, resplendent in a white Renaissance gown with a silver tissue veil, had entered the salon with her husband. "But your guests are here. Surely you don't wish me to leave now, do you?"

The ghost of a smile played about the duke's mouth. "You look splendid, my dear."

Her mother sent her a murderous glower that contrasted with the purity of her costume, white and gold satin with pearls and embroidery in gold and silver. In her right hand, she carried an illuminated gilded torch. The batteries must be concealed somewhere in her costume. How ironic, if she had intended to be the Statue of Liberty. Her mother didn't know the meaning of the iconic statue and what it represented.

Mrs. Fish reached them. A smile replaced the frown on her mother's face as she began the task of receiving the three hundred and fifty guests.

All of New York society queued to fawn over the duke, the guest of honor, and the only person present with noble blood.

Lindy bore the gauntlet with as much grace as she could muster. Many pressed their congratulations on her and the duke. Only when Madeleine approached did Lindy have a genuine smile.

"Darling!" Maddie squeezed her hand and planted a kiss on her cheek. "He's gorgeous, Lindy," she whispered. "What a catch."

"Your Grace, may I present Miss Madeleine Goulet?" The duke took Maddie's gloved hand and bowed over it. "Enchanted. But what exactly are you?"

Maddie giggled. "Guess!"

She wore a black velvet gown with an overskirt that ended in a point front and back, striped horizontally with gold satin. A black silk headband with gold antennae and diamond eyes nestled in her blond curls. Huge gold gauze and lace wings completed her costume, suspended by diamond clasps from her shoulders.

The duke shook his head. "I'm afraid I haven't that much imagination, Miss Goulet. Please enlighten me."

Maddie looked at Lindy. "Darling? Surely you can figure it out."

Lindy smiled. "You're un frelon. A hornet. Am I correct?" Maddie clapped her hands. "Exactly."

Lindy leaned forward and whispered into Maddie's ear. "Could you please sting my mother?"

Maddie dissolved into giggles, and Mama frowned in their direction.

"Best move on, dear." Lindy smiled at her friend. "Before we both get stung."

31

Lindy woke to the murmur of the Atlantic Ocean outside her window. The arrival of the duke had been reported in the papers yesterday, and that meant a steady stream of callers today eager for a glance at royalty.

Her bedroom door opened, and Claudine crept in, then stopped when she caught sight of Lindy. "Alors! Awake already?"

Lindy sat up and pushed the counterpane away. "I can't sleep."

Claudine sat on the edge of the bed. "You've been crying, chérie." She studied Lindy's face.

"For all the good it will do. I'm going to get dressed."

Claudine pressed her lips together and didn't move.

Lindy tipped her head. "What is it, Claudine? You look like the cat that swallowed the canary."

The maid's hand went to her pocket. "The mail came early. There's a letter." Claudine pulled a slim envelope out. "But I don't know if I should give it to you. I'm afraid for you."

Lindy ripped the envelope from Claudine's fingers. It contained another envelope, with Lindy's name written in a bold slanting script. Inkblots marred some of the letters as if it had been written in haste.

She sprang out of bed. "I'm going to go to the beach. Hurry!"

She hastily chose a warm morning dress of blue wool and barely let Claudine pull her corset strings tight. "You must come with me." Lindy shrugged into the heavy, black wool mantle Claudine held out. "Get your cloak and meet me downstairs."

Claudine nodded, and Lindy flew down the steps to the foyer, where she waited impatiently for her maid to appear. The butler emerged from the breakfast room and raised his eyebrows.

"I'm going out for a walk, Percy, if Mama or the duke happens to wake up." There was almost no chance of that. The letter in her pocket burned against her fingers.

Claudine appeared on the staircase and walked sedately down the steps while Lindy wanted to scream at her to hurry. Then Claudine raised an eyebrow and glanced at the butler, who hadn't moved but stood watching Lindy with a frown.

"I'll be fine, Percy. Don't worry. At this hour of the morning, there will be no one awake to accost me. Have no fear."

"I would be remiss in my duty if I didn't send a servant with you."

Lindy opened her mouth to refuse but caught the tiny shake of Claudine's head from her side vision. She sighed. "Very well, Percy. Send for one of the footmen."

A few moments later, Jackson hurried in. He opened the huge glass and iron doors and followed behind them as they took the cobbled path over the hill to the sea and passed through the concrete underpass that opened up to a small stony beach.

Lindy sat on one of the large rocks, and Claudine perched next to her, shielding Lindy from the groom's sight. She turned away still further and pulled the envelope from her pocket and opened it.

DEAREST LINDY,

I RECEIVED your message with great joy. Pack a small bag and meet me tomorrow night outside your home. I will procure a carriage and wait for you outside the gate.

We can be married right away, and then no one will be able to annul our marriage or our love.

Until then, I remain, always and devotedly,

YOURS,

JACK

LINDY CLASPED the letter to her breast and bowed her head over it. Somehow, she must contrive a way to escape. She clenched her fists. She would do it. There had to be a way.

Behind her, Claudine cleared her throat, and Lindy turned. The groom had edged nearer, watching them with narrowed eyes. "Is something wrong, miss? Have you received some bad tidings?"

Lindy shook her head. "No, Jackson, all is well. My aunt

sends me felicitations on my engagement, and her words were so sweet as to draw tears."

The stolid young man pulled his coat closer around his shoulders against the stiff breeze that had risen. "Very well, miss. Please allow me to wish you joy, as well."

"Thank you, Jackson." She rose. "That's enough sea air for one morning, Claudine."

Silently, they returned to the mansion. Once in her bedroom, Lindy flung off her cloak and threw it to Claudine, who caught it and stood rooted to the floor. "What did he say, chérie?" Her usually cheerful face was troubled.

Lindy caught her breath. "I'm going to meet him tomorrow night. We're going to be married." She sank onto the bed and held up the letter. "You must help me, dearest. No one can know."

"Are you sure? Your mother will never forgive you."

"I'm sure. I love Jack. He's all I want."

"What of the duke?"

Lindy snorted. "Let my mother marry him."

The door burst open, and Mama rushed into the room in her dressing gown, her hair in a long braid. "What are you up to, Miss, behind my back?"

In two steps, she pounced on Lindy and plucked the letter from her daughter's stunned fingers. "What's this, then?" Lindy reached to retrieve it from her mother's hand, but her mother slapped her across the face so hard Lindy fell onto the bed, stunned. In all her life, her mother had never struck her.

In a flash, her mother read the letter. She looked at Lindy cowering on the bed, and her lip curled. "How have I raised such a daughter! That you could even think of betraying me so."

Mama pointed a finger at Claudine. "You're fired. Get

your things and get out of this house." When Claudine didn't move, she took a step toward her and raised her fist. "Now!" she screamed.

Her face ashen, Claudine walked out of the bedroom. Mama looked at Lindy, a triumphant smile on her face. "You see how your thoughtless actions affect others, Evangeline?"

Lindy sprang to her feet, her body trembling. "Mama, don't send her away." Her voice broke. "Mama, please."

Mama snorted. "You're more concerned for your maid's feelings than for mine." She tore the letter into pieces and threw them at Lindy. "Your tears do not move me, Miss. You will marry the duke if it's the last thing I accomplish on this earth."

She stalked toward the door and turned with her hand on the doorknob. "Don't push me, Evangeline." She lowered her voice to a whisper. "I swear if you cross me again... I'll shoot him."

Lindy gasped. "What? You can't mean that, Mama. Don't say such things!"

Her mother's lips twisted like a gargoyle's. "You think I wouldn't do it?" Her glare burned Lindy like a torrent of red-hot lava. "There are ways. No one would ever know."

Lindy shook her head. "You couldn't. I don't believe you."

"I never thought you would force me to such an end. But I will do what is necessary."

Lindy's breathing quickened. "Even you—you would never dare..."

"You want to try me, Evangeline?" Her mother's blood-shot eyes flattened like a basilisk. "I meant every word. Defy me once again, and you'll see how far I will go."

Palpable enmity poured out of her mother like a foul cloud. Lindy's mind whirled, trying to reconcile this horrifying apparition in front of her with the woman she thought she knew as her mother.

Would Mama really go that far to get what she wanted?

Her mother waited, the cords in her neck standing out, her chin lowered like a bull about to charge.

I can't take that chance. I can't risk Jack's life.

Her mother would do exactly what she had said to get what she wanted.

"Mama." Lindy broke into sobs. "Don't do anything. I'll marry the duke."

Her mother smiled, and Lindy shuddered at the coldness in her face.

The door slammed, and a moment later, the key turned in the lock.

32

New York City

JACK SPRANG out of bed before the sun rose. He'd packed his valise and laid his clothes out the night before. He hummed under his breath as he washed his face and shaved, then stopped abruptly. He didn't want to wake his sleeping uncle, who would be sure to enquire as to the source of his happiness so early in the morning.

He tucked his shaving kit into the valise and pulled out the blue velvet box tucked underneath his clean shirts. Inside lay his mother's ring. A delicate band of gold etched with posies, with one perfect sapphire in the center. Soon it would rest on Lindy's finger. If only his mother could have met her. But no sad thoughts would tarnish this morning's joy. His mother watched from heaven, of that he was sure.

He propped the letter on his desk for his uncle to find later.

. . .

DEAREST UNCLE:

IT IS with great joy and great trepidation that I write this letter.

Miss Lindenmayer has accepted my proposal of marriage. By the time you read this, I will be with her, and we will be married. I will explain everything later. I know you will not approve, nor will her parents. But we love each other, and we are both of age to make our own decision, and we trust this is the right one for both of us.

RESPECTFULLY,

JACK

QUIETLY, he unlatched the front door and let himself out. Dawn filled the eastern sky with rosy light and tinted the snow pink. His heart gave a happy thump. Soon Lindy would be in his arms, and they'd never need to part again.

He walked briskly through the awakening neighborhood to Second Avenue and hailed a hansom cab. "Grand Central Depot on Forty-Second."

33

N ew York City

REVERENT WINTHROP LOOKED up from his sermon notes when a gentle knock sounded at the door.

"I'm verra sorry to interrupt ye, Reverend." The maid Jenny glanced behind her. "But Mrs. Lindenmayer said it was urgent."

Vera Lindenmayer brushed past Jenny and swept into the room. "I wouldn't call personally if it wasn't."

Reverend Winthrop stood hastily. "Thank you, Jenny." He looked at Vera. "Some tea, perhaps?"

"No, thank you. I prefer to get right to the matter at hand." She took the chair in front of his desk and plopped her fur hat down, sending the stamp box skittering.

"Indeed." Surreptitiously, he pushed the box into place. Jenny shrugged and closed the door, her pursed lips indicating her opinion of Vera Lindenmayer's condescending manner

Reverend Winthrop took his seat. "This is an unexpected pleasure, Mrs. Lindenmayer. I thought you were in Newport for the Christmas season."

She fixed her gaze on him like a whip. "I was in Newport, until a matter of the utmost importance compelled me to take the early train into the city this morning. I've come directly from the station and have no time to spare. I must be at Seaside this evening."

"Of course. How may I help you?"

"It's your nephew I've come about."

Reverend Winthrop frowned. "My nephew?"

"Your nephew, Jack Winthrop. The Jack Winthrop who has been frequenting the library in my home and pressing his unwanted attention on my daughter."

Reverend Winthrop turned a nasty shade of red. He pulled a handkerchief from his waistcoat pocket and coughed into it while Vera Lindenmayer drummed her fingers on his desk and regarded him with narrowed eyes.

"What do you mean, Mrs. Lindenmayer?" He put the hankie away.

"Were you aware Mr. Lindenmayer had given him permission to use the library?"

"Yes, yes. So kind of him."

"But you weren't aware he and my daughter were secretly meeting there?"

"My gracious, no."

"He actually proposed marriage to her." Vera's lips twisted. "The nerve of the rascal."

"I-I-I'm so sorry. I had no idea."

Vera sniffed. "Obviously."

"I'll speak to him immediately."

"Yes. You will." She lifted her chin. "And you will send him away. Immediately."

"Send him away? But... but... how... where?"

"That's for you to determine."

Reverend Winthrop shook his head. "Mrs. Lindenmayer, he's my only nephew. He has no other family since his mother passed away."

"That's no concern of mine." She paused. "Need I remind you how much financial support my husband gives to St. Thomas?"

Reverend Winthrop gulped.

Vera glanced around the comfortable study, the leather chairs, and the cheerful fire burning in the grate. "I suppose you enjoy your life here in New York? It would be a great pity if we had to lose you, Reverend."

REVEREND WINTHROP SAT FROZEN in his chair after Vera Lindenmayer swept out of the room. A cold sweat had broken out on his face, and he pulled out his pocket-handkerchief to mop his forehead. The unmitigated gall of the woman to threaten him like this.

He sighed, pushed away from his desk, and went into the hallway to call up the stairs. "Jack!"

Jenny passed him with a stack of clean linen in her arms. "He isn't here, sir, he went out early this mornin.'"

Oh no. He took the stairs two at a time, burst panting into his nephew's bedroom, and spied the letter on the dresser. Sinking onto the bed, he tore it open and read the contents. Then he groaned and buried his head in his hands. What a tangle.

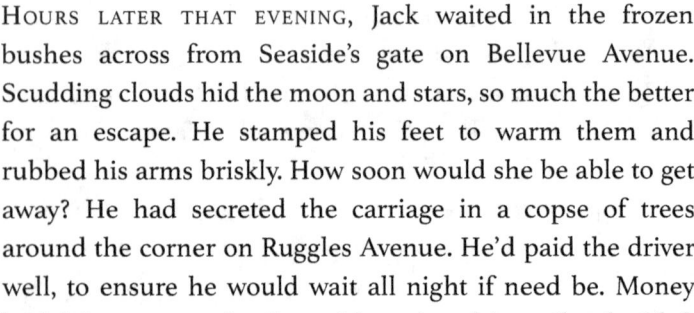

HOURS LATER THAT EVENING, Jack waited in the frozen bushes across from Seaside's gate on Bellevue Avenue. Scudding clouds hid the moon and stars, so much the better for an escape. He stamped his feet to warm them and rubbed his arms briskly. How soon would she be able to get away? He had secreted the carriage in a copse of trees around the corner on Ruggles Avenue. He'd paid the driver well, to ensure he would wait all night if need be. Money hadn't been as much of a problem since his mother had left him a small inheritance.

Wind blew steadily from the ocean, rattling tree branches and carrying the tang of salt. He stared at the lights glowing in the windows of the mansion and tried to imagine Lindy stealthily sneaking along the servant's staircase and out the door. Once he got his arms around her, he'd never let her go.

He hummed a tune under his breath as the minutes and then the hours passed. The clouds blew away, revealing the stars, and the air grew steadily colder. He pulled out his pocket watch and stared at the clock face. Three a.m. He exhaled hard, sending a puff of mist into the air and gritted his teeth. She would come. She would!

34

N ewport, Rhode Island

LINDY STOOD with her face pressed against the cold windowpane while the grandfather clock in the hallway chimed three a.m. No moon or starlight illumined the darkness outside. Now he waited for her in the cold, hidden in the trees. And she a prisoner in her own bedroom. Oh, Jack, Jack.

It was past dawn before Lindy left her post and lay upon her bed, tearless. It was over. Done. When no word came from her, when she didn't spirit herself out of the house and fall into his arms, he would have known the answer was no. Despair must have filled his heart as it had filled hers.

There was nothing else to be done.

She pulled the bell cord at the side of the bed, wondering who would appear now that Claudine had been dismissed.

A key turned in the lock, and then a discreet knock sounded at the door. Her mother's maid, Hortense, peeked in. "You rang, miss?"

"Please ask my mother to come to me."

Hortense nodded, closed the door, and locked it again. It wasn't long before her mother bustled in with her Pomeranian in her arms, her Japanese morning kimono trailing behind her. "You wanted to see me, Evangeline?"

Her eyes were bright. She cuddled the dog, lavishly bestowing kisses on its face while she waited for Lindy to answer.

Lindy swallowed hard. "You can allow me out of my room, Mother. I won't run away. It's over."

Mama tipped her head to one side and considered her. "Will you give me your word?"

"That's funny, Mother, you asking me to give my word." Her mother had the grace to look slightly ashamed.

"Nevertheless, I will have it."

"Very well. You have my word. Mother."

Her mother frowned. "Why do you call me that, Evangeline? I don't like the way you say it. Mother. So coldly."

How can she pretend nothing happened? Had she no feelings, no sympathy for a devastated daughter? Lindy lay on her bed and turned her face away. If only she could fall down a rabbit hole like Alice, and wake up somewhere else.

Her bedroom door closed quietly a moment later. Lindy cried herself to sleep.

JACK STEPPED off the train in a fog of muddled thoughts and made his way through the depot to Forty-Second Street. Hard to believe only yesterday he'd taken the same train to

Newport in a completely different frame of mind. His shoulders slumped. Not knowing what had happened dragged at him like the proverbial albatross. Had she changed her mind? Had they been found out? Had she been prevented from leaving? After the incident in the Lindenmayer salon with Vera Lindenmayer, he believed her quite capable of violence.

Too soon, he reached his street. Now he would have to face his uncle, who was, to put it mildly, sure to be displeased with him. As soon as he opened the door, his uncle walked into the hallway, and a pang went through Jack at his uncle's haggard face and disheveled appearance.

They stared at each other, the overhead lamp casting deep shadows over his uncle's face. It was plain from the puffy bags under his tired eyes that he hadn't slept much the night before either.

"So you're back," his uncle said. "Please come into the parlor."

Silently, Jack followed his uncle into the sitting room. His uncle stirred up the fire, replaced the poker, then sank heavily into the chair opposite Jack. "I read your letter."

Jack nodded.

"So what happened?"

"She never came. I... don't know if her parents prevented her or..." He clenched his fists.

His uncle tiredly ran a hand over his face and frowned. "I warned you about her, Jack. The Lindenmayers are a different class." He stood up and paced in front of the fireplace. "I'm afraid I have some bad news too. Several pieces of bad news, actually." He turned to face him. "I've had some—some financial trouble recently." He shrugged. "Just temporary, I think, but I'm afraid you'll have to leave your classes for a bit. I'm arranging a position for you upstate until my finances allow you to resume your classes."

Jack exhaled hard. If he left New York, it would be even more difficult to see Lindy. "Uncle, I have the small inheritance from my mother. I could use it to finish school."

His uncle shook his head. "You need to save that for the future, Jack."

My future doesn't exist if I can't have Lindy.

"You take it, then, Uncle. Use it for whatever you need."

"That's kind of you. But no. Please oblige me in this."

Jack hesitated. His uncle's hands shook, and the tense posture of his shoulders seemed odd. And there was an undertone of pleading in his words.

Jack sighed. He owed his uncle a great deal. "You've been more than generous to me, Uncle. I'll do whatever I can to help you. You said there were several pieces of bad news?" What else could go wrong today?

His uncle pulled a letter from his waistcoat pocket and held it out. "This came by special messenger."

A spear went through Jack's chest at the elegant handwriting on the cream envelope. Lindy. For a moment, he couldn't breathe. Then he took the envelope and went upstairs to his room.

DEAREST JACK,

BEST TO GET it over with right away, although I never thought I would say these words. Our marriage would be a mistake, Jack. We aren't suited to each other. I should never have accepted your proposal, and I have come to see that in disobeying my parents, I have disobeyed our dear Lord, who calls us to obedience. I realize now it is my duty to trust my parents and marry the duke.

PLEASE FORGIVE ME. I will always think of you fondly.

YOURS, Lindy

HE WHIRLED and hit the wall, his fist crashing through the wooden lathes as if they were matchsticks. Horsehair plaster crumbled to the floor. Jack stared at the gaping hole in the wallpaper, ignoring the pain in his bruised knuckles.

Had she truly changed her mind? Or had her mother somehow intervened? He shuddered, remembering the snarl on Vera Lindenmayer's face before she threw the vase at him. It had to be her doing.

But what could he do now? He'd never be able to get to Lindy again. Her mother would see to that. He fell to his knees against the bed, closed his eyes, and tried to pray through the mess of thoughts fomenting in his head.

An hour later, he was still on his knees with no words left to pray, and no closer to an answer.

35

Jeweled light from the stained-glass window fell across Lindy's lap, turning the pale silk of her afternoon dress to ruby red and emerald green. The martyrdom of St. Lawrence. Surely being roasted alive on a red-hot gridiron couldn't be any more excruciating than sitting here with the duke in her mother's Gothic sitting room.

Forgive me, Lord, for that unlovely thought.

"Miss Lindenmayer." The duke leaned closer; his fair skin ruddy in the dim light. "I believe you know why I am here in Newport."

She nodded.

He searched her face and frowned. "Forgive me, but have you quite recovered from your dyspepsia?"

So that was what her mother had told the duke to account for Lindy's absence the last two days. Heartburn. Close. But her heart didn't burn. It had shattered into a thousand pieces. What did one call that? She swallowed. "Yes, Your Grace, I'm quite well."

And I've become quite a good liar.

He reached into the pocket of his frockcoat. "Your mother gave me to understand this will not be a surprise."

A small box covered in gold embossed red leather appeared. He flipped the top to reveal a rose-cut diamond ring, surrounded by sapphires and nestled in white satin. "I formally ask for your hand in marriage." He pulled out the ring, dropped to one knee, and held it out to her. A smile creased his normally sedate features, only to fade away when she didn't take the ring,

"Miss Lindenmayer?"

A burning heat trapped her voice in her throat. Tears welled, and she drew a ragged breath.

"My dear Evangeline! Tears at such a time." He got up and sat near her. "Take the ring." He held it closer. Cold fire gleamed from its perfect depths, mocking her.

Jack, oh, Jack.

"Is there a problem with the ring? You don't like it? I'll get another. You may have whatever you wish."

If only that were true.

"What is it?" His voice took on a harder edge when she didn't answer. "Is there some other difficulty? I understood that you welcomed my suit." A muscle quivered in his clenched jaw.

Too bad her mother couldn't marry the duke. They would make a perfect couple. She laughed through her tears at this thought.

The duke's shoulders relaxed. "Take the ring, Evangeline, and let the matter be settled." He held it out to her again.

Slowly, she took the diamond and slid it onto her finger. The duke jumped up. "Huzzah!" He quit the room abruptly.

A moment later, her mother's squeal of delight echoed in the hall outside, deepening the emptiness in Lindy's heart.

36

L indy rose early the next morning and rang for Adele, the new French maid who had replaced Claudine.

Did Mama go out of her way to choose the surliest maid available? Adele hadn't a sympathetic bone in her body, and her lips pressed constantly into a prim line, which twisted slightly when Lindy chose an outfit, managing to convey disapproval without a spoken word.

Uncle Henry and her new cousin, Emma, were to arrive at Seaside today for a short visit before Christmas. Maybe getting to know Emma will help keep my thoughts off Jack.

Now she waited inside the marble foyer of the mansion, with Papa, Mama, and the duke, to receive them. Percy and the rest of the staff stood behind them.

The front doors opened, and Uncle Henry walked in on a swirl of snowflakes, holding the arm of a pale, blond beauty with deep hazel eyes and erect posture.

Papa stepped forward and shook Uncle Henry's hand. His hair and mustache had turned completely to silver since

Lindy had seen him last. "Welcome, dear brother." Then Papa turned to Emma. "Welcome to the family, my dear." He kissed her on both cheeks. "I'm sorry for the loss of your father. I hope we shall have a merry time getting to know you."

Mama smiled, her sharp gaze missing nothing about Emma's elegant traveling suit, her boots, and accessories. "Welcome to Seaside."

"Thank you, Aunt Vera." Emma extended her hand, and after a surprised pause, Mama took it, looking even more startled when Emma proceeded to shake it vigorously. "Thank you for inviting us."

Lindy stepped forward. "Hello, Emma. I'm Lindy."

"Evangeline," corrected her mother in a stern voice.

Emma's eyes widened a fraction. "Nice to meet you, Lindy." A spark of amusement flared under her words, and her eyebrow quirked a smidge as if she'd already taken Mama's measure and found it wanting.

Mama stiffened next to Lindy, who repressed a smile, liking Emma immediately.

Papa drew the duke forward. "Please allow me to introduce our honored guest the ninth Duke of Hampshire, James Alexander Bentley. Our daughter's fiancé."

The duke bowed and kissed Emma's gloved hand.

"I'm sure you both must be tired from your journey." Mama smiled and waved her hand toward the staircase. "I will show you to your rooms."

"Oh, let me take Emma, Mother." Without waiting for an answer, Lindy drew Emma away and ushered her forward. "Right this way."

Emma had the guestroom next to Lindy's, decorated to the hilt of course, with blue-brocaded walls and gold touches in the drapes and bed coverlet. The best feature of the room was the tall windows that opened to the sea, the same as Lindy's adjoining room.

"How lovely." Emma removed her hat and admired the view, then leaned forward to examine the window. "Might I open this?"

"Certainly. Let me call one of the maids."

"Oh, please don't bother. I can see how it opens it right here." Emma released the sash lock and pushed up the window. Salt-scented air swept through the room. "I do so love fresh air."

"You are quite self-reliant, Emma, I see."

Emma turned and studied Lindy. "I've had to be," she said quietly. Some of the light in her eyes dimmed. "My mother died when I was eight, and my father..." She sighed and gazed out the window. "He didn't know how to live after she passed away. Much less raise a daughter."

"I'm so sorry."

"Don't be." She smiled then. "I came to enjoy my freedom and independence. Compared to some of my friends, whose parents ascribed to a more conventional bringing up for a girl, I was allowed to come and go as I pleased and read whatever I desired to." She laughed. "After the cooking, the dishes, and the laundry were done, of course. I started keeping house immediately after my mother's death."

"My goodness, you had to grow up so fast. I'm sure it must have seemed strange, leaving one life and entering another."

"Oh yes. Just like Cinderella. Only in this case, Uncle Henry is the fairy godfather. Or would be, if I allowed him."

"Indeed? What do you mean?"

"Oh, Uncle Henry had plans for me when I first arrived, to introduce me to society and find a husband." She covered her mouth with her hand to hide a yawn. "Excuse me."

"Dear me, I'm so sorry." Lindy moved toward the door. "You need to rest after your journey, and I'm keeping you from it. I would like to learn about your life before Uncle Henry and Mahicantuck if you feel inclined to share it. And please don't hesitate to ask me if you need anything. I'm afraid there are going to be some rather stuffy events occurring while you are here. Balls and dinner parties and such."

"Thank you." Emma smiled. "You're very kind." A gentle knock sounded at the door.

"Come," said Emma.

Percy entered the room, followed by several manservants with Emma's luggage. After they left, Emma moved to a small satchel, removed three leather-covered volumes, and placed them on the nightstand.

She likes to read.

Lindy couldn't stop herself from walking over to look at the books.

The Country of the Pointed Firs, The Red Badge of Courage, and The Island of Dr. Moreau.

"Are you reading all of these?"

"Just Dr. Moreau. I'm making notes on the other two."

"Indeed? I haven't yet read anything by Wells. Is it interesting?"

"I don't quite know what to make of it yet. It's certainly different." Emma pulled out a few more books and piled them on the nightstand. "Nothing like Little Women or this, my particular favorite." She held up a well-worn copy of Pride and Prejudice.

Delight percolated through Lindy. "My goodness, I think

we're kindred spirits, Emma. I see you love to read, and so do I."

Emma smiled. "I grew up with a father who loved to read and discuss ideas, and he encouraged me in that direction." Her smile faded. "Although my outspokenness has at times caused some—difficulties—adjusting to my new life."

"I can understand that. For different reasons than yours, I often feel I don't fit in either." Lindy grimaced. "If my mother had her way, I'd never read a book again."

"How dreadful." Emma hesitated. "Your mother is quite —impressive."

"Domineering, you mean? Yes, she is. But somehow, I distinctly get the impression she won't be dominating you, although I'm sure she'll do her best to try." Good gracious, what am I saying? "Oh, please forget I said that. I didn't mean—"

"Quite all right." Emma smiled. "I've already perceived that your mother is something of a martinet."

Lindy's shoulders relaxed. "Exactly right."

"Don't worry about me. I can take care of myself."

Emma certainly looked full of self-confidence. "Perhaps I will learn something from you then."

"Why do I have the feeling there's more to that than you're letting on?" Emma cocked her head to one side. "Have you had difficulties with your mother?"

More than you could ever imagine. Lindy nodded slowly. "Perhaps when we exchange our histories, I will tell you. But right now, I'm sure you'd like to call for your maid and rest. I will see you at dinner this evening."

❧

THE NEXT DAY a constant parade of wagons and delivery vehicles came and went to the basement level of the mansion, conveying crates of chickens, sides of beef, and load after load of scarlet poinsettias and fir garlands to festoon every balcony and balustrade. White candles burned in windows and poinsettias banked walls and staircase steps. Tall Christmas trees abounded in every room on the main floor, covered in glittering ornaments and silver ribbon. It was stunning and magnificent, as her mother intended it should be.

Lindy rose early and dressed for a walk, pleasantly surprised to find Emma already up, waving at her from up the beach.

"Good morning. You're up early, Emma."

Emma smiled. "Have to get my walk in." She wrinkled her nose. "Before all the fuss and feathers start."

Lindy burst out laughing. "You are so refreshing." She linked her arm with Emma's as they strolled down the beach. "This is as good a time as any to tell me about the changes in your life."

Emma shrugged. "There isn't all that much to tell. My father died and left me penniless. I had planned to stay in Brockport and teach, but the law required that I go to the guardian appointed for me years before. Uncle Henry."

"And how are you getting along with him?"

"Very well. I've become quite fond of him.

"He is a dear man. Some of my best childhood memories come from spending summers at Mahicantuck with him." That had been a glorious time. She had been allowed to run free and climb trees, fossil hunt at the river, and make mud pies in the garden.

"Until the will was read, I believed my father had no siblings."

"That must have been a startling discovery."

"It was. And I was quite resistant at first. As I said yesterday, Uncle Henry had all sorts of plans for me. Introducing me to society, et cetera. I put a stop to that, however."

"How?"

Emma shrugged. "I simply told him I wanted no part of it. And after a while, he stopped pushing the idea. Now I teach a small school of poor farmer's children in a building donated by a neighbor." She stopped and turned to face Emma, her hazel eyes piercing. "Why did you sigh like that?"

Lindy frowned. "I'm sorry, I didn't realize I did."

"Shall we sit a while?" Emma gestured to a pile of rocks nearby. They took a seat on a flat piece of jutting rock, partially protected from the sea breeze.

"You're engaged to the duke, so I'm guessing that means moving to England after the marriage."

Lindy nodded.

"I've read about some American girls marrying into the aristocracy of England. France too." Emma leaned down and rooted through a pile of clamshells. "Lady Randolph Churchill was the first, I believe."

"Yes. Jennie Jerome was her American name." And one of the first to bring a huge dowry to her English husband.

Emma held up a whelk shell.

"That's a nice one," Lindy said. "Perfect."

Emma tucked the shell into her coat pocket. "Are you looking forward to moving to England?"

"Not particularly."

"How did you meet the duke?"

"Oh, my mother arranged everything." Lindy laughed bitterly. "I had no say in the matter."

"Oh dear." Emma frowned. "I'm so sorry... I didn't realize.

And here I am, asking you all these questions." She hesitated. "Is this the difficulty with your mother you referred to yesterday?"

"Part of it." Lindy picked up a handful of sand and let it sift through her fingers. "She wants a title in the family. So, she sold me to the duke."

Emma gasped.

"I know that's a horrible thing to say, but it's true." Lindy tried to smile. "Forgive me, I'm not trying to shock you. But I'm seldom able to express what I really think about things." *Except with Jack. I could always tell him what I really thought.* Pain lanced through her chest at the thought.

"Was there someone else?"

"Why do you ask?"

"The look on your face as you said you couldn't normally express your feelings."

"There was. But it's over and done with now." Lindy straightened. "Enough about me. Tell me about yourself and coming to Uncle Henry at Mahicantuck."

"Miss Lindenmayer."

They both turned at the tart, clipped voice. Adele stood on the sand a few feet away, her coat collar pulled close around her neck. "Your mother is looking for you. She requires your presence in her bedroom." She shivered and cast a look about the deserted beach, then frowned when Lindy made no move to get up. "Immediately."

"Thank you, Adele." Lindy stood. "You may tell my mother I will be there shortly." After Adele stalked away, Lindy turned to Emma. "I hope we can continue our conversation later today, perhaps after lunch?"

"That would be delightful. I will see you then."

～

SIX GUESTS TONIGHT, to make the desired number of twelve for a perfect small dinner party. Her mother had kept her busy the rest of the day with small tasks and arranging flowers for the dinner table, so there had been no further opportunity to see Emma.

Her mother used the Grand Salon as a reception room, and here Lindy waited now with her parents, the duke, and Uncle Henry for the guests to arrive. Emma hadn't come down yet.

Dinner would be served at eight-thirty, and it was eight o'clock now. But etiquette dictated the hosts be ready and available early, for the rare occurrence of an early guest.

Papa and Uncle Henry stood near the fireplace, their heads close together, talking about the stock market.

Lindy walked away from her mother's spirited discussion with the duke over the merits of Yorkshire pudding. Snow fell softly outside the tall leaded windows of the salon, and she leaned against the wall, partially hidden inside the heavy silk portieres. Already the steps and balustrades had a thick powdering, and the lanterns on the posts at the end of the drive had drifts of white over their tops, softening their mellow light.

So peaceful. If only she could stay here forever in this little nook.

A gentle hand touched her shoulder. "Are you well, sweetheart?" Papa gazed into her face. When she didn't answer, he took her hand and tried to smile. "I'm sorry about all this, Lindy. But you know your mother..." His voice drifted off, and his lips worked soundlessly, as if he would say more.

Yes, I know my mother. Vera Lindenmayer always gets what she wants and woe to the man or beast that dare stand in her way.

Her father's chin trembled, and Lindy gave his hand a gentle squeeze. "I will be all right, Papa."

"I tried, Lindy. I tried to talk to her about Jack. He's a fine boy, and he'd make a fine husband."

Lindy's throat thickened. "Don't—don't let's speak about him now, Papa. I couldn't bear it."

He nodded. "But I wanted you to know."

She bowed her head. But she wanted to scream. Why? Why couldn't you put your foot down for once and tell her no? What's the worst that could happen?

He answered her unspoken thought. "She said she'd divorce me."

Lindy snorted. "Perhaps that would have been better for all of us." She couldn't keep the bitterness out of her voice.

Her father winced. "You don't mean that."

Lindy sighed. She had no wish to hurt her father. He was as much in thrall to Vera as she was. "Forgive me, Papa."

He put his arm around her, and she leaned against him. "Will you come to see me in England?"

He kissed her cheek. "Of course, sweetheart. As often as I can."

Mama's voice rang out sharply. "Our guests are arriving, Otto."

"The Empress calls," he whispered into her ear.

Emma had come down and now stood next to Uncle Henry for the formal receiving of the dinner guests. Wearing a gown of coral silk, the bodice encrusted with pearls and gold beading, she gave Lindy a warm smile. "Where have you been all day? I looked for you so we could continue our conversation."

"My mother kept me busy with arrangements for tonight."

Emma frowned and leaned in close. "I think she's trying to keep me away from you," she said in a low voice. "I saw her after breakfast and asked where you were. She managed to not answer me."

"Hmm. I wouldn't put it past her."

"And we must leave unexpectedly. Something at the estate requires Uncle Henry's immediate attention."

"Oh no."

"We're taking the early train in the morning."

Madeleine stepped up, on the arm of a strikingly handsome blond man, and pounced on Lindy. "Darling! May I offer my felicitations on your engagement?" She drew the blond man's arm closer through her own. "And please let me introduce my dear friend and escort, Nicholas Stuyvesant." Maddie positively glowed as she gazed at Mr. Stuyvesant, who seemed equally charmed. Lindy sent Maddie a questioning look, and her friend responded with a tiny smile and a slight shrug of her elegant shoulders. Perhaps another engagement would be announced soon. Hopefully, a happier one.

In turn, Lindy greeted Mr. and Mrs. Hermann Oelrichs, old friends of the family. Tessie, a famed New York hostess in her own right, impressive in a regal gown of dark green silk and a dog collar of diamonds and emeralds around her plump throat. White osprey feathers and an emerald clip fastened her chignon at the back, the feathers undulating in the warmth of the candelabras that stood in every alcove.

Percy appeared at the salon door. "Dinner is served."

Papa offered his arm to Emma, as one of the guests of honor. The rest of the party paired off as arranged by Mama. Mr. Oelrichs escorted Maddie, Uncle Henry and Mrs. Goulet, Lindy with Mr. Stuyvesant, Mr. Goulet with Mrs.

Oelrichs, and lastly, Mama escorted by the duke. When they entered the dining room, each gentleman would seat the lady to his right.

A white damask linen cloth covered the rectangular dining room table. Candlelight glinted off the Baccarat crystal wineglasses, the gold-rimmed Spode china, and the sterling silver place settings, and reflected off the crystal chandelier. Lindy was at the short end of the table, with Nick Stuyvesant to her left, and Emma next to him. Name cards with Mama's copperplate handwriting designated each guest's place.

As the gentlemen pulled out the chairs for the ladies, Emma glanced at Papa, holding her chair out, and turned to Nick. "Would you mind awfully if we switched?" She gave him a disarming smile and swapped her name card for his. "I haven't seen Lindy all day." She quickly slipped past Nick and sat down in his place next to Lindy at the end of the table, leaving Papa holding her chair.

Mrs. Oelrichs' and Mrs. Goulet's smiles froze on their faces. Nick's face flushed as pink as the roses in the silver epergne on the table. He cast a quick look around, clearly uncertain of what to do. Mama stared pointedly at Emma. Uncle Henry's lips twitched.

Oh my, she's really gone and done it.

Was Emma aware that the hostess set the seating at a formal dinner party? And that the seating always alternated man, woman, man, woman? Had her cousin meant to create a serious faux pas and enrage her hostess, who, as Lindy well knew, was seething inside—if the shut, cold look on her mother's face was anything to go by? But it would be an even worse breach of etiquette to say something about it.

There was only one thing to be done. Lindy took her

seat, and after a moment's hesitation, the rest of the group followed.

As everyone took their napkins to spread on their laps, Emma leaned over. "I know I'm in hot water now, but I don't know when I'll see you again. And I did want to continue our talk."

"Have you had any formal dinner parties at Mahicantuck?"

"A few." She wrinkled her nose. "And I confess I found them so utterly dull and boring that I asked Uncle not to have any more of them." She laughed. "And I actually think he was relieved because he secretly thinks the same. But of course, he would never admit it."

"You are too much, Emma." She lowered her voice. "We probably won't be able to speak much now, either."

"Why is that?"

"Because at formal dinner parties like this, the hostess 'turns the table.'"

"I'd forgotten about that." Emma's smile faded.

"But I have an idea." Should I do it? Her mother would certainly suspect something. But why not? What could Mama do to me now? "When the ladies go to the drawing room, after a short interval, you could excuse yourself. Leaving early in the morning is a good reason. And a short while later, I will beg leave myself." She leaned in closer. "Our bedrooms have a connecting door. We can stay up as long as we want, and no one will be the wiser."

"Capital idea, cousin." Emma's eyes sparked. "Touché."

Cherrystone clams comprised the first of seven courses, followed by consommé, beef filet with cream of artichokes, oyster patties and celery, turkey with chestnuts and potato croquettes, and lettuce salad. And then, a flaming plum pudding in honor of the duke's English heritage, to end the meal, with ices, bonbons, and almonds.

Emma gave Lindy a conspiratorial wink as the men stood and pulled out the ladies' chairs. And after the women had gathered in the drawing room and had a sip or two of their sherry, Emma approached Mama.

"I can't thank you enough for such a wonderful evening, Mrs. Lindenmayer." She gave Mama a brilliant smile. "But I'm simply a bear if I don't get enough sleep, and we are leaving so early in the morning to return to Hyde Park. I hope you will forgive me if I retire early?"

Lindy bit her lip to keep from smiling. What a consummate actress Emma was.

Mama nodded stiffly. "Of course." She raised her chin. "We will miss your scintillating conversation and..." she paused and smiled coldly. "Your impeccable manners."

Mrs. Oelrichs choked on her sherry.

"Good night then, dear ladies." Emma set her glass down and quit the room.

Mrs. Goulet raised an eyebrow, exchanging a look with Mama. For a moment, no one spoke, and then the inconsequential conversations about nothing of import resumed. Lindy sipped her sherry and waited until fifteen minutes had passed. Then she raised her hand to her forehead and grimaced.

"Are you quite well, my dear?" Mrs. Oelrichs frowned. "You look a trifle pale."

Thank you! You've given me the perfect out. "I... I'm feeling a bit poorly, actually. I think perhaps the cherry-stones haven't agreed with me this evening."

"Sit down, my dear." Mrs. Goulet patted the place next to her on the settee.

Lindy pressed a hand to her middle. "I'm not sure I

should. Oh dear." She gripped the top of the nearest chair and bent over.

"What's this? You're ill, Evangeline?" Mama came closer, eyes narrowed.

Lindy covered her mouth and faked a burp. "Ohhh."

Her mother stepped back. "You'd best go to your room immediately."

One of the most egregious faux-pas a person could commit had to do with bodily functions. "I think that might be best." Lindy swallowed. "I'm so sorry."

"No need to apologize, dear." Mrs. Goulet shook her head. "Clams have the same effect on me. You might consider staying away from them, as I do."

"Excellent advice. Thank you. Good night."

Lindy turned and left the drawing room. Emma isn't the only actress in the family.

Once in her bedroom, Lindy rang for Adele, undressed quickly, and dismissed the maid. She went to the connecting door, knocked softly, and opened it.

Emma jumped off the bed in her nightgown and giggled.

"We did it."

FOR TWO HOURS, they talked and shared their stories and experiences.

"I wish you didn't have to leave so soon." Lindy smiled sadly. "And I wish that we lived closer."

"Perhaps you could come for a visit after you're married?"

"That would be lovely." But I'm sure the duke will want to return to England immediately and put my dowry to work restoring his impoverished estate. "I'm grateful to have had this time with you."

They embraced and said good night.

As Lindy fell asleep, she realized the next time they would meet would be at her wedding to the duke.

AFTER EMMA and Uncle Henry left, Lindy took to spending more time out of doors, especially in the evenings. Undetected, she left by a service door and took the sloping path to the sea. Snow lay serene on the lawns and frosted the marble balustrades. She preferred the murmur of the sea on the frozen sand to the overheated warmth of the house, glistening with color. The blue light of the moon shimmering over the sea beckoned like a balm to her sore heart.

Tonight, she had wrapped up well in a heavy fur coat and a wool muffler around her neck. The bells of Trinity Church echoed faintly over the water. She tried to picture Jack at his books in New York, but he seemed so far away. An icy tear squeezed out as the wind rustled the frozen beach plum bushes on the bluff behind her. Far away, a mournful train whistle called and then faded away on the wind. She'd heard of men who stowed away on trains. Hopped into empty cars and rode the rails to distant destinations to make new lives and seek their fortune in California. What must that be like to board a train with only the clothes on your back and a small sack of possessions?

She sighed. Soon she must go in. Her parents were hosting another dinner party to introduce the duke to more of New York society. The day after Christmas, Mama's wedding planning would begin. She winced at the thought. Marriage to the duke meant she would be living in England.

What would life without her mother be like? At least Lindy would be able to choose her own gowns, even if she hadn't been permitted to choose her husband.

"Help me, Father," she whispered. "Don't allow me to become bitter."

As soon as the words left her mouth, the wind blew them away.

THE DUKE STOOD next to Lindy as they awaited the arrival of the dinner guests. "You're looking fetching tonight. Is that a Worth design?"

Lindy nodded, smoothing the pale rose, cut velvet gown, trimmed with lace insets on the bodice and embroidered crystal roses.

The duke took a closer look at the embroidered crystal roses on the skirt. "His work is fabulous, isn't it?"

"Actually, I don't care for Mr. Worth's designs. I prefer something simpler."

"Indeed."

"You may as well know, Your Grace, that my mother has chosen all my gowns, just as she chose my husband. But after we're married, I intend to use a different designer."

The duke's blond eyebrows rose, and he tilted his head to one side, frowning. "That's quite a challenging statement, Evangeline." He regarded her with a curious smile. "But I suppose we'll have time to work out our differences, won't we? By the way, I'd prefer you call me James."

"Ah, there you are, Evangeline. How lovely you look."

Mrs. Vanderbilt and her husband greeted them. "Congratulations on your engagement, my dear." She held out her gloved hand to the duke, who kissed it and swept her a

disarming bow. "How lovely to see you again, Your Grace."
She moved on to Vera and Otto.

Lindy did everything expected of her. She made
gracious conversation, listened to Mr. Vanderbilt's stories,
and laughed charmingly at Mrs. Oelrichs' jokes. Mama
beamed at her across the dinner table, nodding approvingly
as Lindy graciously inclined her head to hear her fiancé's
comments. But in her head, she was far away in the library
at the chateau on Fifth Avenue, alone with Mr. Winthrop
and her broken dreams.

37

M arch 1898, New York City

THE WEDDING DRESS in all its cream satin magnificence hung on a brass stand in the corner of Lindy's bedroom. And outside her door stood a footman. For insurance, Mama said.

The circlet of fresh orange blossoms brought in by rail from Florida yesterday lay on her dressing table. Lindy absently fingered the sweet-smelling blossoms.

Alone on her wedding day, with only her surly maid, Adele, for company. No loving mother to pin up her hair. No sisters or friends to sweetly exclaim over the bride's blushing beauty. No laughter. No joy.

Tears wet her cheeks. Even the Lord's presence had fled this morning. There was no one to call upon. There was only her filial duty to fulfill her mother's ambitions.

"Tut-tut," said Adele. She had skinned her black hair

into a bun so severe it flattened the corners of her eyes. Lindy shuddered. "Come, mademoiselle, it is time to dress if you are to be at the church on time."

The fifteen-foot train alone weighed ten pounds. Frills of Alençon lace and silver thread embellished the bodice and seed pearl-encrusted skirt. The sleeves were the latest style, chosen by her mother, ridiculously huge puffs that narrowed at the wrist. She'd have to turn sideways to get through the door.

She laid her head on her arms, ignoring Adele. Had Jack moved past the heartbreak and carried on wit his life? She would never know. If only she could bind up her thoughts like the wide silk sash would bind the waist of her wedding gown.

When the French ormolu clock chimed ten o'clock, she straightened and swept it off the dressing table so hard it shattered into pieces against the wall. A sour feeling of satisfaction went through her when Adele gasped and jumped back.

A flurry of French words exploded in the hall outside. "Pour qui tu prends? Open this door at once, idiot!"

"I'm to let no one in, miss. Orders of Mrs. Lindenmayer."

"Quoi? Open it, I say!"

Something scuffled against the door. "Madame, please! Take your hands off me!"

"Let me pass at once, imbécile!" "Ow! Stop! Ow! Ow!"

"Take that! Crétin!"

Lindy snatched the door open to find the footman cowering against the wall while Claudine beat him about the head with her umbrella.

"Claudine!"

Claudine turned and threw her arms around Lindy. "Oh, pauvre bébé, I'm here!" Behind her, the footman rubbed his head dazedly, then recoiled when Claudine turned and glared at him. He beat a hasty retreat, and she sniffed and picked up her bag. "All alone. I cannot believe Madame would—" Claudine burst into a stream of rapid French that Lindy couldn't follow.

"What are you doing here, Claudine?"

"I came to see you on your wedding day since I was not invited to the wedding." She scrutinized Lindy with a sympathetic smile. "But I didn't expect to find you alone, chérie."

Lindy shrugged. "It's her way of punishing me."

"She isn't alone, mademoiselle. I am here to assist her." Adele stepped forward, shoulders rigid, and her prim mouth pressed so tightly that her lips had disappeared.

Claudine shrugged. "Quand même, I am here now."

"I must ask you to leave immediately, madame." Adele's back went rigid. "This is outrageous. Mrs. Lindenmayer will hear of this."

"Oh, get out, Adele." Lindy stood. "I don't want you here." She opened the door. "Go."

Adele's lips worked soundlessly, her face quivering. Then she marched out the door and slammed it hard.

"Have you heard from Jack, chérie?"

"Heavens, no. My mother intercepts all my mail." Lindy sank onto the dressing table bench. "I... I hope and pray he's moved on with his life." *As I must.*

Claudine sat next to her and leaned her head in close. "Your mother can't take me away from you, chérie. I'm coming with you to England. I've brought my bag with me." She pointed to the overstuffed portmanteau.

Lindy gasped. Tears welled in her eyes. "Oh, Claudine? Are you sure? You know you hate England."

Claudine winked at her. "Well, you must travel to Paris for your gowns, non? Without your husband?"

A faint glimmer of comfort rose in Lindy's heart. At least she wouldn't be totally alone. "If you're with me, I think I can bear it."

Claudine nodded. "Now, chérie, I will help you dress." Claudine laced up Lindy's corset and then finished the long row of satin-covered buttons up the back of the gown while Lindy stood in front of the cheval mirror.

Now that the goal had been nearly accomplished, the title almost in the family, her mother had forgotten about her. *Did she ever truly care for me? Or was I only a means to an end? A pawn to fulfill Mama's dreams?*

"Come, chérie, the veil." She held up the clouds of tulle veiling. Using tiny silver hairpins, she attached the wreath of orange blossoms over it.

A heavy knock sounded at the door, and Claudine went to open it. Otto Lindenmayer stood at the threshold, dapper in white tie and tails and striped trousers.

He hesitated, twisting his top hat in his hands. "Are you ready then, Lindy?" His lips trembled.

Lindy sighed. Hers wasn't the only life ruled by Vera Lindenmayer. "Yes, Papa. As ready as can be expected."

Her father blinked when Claudine walked forward. "Good morning, monsieur."

"Er... good morning, Miss Roget. I'm surprised to see you."

"It is a good thing I came, monsieur. Your poor daughter left alone with that, that pisse-vinaigre! She went off into a spout of unintelligible French.

Otto flushed a deep red, and Lindy sighed. "Claudine," she said. "Please stop now."

Claudine looped the train of the wedding dress over her forearm. Papa walked to Lindy and lifted the voluminous layers of the veil with difficulty until he could see her face. "Lindy..."

"Papa, please. Don't say anything."

Her father's head drooped. "I wouldn't know what to say anyway."

He held out his arm. She took it, and with Claudine carrying the train, she left her girlhood bedroom for the last time.

At the foot of the great marble staircase, all the servants stood waiting to see her. Percy approached. "On behalf of all the staff, Miss Evangeline, I wish you great joy in your marriage."

"Thank you, Percy. Thank you, everyone. I hope things will be a bit less exciting after I've left." Titters broke out at this statement.

Percy bowed. "Miss Evangeline, we all want you to know that if you ever have need of any one of us, we'd be glad to leave Madame's service and come to you."

A pang went through Lindy, and her throat thickened. "Why, Percy, that is most gracious of you. I greatly appreciate the sentiment. But England is so far away. I fear you would miss America greatly."

"Nevertheless, miss, you remember what we said." Percy bowed and stepped back.

Another tiny spark of comfort lit in Lindy's heart. Her step felt lighter as her father and Claudine accompanied her to the carriage, decked in white roses.

Papa and the groom helped Lindy into the carriage. Claudine carefully tucked the veil inside.

Lindy glanced at her father. "Claudine is coming too."

His eyebrows rose, but he said nothing and handed Claudine in.

Early forsythia flowered in the hedges, and fat green buds loaded every tree on the boulevard under the pale March sunshine. At the intersection of Fifth Avenue and Twenty-Third Street, a dull roar rose outside the carriage.

Papa leaned out the window. "Good gosh all mighty!"

Lindy laid a gloved hand on her father's arm. "What is it?"

"Most of New York City has come out to celebrate your wedding day, Lindy!"

The day I become chained to the duke for the rest of my life.

A block from St. Thomas the carriage slowed to a crawl. Rows of policemen in navy uniforms and caps linked arms to restrain the crowds surging on the sidewalk. Cheers and shouts of "Lindenmayer!" and "Evangeline!" went up.

More officers lined the steps of the church as a few flakes of snow fell. Otto exited the carriage and held out his hand to Lindy. "Here we go," he whispered into her ear, "steady now."

She was anything but steady as her heart quaked in her chest, and every nerve in her body trembled. But she squeezed his arm and ascended the stairs with Claudine holding her train. The overpowering scent of roses assailed her when she stepped into the vestibule of the church.

Maddie waited for her there. "My goodness, there you are!" She peered through the layers of tulle. "That is you in there, isn't it, Lindy?" Then she noticed Claudine. "Well, my goodness, Claudine!"

Claudine handed the train to Maddie and kissed Lindy through the veil. "I'll see you soon, ma cher."

Lindy barely nodded, holding herself tightly upright, trying not to think. Otto stepped up and took her arm. The notes of Lohengrin's "Bridal Chorus" rose. Ushers opened the great doors into the sanctuary.

JACK WINTHROP SAT in the unused third balcony close to the ceiling of the church. He'd snuck in at dawn when the florists arrived to decorate the sanctuary. They had been at their work for nearly three hours now. Garlands of laurel woven with lilies and pink roses cascaded from the dome above the altar. Spirals of ivy and spider chrysanthemums circled the columns, trimmed with white and gold silk ribbon, and every pew had a spray of ferns and white roses, with pink silk ribbons that trailed to the floor. The ten-piece orchestra arrived and proceeded to set up behind the altar, accompanied by singers dressed in white silk.

At ten thirty, the guests began to arrive.

An usher escorted William Strong, the mayor of New York, to one of the front pews reserved for dignitaries. The British ambassador joined him there. Jack had seen his photograph in the newspaper. This wedding had been the talk of the city for weeks. He couldn't pick up a paper without some mention of it.

Vera Lindenmayer arrived a moment before the bells in the tower struck eleven. Dressed in raspberry satin trimmed with mink, her flushed face matched the hue of her dress. On her head, a ridiculous tuft of feathers bobbed and floated on her lace hat as she addressed various friends and air- kissed relatives. The satisfied smile never left her face.

Eleven o'clock came and went with no sign of the bride.

A faint hope arose in his heart. Has she changed her mind? Then the orchestra broke into the opening bars of the "Bridal Chorus" from Wagner's Lohengrin.

People craned their necks to catch a glimpse of the bride. Guests at the far end of the pews actually stood on the benches so as not to miss anything. The singers stood and began the chorus. The beautiful words taunted him.

Faithfully guided, draw near

to where the blessing of love shall preserve you!

Triumphant courage, the reward of love,

joins you in faith as the happiest of couples!

The Duke of Hampshire came forward to stand with the Reverend Winthrop at the head of the aisle. Stolid and unyielding, with a short, clipped mustache, the duke stood in his full military kit with medals upon his left breast and a blue sash across his chest. Jack searched the man's chiseled features, but no smile of eager anticipation to see his bride crossed the aristocratic face. The violins whirled through the refrain, and the organ crashed again. The bride walked slowly down the aisle on the arm of her father, swathed in a heavy tulle veil. She carried a massive bouquet of white roses, orange blossoms, and ferns.

He checked his pocket watch and grimaced. He couldn't wait any longer. He had barely enough time to make it to the train station as it was. But before he left to start the new life his uncle had arranged, Jack wanted one last glimpse of Miss Lindenmayer's face, and even that had been denied him.

He clenched his fists. Soon his uncle would ask if any impediment or reason existed as to why this marriage shouldn't go forth. He imagined shouting out his protest from the balcony. All heads would turn to gape at him as he begged Lindy not to go through with it.

But his uncle had assured him Lindy was at peace with the marriage, and nothing would stop it. New York City held nothing else for him. This was it then. The first day of the rest of his life without her.

From the balcony, he took the side staircase and exited the church by a little-used door. Hailing a hansom cab, he set off for Grand Central depot.

PAPA'S HAND tightened on Lindy's arm as tears welled and ran down her face under the veil. The heavy train pulled like lead weights at her legs. Somehow, she managed to put one foot in front of the other and keep going. At the altar, the duke held out his arm, and Otto transferred her hand to the duke, who took it and turned toward the altar. Thank God she didn't have to look at him during the entire service.

The candle flames blurred into golden halos behind Reverend Winthrop as he began the service. "Dearly beloved, we are gathered here to witness the union of this man and this woman..."

She closed her eyes while Reverend Winthrop droned on about the significance of marriage and the meaning of the wedding vows. Inside the cocoon of her veil, she remembered Jack's dear face and the morning after the ball when he had declared his love for her. It had all gone so wrong.

The duke gave her a tiny shake. "Evangeline," he whispered.

She started, realizing Reverend Winthrop had spoken to her.

"Please turn and face each other," he repeated in a strong voice.

Trembling, Lindy handed her bouquet to Maddie, who gave her an encouraging smile.

The duke took her gloved hands in his and stared at her. "Repeat after me," said Reverend Winthrop.

"Do you, James Alexander Bentley, Ninth Duke of Hampshire, take Evangeline Marie Lindenmayer, to be your wedded wife, to have and to hold from this day forward, for better, for worse, for richer, for poorer, in sickness and in health, to love and to cherish, 'til death do you part?"

"I do." The duke's voice rang through the sanctuary, sure and confident, as a hum of approval went through the congregation.

Reverend Winthrop turned his gaze to Lindy, and her heart quailed at how like Jack his eyes were. But these brown eyes stared at her with a merciless gaze, and her throat thickened.

"Evangeline Marie Lindenmayer, will you take James Alexander Bentley, the Ninth Duke of Hampshire, to be your wedded husband, to have and to hold from this day forward, for better, for worse, for richer, for poorer, in sickness and in health, to love and to cherish, 'til death do you part?"

Her throbbing pulse roared in her ears, drowning out the soothing violins, and she swayed on her feet. The duke's fingers tightened on hers.

Reverend's Winthrop's brows knit together. "Evangeline?" He spoke in a low tone. "Are you unwell?"

The arrogant smile playing about the duke's mouth disappeared. He leaned toward her. "What is the matter with you?"

"Evangeline?" Reverend Winthrop cleared his throat and started again. "Do you take this—"

"I heard you." Lindy wrenched her hands out of the

duke's and lifted her veil. A gasp went through the congregation.

The duke shook his head. "Don't do this, Evangeline."

Lindy ripped the veil off her head and threw it to the floor. "Do I take this man?" Her voice rang through the sanctuary. "As a matter of fact, I don't."

38

Mama shrieked like a steam whistle and fainted dead away. The violin's limpid notes veered off into a jarring screech as a cacophony of cries and exclamations swirled through the scented air.

All color drained from the duke's face. His lips quivered as he clenched his jaw, making the tendons in his neck stand out like cords. "You'll pay for this," he snarled. He ran toward his mother, who had collapsed into the pew. The bridesmaids huddled together like a gaggle of confused sheep, eyes wide and their mouths agape.

"What's the matter with you, Evangeline?" Reverend Winthrop grabbed her arm. "Have you lost your senses?"

Lindy wrenched her arm out of his grasp. "I've regained my senses, actually. And just in time." She turned and faced the guests. "Go home now."

A clamorous buzz rose as the guests dispersed, shaking their heads or whispering behind their gloved hands to each other. Well, I've done it now. New York society would never get over this. She could almost see the headlines on the society pages of the morning newspapers: "Dollar Princess Jilts Duke at the Altar!"

Mama had regained consciousness and was pleading with the duke, who refused to speak to her, turned his back, and stalked away with his family.

Only her father hadn't moved from his place in the first pew, oblivious to his steaming wife. He stared at Lindy and then shook his head, a tiny smile at the corner of his mouth. She shrugged her shoulders and tried to smile at him, while the flash of adrenaline that had powered her through the last few minutes seeped away and left a sick quivering in her belly.

Mama charged at her then, the loose flesh of her neck and jowls shaking, and patches of red high on her cheeks. "How could you? You've ruined us!" She shook her fist in Lindy's face. "After all I've done for you! All these years, all our plans!"

Lindy straightened her trembling limbs and faced her mother. "They were never my plans, Mama. I tried to tell you."

"Oh, you'll be sorry, my girl." Her mother's lips twisted. "I never want to see you again. You're disowned! Out of this family," she screeched. "Do you hear me? Out!"

Papa came forward and put a restraining hand on his wife's plump arm. "Don't say things you might regret, Vera."

Mama shook him off. "I mean every word! You won't get a penny, do you hear me?" Her spittle hit Lindy in the face.

Lindy swallowed hard. "I couldn't marry him."

Her father managed to get an arm around Mama and dragged her off. "Not a penny, Miss!" she screamed over Papa's shoulder. "Do you hear me? How could you? How could you? Ohhhhhh..."

Her wails echoed through the empty church and then faded to a moan. The orchestra finished packing up their instruments and left.

Reverend Winthrop had withdrawn to the sacristy to wait out the kerfuffle. Now he walked into the sanctuary, plucked his Bible off the podium, and glared at Lindy. "You've accomplished nothing, Miss Lindenmayer. Jack's gone out west. You'll never see him again."

The words slashed through her heart like a sword thrust. "Out west? What do you mean?"

His lip curled. "Far away from you. Heaven help you, now you've defied your parent's wishes so publicly." He shook his head. "What were you thinking?" Muttering under his breath, he turned and marched away, his shoulders stiff. Lindy sank onto the carpeted steps, heedless of her expensive gown. Jack gone? How could she find out where? Her heart thudded in her chest. She had defied her mother in the most public way possible. Vera would never forgive her.

But it will all be worth it if I can find Jack.

Footsteps pattered in the sanctuary. Papa and Aunt Gertrude had returned.

Lindy rose on shaky legs and threw herself into her father's arms. "Papa, I'm so sorry." Tears poured out. "I couldn't do it. I just couldn't. Please forgive me."

She wept until there were no tears left. Papa guided her to the front pew and sat, drawing her close. "There, there, liebchen, don't cry anymore."

"What am I to do, Papa? I can't go home. Mama is so angry with me."

He pulled a handkerchief out of his pocket. "Dry your tears. I have a plan."

Aunt Gertrude took Lindy's hand. "You can come to Buffalo while we try to find out where Jack has gone."

Papa nodded. "I've already sent Claudine home to bring your luggage to the train station."

"You're not angry, Papa?"

Her father shook his head. "No, sweetheart. You did what I've never managed to do—stand up to your mother. But now we must deal with the consequences. Even if I could persuade your mother to allow you home, it wouldn't be pleasant. The best thing is to go to Buffalo with Gertrude while we try to sort it all out. But right now, we must sneak you out of the church. I persuaded Reverend Winthrop to lock the front doors. The press will be mad to get in here."

"Stand up, dear." Aunt Gertrude turned Lindy around, detached the train from the wedding gown, and folded it over her arm. She held out her own velvet cloak. "Put this on."

Lindy allowed her aunt to throw the voluminous cloak around her shoulders. It had a large hood, meant to go over a lady's elaborate hairstyle, and Gertrude pulled this forward to hide Lindy's face, then quickly buttoned the cloak over the wedding dress.

"Come now. We'll go out another way." Papa pulled her cold hand through his and hustled her up the steps, through the sacristy, and along a hallway.

"Hurry, sweetheart," her father urged. "Hold on."

Her father's closed carriage waited at the bottom of the church's rear entrance. Papa helped her traverse the steps, then assisted Gertrude into the carriage while snowflakes drifted through the air.

"Goodbye, Lindy." He kissed her forehead. "I'll be in touch soon. I'll arrange an allowance for you, through Gertrude's bank in Buffalo."

"Please, Papa, try to find out where Jack is?"

Her father pressed his lips together. "I'll do my best."

"She said she'd shoot him."

"What?" Her father's jaw gaped.

"Who said that?"

"Mama."

Aunt Gertrude pressed her lips together and shook her head. Her father's eyes widened. "You—you must have misunderstood her, darling."

"No. She said it. She meant it."

He rubbed a hand over his forehead, frowning.

"Find him. And don't tell her. Please, Papa. I love him." She squeezed her father's hands. "Please try."

He sighed. "I will. Now, off with you."

He helped her into the carriage, firmly closed the door, and nodded at the coachman.

Aunt Gertrude pulled the window shades closed as Lindy sank against the cushions in a daze. When she had awakened in her bedroom this morning, she'd had no idea the turn her wedding day would take. She shuddered to think of the anger her mother would take out on the servants.

Outside the old Grand Central Depot, the carriage joined a line of other vehicles waiting to discharge passengers. Snow fell in earnest now. The station bustled with passengers waiting to buy tickets, surrounded by their bags. Children cried, men shouted, and an occasional lapdog barked from its basket. Through the gates came the shriek of train whistles and the hiss of steam brakes.

They entered the train shed with its massive glass and

iron arches soaring overhead. Aunt Gertrude's Pullman car waited on its own track. Painted in a classic green, with ornate gold lettering on the side that spelled out "Pullman Palace," it had to be eighty feet long. A butler appeared on the porch with brass balusters and a striped awning at the end of the car. He bowed.

"Do you remember Polden?" Aunt Gertrude smiled at her butler.

The neat black mustache had turned white, and his eyebrows too. Polden bowed.

"I do remember. So pleased to see you again, Polden." He offered her his gloved hand to assist her up the platform steps.

Claudine waited behind him. "Oh, chérie." She embraced Lindy. "I've always wanted to see Buffalo."

Lindy laughed, and then nearly sobbed. "Dearest Claudine. Are you sure?"

"Oui!"

"Do let's go inside, dear," Aunt Gertrude said. "Let me show you the rest of the car, and then perhaps you'd like to rest?"

Lindy nodded. She had been in Pullman cars before, on trips to Philadelphia to visit Aunt Julia. But Papa hadn't seen the need to have his own private car, and surprisingly Mama had agreed with him.

It was blessedly warm inside. Lindy tried to pay attention as Polden showed her around the Pullman. Her legs seemed frozen, and every other moment, a sick quivering stabbed through her spine to the pit of her stomach. The wedding was well and truly off, ruined by her refusal.

Polden's lips moved, but she barely understood him. She tried to concentrate, her numb brain absorbing some of the tour. A corridor with oak-paneled walls ran the length of the car, with windows facing it. To their right were small compartments for servants.

A small dining room adjoined the kitchen, illuminated with a crystal chandelier, walls of burnished mahogany, and an oriental rug underneath the table. Pastoral landscape scenes adorned the curved ceiling, and intricate marquetry in patterns of fruit and flowers decorated every cabinet. The parlor had overstuffed club chairs and padded footstools, placed to view the passing scenery. Decorative leaded glass crowned every window.

Lindy inspected one of the bronze sconces on the walls. "Electric?"

"Yes, miss. The entire car is electrified."

"It certainly is impressive, Auntie."

A knock sounded at the door, and the conductor entered and doffed off his cap. "Are you ready to leave, Miss Lindenmayer?"

Gertrude glanced at Lindy. "Quite ready, my dear?"

"I'm ready. Thank you."

The conductor nodded and left the compartment.

Lindy swayed on her feet. The weight of the wedding gown dragged at her legs and spine. "I—I think I will lie down for a bit."

"Of course, my dear. Why don't you take a nap? I'm sure you must be exhausted."

Aunt Gertrude, Claudine, and Polden all gazed at her with sympathetic expressions. Suddenly she wanted to rip the suffocating dress off her body. "I have to get this off." There was a note of hysteria in her voice. She ran a finger around the tight neckband of satin at her neck and wrenched it away from her skin.

"This way." Claudine laid a gentle hand on her shoulder and steered her toward the back of the Pullman. Beyond the sitting room were two separate staterooms, complete with their own bathrooms. Claudine turned aside at the second door. Curved windows on both sides provided a panoramic view. Rose silk-shaded lamps glowed on the brocade-papered walls, and there was a small, attached dressing room.

The Pullman lurched, and steam hissed as the locomotive chugged out of the station. The dim interior of the stateroom brightened as they emerged into the daylight. The tall buildings of New York City sped past and then were left behind as the train picked up speed.

Claudine couldn't undo the tiny buttons of the dress fast enough for Lindy. She clenched her fists and willed herself to stay calm as Claudine lifted the tight-fitting bodice over her head, and she could finally step out of the skirt.

"Unlace me, please." She kicked her wedding slippers off. Every tight and restraining garment had to come off, including her unmentionables, silk stockings, and jeweled garters, until every piece of wedding finery lay on the floor. Claudine had a simple nightgown waiting. One of her old ones. "Thank you, Claudine." She sighed as the soft folds of the old nightgown swathed her limbs.

Claudine turned the bed covers down. But Lindy walked to the bank of windows and unlatched one.

"Chérie? What are you doing?"

Lindy didn't answer, struggling with the window catch. When it came free, she pushed the sill up as far as it would go. Snowflakes streamed into the room on the rush of cold air, taking her breath away. The iron tracks stretched out behind them and disappeared into the falling snow. She turned and snatched the pieces of her wedding gown off the floor.

Claudine's hand went to her mouth. "No, Lindy. You can't."

Lindy didn't answer. She rolled the heavy bodice and skirt into an awkward bundle.

"It's worth a fortune, chérie."

Lindy knew that. Her mother had crowed about the expense of the Worth gown, noting no heiress had ever had as expensive a gown as Lindy had. Even the newspapers had speculated on its cost and had even dared to suppose her garters would have diamonds in them. It mattered nothing now. She retrieved the silver and pearl-studded wedding slippers and wrapped them in a fold of the satin.

"Don't do it," begged Claudine.

Lindy ignored her and tried to stuff the gown through the window. It was too wide, and she partially unrolled it and fed it through the opening, until finally it burst out of the window and the wind snatched it. The shoes and bodice went one way, the ridiculous puffs inflated like balloons, and the skirt sailed into the air and belled out, the silver embroidery flashing before the dress disappeared into the white curtain of snow.

Lindy heaved a sigh. Now perhaps she could sleep. Heaven knows the day had been exhausting enough. She closed the window, sank into the featherbed, and pulled up the rose silk coverlet.

Claudine turned off all the lamps but one in the dressing room. "Ring if you need me." She shut the door quietly behind her.

Lindy closed her eyes, grateful for the silence and lulled by the rocking motion of the car. The future stretched before her like a vast empty plain. All the plans and way of life mapped out for her by her mother and the duke had vanished. Wiped out like chalk on a blackboard.

The future was one big question mark.

"Oh, Jack," she whispered.

LINDY WOKE when the rocking motion of the train slowed. A short while later, the hiss of the brakes announced their arrival in Buffalo. Snow still fell heavily.

A gentle knock sounded at the door, and Claudine peeped in. "Chérie?"

"I'm awake. Come in." She sat up and pushed the covers off.

Claudine entered carrying a tray with cups and a silver pot, with steam curling from the spout invitingly. "Coffee?"

"That would be heavenly." Lindy sighed. Maybe hot coffee would penetrate the layer of ice that encased her from head to foot. She stirred sugar and cream into her cup and took a sip.

"We won't detrain for a bit." said Claudine. "There's so much snow your aunt has sent to the house for a sleigh."

"I've done it now, haven't I?" The cup clacked against the saucer in her hand, and Lindy set it down before it could spill.

Claudine nodded, a warm look in her brown eyes. "I'm proud of you."

"She'll never forgive me."

Claudine shrugged. "Perhaps in time."

"I hope she won't be too beastly to Papa."

Claudine arched an eyebrow delicately. "I'm sure he will be spending beaucoup time in the stables."

"Perhaps he'll move to the stables!" The layer of ice around her heart melted into sudden laughter, and Claudine joined in, convulsing in giggles and gasps until tears ran down their cheeks.

Lindy wiped her eyes. "Yes, I've done it now. It wasn't a dream."

"Oublie le passe—à l'avenir, chérie," said Claudine. "On to the future. Are you going to finish your coffee?"

Lindy shook her head, and Claudine picked up the tray. "I'll return to help you dress."

Lindy sank against the cushions. How long would it be before the quivering stab of apprehension no longer speared her insides every time she thought about what had happened today? At what she had caused to happen. If she had gone through with the wedding ceremony, she'd be in a Pullman car right now alone with the duke. Headed for her honeymoon. It was definitely better to be alone, even with her future ruined and no knowledge of where Jack was.

When Claudine knocked on the door and entered the room, Lindy gave her a brilliant smile. So much better to see Claudine entering the bedroom than the duke.

After Claudine helped her dress, Lindy went into the parlor where Aunt Gertrude sat in a chair, her feet propped up, reading the newspaper.

She rose and kissed Lindy's cheek. "Did you get some rest, dear?"

Lindy nodded.

"Are you hungry?"

Lindy didn't know whether the constant quivering of her stomach was hunger or... something else. Fear for the future, perhaps. The tiny pang that ran through her nerves every time she thought of Jack wasn't going away anytime soon. "I suppose I should be."

"Excellent. I've asked Polden to make us something light while we're waiting for the sleigh."

Polden appeared with a large silver tray.

"Here, Polden. The dining room seems too formal after such a day."

The butler deposited the tray onto a low table. Aunt Gertrude lifted one cover to reveal a mound of buttered toast. Underneath a cozy, a silver pot held cocoa, delicately spiced with cinnamon, and an enormous apple pie lay under the third, still warm from the oven.

"Mmm." Lindy's mouth watered. "I think I am hungry after all, Auntie. Thank you."

They ate and drank for a while in silence. Finally, Lindy put her napkin away and sighed. "That was delicious."

Polden appeared. "The sleigh has arrived, madame."

They tucked themselves into the sleigh, well-wrapped with lap robes and mufflers around their faces. The snow had finished its dizzy dance after coating every tree and branch.

The coverlet of snow had hushed the city streets and even dimmed the streetlights' yellow glow. Only the bells on the horses jingled sweetly, and the peaceful silence swallowed that up too. Soon the sleigh turned onto Delaware Avenue, a broad street with spacious mansions, wide lawns, and tree branches arching to meet overhead into a perfect colonnade.

The sleigh pulled around the rear of the mansion. Aunt Gertrude waved at snow-covered flower beds. "It's difficult to believe, but there are tulips blooming under there."

There was no line of servants to meet. Aunt Gertrude had said she could meet them in the morning, for which Lindy had been grateful. Gertrude showed her to a bedroom with a small fire in the grate, softly lit with silk-shaded lamps.

"I'll see you in the morning, dear."

Claudine helped her undress and left quietly.

Even though Lindy had slept on the train, her limbs were heavy. A vague headache beat at her temples. She pulled aside the silk drapes from the window opposite her bed. A crescent moon glowed high on the horizon, surrounded by glittering stars. She left the curtain open, and a silvery beam of light fell across the room.

She got into bed and pulled the covers up. Hot tears ran down her cheeks. "Oh, Jack," she whispered into her pillow. "Where are you?"

39

B uffalo, New York

LINDY COULDN'T SEEM to stir out of bed the next day and stayed in her room. She told Claudine to take the day off. Poor Claudine. Her life had changed too, although she was her usual cheery self.

On the second day, the clatter of china woke her. Sun streamed through the window. Aunt Gertrude bustled in, followed by Claudine carrying a tray.

"Morning coffee and croissants in bed," said Aunt Gertrude. "And then up! It's a beautiful day."

Claudine placed the bed tray in front of her and poured a cup of coffee for her. It did taste delicious, as did the fresh flaky chocolate croissant.

"I want to show you the city this morning, and then I have a meeting to attend. Perhaps you'd like to come with me."

It didn't sound like a question. Claudine winked at her behind Aunt Gertrude and went into the dressing room.

"The snow's nearly gone." Gertrude nodded at the tray in front of Lindy. "Drink up now. We'll have dinner out."

"The snow is gone? But there was so much of it."

"The last gasp of winter. It's nearly April, although there have been several springs where snow covered my tulips. You never know in Buffalo, with Lake Erie so close. But I think this is it. Spring is here." She rose. "I'll see you downstairs when you're ready."

IT WAS warm enough for an open carriage. Green grass poked out through the melting snow, and the tulip beds lining the gravel drive of the house were full of glossy green leaves and green buds ready to pop.

"The grass is so green already."

Aunt Gertrude nodded. "Poor man's fertilizer."

"Excuse me?"

"Late snow," said Aunt Gertrude. "It's called poor man's fertilizer here."

"I suppose that makes sense."

Spring had arrived overnight. The trees all wore a hazy veil of green, robins sang, and the smell of wet earth permeated the air. Lindy's heart lightened. Perhaps all would be well, as Papa had said.

The carriage headed south of Delaware Avenue into the heart of the city. The skyline wasn't as impressive as New York City, but the buildings her aunt pointed out to her were individual works of art. The Guaranty building. The Buffalo State Asylum for the Insane with its soaring towers.

"I've saved the best for last." Aunt Gertrude smiled as the

carriage turned off into a sloping park of green lawns, tree-shaded walking paths, interspersed with ponds and fountains and beds of yellow and white daffodils and blue hyacinth. The noise of the city gave way to birdsong as they drove deeper. "It's called, simply, the Park."

"Hmm. Something about the layout seems familiar—the sweep of the lawns and the placements of the ponds and the stone walls."

"I wondered if you'd notice. The same architect designed Central Park. Frederic Law Olmsted. I think this park is every bit as beautiful as Central Park."

"I must agree with you. It's lovely."

Aunt Gertrude pointed to a lake on their right, where a magnificent wooden structure three stories tall with a double row of enclosed balconies stood. A wide staircase of stone steps led to the edge of the lake. Pennants fluttered gaily from its turrets. "That's the boathouse. In the summertime, we can rent a canoe there and paddle ourselves around the lake."

All sorts of people were out walking the shaded paths in the park. Mothers pushing prams, young boys on their way to school with their books strapped together over their shoulders, and young ladies strolling arm in arm.

"We'll come back on Sunday," said Aunt Gertrude. "We'll get an ice cream, and walk for miles. That's the sort of thing I love to do."

"I can see why." How delightful it would be to ramble through these verdant grounds without worrying about her mother. "The day you and I walked in Central Park last October? That's the first time I'd ever visited it."

"No!" Aunt Gertrude's jaw dropped. "Your mother kept you that immured?"

"You don't even know the half of it."

"Actually, I do." Her aunt stared down her long nose at Lindy. "How she could have locked you in your room for weeks on end... Well, it's insufferable, is what it is. If I had known, I would have come in a flash." Her pince-nez bounced indignantly on the end of her long nose.

"It's even worse than that." Lindy's heart beat faster at the memory of Vera finding Jack's letter. "I told you and Papa that she threatened to shoot Jack."

Gertrude shrugged and shook her head. "No, Lindy..."

"I couldn't believe it either. But if you could have seen her eyes, Auntie. Cold as a snake." Lindy shivered. "How could she say such a thing?"

Gertrude shrugged and adjusted the pince-nez on her nose. "It's no secret there's no love lost between your mother and me, dear. But she is your parent, so I will not speak evil of her. You're here now, and we must make the best of it." She leaned forward. "Drive on to Statler's, Cooper." She turned to Lindy and smiled. "It's a new restaurant in Buffalo I want you to see. I admire its proprietor greatly.

The carriage reentered the main part of the city, where streetcars ran the length of the avenue. Horse and carriages occupied the lanes next to sidewalks full of women shopping and businessmen carrying briefcases. Storefront shops, some with colorful awnings stretched over their display windows, did a hearty business.

"That's the Ellicott Square building." Gertrude pointed to a massive structure of pearl-gray granite and iron. "Statler's is on the lower level."

"My goodness, it's huge."

"The largest office building in the world, so they say." James helped Gertrude, then Lindy, from the carriage.

Lion heads adorned the top of the projecting cornice, staring at the sidewalk below. Marble steps led to an imposing facade, with banded columns and elegant sculpture. The glass and iron doors opened into a sunny, interior central court- yard, with a mosaic floor and a soaring, curved skylight of glass and iron.

"The walls are Italian marble, and the floor also, all imported."

"It's very grand."

At each end of the main floor, two grand staircases rose to a balcony that circled the second floor.

"The second floor is reserved for banking, this floor for shops, and the rest are offices. There's even a new gentlemen's club on the top floor."

"And the restaurant?"

"In the basement. This way."

A long flight of marble steps led downward and opened up into a spacious room filled with octagonal tables covered with white linen. A pleasant buzz of conversation rose above the tables.

Lindy's stomach rumbled, and Aunt Gertrude laughed. "My sentiments exactly."

Soon they were seated in a snug corner examining the menus.

"We'll have our dinner here," said Gertrude. "I've given the cook the night off to visit her family in East Aurora." She lowered the menu. "Another fascinating village. I'll take you there soon."

A waiter in an immaculate white apron appeared to take their order.

"I'll have a dozen blue point oysters, please, and the broiled lobster. Lindy?"

"The porterhouse, please, with mushrooms. And coffee."

"Very good."

Lindy glanced about the dining room. "It looks to be a successful enterprise, Auntie."

"It does, doesn't it? But actually, Mr. Statler's first restaurant here failed almost immediately."

"Oh?"

"Yes, he was advised to go into bankruptcy. To give up. Instead, he convinced his creditors to wait a year for their payments. And he began to advertise. And this is the result." She waved her hand at the bustling restaurant. "Ah, there he is now, at the next table."

A slim man with a thick mustache stood in conversation with two of his customers. He wore impeccable black broadcloth, had straight-backed posture, and a grave manner. He ended his conversation, turned, and caught sight of them.

The serious expression dropped from his face, and he came immediately to their table, beaming. "Miss Lindenmayer! How lovely to see you."

"Thank you, Mr. Statler. May I introduce my niece, Miss Evangeline Lindenmayer?"

He bowed low. "Very nice indeed to meet a relative of Miss Lindenmayer's. Are you in town for a visit?"

"I'll be residing with my aunt for a season. She's been telling me of your business success."

He laughed, his smile lighting up his face. "Only after much trial and travail."

"Tell me about these odd-shaped tables." Lindy patted the wood under her fingers.

"Oh, the octagon shape? They ensure easy conversation, and allow me to fill the room to capacity without sacrificing privacy."

"You have put much thought into your establishment, sir."

"Thank you. I hope to see you both again soon." He bowed and left.

When they had finished their dinner and left the restaurant, Aunt Gertrude paused at the carriage. "Do let's walk for a bit." She linked her arm through Lindy's. "The oysters have positively given me some extra energy."

Stores filled every space on Main St. A millinery shop, a florist, and then a store with windows that reached to the second story, filled with all manner of items for sale. A brightly painted sign hung from chains over the door. "Woolworth & Knox 5 & 10 cent store."

"Oh my." Lindy couldn't resist pressing her nose close to the glass to peer into the store.

"Can we go in here, Aunt Gertrude?"

Her aunt nodded, and an obliging young man opened the door and ushered them in.

"I know you've never been in a store like this, Lindy. Look around. I'll meet you in the notions department." Lindy didn't know where to start. Kitchenware and sewing supplies filled the shelves to her left. She had shopped with her mother in New York and Paris, but those elegant shops had nothing in common with this amazing spectacle of a store.

As she wandered around examining the merchandise, another interesting thought occurred to Lindy—no shopkeeper had approached her. Clerks in neat uniforms stood behind counters and display tables, but no one followed her, pointing out expensive items, as they did in the exclusive shops her mother visited. How refreshing.

In the middle of the long main aisle stood a table covered with bright red cloth. Above it hung a sign that announced "5 Cent Table" in bold black letters. It had everything from baby bibs to button hooks, pencils to harmonicas. Everything on this table was five cents? Before this, she had had no idea what five cents could buy.

She lingered longest in the toy aisle, where she marveled at the displays of dolls in lacy dresses. There were bags of marbles, small sets of dolly dishes, and miniature feather dusters perfect for a little girl's hand. She couldn't resist buying a set of white china dishes covered with pink rosebuds, and a little dustpan and broom. She met her aunt in the notions department, where Gertrude had finished selecting thread from a rainbow of colors on a revolving stand. Carrying their purchases, they left the store, and her aunt hesitated on the sidewalk. "What is it, Auntie?"

"Well—I thought I'd sworn it off but... oh, let's go back in. It's my one vice."

Mystified, Lindy followed her aunt into the store and across the main aisle to a glass-fronted cabinet where two young ladies dressed all in white stood. The warm scent of sugar wafted over them.

"Sweets," sighed Aunt Gertrude. She gazed longingly at the display trays. "My downfall."

"My goodness," said Lindy, "There's so many!"

She chose Tootsie Rolls and caramels while Aunt Gertrude bought several pounds worth. She pulled a chocolate-covered cube out of one white paper bag. "Try one."

Lindy took the candy and cautiously bit into it. Inside was a honeycomb filling that melted with the chocolate in her mouth into a luscious concoction of sticky sweetness.

"Mmm," she said when she could speak again. "What is it?"

"Sponge candy. A Buffalo invention. My absolute favorite."

∾

AUNT GERTRUDE KEPT Lindy busy the next few days, continuing the tour of Buffalo and introducing her to some of her friends. By the end of the week, Lindy had settled into a new routine. But it didn't stop the whiplash-sharp dart of pain that crushed her heart when she least expected it. Out walking with Aunt Gertrude, memories of Jack would intrude on her conversation, an ache of her heart so intense, she had to steel herself not to wince. Each night alone in her bed, she would see him in her mind, his brown eyes gazing at her, that lock of blond hair she always wanted to tenderly brush off his forehead. In her dreams, she would hear his voice and wake with her heart thudding, only to realize it was a dream, and Jack was gone.

"Help me, Lord," she prayed. "Make for me the way of escape, that I might be able to move ahead in faith that You know what You are doing in my life."

At the end of the week, the weather had continued fine, and on Sunday after church, restless in the quiet house, Lindy put on some sturdy boots and went to investigate her aunt's garden at the rear of the house.

It spread over several acres and included a tiny apple orchard. Espaliered pear trees grew against a sunny stone wall, and beyond this, a graveled path split into two lanes. The one to her left led into a copse of beech trees. The path turned sharply, and she gasped. Underneath the feathery green foliage of the beech trees, a carpet of nodding blue flowers stretched to the far end of the path. Bluebells. In every shade of lavender blue clustered so thickly under the trees, she could see only the barest trace of green grass. Enchanted, she walked on, inhaling their delicate scent. She stooped to pick a cluster, bound them with a blade of grass, and tucked them into the neck of her jacket.

An old German hymn her grandmother used to sing rose up within her at this little bit of unexpected heaven.

Jesu, deine tiefen Wunden,
    Deine Qual und bittern Tod
    Laß mir geben alle Stunden
    Trost in Leib'sund Seelennot.

"Oh, Lord," she whispered. "How can I be sad among the beauty You've placed before me?" She hummed the old tune, and the words came.

Jesus, grant that balm and healing
    In Thy holy wounds I find,
    Every hour that I am feeling,
    Pains of body and of mind.

"Amen."

40

M ay 1898, Chautauqua, New York

JACK WINTHROP STRODE through the wooded grounds of the Chautauqua Society camp. The sharp scent of pine and cedar refreshed his rumpled mind, and he stopped to take another bracing lungful of the fragrant air.

"Camp" was a misleading word. The buildings of the Chautauqua Society were impressive rather than rustic. The amphitheater, for instance. He stopped in front of it, admiring the circular wooden structure that, according to Bishop Vincent, could comfortably seat five thousand people. The camp itself was huge, bordered on one side by the blue waters of Chautauqua Lake, and on the other by streets of quaint Victorian cottages. Threaded among the bungalows and cottages stood great buildings dedicated to the study of various religions, arts, and sciences. A few steps from the amphitheater stood the Hall of Philosophy, modeled on the Parthenon of Athens.

But void of people and with only a skeleton staff present at the moment, it seemed empty. As empty as he felt. He'd been here for two months. His position as assistant to the camp director was moderately interesting, and perhaps after a while he would settle in, but—he closed his eyes, fighting the ever-present ache in his heart for Lindy.

"Are you quite alright, Mr. Winthrop?"

A pert young lady stood a few feet away, dressed in a cornflower blue walking outfit that perfectly matched her eyes. He'd seen her at a distance the night before in the communal dining hall, surrounded by a bevy of clearly besotted male staffers.

"Ahh... yes, thank you, I'm fine, Miss...?"

She smiled, revealing rows of perfect teeth. "Miss Vincent. I'm the niece of the camp founder, Bishop Vincent."

"Yes, of course." He'd been introduced to all the staff and their families when he'd first arrived, but hadn't yet committed their faces and names to memory. "Forgive me."

"Nothing to forgive, sir. You're new here. We've only to learn one new name while you must learn fifty, at least."

Jack smiled back. "You're very gracious, Miss Vincent."

"Are you on your way to dinner?"

"Actually, I was."

"May I join you?" She smiled again. "Please don't think me too forward. We are quite informal here at Chautauqua."

He offered his arm, and she laid her gloved fingers on it, the touch as light as a butterfly.

"How do you find Chautauqua so far, Mr. Winthrop?"

"Everyone has been extremely welcoming."

"Yes, we're good at that. We'll kill you with kindness until you never want to leave."

Startled, Jack burst out laughing. "Very droll, Miss Vincent."

"Call me Gillian. Remember, we're not formal here. I think you'll find it a pleasant refuge from the city."

The old Athenaeum Hotel at the center of the grounds served dinner. A fire roared in the great stone fireplace, and wood-beamed ceilings, overstuffed chairs, and plump sofas filled the cozy space.

Gillian asked for a table in the corner. Once they were seated, she fluffed her napkin out and laid it in her lap. "I'm ready now," she said.

"Ready, Miss Vincent?"

She leaned in closer. "Gillian, please. To hear your life story. Or at least the part about why you came to Chautauqua, John."

Jack winced. "Call me Jack." *He had said the same words to Lindy. I couldn't possibly, sir.* He smiled at the thought.

"John is much more impressive a name. What's so funny?"

Jack sighed. "Nothing. What do you wish to know?"

"Why you chose to come to Chautauqua and leave New York City."

It wasn't my choice. "My uncle arranged the position for me."

"Indeed."

"He's experienced a temporary reversal of his fortunes, so I had to leave seminary for the time being."

"He was putting you through school?"

Jack nodded. "He took my mother and me in after my father died. Now, what about you?"

Gillian scrutinized him and smiled slightly, acknowledging his deft handling of the conversation. "Not much to tell. Our stories are somewhat similar. My parents died when I was a child, and my uncle raised me. I've spent every summer in Chautauqua since the age of seven."

"It's a magnificent place."

"And world-famous. People from all over the world visit each summer. You never know who you'll meet."

"And it all started as a sort of 'summer' school for Sunday school teachers?"

"That was the initial vision. And then the response to the quest for learning soon broadened into science, music, and the arts."

"It's refreshing such an idea took root here."

"Here? You mean in such a rustic place? I assure you, Mr. Winthrop, we may be informal here, but we are certainly not backward!"

Jack coughed. "Forgive me. I never meant to imply such a thing."

"Didn't you?" She lowered her menu and scorched him with her glare. "Don't let my uncle hear you voice such sentiments. He'd send you packing."

"My dear Miss Vincent, might we start over?" He held out his hand across the table. "Hello. I'm Jack Winthrop."

The scowl dropped off Gillian's brow, and she laughed— a pleasant sound. "Of course." She shook his hand firmly. "Gillian Vincent. Delighted to make your acquaintance."

JACK RAN into Gillian regularly after that evening, and they would stop and exchange a few words of conversation. They began to meet for tea once or twice a week until his responsibilities increased as the opening day of the camp approached, and several days passed when he didn't see her at all.

"There you are!"

Jack looked up from his book as Gillian strode along the library aisle, followed by an older blond woman dressed in black silk. "I've been looking everywhere for you."

Jack stumbled to his feet. "Is something wrong?"

"Did you forget our tea?"

Jack clapped a hand to his forehead. "Oh, I'm sorry! It went completely out of my head. With the camp opening soon I've been working on the lecture for the—"

"Fiddlesticks, I don't care. Although if you can forget a girl that easily, I don't know what that bodes for me." She arched an eyebrow at him, then laughed. "I'm only joking, John, don't look so puzzled. Mightn't a girl have a sense of humor as well as a man?" She drew the older woman forward. "This is my Aunt Pearl. She'd like to have tea with us."

"Very pleased to make your acquaintance, ma'am." Jack bowed.

"Likewise, Mr. Winthrop." She smiled at him.

Gillian stood opposite him, shaking her head with a bemused smile, a vision in pink silk and lace. "We can still go if you'd like."

When he hesitated, her lower lip curled into a pout. "I'm not used to being told no, young man."

"Of course." He gathered his books and papers and held his arm out to Gillian. They made their way through the camp to the hotel and took a table in front of one of the wide windows framing a view of the lake, glittering in the early June sunshine. Once seated, Aunt Pearl pulled a slim book out of her reticule and engrossed herself in it.

"What are you lecturing on, John?" Gillian insisted on

calling him by his given name, though he preferred Jack. She certainly has a stubborn streak.

"The principles of divine eminence. Your uncle's request."

She poured him another cup of tea and added cream and one lump of sugar, as he liked it. When did she begin to do that?

"Sounds perfectly boring."

"It's not. But what about your reading list?" A week ago, Gillian had asked him to suggest some reading material, and he had obliged.

"The Picture of Dorian Gray isn't too bad." She took a sip of tea and shook her head. "But honestly, John, The Time Machine?" She frowned. "Don't you think we should be spending our time on books that will improve our minds? Help us live a better Christian life?" She sniffed and then pressed her pretty lips together as if to stop herself from saying more.

Jack chuckled. "Of course. But I also read to improve my mind, widen my world, and stretch my imagination. Have you no sense of adventure?"

Gillian shrugged. "I'm a trifle surprised to find you read such things."

Jack stifled a sigh. "Well then, what about Pascal's Pensées?" He leaned forward, eager to hear her thoughts on it.

"Oh, that." She waved a languid hand in the air. "I had to give that up almost immediately, John. All those big words! I needed a dictionary just for the first paragraph."

Jack blinked. Well, what did you expect? That Gillian Vincent would have the thoughtful intelligence and beauty of Lindy? Gillian did have beauty, with her flaxen hair, porcelain complexion, and tiny waist. He'd noticed the attention she attracted as she entered the inn. And the envious looks on the faces of the young men when they glanced at him. But in all honesty, she seemed no different from the young women in his uncle's church, who tittered behind their gloved fingers and made cow eyes at the young men.

"John!"

He started. "Pardon me—what?"

A tiny frown creased the perfection of her smooth forehead. "The waiter is here. He asked what you'd like with your tea?"

"Oh."

The young man in the white apron held his pencil poised over his pad. "Sir?"

"Let's see. Actually... I—don't care for anything, thank you."

The waiter bowed and left.

Gillian snapped her fingers in front of his face. "John, is something wrong? You're a thousand miles away this afternoon."

He certainly couldn't tell her what he'd been thinking. "Nothing is wrong."

She slumped in her chair. "I suppose I shouldn't have asked you to go to tea with me. It's obvious you'd rather be shut up in the stuffy library." She gathered her parasol and rose to her feet. "I'm not accustomed to being treated in this way, John, and I don't appreciate it." Her voice rose a full octave. "As if I'm some vapid female you must put up with."

Jack stood. "Forgive me, Gillian." Staff at nearby tables turned in their direction. "Please sit down. Can we begin again?"

Gillian stood for a moment, pouting.

"Please," he said, wondering if she had the ability to read minds.

She sat and smoothed her skirt. "It's not as if I go around throwing myself at men."

"Of course not."

"When we're together, you always seem to be thinking about something else."

Jack picked up his cup and sipped his scalding tea. She was correct, but he couldn't admit to that.

"And you never wish to discuss anything of your life before you came to Chautauqua."

He cleared his throat. "I'm not used to having these sorts of discussions with young ladies, Gillian."

"Ha!" she scoffed. "I don't believe you. Surely you have had your share of girlish admirers?"

Jack shook his head. "Indeed, no. I haven't." He grinned at her. "But you have, I dare say."

Gillian tossed her head and preened like an exotic bird. "So, you have noticed some things, John." She smiled at him. "Perhaps you're not as obtuse as I'd previously thought."

After they finished their tea, they left the hotel, followed at a discreet distance by Aunt Pearl.

"I know my uncle has already given you a tour of the grounds, but I wonder, did he show you Palestine Park?"

"No, actually. It was raining that day, and your uncle didn't care to brave the mud puddles without his galoshes."

"Come then. I'd like to show you."

A pleasant stroll brought them to the lakeside, with Aunt Pearl walking ten or so steps behind them.

Jack leaned closer to Gillian. "Is Aunt Pearl your chaperone?" he whispered.

Gillian laughed. "We don't use that word out here in the

country. She's playing chaperone for me. A **young lady** mustn't be seen alone with a young man, **surely you realize** that, John? Aunt Pearl is giving a courting **couple the** respectability they require. Here we are now. **See that hill?**"

Wh-what? Is that what we're doing?

Numbly, Jack tried to focus on the **piece of ground** Gillian pointed to, but his head spun like a **merry-go-round.**

Courting?

41

That night Jack barely slept after Gillian's courting comment. Normally, he dropped off to sleep as soon as he lay his head on the pillow, but instead, he tossed and turned until the birds started singing in the morning glory vine outside his window. It seemed only a moment later when the full-throated drone of a steam whistle reverberated through the bedroom, and he jerked upright in bed, narrowly missing the sloping gable above his head. What the deuce? Before his hammering heart recovered, clanging bells pierced the air, and another low-pitched whistle filled the morning. Jack jumped out of bed and peered out of the window. Today was the official opening day for Chautauqua, but campers arriving this early?

He shaved and dressed quickly, then went downstairs and through the front doors of the hotel. Horse-drawn wagons clopped past, fellows carrying large valises and suitcases, families with children clutched to their side. More steam whistles, more bells ringing, and a dull roar of conversations, greetings, and excited shouts rose above the moving crowd. Dogs barked, children cried, and was that a rooster crowing? Jack descended into the bustling maelstrom and fought his way upstream through the throng to the wharf. The City of Cincinnati had moored dockside. Right behind it, the City of Mayville had tied up, and passengers streamed off its gang- plank onto the dock.

Two more steamboats approached the wharf, the steam whistles and bells announcing their impending arrival echoing across the lake. Piles of trunks and grocery boxes loaded the wooden dock. Peeking out from a pile of suitcases stood an iron cookstove, a feather bed, and various chairs, desks, and other furniture. Kegs of nails and bundles of campfire wood littered the dock. People swarmed over the unloaded paraphernalia, claiming their property, calling for children, raising hands to summon a steamboat employee's help to move their belongings onto a wagon, all amidst the continued pealing of the ship's bells.

He spied Gillian in the mix, with a clipboard and pencil, directing campers to various places. "Isn't it grand?" she called out to Jack. "Just wait until tonight!"

Seemingly overnight, the quiet pine woods of Chautauqua transformed into a bustling city of campers, students, teachers, and seekers. The Chautauqua Press published its first edition of the season that afternoon, The Chautauqua Assembly Herald, and Jack soon found "The Drift of the Day" became his favorite part of the Herald, written by an anonymous wag who made droll and witty observations of the campers.

Opening ceremonies took place in the amphitheater that evening. Jack sat at the rear of the five thousand-seat theater, enjoying the excellent acoustics of the concave-roofed wooden structures which conducted the speaker's voice most admirably to the farthest top seats.

Bishop John Heyl Vincent, one of Chautauqua's

founders, welcomed everyone to the twenty-fifth Chautauqua assembly. "We are anxious in striking the keynote of
this summer assembly to remember that we depend utterly
upon the Divine Spirit for all the work we attempt to do in
the study of the Divine Word, and for all our investigations
into the Divine Works. In nature, in literature, in art, in
science, our hope is in the Spirit of the Living God. If our
theory is true, God, whose we are and by whom we live, is
present, nearer to us than the air we breathe. That our
spirits may be in harmony with His Spirit, that His spirit
may enter, possess, and dominate our spirits, this is the high
end of all worship."

Then he gave a short and snappy teaching on The Cause
and the Cure of Superficiality in Religious Teaching.

A Venetian fête on the lake would cap off the evening.
Gillian had refused to explain it to him and would only say
he must experience it for himself.

Now, far above the lake, heat lightening flickered
through the clouds. Campers streamed along the path to the
beach, lit by fairy candles in sparkling glass jars. Rumbles of
thunder heightened the anticipation as the lake filled with
yachts, steamers, and rowboats, fitted out with Chinese
lanterns blazing in rainbow hues. Gold, scarlet, emerald,
and sapphire-colored fire burned on their decks, and strings
of lights outlined their hulls.

Some of the larger ships had their names emblazoned
on their masts. The lights cast a gorgeous, golden light
across the water, mirrored in the surface of the lake. At ten
o'clock, the boats discharged Roman candles and rockets
from their decks and circled about the lake as fireworks
were set off from the beach at the same time, adding their
pyrotechnic splendor to the scene. The Chautauqua search-
light flashed across the sky, and the colored fountain added

its sparkle to the view as lighted candles floated on the water.

Seated next to Jack on the bench, Gillian squeezed his arm. "Didn't I tell you it would be spectacular?"

"You did. It's dazzling. And most likely, the closest thing to a real Venetian fête I'll ever get to."

She nestled closer. "Oh, I don't know about that. Venice would be a wonderful place to honeymoon."

Jack's jaw fell open. "Gill—"

"Don't say anything," she said. "I only want you to know that all this"—she waved toward the fireworks and shooting stars— "is how you make me feel inside."

"I can't promise you anything," he said hoarsely, finding his voice with difficulty.

"I'm content to wait." She lay her head against his arm and turned to the fireworks.

Another hour passed before Jack could say good night and retire to his room at the hotel. How had it come to this? He'd been friendly, nothing more.

He had to speak to her tomorrow and set the matter straight.

42

J une 1898

TWO DAYS LATER, Jack sat in a comfortable leather chair in the hotel, his feet on a stool and the Chautauqua Herald Assembly and The Buffalo Evening News in his lap. Rain poured in sheets outside the inn, hammering off the roof into the mud below, while he basked in cozy warmth near the massive stone fireplace. Rain hadn't diminished the fervor of Chautauqua's campers but only sent them inside for the afternoon. The flames occasionally hissed when an errant raindrop found its way inside. Gillian sat nearby, curled up in a lounge chair, engrossed in the latest issue of Godey's Lady Book.

He hadn't found the courage or the words yet to confront Gillian. Distractedly, he picked up the Herald while thinking about the matter and went to "The Drift of the Day."

. . .

MY DEAR! What were you thinking of? To walk across the top of the choir while Mr. Plagles was giving a lecture in the Amphitheater! Can't you see how rude it was? And your footsteps, sforzando staccato! How sweet of you it would have been if you had crossed the rustic bridge instead of intruding on the lecture.

To be sure the audience would never have known how thoughtful you were—but what of that?

You would have known.

HE CHUCKLED and picked up the Buffalo paper. The second Boston Marathon had been run yesterday in Massachusetts. He turned the page, and a headline jumped out at him. "It's a Sad World When Children Disobey their Parents and Scorn their Judgment!"

Hmm. That sounded interesting. Jack folded the paper in half and continued reading.

WHAT IS this world coming to? Has it anything to do with the turn of the new century fast upon us? In quieter days, children respected their elders and undertook to please them in every respect. However, this spring in New York City has seen an unprecedented number of grooms jilted at the altar by reluctant brides.

It started in March of this year, when Evangeline Lindenmayer, daughter of business baron and socialites Otto and Vera Lindenmayer, repudiated her fiancé, the Duke of Hampshire, in an unparalleled act of rebellion at the altar. Miss Lindenmayer refused to say "I do" in front of the highest of New York society, the mayor of New York, and members of the British aristocracy who had traveled across the pond for the ceremony. The whole scene caused her poor mother to faint in anguish.

Furor has raged in society circles all over the city, and Miss Lindenmayer has disappeared from sight, and well she might! A second and then a third wave of reluctant brides have followed her lead, leaving heartbroken parents in the lurch and city elders shaking their heads, to say nothing of the jilted grooms.

"No!" Jack dropped the newspaper and jumped to his feet.

Gillian started. "What is it?"

Jack gulped. "Nothing—I was—surprised about something."

"My goodness, you have the reflexes of a boxer, John." She rose and retrieved the newspaper, still open to the society page. She held it out to him, then stopped, frowning. "John, are you quite well? You've turned as white as a sheet."

Jack shook his head, trying to clear the spinning sensation in his brain. She hadn't married him! Lindy, oh, Lindy, my darling! He swallowed hard and took a deep breath. "I'm fine." He held out his hand for the paper.

Gillian's eyes narrowed, and she stepped back, scrutinizing him. "Whatever upset you, it's in here, isn't it?" She scanned the page. "I didn't know you read the society pages, John. How funny." Then the smile dropped off her face. She collapsed into her chair, still reading.

Jack righted the footstool and sat down. Couldn't run away now.

A moment later, she looked up from the page. "Why did this story upset you so?"

He shrugged.

"Did you know this girl?" He nodded.

"John, talk to me. Tell me about it."

"I'd rather not."

Gillian smiled at him. "It might help."

What had Lindy said after his mother's death, quoting one of the poets? Shared joy is double joy; sorrow shared is half sorrow.

But he had no desire to share his thoughts with Gillian. Even though she emanated sympathy—all smiles and graciousness. She'd made it clear in these last few weeks she had set her cap for him. And he'd been glad of the companionship until her courting comment the other night.

He gripped the arms of the chair. Who had he been kidding? He wanted to rush out and start searching for Lindy immediately.

He pressed his lips together and then sighed. "We were secretly engaged. But her parents wouldn't hear of our marrying. I'm far out of her class."

"Then how did you meet her?"

"My uncle pastors St. Thomas Episcopal in New York City. The Lindenmayers attended there, and Mr. Lindenmayer offered me the use of his library. That's where we met."

"How curious."

"What's curious about it?"

"That she'd be in the library."

"She loved to read, as do I. We had many conversations about books."

Gillian scowled. "Oh, you and your books." She waved a dismissive hand. "I've heard a great deal about those rich families in New York. Such excess! Wait—" She picked up the paper again, and her eyes widened. "I've heard of this girl. Of course! All the papers were speculating about the cost of her trousseau, her wedding dress, and her diamond-trimmed garters. Oh my!"

Jack stiffened. "She had no interest in any of that." He couldn't keep the coldness out of his voice.

"And to forsake her fiancé at the altar. A duke, imagine."

Jack gritted his teeth.

Gillian sniffed. "Well, it's obvious you're better off without her, John. You've had a narrow escape, I must say."

He nearly choked then. "What on earth do you mean?"

"Apparently, she's unreliable if she could do that to her parents and her fiancé. How could you ever trust her?"

"You know nothing about her, Gillian."

She frowned. "You sound as if you're still in love with her." She raised her hand to her throat, and her lower lip trembled.

Jack reached for the paper, touching her hand, and Gillian blushed a rosy pink.

He stood. "I am still in love with her, Gillian. I'm sorry. And I have to find her."

43

B uffalo, New York

AUNT GERTRUDE REPLACED her coffee cup and peered over her pince-nez at Lindy. "I've a meeting this morning at my women's club. Perhaps you'd like to attend with me?"

It didn't sound like a request. But Lindy did need to get out of the house and do something besides think about Jack. She smiled wryly at her aunt. "It isn't a committee to screen who's rich and fit enough for an invitation to the Patriarch's Ball, is it?"

"I suppose you're thinking of your mother?"

Lindy's lips twisted. "Who else? She fought hard to get into that society circle, and now she decides who to keep out."

Gertrude shook her head. "And I helped her. I had no idea how far she'd go."

Lindy pushed her plate aside. "Let's not speak of her on such a beautiful morning. Tell me about your club."

"I'd rather show you, dear."

An hour later, they were in the carriage headed for downtown Buffalo. The drive took them through Niagara Square with its lovely circular flower bed filled with flowering crabapple trees, heavy with pink and white blooms.

"That's our building, Lindy. The left half of the block." She pointed to a grand five-story building with a soaring roof, classical lines, and rounded archways. "We call it the Women's Union, or simply 'the Union.'"

The letters WEIU had been chiseled into the granite stone above the lintel of the main door. And underneath that "Women's Educational & Industrial Union, Each for All and All for Each." A flight of granite steps led to a vestibule with marble walls, and a lovely mosaic floor. This, in turn, opened to a spacious foyer with oak wainscoting and a rich oriental carpet.

"Everything you see has either been donated by benefactors or paid for with money we've raised. We have a gymnasium out back, a club room on the second floor, and a live-in superintendent with her own apartment."

Aunt Gertrude gave her a tour of the building, which ended on the third floor. "This is the Domestic Sciences Department. I'll leave you here for an hour while I attend my meeting. I think you'll find it quite interesting."

The entire third floor had been divided into classrooms and work areas, all open to each other. A child-sized laundry had been set up in one, with miniature tin tubs, washboards, and low shelves filled with laundry soap, bluing, starch, and everything a little laundress would need. Diminutive ironing boards were in another cubicle.

But the kitchen attracted Lindy's immediate attention.

Fully equipped with the latest in ovens, stoves, and sinks. Shiny copper pots and pans hung neatly on the walls. Young girls, about fifteen in all, some with dirty faces and scuffed shoes, and dressed in hand-me-downs either too large or too small, as evidenced by the scrawny arms that poked out from threadbare sleeves, filled several tables built at just the right height for small children. But despite the shabbiness of their pinafores and blouses, each child shared the same identical look of rapt attention on their grubby faces. Lindy found a chair in a quiet corner to listen.

The preparation of a simple pudding was the lesson today. The teacher stood in front of the class and demonstrated the proper way of cracking an egg. The little girls intently followed her actions as she took up a whisk.

"Remember, children, always wash your hands before you begin." The girls nodded in unison. "And now we'll practice what we have learned."

The girls jumped up and milled together at the long low counter, where small mixing bowls and tiny whisks had been arranged.

The teacher, a slender young woman with shining brown hair and an immaculate white shirtwaist, came over to greet Lindy. "Good morning. Are you new here?" She had a pleasant, well-modulated voice and a kind face.

"I'm with my aunt, actually, Gertrude Lindenmayer."

"Oh yes, she's one of our directors. Are you going to become a member of the Union?"

"Possibly."

"Welcome. I'm Jane Ryan."

"Thank you. Evangeline Lindenmayer. But please call me Lindy."

"Certainly." She gave Lindy a broad smile. "I saw you

observing the children, Lindy. Are you perhaps thinking of working with them?"

"Perhaps." Jane's expectant smile seemed to require a response. "How do you like teaching here?"

"I greatly enjoy it. But we always need more teachers. Might you be interested?"

Lindy laughed. "My goodness, Miss Ryan, you are so direct! I hardly know what I'd be able to teach these children."

"You never know." Jane gave her a mischievous glance. "This is my group, the Kitchen Garden girls. I teach them the things they will need to know when they apply to be a maid or a housekeeper or to be a wife."

While Lindy struggled to find an answer to this observation, one of the older girls helped a tiny girl up onto a stool a few feet away from them.

"You haff it now. Reach a little further, mausi." The little girl giggled as the older girl helped her whisk the eggs.

Jane nodded at the two girls. "We have the kindergartners today. Some of the older girls must bring their smaller siblings."

The older girl was as slender as a young willow tree, with thick blond braids tied up under a white kerchief. Her fingers were long and slender too, with nails bitten to the quick.

The girl smiled and bobbed her head when Lindy stepped closer. "Gut morning, fräulein."

"Guten tag."

The girl's brown eyes lit up. "Sprechen Sie Deutsch?"

Lindy shook her head. "No. But I understand a little. My grandmother was German."

"Ah."

"Is this your little sister?"

"Gia?" The girl glanced at the small tot with olive skin and a mass of wild black curls industriously beating the eggs. "Nein, nein. She is..." She looked at Miss Ryan and shrugged.

"Italian," said Miss Ryan. "Gia's family is from Italy."

"Ja." The girl ducked her head and smiled. "It-TAL-ee."

Of course. Any fool could see they looked nothing alike.

Lindy tried again. "And what is your name?"

"Minna Schneider."

"Well, Minna, you're doing a fine job with Gia."

The girl beamed. "I am already cook. At home."

"Oh?"

"For mein papa." She reached out and took Lindy's hand. "Come. I show you."

She led Lindy over to a corner of the kitchen where baked goods lay stacked on a table, wrapped in waxed paper and tied neatly with string.

"Mein."

"All these. Yours?"

"Ja. For the exchange. I sell."

"My goodness."

Minna picked up a parcel. "I give to you. Mein new friend." She held the package out to Lindy. Her thin face shone with pride.

How could Lindy refuse? "Thank you, Minna. I shall bring it home with me."

"Lebkuchen." Minna nodded her head. "Very good. I make."

Gia called to Minna then, and the blond girl skipped across the room to her little friend. The mouthwatering scent of cinnamon, clove, and possibly cardamom drifted up from the package.

Jane walked over. "You've made a new friend. I've never seen her do that before."

"What's that?"

"Give away one of her baked goods."

"She mentioned the exchange?"

"Oh yes. Come downstairs."

Lindy followed Jane to the first floor, where a room had been set aside off the spacious foyer. Fancy work and baked goods produced by the girls and the women of the Union were displayed here for sale, with the proceeds used to help their families. Lindy fingered a fine piece of needle lace. "This is lovely."

Jane nodded. "We have some talented women in the city, and they had no place to showcase their work. So the Union provided one."

"What do you suppose this strudel would sell for?"

"Ten cents." She pointed to a neat mound of packages wrapped in white paper and tied with string. "Those are Minna's. See?" She turned over the white price tag. The tiny initials "MS" had been printed on the underside.

Ten cents could buy a quart of milk or half a pound of butter. What an expensive gift Minna had so freely given her. Lindy chose another strudel and several packages of lebkuchen. A white parcel labeled "springerle" caught her gaze.

She lifted it to her nose, detecting the faint scent of anise. "My grandmother used to bake these at Christmas." Lindy smiled at the memory of her plump, German grandmother, busily baking during the Advent season in the cozy house the Lindenmayers had lived in before her mother built the monstrosity on Fifth Avenue. "I'll take all of these."

～

THE ARRIVAL of the baked goods caused consternation in the kitchen of Aunt Gertrude's home. After Lindy deposited them on the kitchen table, the cook, Mrs. Hedwig, flushed dark red and drew herself up ramrod straight. "Is Miss Lindenmayer displeased with my baking?"

Lindy blinked. "Of course not."

Mrs. Hedwig looked down her long nose at the packages. "Then why does she feel the need to bring"—here she paused, and her nostrils flared— "these?" The gray curls clustered around her face quivered.

"Mrs. Hedwig, your pies and cakes are wonderful, as you surely must know. I bought these to help support some of the poor children at the Union."

"Humph."

"She's a German girl, Mrs. Hedwig. Surely you could feel some sympathy for one of your unfortunate compatriots?"

Mrs. Hedwig didn't budge.

Lindy wasn't averse to using a bit of subterfuge. "She has no mother, the poor dear. All she has is her mother's recipes." She stole a sideways look at the cook. "She used her mother's springerle board to make these."

Mrs. Hedwig's face softened. Lindy unwrapped the parcel, and the scent of anise drifted up.

The cook reached out and picked up a cookie, a plump heart embellished with dots and scrolls. "I used to make them with my mother too." She took a bite. "Mmm. Perfect." She looked at Lindy. "Would you like a nice cup of coffee to go with the springerle?"

Lindy grinned. "I would indeed!"

44

Lindy began attending the Union several days a week, assisting Jane Ryan with the Kitchen Garden girls. Today they were learning the proper way to make a bed. All the regular girls in the class were there except Minna. Lindy missed her sparkling hazel eyes and hoped nothing had happened to her.

The little girls were fighting over who got to make the bed next when Minna appeared at the edge of the group, towing a petite blond girl with braids wrapped around her head. The new girl's complexion was waxy white, and she was slender to the point of skeletal.

"Oh, Fräulein Lindenmayer, I am so glad you are here." She pulled the other girl forward. "This my friend, Kasia Kovaleska."

"So nice to meet you, Kasia." Lindy held out her hand, but the girl shrank away and coughed into her sleeve.

Minna beamed. "For so long, I try to make her come, and she never come until today." Minna gave her friend a squeeze.

"It's a perfect day to bring a friend, Minna." Jane smiled at the girls. "We've finished our lesson, and we're having cocoa and cake. Why don't you find a seat for yourself and Kasia?"

Arm in arm, the two girls went to a table, while Lindy helped Jane serve the refreshments. From the excited chatter and shining eyes of the girls, Lindy understood an event like this happened rarely. For the next half hour, she couldn't help noticing how often Kasia Kovaleska coughed, her narrow shoulders shaking under the thin cloth of her threadbare dress. Perhaps some medicine from the druggist would help that cough. Now that she thought about it, many of the children had coughs or runny noses.

SOON LINDY WAS SPENDING NEARLY every day at the WEIU with the younger girls. Jane welcomed the help and set Lindy to various tasks in the practice kitchen as an assistant. One morning as she put away clean dishes, Minna ran in, her face glowing and her arms full of packages.

"Ah, fräulein, so happy you are here this morning. Today I make apfelstrudel. And I teach you." Her wide smile made Lindy laugh.

Jane found an apron large enough to cover most of Lindy's dress. A peck of fresh apples in glorious shades of green and red waited for them. Minna attached an odd-looking iron instrument to the edge of the counter and urged Lindy forward.

Lindy picked up an apple and studied the contraption. "Um... what do I do?"

Minna's eyes widened. "You not know how to peel?"

Lindy shrugged and laughed. "I'm afraid I wasn't ever allowed into the kitchen to learn."

"Nein? Your mother not teach you?"

A pang went through Lindy at the girl's innocent question. Lindy tried to smile. "No, Minna. But she taught me other things."

"Not to worry, fräulein." Minna took the apple and gave a demonstration of its workings. "Now, you try."

Lindy positioned the apple on the iron pin and turned the handle. To her delight, the skin fell off in one long perfect spiral.

"Gut!" Minna mixed a pile of flour with oil and water and kneaded the dough. Her heart-shaped face flushed pink with the effort, and she had flour up to her elbows, on her cheeks, and in her hair.

She rolled the mound of dough over and gave it one final pat. "There!" She brushed the flour off her hands. "Now, ve must let the dough rest." She took a paring knife and helped Lindy finish peeling the apples. The scent of the fresh fruit made Lindy's mouth water, and she couldn't help popping a slice into her mouth. Minna chopped the apples and filled a great mixing bowl to the top. From small folded papers, she pulled cinnamon, nutmeg, and salt, and added them to the apple mixture. Then she melted butter and combined it with toasted bread crumbs. "For the juices," she explained. She stirred the mix- ture and covered it with a clean white cloth.

"Now ve vait."

Jane clapped her hands for the attention of the girls who had finished their ironing lesson. "Now, girls. We have a special surprise today. Cocoa and hot cross buns."

She went to the pantry and pulled out the large box

Lindy had brought with her. Earlier she had stopped at the Broadway Market and bought every bun in Al Cohen's Bakery before coming to the Union.

The little girls squealed and hurried to clean up. Before long, they were seated at the tables with their cocoa, feasting on the buns, their excited giggles and conversation buzzing.

"Fräulein?" Minna stood in front of Lindy, her hands deep in the pockets of her voluminous apron. "If there are any buns left, might I haff one to giff to my friend?"

"Kasia?"

Minna nodded shyly.

"Of course. Is she sick today?"

The smile left Minna's face. "Ja. Very sick. She cough all the time."

"Oh, I'm so glad you reminded me, dear. I have something for Kasia." She fetched her pocketbook from the cloakroom and retrieved the glass bottle of cough syrup. Hurrying upstairs, she found Minna and put the bottle in her hand. "Here, for her cough."

Minna's eyes lit up. "Danke, danke, fräulein. This vill be vat she needs to get better so she can come vit me to the Union."

"I hope so." Lindy smiled at the girl, who carefully tucked the bottle in her pocket. "Now, let's go and see how many buns are left."

Minna clapped her hands when she peered into the box. "So many!"

There were eleven buns left over, enough for each girl to take one, with one extra for Minna to give to Kasia.

"Oh, she vill be so happy ven I bring these to her. And mine I vill give to mein Papa. Now ve must check the dough."

Minna nodded in satisfaction when she saw the dough had risen and brought out a white cloth. "This is special cloth. You vill see. Now ve must push two of the little tables together."

Lindy helped her pull around two of the smaller tables to make a square.

Minna spread the cloth out. "Das mehl." She pointed to the white substance encrusting it. "Flour."

She turned the mound of dough onto the floured cloth and used a long rolling pin to smooth it into a large circle. "Now, ve stretch it."

Slowly she worked her way around the table, taking the edge of the dough and stretching it out, again and again on the tips of her fingers, until the thin dough appeared almost translucent.

Minna's teeth caught in her lower lip as she concentrated on the dough. "Mama always said it had to be thin enough to read through."

Although she spoke frequently of her 'Papa,' Minna had never mentioned her mother. "Minna." Lindy hesitated. "Is your mother alive?"

The girl didn't look up. She hunched her shoulders and concentrated even more fiercely on the dough. Then she shook her head. "Nein." She surveyed the round of dough. "I think it is ready." She fetched the bowl of apples and spices, drained off the juices, and mixed them with the bread crumbs toasted in butter. From her apron pocket, she took a piece of cloth and unrolled it to reveal a sheaf of feathers tied together at the ends of their quills. "Gans Gefieder," she said, waving it.

Lindy shook her head, laughing. "Gans what?"

"Gans Gefieder." Minna stopped, frowned, and screwed

up her face, thinking. "Feathers, fräulein, goose feathers. Gans."

"Ah. Goose feathers." What a sweet girl. Her dress was threadbare. Her hair hadn't been washed in who knew how long, and she didn't have an ounce of extra flesh on her thin frame. But she had the smile of an angel. A pang twisted Lindy's heart. This child had nothing, and Lindy had been given everything. And what had she done with it? Nothing.

"And what do you do with that?" Lindy stepped forward as if she could blot out the stab of pain that had pierced her like a knife. "What can I do to help?"

Minna had melted butter in a small pan. "Now ve spread the butter. Vorsichtig. Carefully." Using the goose feather brush, she spread the melted butter over the stretched dough, careful not to tear it. "Now, you do." She handed the feather brush to Lindy. "Vorsichtig."

As gently as she could, Lindy spread the butter in a thin layer over the rest of the dough. Minna clapped her hands. "Very gut, fräulein. Perfekt. You haff made strudel before?"

Lindy shook her head. "No. Never."

"Nein? But you do it so vell, fräulein."

"Only because you showed me, Minna."

Minna smiled, her grin stretching her cheeks wide. "Now, the crumbs." Carefully, she sprinkled the crumbs over the buttered dough. "And next, the apples." With deft hands, she spread the fragrant mixture of apples, cinnamon, and nutmeg over the crumbs. "And now, ve roll."

She lifted the edge of the floured cloth and ever so carefully rolled a third of the filled dough over on itself. With the goose feather brush, she buttered the exposed edges of the dough. Then she ran around the table and took the other side of the cloth and rolled the last third of the dough onto the roll. "There!" She tucked the ends under the roll and gave it a pat. "Ready for the oven." Using the cloth, she maneuvered the large roll of filled dough onto a baking pan. After checking the oven temperature, she placed the pan in the oven. Then she swiped her hand across her forehead, leaving a dusting of flour on her pale skin. "Now it bakes for a good, long time, and then it will be done. Ready for the exchange."

AUNT GERTRUDE HAD another engagement the next morning, so Lindy took the carriage alone. Rain poured from sodden skies, but everywhere a sheen of green shone on the lawns, and fresh green shoots pushed up from the hedges toward the sky.

Lindy arrived at the Union, hung her wraps in the cloakroom, and hurried upstairs, hating to be late for the Kitchen Garden class. The girls already stood at their stations, measuring out flour for the day's lesson. Jane smiled at her and then nodded toward Minna, who sat by herself at the end of a table, her head down.

As Lindy drew closer, she realized the girl clutched a handkerchief and repeatedly wiped her eyes. "Minna?"

The girl turned and burst into sobs. "Oh, fräulein."

A pang went through Lindy. "What is it, sweetheart?" She couldn't resist the endearment, wanting to comfort her.

Minna sobbed harder. Tentatively, Lindy put a hand on the girl's shoulder, and Minna turned to her in a torrent of sobs, burying her face in Lindy's dress. Her thin shoulders shook so dreadfully Lindy put her arms around the child and drew her out of the classroom into the hall where a few chairs stood.

"What is it, liebchen?"

Tears streamed down Minna's face. Lindy sat and gathered the child into her arms to wait until the sobs lessened.

Minna pulled back, wiping at her eyes with the grubby handkerchief. "Sie ist tot," she whispered.

Lindy shook her head. "I'm sorry, Minna. I don't understand."

The child's body shook in a fresh spasm. "She is dead. Dead! Ach, du Lieber!"

A spear of dread went through Lindy. "Who's dead, Minna?"

The girl's face screwed up, and she burst into tears again. "Kasia."

Oh no. Kasia Kovaleska? Dead?

"Oh, my poor darling." Tears smarted in Lindy's eyes, and she closed her arms tight around the girl. "Oh no, no, not Kasia." Tears ran down Lindy's face as she held the sobbing child.

Finally, Minna sat up and wiped her eyes with a corner of her apron. "She has no one, fräulein."

"No family?"

"Nein."

"What happened, Minna?"

Minna shook her head, and fresh tears slipped down her pale cheeks. "Her cough. It was getting worse. And then, last night—" The girl dabbed at her eyes. "She coughed and coughed, and—blood came up. So much blood." Her body shook with repressed sobs. "Mein papa took her to the hospital in his wagon. But they could do nothing." She looked up at Lindy, tears brimming afresh in her eyes. "I stayed with her. She died this morning."

Pain tore through Lindy's heart. Could this have been prevented? What could I have done?

Minna shook her head. "She is mit Engeln now. With the angels."

Lindy gathered the girl close. "Liebchen," she murmured. "I'm so very sorry."

KASIA KOVALESKA indeed had no one. After questioning Minna, Lindy realized she had to do something. Leaving Minna with Jane, she went home to consult her aunt.

Aunt Gertrude knelt on a mat in a flowerbed, splitting clumps of iris roots. Her welcoming smile turned serious as Lindy approached. "What is it, dear?" She rose to her feet and brushed mud off her apron.

"It's Minna. The little German girl I've told you about?" Her aunt nodded. "Has something happened to her?"

"Not to her. A friend of hers. A young Polish girl. She died this morning at Buffalo General. Of consumption."

Her aunt sighed. "Oh my. So sad."

"I want to help. Minna says there is no family here in Buffalo to take care of the funeral. After her older sister died, Kasia lived alone in their garret. They were lacemakers."

Gertrude nodded. "What do you propose to do?"

"I want to buy a coffin for her and pay the funeral expenses."

"Very generous of you, my dear."

Lindy shook her head as hot tears welled up. "It's not! It's selfish. I want to do something because I can't stand that she died so far from home, with only poor little Minna to keep watch." A sob caught in her throat. "I feel guilty I have so much and others have so little."

Her aunt gave her a long, level look. "Your desire to help does you credit."

"You don't object, then?"

"Not at all. I'm happy to see you taking an interest in the children's lives. Let's go in. I'll write up a list of the arrangements you'll need to make."

Lindy returned to the Union to speak with Jane. Then she went to find Minna.

"Liebchen."

Minna's pale tear-stained face brightened when she saw Lindy. "Yes, fräulein?"

"I want to do something for Kasia. Could I bring you home this afternoon so I might speak with your father?"

~

THE ELECTRIC STREET lamps were burning by the time Minna directed James to her home on Strauss Street, near the Broadway Market. They passed St. Stanislaus Church. On the next block, Minna and her father lived in a tiny two-room flat, in the cellar of a tenement building.

Minna's father met them at the bottom of the stairwell. The odor of frying onions and ammonia permeated the air. "There you are, mausi!" He scooped Minna into his arms. "I was getting worried."

"Papa, this is Fräulein Lindenmayer. One of my teachers."

Deep lines creased Mr. Schneider's face, and there were dark smudges under his eyes, but his warm smile welcomed Lindy. "I am pleased to meet you, fräulein. Please." He stepped aside and gestured toward the crude kitchen table against one wall. "Sit, please."

Lindy hesitated, then caught the shy, eager look on Minna's face. "Thank you."

Minna filled a battered teapot with water from a bucket and stirred up the fire in the cookstove. A small pallet lay on the floor next to the stove, made up with a tattered blanket. On the wall above the pallet, colorful advertisements for flower seeds had been pasted. A calendar from Mazurek's Bakery hung on another wall. Wooden shelves above the stove held a few china bowls and a chipped enamel pot. At one side of the room, laundry hung on a line strung across the corner. There were only two chairs, and Mr. Schneider stood next to the stove.

Minna went to a carved wooden chest with the date 1790 carved into the top and took out a tin. "Lebkuchen."

Lindy waited while the teapot boiled. There had been no sign of supper when she entered the flat with Minna. Do they eat supper? Can they afford supper?

Minna made tea for the three of them, proudly handing out the cracked teacups and serving the gingerbread. All Lindy could think about was that she was taking sorely-needed food out of their mouths. The cold chill in the room crept under her skirts, up her backbone, and curled around her chest. It was colder in this basement than it was outside. Damp too.

"This is delicious, Minna."

Minna smiled and ducked her head. Her father gave her a loving glance.

Lindy cleared her throat. "I've come to speak to you about Kasia Kovaleska."

"Ja. The smile left his face, and he shook his head. "Poor Kasia." He glanced at his daughter, and a muscle tightened in his cheek.

"Minna tells me she has no family here in Buffalo."

"Nein. No family."

"I'd like to—" Lindy swallowed. Am I overstepping my bounds? "I'd like to pay the expenses for her funeral."

Mr. Schneider's eyes widened. "That would be most kind of you, fräulein."

"Could we do the wake here?" "Ja, ja." Of course."

Lindy stood. "Then I will speak with the pastor at St. Stanislaus tomorrow and make the arrangements."

She embraced Minna before she left. "I will see you tomorrow night, liebchen."

THE NEXT MORNING, Lindy rose early and took the carriage to Buffalo General Hospital to sign the necessary papers to release Kasia's body to the Schneider's home. At the National Casket Company, she chose an oak coffin to be delivered and went on to Wedekindt's Funeral Home on High Street. There Lindy paid for an undertaker and the rental of potted palms, chairs, flower stands, candlesticks and tall white candles, a bier with a back drape, and the wagon to transport Kasia to the cemetery. At Palmer's Florist on Main Street, she chose floral arrangements of white roses and calla lilies and arranged for their delivery.

Her next to last stop was Hengerer's Department Store. She made her way to the children's area. Rows of dresses hung neatly on racks. She was examining one of fine white silk, with a pin-tucked bodice and satin ribbons on the skirt when a clerk approached.

"May I assist you, miss?" A young lady with a pompadour, in a starched white blouse and trim black skirt, approached. "Anything in particular you're looking for today?"

Tears blurred the details of the dress, and Lindy's throat thickened. This would most likely be the finest dress Kasia had ever worn. And it was for her funeral.

Lindy groped for her handkerchief in her reticule.

"Is something wrong, ma'am?" The clerk stepped closer. "Are you unwell?"

Lindy shook her head. "No. No. It's just—this dress is for a young girl who died yesterday."

"Oh, I am so sorry. A relative?"

"No." Just a young girl with no family, who lived in a hovel far from home, and didn't have enough to eat.

"It's beautiful." The clerk gently touched the deep yoke of lace at the neckline. "Do you know what size you need?" Lindy shook her head. "She's just a tiny thing, really, but I'm not sure."

"How old was she?"

"About fourteen. But... but undersized for her age."

The clerked examined the dress. "I think the one you've chosen will work. If needed—" The young woman hesitated. "If needed, the dress can be cut up the back, for the undertaker to... to..."

"I understand." Lindy winced. "Please wrap it up for me."

At noon she met with Father Pitass at St. Stanislaus. The church secretary ushered Lindy into the rectory study, a spacious room with bookshelves covering three walls and a plain mahogany desk. Father Pitass rose to greet her, a man of about fifty with firm lips, a long nose, and intent eyes under thick black eyebrows.

"Ah, Miss Lindenmayer, how nice to meet you. Please, sit."

He gestured to one of two chairs in front of the desk, and instead of returning to his own chair behind it, he took the one next to Lindy and sat to face her. "So, you are here to discuss a funeral for a young Polish girl?"

After the morning spent choosing Kasia's coffin and dress, the warm kindness in his face undid her, and tears welled up. Horrified, she retrieved her handkerchief. "Yes." She dabbed at her eyes. "I'm not sure that she was a member of your church, but yes. Kasia Kovaleska."

"Ah." Father Pitass shook his head. "I know of Kasia and her sister, Edyta, I'm afraid. Occasionally they would come to Mass, but after Edyta died, Kasia no longer attended. Some of our Felician sisters went to see her and brought food. We tried to place Kasia with one of our parish families, but she refused. She did not want to be a burden."

So she continued to live in an unheated garret, alone.

Lindy signed. There was nothing she could do for Kasia now except purchase a burial plot and plan her funeral.

A SMALL AND strange gathering met that night in the tiny Schneider home. Minna and her father. Lindy, Aunt Gertrude, and Jane Ryan. Father Pitass. And a few ladies from St. Stan's parish, moved by the plight of the young Polish girl.

Tall white candles burned around Kasia's coffin. They said prayers. Father Pitass and the ladies from the parish sang hymns in Polish.

Kasia lay in the oak coffin on a white satin pillow, her curly blond hair spread over the pillow instead of the usual braids she had worn around her head. Lindy had brought white rosebuds to weave into Kasia's curls with the blue silk ribbons. The girl's pale face on the pillow seemed at peace.

The spray of white roses in her arms filled the tiny basement flat with their scent.

"She looks beautiful, fräulein." Minna smiled, and the pain in Lindy's heart eased a little. Kasia did indeed look beautiful. Death had smoothed out the shadows under her eyes and erased the lines in her face.

Lindy fished in her pocket for the tiny pair of sewing scissors. "I have her mother's address in Poland, liebchen." She held out the scissors. "Do you think you could cut a few of Kasia's curls to send to her?"

Minna nodded and took the scissors. She approached the coffin and carefully cut two ringlets of blond hair.

Lindy tucked the curls into a small envelope. Then she kissed Minna's cheek. "I will see you in the morning, liebchen."

Father Pitass had told her they would sit up all night with Kasia's body.

THE NEXT MORNING Lindy and Gertrude took the carriage to St. Stan's. Lindy had never been in a Catholic church before. A few mourners had gathered at the front of the church and knelt with heads bowed. Candlelight reflected off the shining marble floors and gleamed from the gold stenciling on the walls. A faint scent of incense lingered in the hushed atmosphere.

Kasia's coffin stood before the altar, covered by a white cloth. Father Pitass celebrated the Catholic mass, and although Lindy understood none of it, a quiet peacefulness communicated itself to her through the prayers and responses of the people.

A wagon transported the coffin to the church cemetery, five miles outside of Buffalo on Pine Ridge Road.

Father Pitass intoned the invocation at the graveside. "Wieczne odpoczywanie racz jej dać, Panie." Eternal rest grant unto her, O Lord.

The Polish mourners replied, "A światłość wiekuista niechaj jej świeci." And let the perpetual Light shine upon her.

Father Pitass blessed the coffin with holy water and threw a clump of soil on it. "Prochem jesteś i w proch się obrócisz, ale Pan Cię wskrzesi w dniu ostatecznym. Żyj w pokoju."

"Dust you are, and to dust you shall return, but the Lord will raise you on the last day. Live in peace."

One by one, the attendants filed past the coffin and threw a handful of dirt onto its shining surface.

Minna waited until the end. She tossed the dirt on the coffin and then laid a white rose on top of it. "Goodbye, my friend," she whispered.

Father Pitass approached Lindy. "Some of the ladies from the church have taken the liberty of preparing lunch for your group."

"How thoughtful of them."

The priest smiled. "It's Polish custom, and I think, German as well?" He looked at Mr. Schneider, who nodded.

Minna's father hadn't said much during the wake in his home, the Mass at the church, or the graveside service after. Now he sat next to Minna, watching as she tasted the Polish food and chattered to the ladies, who were trying to teach her the names of the dishes and laughing at her pronunciation. Mr. Schneider didn't join in the laughter, only glanced occasionally from his daughter to Lindy, his face a solemn mask.

Lindy sat at her desk that evening to compose a letter to Kasia's mother in Poland. She tucked one golden ringlet in the envelope. When the grieving mother opened it, that lock of hair would be all she had left of her precious child. The other ringlet Lindy intended to have placed into a gold locket for Minna, as a memorial of her friend.

Lindy thought of her expensive wedding dress, thrown out of the train into the snow. The cost of that dress alone could have fed the children at the Union and their families for a year, at least.

Perhaps more.

45

July 1898, Chautauqua, New York

JACK THREW the letter in the trash, shaking. He'd written his uncle and Otto Lindenmayer, enquiring about Lindy's whereabouts and telling them he had discovered Lindy hadn't married the duke. His uncle wrote to say he knew nothing and wouldn't dare interfere by asking the Lindenmayers where she was. Even his letter to Otto Lindenmayer returned to Jack unopened. Who else could he ask?

He paced the confines of his small bedroom and then whirled and smashed his fist on the desk, sending papers flying.

A knock sounded at his door. "Come," he said.

Gillian Vincent drifted in, a cloud of white batiste, a lace parasol over her arm, and an enchanting smile on her face. "I've come to rescue you."

Jack groaned inwardly. "Indeed." What now?

"And what makes you think I need rescuing?"

She glanced from the untidy desk to the papers on the floor and the stacks of books in every corner. "You've been immured here far too long. You missed the concert in the grove, the picnic at the beach, and I refuse to let you miss the fireworks."

Jack sighed. He hadn't left his room for the last few days except to use the necessary room and eat his meals. Preferably very early or late, avoiding company.

"Honestly, John, this room is a disgrace." She dropped her parasol on his chair and bent over to retrieve the letters on the floor. "Oh." She gazed at the letter from his uncle, who unfortunately had the large, sprawling handwriting of a child, easily readable. Her lips tightened, but she said nothing, only dropped the letters on his desk, sniffed, and brushed her fingers off as if wiping away dirt. "Come now. I'll not take no for an answer."

By sheer force of will, she got him downstairs, his cravat tied appropriately and his frock coat on. They walked through the hotel as people bowed and greeted Gillian, who was well-known throughout the camp.

It did feel good to be outside. He hadn't realized how stuffy his room had become. The weather had warmed this week, at times almost too humid for May. The grounds took on a golden glow as the sun went down, slanting through the pines. Families and visitors jammed the lakefront.

Wooden chairs had been set up on the beach, and the camp band played popular tunes. Gillian chose two chairs and sat down, stowing her parasol under her seat. "Now, isn't this better than mooning about in your room?"

Jack squeezed his eyes shut for a moment and sighed. "I wasn't mooning, Gillian, I was thinking."

"You've got no right to think about her."

Jack stiffened and turned to her. "Pardon me?"

"She doesn't deserve you." Gillian shook her finger in his face. "And that's that. You'll have to stop this nonsense if you're going to remain at the camp."

Was that a threat? "You're the one who must stop, Gillian. You can't pretend nothing's happened."

She didn't reply, but lifted her chin and stared out over the lake, her lips tight and her profile cold as ice.

The sun hasn't gone down yet, but the fireworks have already started.

JACK HAD FINISHED his final lecture on the use of Sunday school materials, and the last student had left the lecture room when the white-bearded figure of John Heyl Vincent appeared at the door. "Just finishing up, Jack?"

"Yes sir." What was he doing here? It could only have something to do with Gillian. After the initial round of introductions when he'd first arrived, he didn't see Bishop Vincent for weeks and instead worked under the direction of another senior member of the staff.

"I'd like to speak with you."

"Of course, sir."

Jack gulped, gathered up his papers, and followed Bishop Vincent out of the Hall of Philosophy toward the brick quadrangle in front of the building, rimmed with wooden benches.

Bishop Vincent chose a bench away from the quadrangle, under a mass of purple morning glory. Jack took a seat a few feet away and waited.

Bishop Vincent stroked his long white beard. "Tell me, Jack, how are you faring here in Chautauqua?"

Jack cleared his throat. "I'm... enjoying it. It's different from anything I've ever done."

The bishop laughed. "To be sure. Nothing like Chautauqua has ever existed before. Many of the same teachers and students return year after year."

"I can see why. It's a lovely spot, and there are so many opportunities for learning."

"Exactly. You've hit the nail on the head. Opportunities for learning. And perhaps, opportunities to learn from our mistakes, eh?"

Jack's face grew warm. "I don't know what you mean, sir."

"Come now. Gillian has told me all about your situation." He hooked his fingers in the pockets of his waistcoat and gave Jack a stern glance. "I don't think you're seeing clearly, my boy. The Lord has placed a virtuous woman in front of you, groomed for ministry from a young age, who would be an excellent wife and helpmate."

Gillian? She doesn't do anything about the camp except preen over her clothes and seek out my hiding places. "I'm not seeking a helpmate, sir."

Bishop Vincent sat upright, and his lips thinned. "Surely, you have given up hope of finding her?"

"To whom do you refer, sir?"

Did Gillian really run to her uncle about this?

"The girl who left her groom at the altar—the New York society girl. She wouldn't be any good for you. Surely you must see that?"

Jack stood, his chest tight. "Perhaps I could be of some good to her."

"I think you're missing what God is doing here, Jack. I believe He has put you and Gillian together."

"Then I'm sorry, sir. He hasn't spoken that to me." He relaxed his shoulders. "Please excuse me."

He strode away, heedless of where he was going, and ended up at the beach. The breeze cooled his hot face but did nothing for his thumping heart. Lindy, where are you?

"John!"

He turned. Gillian hurried across the beach toward him. Without thinking, he ran into the water and swam away as fast as he could.

TWO MORE OF his letters came back. This time he had written directly to Otto Lindenmayer at his office. A week apart. And now both had been returned, unopened. Return to sender. Otto Lindenmayer obviously had no intention of revealing his daughter's whereabouts.

He dropped to his knees against the bed and bowed his head. Dear Lord, is this then Your will for me? You've closed the door. There's nothing left I can think to do. So, I turn it over to You. May Your will be done in my life. Amen.

In his desk drawer, he retrieved the other returned letters. Bit by bit, he tore them into tiny pieces and dropped them in the wastebasket.

46

B uffalo, New York

THE DAYS FOLLOWING Kasia's funeral left Lindy feeling at odds. Although one perfect summer day after another followed, she found it difficult to reconcile the flourishing life all around her with the knowledge that Kasia had departed it.

On one of these beautiful summer mornings, Lindy found her aunt studying a thick booklet at the breakfast table.

"You need a change of scenery, my dear." Aunt Gertrude peered over her silver pince-nez at Lindy. "You're too pale, and you're not eating enough." She glanced at the poached egg Lindy had chosen from the sideboard.

"What do you suggest?" Lindy poured a cup of coffee from the silver carafe. "I know I've been melancholy."

"Chautauqua."

"Chautauqua? You mean the lake?"

"Well, yes, the lake is part of it. I meant the Chautauqua Institution. It started as a teaching camp years ago, for Sunday school teachers. Now it offers lectures on all kinds of subjects. There are classes, music, even drama. A few years ago, they did Ben Hur. It was marvelous." Aunt Gertrude pushed the booklet across the table toward Lindy. "They have a lovely hotel, the Athenaeum. I think you'd enjoy it."

"Very well, let us go to Chautauqua then."

It might be a good thing to get out of Buffalo for a while.

CHAUTAUQUA WAS INDEED LOVELY. Set on the shore of the pristine lake, there were all sorts of amusements to be found besides lectures and classes, and Lindy found herself enjoying life again. They had booked their room at the Athenaeum for two weeks.

Now in the middle of the second week, Lindy walked along the brick path with Aunt Gertrude toward the amphitheater, enjoying the patches of blue sky that shone through the leafy branches overhead.

Her aunt had selected a lecture on Dante's The Divine Comedy for the morning class. "Why don't you choose the afternoon lecture, Lindy?" Gertrude waved the program at her niece. "Don't make me do all the work."

"Oh, Auntie, you know you've been dying to hear Jane Addams's discourse on 'The Social Obligations of Citizenship—'" She halted stock-still in the middle of the path, causing several people to swerve around them with mutters of irritation.

"What is it?" Gertrude asked.

Lindy didn't answer. She couldn't move or speak.

Is it him?

A tall blond man walked toward them, with a pretty girl on his arm, laughing up into his face. It can't be. But her hand went to her throat where her breath had caught with a stab of pain. The adoring look on the girl's face sent a dart of ice through Lindy's heart.

A moment later, the couple stopped in front of her, and it was the man's turn to freeze, all color draining from his face. "Lindy?" Jack choked.

LINDY'S VISION went dark and sparkly at the edges.

"She's going to faint!" shrilled Aunt Gertrude, and then someone caught Lindy and lifted her to a bench. When she opened her eyes, Jack was fanning her with his hat. Behind him, the pretty blond girl glowered at her, her gaze narrowed, while Aunt Gertrude hovered in the background.

"Oh, thank goodness." Jack sat next to her and stared into her face. "Dearest Lindy, where have you been all this time? I've been desperately trying to find you."

The familiar scent of sandalwood enveloped her, and she nearly swooned again. "Jack," she whispered and clutched his sleeve.

"You didn't marry him." He smiled at her, and her heart gave a queer, little jump. "What a brave thing to do."

Lindy sat up, trying to collect herself, and moved to the end of the bench, aware of the pretty blond girl listening to every word. "You know? How?"

"I only found out recently. An article in The Buffalo Evening News. The society pages, for pity's sake."

"Oh, that horrid piece."

Behind Jack, the blond girl stepped closer, eyeing Lindy.

"I was there, you know," Jack said, his intent gaze making her feel dizzy all over again.

"What?"

"At the wedding. I snuck into the third balcony early that morning. I wanted to see you one last time. And then you had the ridiculous veil on. I couldn't see a thing."

Lindy's head reeled. "Then you saw—?"

"No, I had already left." Jack smiled crookedly. "If only I had stayed."

"Darling." The blond girl laid a proprietary hand on his coat sleeve. "Aren't you going to introduce us?"

Lindy's jaw fell open. Darling? The smile on the girl's face changed from pleasant to triumphant. Lindy managed to clamp her mouth closed and get to her feet. "Yes, please do introduce me to your charming companion."

"Yes." Jack stared at Lindy and gulped. "Uh, yes." He stood, and the girl immediately entwined her arm into his, never taking her gaze from Lindy. "Miss Lindenmayer, may I introduce Miss Gillian Vincent."

Gillian lifted her chin. "His fiancée." She shot Lindy a smug look.

Lindy choked and stumbled backward. Somehow, she managed to regain her balance and walk away. Her spine straight, she took one step, then two, and then as fast as her corset would allow, she raced back to the hotel and up the stairs to her room, where she burst through the door and threw herself on the bed. No tears came. All she could do was shake her head and moan. How could this be? Had he been here all along? In the same state? Had her father known?

The questions beat through her mind like a relentless

drum. Bitter fluid rushed into her mouth, and she lurched
to the bathroom, violently sick.

JACK FLUNG GILLIAN'S hand off his arm and turned on her.
"Why did you say that? It isn't true!"

"It's almost true. Isn't it?"

He hesitated, and she smiled then. "Be honest, John."
Perhaps he had been drifting that way in the beginning. But
only because he'd thought Lindy was gone, married to the
duke, and living in England. Everything has changed now.

He took a step back, his mind reeling. "I have to find
her," he said hoarsely. "I'm sorry."

He turned and ran, searching for the pale green dress
that had made Lindy's eyes the color of the sea. "Excuse me,
please," he said, pushing through the crowd of people who
swarmed the path. "Let me through, please." It was an
uphill battle, as most of the campers headed toward the
amphitheater and the classrooms after breakfast. The camp
was in full morning operation, and he was going against the
flow.

AUNT GERTRUDE CREPT into Lindy's bedroom a short while
later.

"I can't stay, Auntie. I have to get away from here."

"I understand, dear. Of course. We'll leave today."

Lindy sat up. "There's no need for you to go."

Gertrude shrugged. "I've heard most of the lectures I
planned on. No matter." She hesitated. "So... that was Jack?"
Lindy nodded. "His uncle said he'd gone out west. All this

time, I thought him in California. And he was here, at Chautauqua." She bit her lip. "Engaged." Her throat thickened again, and she swallowed hard. She had to get out.

She jumped off the bed and dragged her suitcase out from under it. Never had she packed so quickly, jumbling dresses and waists and ribbons together in her haste.

An hour later, they were on the City of Cincinnati, headed toward Buffalo.

JACK HAD COVERED ALL the open areas of the camp when he stopped, his breath ragged, and slapped his head. He wasn't thinking clearly. She'd probably have gone to her lodgings, obviously being upset when she ran from him. And here he was at the tail end of the camp. He sprinted toward the Athenaeum Hotel but had to stop at the bottom of the staircase to catch his breath while his pulse thumped painfully at his temples. Retrieving his handkerchief, he wiped his sweaty face and straightened his coat. Please, Lord, let her be here.

The desk clerk at the hotel shook his head at Jack. "Checked out, sir, about twenty minutes ago."

"Did they leave a forwarding address?"

"One moment." He turned to search the file behind him and then smiled regretfully. "I'm sorry, sir. No forwarding address."

This couldn't be happening. Once again, he had just missed her. He left the hotel and ran pell-mell through the grounds toward the beach and the pier. Maybe they hadn't left yet.

"Long gone, sir," said the ticket master. "Next one due in at two thirty."

Jack swallowed hard and took the path to the beach. Boats and trains reached Chautauqua from nearly every point in the eastern United States. No telling where they had gone. His fist shot out and hammered a tree trunk until the pain stopped him. Gasping, he sank to his knees.

HE SKIPPED supper and took a canoe out, paddling hard along the western shore of the lake until his shoulders ached. The shouts of children on the beach and the faint snatches of music practice receded behind him. Only the waves purling on the shore, and his rapid breaths reached him. He shipped his paddle, letting the canoe drift, and watched a water bug skate across the surface of the lake.

Now what? Lord, how could I have lost her again? What do I do now?

And Gillian. There was no doubt in his mind Gillian's announcement of their engagement had caused Lindy to run away.

He had to get out of the camp. He hadn't left its confines even once since his arrival in March. It truly was a large town sufficient unto itself, complete with its own post office, grocery store, newspaper, a sewage system, power plant, and waterworks. But right now, he had to get out of Chautauqua. After beaching the canoe, he went to the train station and booked a ticket to New York City for the next morning. Perhaps he could muscle his way into Otto Winthrop's office and confront the man directly. He packed his suitcase and sent a note to Bishop Vincent, requesting a short leave of absence.

But what to do about Gillian? He was writing her a note when a knock sounded at his door. Gillian stood outside.

She looked at the pen in his hand and sighed. Then she turned and walked a few steps to the sitting room at the end of the hall. He followed her.

She turned abruptly to confront him, her fists clenched. "You're leaving?"

How can I explain it to her? "I must, Gillian. I have to figure out what I'm doing."

"Are you having doubts?" Her lower lip trembled. "About us?" She put her hand on Jack's arm. "Don't make a decision now. You're overwrought."

"I am that."

"Did you know she would be here?"

He shook his head. "I had no idea. I didn't even know where she was."

Gillian's chin lifted. "And now you do? Know where she is?" Her gaze didn't falter, but the pulse beating in her throat gave her distress away.

He sighed. "No. I don't."

"And why is that?" Her hand tightened on his arm. "Why, John?"

He didn't answer.

"Shall I tell you?" Her blue eyes were steady on his.

Jack pressed his lips together and met her defiant gaze. "Tell me."

"She's run away again. From you this time."

He clenched his fists and tried to control his anger. "She ran away because you lied, Gillian. You told her we were engaged, and it's not true."

Gillian shook her head. "Why didn't she stay? Stay and fight for you?"

He stared at her, his thoughts tumbling over one another. "She's not like—She's..."

"I'd have stayed. I wouldn't have let you slip away again."

Jack sighed, and his shoulders slumped. "I need to be alone, Gillian.

"Face it, John! She ran away because she didn't want you to find her."

"No."

"Yes." Her voice turned gentle. "I know you don't want to hear this. But it's clear to me she wants nothing to do with you. Why else would she have left so abruptly? Why wouldn't she have stayed, at least to discover what had happened to you?"

He bowed his head. He had asked himself the same question at least a hundred times in the last few hours. "I don't know. But I need to get away. To think."

She patted his hand. "Of course you do. Just come back." She stood as if everything had been settled. "Where will you go?"

"New York. To see my uncle."

"Very well, darling."

47

New York City

It felt odd to be back in his uncle's home. As if four years had passed instead of four months. His uncle had been pleasantly surprised to see him and welcomed with open arms. He had ordered a roast beef for dinner in honor of his arrival, and then, comfortably replete, they sat together in the library.

"I've taken a week off, Uncle, to consider some things. I need your advice."

"Certainly, my boy. Everything going well at Chautauqua? How is the Vincent girl?"

Jack had dutifully written his uncle each week, detailing his assignments and progress at the Chautauqua Institution. He had mentioned Gillian, and his uncle had written back, urging him to cultivate that relationship.

"She is well. She wants us to marry."

Reverend Winthrop sat up with a thump of his feet. "You don't say! Congratulations, Jack. Capital news."

"Well... there's a problem."

His uncle's brow furrowed. "What sort of problem?"

"Do you know where Evangeline Lindenmayer is?"

Reverend Winthrop's eyes bulged, and he nearly choked. "Lindenmayer? What the deuce—what's she got to do with anything?"

"I've tried everything to find her, with no success. And then this week, she showed up at Chautauqua."

His uncle frowned. "Did you speak with her?" A worried look stole over his wrinkled face.

"That's just it. She left before I could. Gillian was with me and... and even though there's no formal arrangement yet, she told Lindy we were engaged."

Reverend Winthrop snorted. "Oh my." He smiled. "I can see what a kerfuffle that would cause."

"Yes. Lindy ran away before I could say anything." "Then what's the problem, my boy? You should be

counting your blessings."

"I'm still in love with Lindy, Uncle. I can't marry Gillian."

His uncle bolted upright. "Nonsense, Jack. You can, and you must marry Gillian."

"Why?"

"Because from everything you've written about her, she's perfectly suited to be your wife."

"But I don't love her."

"Pshaw! Love, love, love. You can grow into love. You've made some excellent connections through Gillian. Think of your career, my boy."

Jack shook his head, scarcely able to believe his uncle's words. "But how can that be fair to Gillian? How can I marry a woman I don't love while I love another?"

His uncle chuckled. "You're going to have to get over these adolescent ideas. You're speaking of infatuation, not love."

Jack sprang to his feet. "It's not infatuation, Uncle. We were of the same spirit, the same mind. I'm not a whole man without her."

"Then why did she leave without telling you if you're of the same spirit?"

The same question Gillian had so calmly asked. Is it possible I'm deluded? That Lindy no longer felt the same toward him?

Jack clenched his jaw. "I don't know. But I have to find out."

"Don't be foolish and throw your future away. Marriage is a business transaction. Take Gillian Vincent and move on with your career. That's my final word."

Jack studied his uncle's placid face. "Is that how you felt about my mother?"

His uncle's jaw fell open. "What's your mother have to do with anything?" He spluttered, trying to regain his composure.

"Wouldn't you have married her if you'd had the opportunity?"

His uncle's lips worked, and he turned away. "I didn't have the opportunity."

"But what if it had presented itself? What if she had loved you in return?"

His uncle tensed and gripped the arms of his chair. "It was a long time ago, Jack." Then he drew a deep breath. "But... if she had loved me..." A wistful smile stole over his face, and Jack caught a glimpse of his uncle as a young man. "I wouldn't have let anything stand in my way."

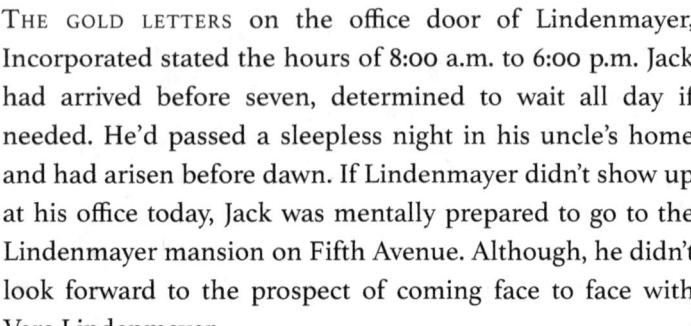

THE GOLD LETTERS on the office door of Lindenmayer, Incorporated stated the hours of 8:00 a.m. to 6:00 p.m. Jack had arrived before seven, determined to wait all day if needed. He'd passed a sleepless night in his uncle's home and had arisen before dawn. If Lindenmayer didn't show up at his office today, Jack was mentally prepared to go to the Lindenmayer mansion on Fifth Avenue. Although, he didn't look forward to the prospect of coming face to face with Vera Lindenmayer.

At a quarter to eight, a middle-aged woman in severe black broadcloth and a white shirtwaist came along the hall to open the office.

"Good morning, sir." The secretary scrutinized his frock coat and cocked an eyebrow. "Do you have an appointment?"

"No. But I'm hoping to see Mr. Lindenmayer today."

"Your name?"

"Jack Winthrop."

The woman's eyes widened. "Oh.

"Is there a problem?"

"Oh, no, sir. Please wait in there." She pointed to another door.

Jack took a seat in the room, cozy with its red-brocaded walls. But he couldn't sit for long and ended up pacing the room, end to end, over and over. His stomach rumbled. He'd barely been able to eat since coming to New York. One way or the other, he had to get this settled.

The secretary sat at her desk behind a frosted glass panel. Soon he heard voices, and a moment later, Otto Lindenmayer strode into the waiting room.

"Mr. Winthrop! What a surprise."

"I hope not an unpleasant one."

"No, no, no. Come into my office." He stopped at the secretary's desk. "Send some coffee in, Miss Haskell."

"Very good, sir."

Otto led Jack into a room richly paneled in walnut and indicated a chair. "Sit, Jack. I've been searching everywhere for you. And here you are in my office, come from nowhere."

Jack could hardly believe his ears. "You've been looking for me?"

"For months. I even hired a private investigator, but he couldn't turn up a trace of you."

"May I ask why, sir?"

"Why, for Lindy. What else?"

Jack sat, his knees weak. Lindenmayer actually seemed happy to see him.

Otto regarded Jack with a quizzical glance. "You know she never married the duke?"

"I've only recently discovered that, sir. Since then, I have been desperately trying to find her. I sent you many letters. They were returned to me, sir. Unopened."

Otto frowned. "I never received any letters."

"Five letters, sir, to be exact."

A glint came into Otto's eye. He went to the door of his office and opened it. "Miss Haskell? Would you please come in here a moment?" He looked at Jack. "We'll get to the bottom of this."

Miss Haskell came slowly into the office, avoiding Jack's eyes.

"Please sit down, Miss Haskell."

She perched stiffly on the edge of a chair and folded her hands.

Otto cleared his throat. "I'm trying to solve a mystery."

He fixed his secretary with a stern glance. "Have any letters from a Mr. Jack Winthrop arrived at the office?"

The secretary stared at the floor and twisted a ring on her finger. "W-Winthrop?"

"Yes, Miss Haskell. Winthrop."

"T-There may have been one. Or two."

"Indeed." Otto tapped his fingers on the desk. "And what happened to those letters?"

Miss Haskell swallowed hard. "I—"

"Come, come, Miss Haskell, must I remind you, as your employer, I am entitled to an answer?"

"No sir," she stammered, "I mean, yes sir."

"Well? Come, be smart about it if you value your position."

"She made me do it!" Miss Haskell burst into tears. "I didn't want to, but she said she'd have me fired!" She pulled a hankie from her pocket and wept into it.

"If there's any firing to be done, I'll be doing it. But I wouldn't dream of firing you."

Miss Haskell raised a tear-stained face. "Truly, sir?"

Otto nodded. "Why would I fire the best secretary I've ever had? Now dry your face and explain yourself."

The secretary blew her swollen nose with a loud honk. "It was months ago, sir. In the spring. Mrs. Lindenmayer came to see me. She gave me strict instructions to watch for any correspondence to you from a Jack Winthrop."

"And?"

"And if a letter came, I was to return it unopened."

"I see."

"I tried to tell her it wasn't right, sir. But she cut me off and..." she hesitated, twisting the damp handkerchief between her fingers.

Otto shrugged. "I well understand how terrifying my

wife can be," he said kindly. "You're excused. And not a word to Mrs. Lindenmayer about this conversation."

"Yes, sir. Thank you, sir."

Miss Haskell hurried out, and the next minute they heard the happy clacking of her typewriter.

"Mystery solved." Otto looked at Jack. "Lindy is at her aunt's house in Buffalo, New York. Here." He snatched a piece of paper and scribbled the address down. He blew on it and handed it to Jack. "There you go."

Jack could scarcely believe his ears. "You've no objection then, sir?"

"I'm looking forward to welcoming you into the family." He gave Jack a firm handshake. "Go get her, son."

48

B uffalo, New York

LINDY TOOK her morning coffee to the gardens. The roses were in full bloom, and the air delicious with their scent. She sipped her coffee and sighed. It had been almost a week since she'd come face to face with Jack at Chautauqua. After thinking about him every day since she left the duke standing at the altar. All Papa's efforts to find him had come to nothing.

And then, what had she done? She'd run away like a child, as fast as she could. Back to Buffalo without another word. The girl with him had disconcerted her. Gillian Vincent.

His fiancée. Fiancée! Obviously, he had forgotten Lindy altogether if he could become engaged to another girl so quickly. But there had been shock on his face too. And when he sat next to her, he had a pleading look in his eyes and hesitated when he had to introduce Gillian.

And the pain in his voice when he cried out her name as she ran away.

Lindy snorted. Fuss and feathers. It didn't amount to anything. He was engaged to be married to another woman, and that was that.

Or was it? She couldn't get the sound of Jack's voice calling her name out of her head. What might have happened if she hadn't left?

Oh, why did I run away? Silly girl.

Maybe there was an explanation? But he had known she hadn't married the duke. He had said so. Was it possible he had searched for her, as she had searched for him? She stopped cold. Mama. Her mother hadn't spoken to her since the wedding fiasco, returned Lindy's letters unopened. What if her mother had engineered something of the same regarding Jack?

Claudine greeted her, smiling. Lindy made up her mind. "Find something cool and light, please. I'm going to Chautauqua."

Two hours later, Lindy stood first in line to disembark and fidgeted while the crewmen tied the boat up. She fairly flew across the gangplank, ignoring the questions of the dockworkers as to the whereabouts of her trunk. She walked as quickly as she decently could toward the hotel.

"Oh, please, please, please," she prayed under her breath. What did she have to lose? She should never have run away from him. He hadn't known she had refused the duke until he read the opinion piece in the newspaper. She should have stayed and tried to explain, but she'd been so taken aback by his introduction of the beautiful blond girl as his fiancée she'd had no other thought than to run as far away as she could.

Finally, she reached the hotel and approached the desk, gathering her manners and trying to still the urgent thumping of her heart. "Is Jack Winthrop in?"

The desk clerk examined his records. "He's away for a few days. Would you like to leave a message?"

"Do you... do you have any idea where he has gone?"

The desk clerk shuffled his feet. "Miss, I only man the desk."

Lindy gulped. "Of course. Please excuse me." She turned away and sank into a chair in the lobby. *What do I do now?* She couldn't wait, having no idea of when he would return. She approached the desk, asked for ink and paper, and held the pen poised in her hand. *What did one write at such a time as this?*

JACK,

I shouldn't have run away. I'm desperate to see you. I love you. Please come.

Lindy

SHE WROTE her address under her signature, folded the note, and gave it to the clerk.

There was nothing else she could do. She made her way through the camp toward the pier and booked a ticket to Buffalo on the three o'clock ship, then found a place to wait on a long wooden bench in front of the station. The late afternoon breeze picked up, making whitecaps on the lake. A blue heron flew low over the water, slender and graceful, as another steamship chugged its way toward the dock.

Lindy leaned her head against the wall. She couldn't have been any plainer in her note. I love you. Please come. She blushed to recall her words. If only Jack would read them and respond.

Please, don't let it be too late.

49

C hautauqua, New York

THE NIGHT TRAIN couldn't return to western New York fast enough for Jack. Every nerve in his body twanged on alert, ready to rush off to Buffalo. But first, he had to speak to Bishop Vincent. And Gillian.

He left his suitcase in his room and went in search of Bishop Vincent, not caring that his haste and hurried movements were the exact opposite of everyone else on the grounds, leisurely going about their day. After checking the bishop's office, the amphitheater, the meeting rooms, and classrooms, he finally came upon him walking to his office from the dining hall.

"Good morning, Jack. Back already? That was a short trip."

"Yes sir. Do you have a moment? I need to speak with you."

"Of course. Come up to my office."

Jack's heart thumped in his chest, and his palms were moist as he followed the bishop up the stairs.

Bishop Vincent ushered him in. "Have a seat."

"No, thank you, sir." Jack straightened his shoulders and took a deep breath. "I'm sorry to have to say this. I cannot marry your niece. It was wrong of me to think I could."

Bishop Vincent frowned and drummed his fingers on the blotter. "I'm disappointed to hear that, son. What's happened? Have you had a tiff?"

"No, sir. Nothing like that. Gillian has been a model of feminine grace and sweetness."

"Indeed?"

"It's me. I'm the problem." Best to get it out bluntly. "I love someone else, sir."

Bishop Vincent grimaced. "Oh dear." He pulled a handkerchief from his pocket and wiped his forehead. "Have you told Gillian?"

"No, sir. I came to you first."

"I appreciate that." He fixed Jack with a stern glance. "I suppose this means you're leaving Chautauqua?"

"Yes sir."

"Is there any chance you might change your mind?"

Jack shook his head. "No. Sir."

"Then I won't try to persuade you." He stroked his white beard and sighed. "Gillian is set on you, young man. You're going to break her heart."

Jack swallowed. "I'm aware of that, sir. And I'm truly sorry."

Bishop Vincent clucked his tongue. "I'm afraid you will be sorry, my lad. I wouldn't want to be you right now," he muttered.

"What was that, sir?"

"Nothing, nothing... just thinking aloud." He waved at Jack. "Go, then. God be with you."

"I will, sir. And thank you for understanding." Bishop Vincent nodded.

Now for the hardest part. Telling Gillian.

Jack took the brick path through the village and paused on the footbridge over the creek. Pleasant conversation and laughter floated around him, as people came and went to their classes and outings. Musical notes drifted on the breeze as the camp orchestra practiced in the amphitheater. It was a beautiful day. And now he had to go and break the devastating news to one of the sweetest girls he had known. He prayed for wisdom and grace. And peace for Gillian.

He went directly to her home, a delightful Victorian cottage with elaborate gingerbread trim, not far from the amphitheater. What a pretty picture she made, in her pink dress, sitting at the wicker table on the porch, with her blond curls loosely pinned up and her chin propped on her hand, peacefully reading her Bible. And he was about to disturb that tranquility.

She glanced up at his hesitant step on the stair. "John! You're back." She sprang up, her whole countenance full of restrained longing, and took his hands.

"Yes." He dropped her hands and stood back. "I need to speak with you." He kept his tone solemn.

Her eyes widened. "Very well. Come and sit." She patted the wicker chair next to her. "Would you like some tea?"

Be gentle, her uncle had said. How he hated to hurt her. "Yes, please."

She busied herself with the chintz teapot, pouring the fragrant liquid into a delicate cup and adding milk and one lump of sugar.

He cleared his throat. "Gillian, I think you know I find

you a beautiful and gifted young woman. You've made my stay here quite pleasant."

She smiled, her pink cheeks blushing rosier. "I'm glad you appreciate me, John."

He took the cup of tea she offered him. "I do. And I think highly of you."

She beamed.

"And... that's why—" He swallowed hard as the smile on her face ebbed away. "Gillian... I can't marry you. I'm so sorry."

She went stock-still. "What do you mean you can't marry me?"

"I'm sorry." Jack shook his head. "I never meant to hurt you." His fingers trembled. Carefully he set the brimming teacup down.

Two spots of bright red appeared high on her cheekbones, and she clutched her hands together tightly, her knuckles white. "Is it because of her? The Lindenmayer heiress?"

What else can I do but tell her the truth? Gently, her uncle had said. "Yes."

Her eyes looked suspiciously shiny, and her entire face flamed red. *Poor thing, she must be dreadfully humiliated.* He stood up. "I'll go now and leave you in peace. I hope you can find it in your heart to forgive me."

Gillian wrapped her fingers around the teapot handle. "Forgive you?" She leaped up and smashed the teapot on the porch floor at his feet. Boiling liquid splashed his trousers and feet, penetrating his bare skin.

"Ow!" Jack recoiled. People breakfasting on the porch next door glanced over at the noise and stared. He stumbled to his feet and snatched the steaming fabric away from the tender skin of his ankles.

Gillian grabbed his teacup. "How can you do this to me?" She threw it against the far wall where it shattered with a crash, spewing brown liquid. "You... you brute!"

She turned to him, her bosom heaving. The whites of her eyes showed all around her pupils like an enraged bull, and involuntarily he backed away. She bared her teeth and came at him with her fists

"I'm so sorry, Gillian." He fended her punches off and tried to retreat toward the steps, his head reeling with the ferocity of her sudden attack. "Please try to understand," he panted. "I never meant to hurt you."

The Vincent's housekeeper opened the screen door and peeped out. "Miss Gillian? Is something wrong?"

Gillian whirled. "No!" she screamed, stamping her foot. The housekeeper ducked into the house as another teacup shattered against the door frame. The door slammed, leaving Jack to fend for himself.

Gillian grabbed the last teacup and turned toward Jack, snarling like a cat.

Dear Lord, what was happening? "Gillian, stop! Please." He ducked as the teacup sailed over his head and crashed on the sidewalk behind him. "Can't we talk about this calmly?"

"Calmly?" she spat out, her lip curling. "I'll give you calm." She grabbed the edge of the wicker table and flipped it over. Spoons, plates, and napkins went flying. The campers eating breakfast on both of the neighboring porches were standing now, gawking, and people passing on the path below had stopped to watch in horrified fascination.

"Gillian. You're making a scene. Please stop." He rubbed his legs where the tea had scalded his skin.

The veins in Gillian's neck stood out. She grabbed a wicker chair, lifted it over her head, and took a swing at him.

He ducked. "Get hold of yourself!"

"Get hold of myself? Oooooh! I'll get hold of you!" She smashed the chair on the porch railing and picked up another one. "Get out!"

He raised his hands in defense, and she brought the chair down on his head. He staggered back, seeing stars. "Stop this at once!"

"I'll stop you! Forgive you?" Her face murderous, she came after him with the chair. He tripped backward down the stairs and somersaulted off the bottom step. Then he ran for his life.

He made a beeline through the camp for the pier. "Thank you, God," he panted, as he saw the City of Cleveland lying at anchor and people boarding for the eleven o'clock trip. Praise the Lord he had his pocketbook on him. He bought a ticket for Buffalo and sat down to wait, nervously watching the beach for Gillian to appear waving her chair or some other weapon. But she didn't, and soon the boat cast off, headed toward Buffalo. Only then did he allow himself to relax.

He didn't know which hurt worse, the scalded burns on his ankles or the tender lump at the back of his head. How in the world had he misjudged Gillian so badly? She'd said he had a narrow escape from Lindy. But between his burned ankles and his bruised head, he couldn't help but feel it was he who had made the narrow escape.

The two-hour trip meant the steamship would dock in Buffalo at one o'clock. He straightened his shirt and brushed grass off his trousers. It seemed to take hours before they tied up at the city pier, and he could run off the boat to hail a carriage. It seemed another hour before the carriage pulled up before III Delaware Avenue. Hurriedly, he paid the driver and asked him to wait. He ran up the manicured path and beat on the front door until the surprised butler opened the door with an insulted look.

"May I help you, sir?" he asked, his nose in the air. Jack realized he must look a sight—out of breath, no hat, and more than likely a wild expression on his face.

Jack drew a deep breath and straightened his posture. "Is Miss Lindenmayer at home?"

"Whom shall I say is calling..." The butler gave Jack the once-over. "Sir?"

"Jack Winthrop."

"I regret to say Miss Lindenmayer is out. Good day, sir." He started to close the door, but Jack threw his hand out.

"Wait!"

The butler frowned.

"Do you know where she is? Please! It's very important." The butler's lip curled. "Even if I knew, sir, I'm not at liberty to say." He tried once again to close the door, but Jack shoved his boot between the door and the jamb. "Wait. I've just come from New York. I met with her father, and he's given me his blessing to ask for her hand in marriage. Please! I beg of you—tell me where she is!"

The butler's lip curled. "You met with her father?"

"Yes, yes, her father."

The butler's eyes narrowed. "And what does he look like, pray? And what's his name?"

"Otto! And he has silver hair, a silver mustache, and he's given me permission to marry his daughter!" He shouted the last phrase at the top of his lungs.

The butler's eyes widened, and he took a step back. "Very good then, sir. Miss Lindenmayer left a short while ago for Chautauqua."

Jack ran to the carriage. "Quick! Back to the docks."

The cabby's lips twitched, but he said nothing and clicked at the horses.

I can't miss Lindy again. But if she had gone to Chautauqua—what other reason could there be except to see him? He prayed it was so. And kept praying until he reached the docks and purchased another ticket for the twelve thirty sailing of the City of Pittsburgh.

A maddening two hours passed while he alternated between pacing the boat deck and stopping to pray fervently. Long before any of the figures on the beach and at the pier could be seen clearly, Jack stood at the rail, ready to search. As soon as the steamship pulled alongside the dock, he sprang up and over the rail, eliciting shocked gasps from the surrounding passengers.

A dour-faced elderly lady waiting on the dock fixed him with a disapproving glance. "Just what do you think you're doing, young man?" She waved her cane in his face. "Rowdy behavior isn't tolerated at Chautauqua!"

"Excuse me, ma'am," he said, trying to dodge the cane. "I'm looking for someone."

"Humph." She sniffed. "Young people these days."

The camp orchestra was practicing near Palestine Park, and as he ran up the slope, the orchestra burst into the crashing strains of Stars and Stripes Forever. He turned every which way, trying to see everything at once while keeping an eye out for Gillian at the same time.

Where would Lindy have looked for him first? He stopped and slapped his forehead. Of course, she would have gone to the hotel. He sprinted off, weaving in and out of the newly arrived campers streaming toward the main grounds. A stitch in his side throbbed as he ducked under tree limbs and skirted a wagon carrying children singing at the top of their lungs.

The crowd grew denser as he careened through it. He reached the hotel and lurched to a halt to catch his breath. Several young ladies passed him, nudging each other and giggling when they looked at his feet. Oh no. Tea stains decorated the bottom of his light summer trousers. He ran his hands through his hair—no telling where he had left his hat—and realized his hair was standing on end. This wouldn't do. He mopped his sweaty face with his handkerchief, smoothed his hair, and ascended the stairs to wait while the minutes ticked by as the desk clerk checked in three families with assorted children.

Finally, he stepped up to the counter. "Any messages for Jack Winthrop?"

"Yes sir." The clerk plucked a single envelope from the key slot. "Here you go."

Jack ripped it open and read it quickly. "Hallelujah!"

Then he closed his eyes. *I know she's here, Lord. Help me find her.*

"Did you see the lady who left this note?"

The clerk nodded. "I did indeed, sir. Quite the lovely young lady."

"Do you remember the color of her dress?"

"Rose pink, sir. A lovely rose pink."

"Thank you."

Jack hastened through the grounds in front of the amphitheater and scanned for any vestige of pink. Peacock blue, emerald green, dark purple, black and white stripes, polka dots. He'd never paid this kind of attention to a lady's dress. Thankfully, there didn't seem to be too many ladies in pink. What would Lindy have done after she left the note?

He set off for the pier where the crowds had dispersed for the moment, although another steamship headed for the shore, blowing its steam whistle. Soon the dock would once again be a sea of people.

There! Just ahead, he spotted a woman in a pink dress with a matching hat. He strode toward her. "Lindy!"

The figure in pink turned at his cry, and Jack gasped. "Gillian!"

GILLIAN LIFTED her chin and regarded Jack with a cool smile. "Did you really think you'd escape me that easily, John?"

Fortunately, she hadn't any sort of weapon clutched in her hand, but he wasn't taking any chances and retreated a step. "There's nothing else to say. I love another."

Her lips trembled at his last words, and he softened his voice. "It wouldn't be right to marry you when I can't love you that way."

"People can learn to love, can't they?"

He nodded. "I believe so. But I won't do that. You must accept this."

"I won't accept it." The veins in her neck bulged. "You're going to marry me."

"No."

"Yes!"

"Jack?"

Gillian froze, staring over his shoulder. He turned, and there she was. "Lindy!"

Jack took her hands, and Lindy's heartbeat pulsed down to her fingertips. He beamed at her, holding her hands tightly. She couldn't stop smiling while tears welled in her eyes at the same time.

"Finally," Jack said. "I've found you." He pulled her closer. "We'll never be parted again if I can help it."

Gillian stood a few paces away, her face frozen in shock. Then she drew a shaky breath. "You truly do love her, don't you?"

Jack turned. "Gillian—"

"You don't have to say anything, John. I—you've never looked at me that way. I understand now." She smiled ruefully. "I release you. Go in peace, be well, be blessed."

Back straight and her chin held high, she walked away and called a greeting to a handsome young man who stopped to speak with her. A moment later, they strolled on together, her hand tucked into his arm while she smiled up into his face.

Jack laughed and shook his head. "That's exactly what happened the first time she laid eyes on me." He captured Lindy's hands again. "Now, you. That's another story. I'm not letting go of you again."

She touched his cheek, and he turned his face into her palm and kissed it. She felt the touch of his lips all the way to her toes. "I don't want you to." Her face grew warm. "How often I thought about you all these months..."

"And now here we are together." He finished her sentence.

"And it's real."

He drew her closer. "So real. I love you, my darling."

"And I love you—so much I scarcely know what to do."

He smiled and planted a kiss on the tip of her nose. "I know precisely what we're going to do, sweetheart. We're going to plan our wedding."

. . .

RENEE YANCY IS a history and archaeology nut who works as an RN when she isn't writing historical fiction or traveling the world to see the exotic places her characters have lived.

A voracious reader as a young girl, she now writes the kind of books she loved to read—stories filled with historical and archaeological details in every aspect of life in a different time period, interwoven with strong characters and a tale full of pathos and conflict. Her goal is to take you on a journey into the past so fascinating that you can't put the story down.

Find out more about Renee and her books at

THE AUTHOR gratefully acknowledges the use of the following trademarks:

Louis Vuitton: LOUIS VUITTON MALLETIER Société par actions simplifiée FRANCE 2 rue du Pont-Neuf Paris FRANCE 75001

The New York Times: Company CORPORATION NEW YORK 620 Eighth Avenue New York NEW YORK 10018

IF YOU ENJOYED READING A Test of Gold, I would appreciate it if you would help others enjoy this book, too. Here are some of the ways you can help spread the word:

Lend it. This book is lending enabled so please share it with a friend.

Recommend it. Help other readers find this book by recommending it to friends, readers' groups, book clubs, and discussion forums.

Share it. Let other readers know you've read the book by positing a note to your social media account and/or your Goodreads account.

Review it. Please tell others why you liked this book by reviewing it on your favorite ebook site.

Everything you do to help others learn about my book is greatly appreciated!

RENEE YANCY